Seeing
DOUBLE

OTHER TITLES BY TAMRA BAUMANN

It Had to Be Him

It Had to Be Her

It Had to Be Fate

It Had to Be Them

Kindle Direct Publishing

Matching Mr. Right

Perfectly Ms. Matched

Matched For Love

Seeing DOUBLE

TAMRA BAUMANN

Montlake
Romance

Published by Montlake Romance, Seattle

www.apub.com

Amazon, the Amazon logo, and Montlake Romance are trademarks of Amazon.com, Inc., or its affiliates.

ISBN-13: 9781542046091
ISBN-10: 1542046092

Cover design by PEPE nymi

Printed in the United States of America

This book is dedicated to my agent, Jill Marsal.
Thanks for always believing.

Chapter One

Having prophetic dreams on a regular basis wasn't nearly as fun as one might think, especially when only half of them made sense, but Dani Botelli wasn't complaining. Instead, she intended to make the next thirty years of her life better than the first thirty had been. Wasn't thirty the new twenty-five anyway?

As she raced for the courthouse steps, she vowed that this time around she'd search for a more compatible man, she'd hold down and thrive at her job, and she'd do her level best to stay out of harm's way for more than a day or two at a time. When a person was on a first-name basis with most everyone at the police station and the emergency room, it probably wasn't a good thing. Unless you actually worked there.

The first item on her self-improvement list involved convincing her detective almost-ex-husband, Jake, to sign their divorce papers. She'd finally gotten serious about the divorce and cut off the sleeping-together part about three weeks ago. They'd never gone that long before, so it was a new record, but he still hadn't signed.

Next, she needed to make a success of her job as a Realtor and stop living off her famous mother. The living-off-her-mom part wasn't going to be so easy. Shopping in designer boutiques and traveling to exotic places had become commonplace in her past life.

Actually, it had been the best part of her former life, but she'd been too young to appreciate it before she got married. Paying her own Visa bill that first time had been a life-altering experience. Those statements should come with some kind of health warning like cigarette packs do: "Your risk of a heart attack may increase after you see how irresponsible you've been this past billing cycle."

But in order to keep her job and earn enough money to move out of her mother's guesthouse, she planned to ignore the unwanted visions that kept popping into her head, the ones compelling her to share them with her ex.

Let Jake figure out "who done it" all on his own.

Jake never missed an opportunity to take advantage of her odd dreams and mostly right hunches about things, but sometimes her visions, ones that seemed to come out of nowhere, could be as confusing as sudoku puzzles to the math impaired.

Her little "extra abilities" were an unwanted burden, and keeping them a secret had always been a daunting task. But, by ignoring her secret woo-woo skills, she'd be able to put some distance between herself and Jake and stay out of the crosshairs of the criminals who loved to hate her after she helped throw them into jail.

Dani lengthened her stride as she approached the courthouse in downtown Albuquerque—yes, the same place *Breaking Bad* was filmed—to testify for the prosecution in another, and hopefully the last, of Jake's stupid cases. A glance at her watch showed she was late.

Being on time was absolutely not on her self-improvement list because everyone needed a *few* vices to keep them interesting, didn't they? But judges tended to be picky about that sort of thing, so she needed to get a move on.

Just as her stiletto landed on the bottom step, a familiar voice called out, "Dani?"

Michael Reilly.

Crap. Now what?

Michael was the first man she'd ever slept with—to her undying regret—and in a strange chain of events, he had become one of her mother's many lawyers.

It was something they never talked about. The sleeping-together incident, not the lawyer aspect.

He looked like an extremely buff Ben Affleck, and she'd always been insanely attracted to him. But their complicated past threw a bucket of cold water on those desires.

Most of the time.

Pretending she didn't hear him, Dani picked up speed, taking the slick stone steps two at a time. No easy task in three-inch Manolos. Michael had once been a starting quarterback for the Dallas Cowboys, however, and she was no match for his powerful strides.

"You're a little overdressed for a jog, aren't you, Botelli?" A large hand gently wrapped around her arm, thwarting her plans for escape.

She turned and stared into his gorgeous jade-green eyes. "I'm so late, Michael. Can we do whatever tedious lawyer thing you have in mind later?"

"Sure." He smiled, exposing deep, sexy dimples. "If we wait until next week, I can just visit you in jail." His eyes danced with mischief as he leaned so close his breath tickled her lips. "I bet you'll look extremely hot in one of those orange jumpsuits."

Okay, maybe it'd be worth her while to hear what the man had to say. While trying to keep her rising panic in check, along with her hormones, she gave him a casual shrug. "What's the problem?"

He tugged her toward the courthouse, his hand still wrapped around her arm. She wasn't going to think about the zing of pleasure his touch sent through her. The last time she'd let that affect her, they ended up sleeping together that one and only time.

She hadn't meant to sleep with him, and every time she replayed it in her head, she still couldn't remember what made him so irresistible that night.

It probably had to do with how they used to be such good friends, his killer smile, and how he could kiss like no one else.

He lengthened his stride and said, "Let's walk and talk. You were scheduled to testify five minutes ago." His hand moved from her arm to around her shoulder, but it was no tender embrace. He was probably trapping her against his hard body so she couldn't slip away.

He added, "Your mother is eager to clear up that pesky trespassing charge against you. And thank you for ignoring the three messages I left on that particular subject." He slipped his large hand to her lower back, gently guiding her toward the metal detectors.

"Um . . . I've had a little problem with my cell, but it should be fixed soon."

"It helps if you pay your bill on time."

"Thanks for that clever tip." Dani raised a brow, hoping to look indignant, but he was right. She wasn't getting her next real estate commission check until Friday. And it was only Tuesday.

He blew out an impatient breath as he stepped through the metal detector. "Look at it this way. If your phone works, we don't have to see nearly as much of each other."

"Oh, but I *so* look forward to seeing your sneer in person." She batted her eyelashes at him. "What were the calls about?"

The corners of his mouth tilted as he opened the heavy courtroom door, waiting until she entered first. If nothing else, Michael was the consummate gentleman, even when he was giving her a hard time.

"We'll discuss it after your testimony. I'm looking forward to the show."

She sent him an eye roll as a parting shot, then made her way toward the district attorney and Jake. Michael's deep voice rang out behind her. "Knock 'em dead, slugger."

Dani didn't have time for a clever retort because a very rude and impatient man grabbed her arm and yanked her along with him to the front of the courtroom.

After she was seated on the witness stand, the court registrar asked, "Do you, Daniella Francesca Botelli, swear to tell the truth, so help you God?"

She hated when anyone used all of her names. It made her sound like one of those frozen Italian meals in a bag. "I do." And this was going to be the last time she'd ever do this for Jake.

Really.

This time she meant it.

~

Michael settled into his seat, prepared to watch the curvy, olive-skinned Italian beauty testify. What had Jake dragged her into now? She'd been involved with the most bizarre legal tangles since she'd been with him. Divorcing that guy would be the best thing Dani could do for herself.

Not that he cared one way or the other.

It was days like this that he missed professional football, when all a guy had to do was win a ball game. Now he had to deal with the likes of Dani Botelli.

He tried to focus on her testimony but found it hard to concentrate when nerves had her chewing on her sexy, full bottom lip. She tossed her light-brown curly hair back and drew a deep breath. "I was making a deposit at the bank, and then that man"—Dani pointed to the defendant—"came in with a gun and told everyone to hit the floor."

She'd just proven his point. How could anyone be at the scene of a crime as often as she was? She'd been an eyewitness three times in the last year. It was as if she knew the crimes were going to happen, then showed up to watch. What were the chances? But then, it was Dani. If there was trouble within a ten-mile radius, she had always ended up right in the middle of it. Ever since they were kids.

When she shifted her slender legs, causing her short skirt to rise higher on her thighs, he turned his attention to his phone. He needed to block the memory of those long legs wrapped around him.

He wasn't there to lust after her. He was there to get Dani's mother, Annalisa Botelli—not only one of the greatest actresses of all time but the most persistent woman on earth—off his back about Dani's latest legal problem. Why Dani had felt the urge to scale the wall of the mayor's mansion was still a mystery. One he wasn't sure he wanted to solve. But one phone call from her powerful mother had soothed everyone's ruffled feathers, and they'd struck a deal to keep Annalisa's little princess out of the slammer once again. However, this time there was a deadline to keep, and the police were growing impatient.

The defense lawyer's voice rang out. "So what happened next, Ms. Botelli?"

As Dani recounted the crime, Michael stared at her again, not hearing her words. The timbre of her low, silky voice slipped into his mind, bringing back unwanted memories of how he used to love her. Like he'd never loved anyone else.

That was a painful road he'd never travel again, no matter how breathtaking the view.

After her testimony, Dani slipped through the retreating crowd, hoping to find Michael, avoid Jake, and then make a quick escape from the courthouse. She squinted into the bright midday New Mexico sunshine, spotting the angry goon who'd sent her death stares the whole time she'd testified against his twin brother. He stood across the street banging out something on his phone.

Quickly changing direction, she slipped behind the protection of the courthouse's huge columns.

When she bumped into a hard chest, her heart nearly stopped. But then she recognized a familiar tailored gray suit, white shirt, and red power tie. "Oh, there you are, Michael." Before she could ask what needed to be done to keep her out of jail, her name rang out behind her.

She turned as her ex strode toward her.

"We need to talk, babe." Jake turned his attention toward Michael and lifted his chin in greeting. "Hey there, Counselor. Would you excuse us for a minute? I need to talk to my *wife* about something."

Michael didn't bother to respond. Instead, he dug out his cell and got busy reading the screen. Jake and Michael had always disliked each other. She wasn't entirely sure why.

"It's *ex*-wife, Jake," Dani growled as he dragged her out of Michael's earshot. "That is if you'd hurry up and sign the papers."

No response from him. As usual.

When they were a few feet away, she stopped and slammed her hands onto her hips. "Ignoring this and hoping it goes away isn't going to work this time, Jake. I haven't changed my mind about the divorce, and I meant what I said about not sleeping with you anymore, *babe*."

Jake's response was a slow, patient grin that had her reconsidering the sleeping-together part. So sue her, he was damn cute. He stood there—all blond, six feet of him in his tight jeans, a badge tucked at his waist, chambray work shirt, and cowboy boots—knowing full well she was wavering.

Luckily, her new-and-improved sensibilities kicked in, reminding her that Jake was not going to be part of her future. At least not romantically, but she hoped they'd always be friends.

Jake's gravelly voice lowered before he said, "Thinking about ways to get you into bed is one of my favorite pastimes, but this isn't one of those times. There's this new case—"

"No." She crossed her arms and shook her head. "I'm not doing this anymore. I'm done."

"Work this case with me, and I'll never ask for your help again."

She gritted her teeth. "No, Jake, I mean it. I don't want to do this anymore. And because of that big fancy speech you gave me about growing up and being responsible for myself, I have to spend some time actually listing and selling homes. Not solving crimes."

"You may have seen this one on the news. The scumbag claims three men broke into his home, stole some electronics, then shot his wife and child. Said scumbag will conveniently receive enough from the insurance settlement to cover his massive debts with just enough left over to buy the twenty-one-year-old he's been banging on the side a new diamond ring."

Dani stared into Jake's eyes. He had that look: the one that told her he'd not give up until he found the truth. It was the reason she'd fallen head over heels for him in her past screwed-up life. Jake was a rare person, who believed his gut instincts were really no different from her dreams and visions. If they could have gotten along as well out of bed as in it, they'd still be together. "You think the guy shot his wife and then his own child?"

Shaking his head, Jake replied, "Stepkid. But I can't find the gun. It has to be somewhere in the house. The neighbors heard gunshots, and within eight minutes, 9-1-1 was called by the guy himself. Claims he fell asleep in front of the television in the basement and, when he heard the shots, raced upstairs, catching only the backs of the intruders as they ran away."

"What about the gunshot residue test?"

"Negative. I say he wore gloves, threw them into the fire—conveniently burning at ten fifty at night—and then hid the gun. I've had the home sealed off, but I'll have to let him back in soon. He's guilty, babe. I can feel it."

Dani chewed her lower lip as she considered Jake's request. His gut feelings were solid; he was never wrong. But she was trying to live a somewhat normal life. And that didn't include invoking confusing visions of crime scenes.

And why did there have to be a little kid involved in this particular crime? What kind of person would she be if she didn't help put anyone who'd harm a child behind bars? "So you just want me to make a quick run through the house and see if anything pops?"

He beamed a sweet, triumphant smile. "Yep. It'll just take a few minutes."

"Fine, but this is the last time, Jake," she muttered and then turned and marched toward Michael as he ended a call. "Hey, Mr. Ever-Efficient Lawyer, when you go back to the office, would you ask Ron if we can get Jake another copy of our divorce papers? He keeps misplacing them."

"Okay." Michael stared into Jake's eyes for a moment, then turned back to her. "But only if you'll grace me with your presence at three o'clock this afternoon."

"Fine."

At the sound of breaking glass, she peered around Michael. "Hey! What's he doing to my car?" She grabbed Jake because Jake was armed, and she wasn't stupid—the guy had a bat in his hands—and ran toward her car.

The same man who had glared at her in court was slamming a baseball bat into the windshield of her ugly green Ford Taurus. "Die Bitx" was carved across the hood.

Strangely, she was more upset about what was carved on the hood than the fact that the guy was beating the crap out of her car. Did he mean "bitch"? She wasn't a bitch. Well, not most of the time, anyway.

Another cop beat them to the scene and wrestled the bat out of the thug's hands.

Dani slowed her pace as Jake rushed forward to help contain the man. The officer lifted a hand to stop him. "I've got him, Detective."

Jake bent to pick up the bat, and the goon punched the officer in the stomach, slipped out of the cop's hold, and ran right toward her.

Panic nearly stopped her lurching heart. He was on her in seconds, and she didn't have time to run before he was directly in front of her. She flailed backward, tripping over a curb as the car smasher lifted a hand to strike her. Out of the corner of her eye, she saw Michael swinging his briefcase at the man's head, but before it hit him, a fat open hand made contact with the side of her face.

She flew sideways, skidding across the hard pavement. It felt as though she'd been clocked with an anvil, and the skin on her scraped hands and legs burned as if on fire.

As she scrambled to get away, she hoped Michael or Jake would contain him before he could do more damage. She'd crawled a few feet before the sound of a low moan stopped her.

She took a tentative glance over her shoulder. The guy who'd hit her lay on the ground, with Michael's briefcase beside his head.

Dani released the breath she'd been holding as Jake and the officer cuffed the man. Jake growled at the cop, "Now he's under control, Officer. That's my *wife* he hit!" Then he glanced her way. Using his cool, cop gaze, his eyes did a quick up and down, assessing the damage before he turned his attention back to the still-struggling assailant. The fact that he didn't comment on her condition probably meant she'd live. But the ache in her head had her eyes stinging with tears.

When she tried to stand, the ground tilted, so she sank her butt to the hard pavement, waiting for everything to stop spinning.

Michael knelt beside her as she held her battered face. He whispered, "You okay?"

She cleared her throat and squeezed her eyes closed to contain her unshed tears. He was the last person on earth she'd cry in front of.

Lifting her chin, she opened her eyes and stared into his. She blinked in confusion at the genuine concern reflected in his gaze. If Michael was worried, then maybe she was worse off than she'd feared.

Before she could ask how bad the damage was, he laid a finger under her chin, gently tilting it. "If I were you, I'd postpone that photo shoot for your new business cards. A big red handprint on your face may be a little off-putting to potential clients."

She shot him a weak grin as relief filled her. She'd be all right if Mr. Responsible was making jokes. "More sound advice, Michael? Be sure and bill my mother for it." She accepted his offered hand.

After Michael tugged her to her feet, a wave of dizziness hit her, but his big hands were there to steady her. "Seriously, Dani. Do we need to take a trip to the emergency room?" He glanced down and surveyed the damage.

"You probably just want to go to the emergency room so you can increase your client base. I always suspected you were an ambulance chaser."

"Damn, you're onto me. But maybe we should make a trip over there, just for fun. I could use the extra money."

When she chuckled, the worry lines etching his forehead relaxed.

"I'm fine, Michael. Really."

"Okay." He released her, but then her brain took a spin around the perimeter of her skull, and she tottered.

Michael quickly slipped his hands around her waist, pulling her firmly against his side, then turned toward her battered vehicle. "Is your Porsche in the shop?"

"No. It wasn't practical for running families around to look at houses, so I sold it." And paid off a big chunk of her debts in the process, but he didn't need to know that. Michael thought she was a spoiled brat. It still pained her to think about how their relationship had taken a 180 in high school.

Once they'd parted ways, it'd become her full-time job to avoid him because Michael's mother had been Annalisa's assistant at the time. He and his mom had lived in the guesthouse on her mother's estate. But from ages ten to sixteen, Dani and Michael had been inseparable. They'd traveled the world together, teased each other constantly, and could always make the other laugh. They'd had the easiest relationship she'd ever had with a boy. But then somewhere along the line, her feelings had changed for him. He went from being her best friend to being the only man for her.

On the night before her sixteenth birthday, she'd lain in bed, staring at the ceiling as she tried to find a way to tell him how she felt about him. Unfortunately, she'd fallen asleep and had a dream that night. In it, Michael was walking down the aisle with a woman who wasn't her. When she awoke, she'd felt devastated by the thought of Michael with another woman, and she'd parted ways with him that day. It had hurt too much to even look at him.

That dream was the clearest and most straightforward one she'd ever had. Like the universe slapping her in the face and laughing at the idea of a screwup like her ever being good enough for a great guy like Michael. Her heart had never recovered from that blow.

Shaking off her bad memories, she said, "This car makes a lot more sense than a sports car." And it was butt-ugly, but it was all she could afford at the moment.

Michael nodded. "I suppose it does."

Her face ached, and the scratches on her arms and legs stung, but they didn't pain her nearly as much as the idea of coming up with the money to fix her car. The insurance deductible was five hundred dollars, and she had only twenty-two bucks that had to last until her next closing.

While the officer and Jake got the guy from the courtroom onto his feet and under control, she studied the profanity scratched into her car. *Nice.*

The "Die Bitx" was etched deeply into the hood, and she doubted she'd ever be able to get rid of it entirely.

A soft sigh left her lips as she suddenly realized she was still snuggled up against Michael Reilly's long, solid former-football-player body. It wasn't a hardship. He obviously still worked out.

Afraid she was enjoying his comforting touch a little more than was wise, she quickly pulled out of his embrace and leaned down to pick up his scarred briefcase. "Sorry about this. It was probably worth more than my car." Dani knew her leathers. She hadn't grown up the daughter of one of the richest women on earth without knowing quality when she saw it. She just couldn't have nice things like that anymore now that she was supporting herself.

He glanced at her car, then solemnly met her gaze again. "I think it's still worth more, even battered."

She snorted out a laugh and handed over the case. "Wait a minute. Did you just make another joke? That makes three in the last five minutes. Are you taking Prozac these days?"

He sent her a bored look, but the gleam in his eyes gave away the fact that he was fighting a grin. He reached into his pocket for his cell. "Since the blow to your head hasn't affected your quick wit, I'll trust you'll remember to stop by my office at three o'clock today." After punching their appointment into his phone, he glanced at her car. "Or, you could just ride back with me, and I'll run you home after?"

As the cop led that vile man away, Jake slid beside Dani and wrapped his arm possessively around her shoulder. "Nope, Dani's all squared away, Counselor. She's going to help me with a case I'm working on, so I'll take care of her."

Obviously understanding Jake's back-off gesture, Michael raised a hand for peace and said, "If you want to avoid jail time, I'll see you at three Dani." Then he turned and walked away.

"I'll be there." She turned to Jake. "Where are you parked?"

After Dani slid gingerly into Jake's police cruiser, she laid her head back against the seat and groaned. "I can't afford to get my car fixed until Friday, this was one of my favorite skirts—*was* being the operative word—and I feel like I've been in a bar brawl. Is it too much to ask to live an ordinary life without all the drama?" After she tilted her throbbing face toward his, she added, "I would've never had to testify against that insane man's brother, and I wouldn't have to go to some gruesome crime scene, if it weren't for you, Jake."

He shrugged. "Yeah, but you do it because you love me."

God help her she did, but not as a husband. Sadly, they wanted different things from marriage, and it was never meant to be. After she and Jake had separated earlier in the year, a dream revealed a man her heart recognized as the one she'd always love.

Well, she'd seen the back of him anyway. It would have been way too much to ask to actually see the man's face rather than his backside, although a fine rear view it was. He had a strange jagged scar, like a long squiggle, on his right shoulder. Even she should be able to identify him when she finally met him.

Her mother, who was afflicted with similar prophetic dreams that no one knew about, insisted Dani would meet the man soon, but he was going to hurt her, because he'd been walking away in the dream, ending their relationship. He might not be the man she was meant to spend her life with. Either way, the man in her dream hadn't been Jake.

Dani laid her hand on Jake's forearm and gave it a gentle squeeze. "I do love you, Jake, enough that I want you to be happy. You need to get back out there and find that *one woman* who actually wants to be barefoot, pregnant with your fourth or fifth child, and have a perfectly prepared meal on the table when you return home each night." She sent him a stern look. "That is, if you can pry your dedicated little self away from work long enough to actually come home."

He tore his gaze from the road and met hers. "I know I work too much. I can be better about that. And you say you don't want kids, but you'd be a great mother. It isn't certain if we had a child it would have extra abilities. You always seem to conveniently forget that your sister doesn't have them." He shot her a grin. "And look how well we've gotten along in the past few months. It shows we're meant to be together."

"That's only because we haven't lived together for the past few months." She rubbed at the tension headache brewing behind her forehead. "Do you realize we've been separated almost as long as we were married?"

Jake shook his head, waving off the facts. "Actually, I just read an article on the Internet that said in the United States, there are three-point-eight million married couples who don't live under the same roof. If they can do it, so can we. But I'd rather you come home and forget about the divorce."

"Are you having a complete memory lapse?" Dani threw her hands up in frustration. "We drive each other crazy. You lost all your ability to cook, clean, and pick up after yourself when we were together. That is, when you decided to come home. And I distinctly remember you saying that I needed to grow up, stop taking handouts from my mother, quit spending money faster than you earned it, and pick up the damn books I leave stacked on the floor for you to trip over. If we had a kid, I'd probably get so lost in a book or on the Internet researching something that I'd forget to feed it. I was a lousy wife, and I'd be a horrible parent, Jake." She crossed her arms and huffed out a breath. "And so would you. Your nurturing skills suck."

Even Michael, who was constantly annoyed with her, had at least been kind earlier. Jake hadn't even mentioned the attack she'd just endured because of his dumb case. Granted, he'd been a little busy containing the car-battering thug, but still.

"I can be nurturing just as much as the next guy." He put a pathetically sorrowful expression on his face. "I'm extremely sorry you've been hurt, and wish I could take away your pain and make it my own." He barely suppressed a grin before he added, "There's a bottle of aspirin in the glove compartment."

She shook her head in utter frustration, sending a whole new wave of pain to her face, and dug the bottle out. "A little ice would be nice, too." She tossed back three pills and gagged as she tried to dry swallow them.

He glanced in the mirror and made a quick lane change. "It's lunchtime anyway. How about we swing by a drive-through?"

"Whatever," Dani groused, ignoring the acidic flavor coating her tongue.

"Honest, Dani, thanks for all your help, and I am sorry about today. You know I appreciate all you do for me. And I'll bet you're hungry because you spent your lunch money on something sparkly in lieu of eating. How about I buy you a supersize combo meal *and* a cup of ice as a reward for another of your good deeds?"

"My hero," she muttered and leaned her head against the seat. She hated to admit he was right. That's how she'd justified her new earrings. They were on sale and only cost as much as three or four lunches. Some women used Atkins or South Beach diets to keep their figures. She used the jewelry diet. It worked for her.

Jake sent her a cocky grin. "You're going to think I'm a hero when I arrange for the department to pay for the repairs on your car. It's the least we can do, since you won't accept a consulting fee."

"Thanks." She sighed with relief, hoping he wasn't going to engage in another argument about her taking money for his use of her visions and dreams. If she took payment from the police, it'd be public record, but her mother insisted that no one know of their extra abilities. It might not be so good for her mom's ticket sales.

Being the daughter of a celebrity sucked sometimes. Like the time she'd been kidnapped for ransom at the age of four but, luckily, hadn't been harmed. Because of that, she'd had annoying security guards following her every time she set foot outside her mother's gated compound, until she'd graduated from high school. Having constant tattletales sure curtailed her adolescent fun. But worse, it was hell living with a huge secret your whole life, with only a handful of people who knew the truth. Because of that, she had to decipher her visions and dreams, trying to arrive at the scene of the crime in time so that she or the police could witness the act, thereby, keeping her secret. But she was going to stop sharing what she saw . . . soon.

Jake was blissfully quiet for a few moments, and she'd almost fallen asleep when he said, "Michael wants you. What's up with that?"

Dani shifted slowly to meet his stare, her head still pounding. "Michael thinks I'm a ditz. He doesn't want me." Anymore, but she kept that part to herself. She took pride in the fact that Michael had been the first of only two men she'd been with before Jake. Her mother was notorious for sleeping around, and because of it, Dani was very selective with her bed partners.

The muscles in Jake's jaw twitched, indicating he was being serious for a change. "Trust me, he wants you. Bad. But there's another man you need to worry about more than the tight-assed Michael Reilly. His name is Carlos Watts."

At the gravity of his tone, Dani forgot all about Michael. "Is that the guy who attacked me?"

"Yeah. He's no criminal mastermind. He showed that when he beat the crap out of your car in front of a courthouse swarming with cops. I don't know how long I can keep him locked up. Maybe forty-eight hours, tops. The fact that he hit a cop will help, but his grandparents have money and have been bailing him and his brother out of trouble their whole lives. He may cool off after a few days and forget about you, but then again, he may not. We need to come up with a plan to keep you safe."

Chapter Two

Michael rubbed his shoulder as the elevator doors slid closed. His damaged rotator cuff throbbed, bitterly reminding him of the reason he'd retired early from the NFL. Clocking that guy with his briefcase had irritated the injury, but it took him down, so it was worth it.

When the doors parted, he lifted a hand in greeting to the receptionist, then headed down the long, quiet hall toward his office. The light scent of Dani's perfume clung to his jacket just as thoughts of her lingered in his mind. What kind of a case could she be helping Jake with?

Maybe there was a piece of art or jewelry that needed identifying. Besides being rich and having luxuries growing up, Dani had been a full-time college student since high school, earning four advanced degrees. No one could call the lady stupid—she'd always been a genius with computers—but her degrees were all in incredibly impractical subjects like history, art, philosophy, and some sort of cinematic-appreciation thing. Being a professional student had probably been her way of keeping Annalisa's money coming so she could put off the inevitability of growing up and getting a real job.

As soon as he entered his office, his assistant's voice rang out through the intercom. "Ron wants to see you right away."

Swearing under his breath, he tossed his beat-up briefcase onto his desk, and then headed down the long hall adorned with leather furniture and expensive art. He'd partnered with Ron because Ron was the most successful lawyer in town, and because Ron was his stepfather. But as the years passed, Ron's true colors had shone through, so Michael was actively seeking a way to end their partnership.

Knocking on Ron's doorjamb, Michael stuck his head inside, dismayed to see his stepbrother, Chad, there, too.

Ron, a vain, sandy-haired man, looked up from his desk. "Ah, Michael, there you are. Come in." When Ron forced a smile, there was barely a wrinkle on his face. He'd gone under the knife to hold off the ravages of aging one too many times. He looked as fake as his spray tan. "We need to discuss Annalisa's latest request."

His stepbrother sat with his arms crossed, looking like a beach bum in an expensive suit. He sent Michael a sneer. "You lucky dog. I might divorce my wife just so I can fulfill all of Annalisa Botelli's *needs*."

Wary, Michael glanced at Ron, who was chuckling. The man would bill his own mother to write up a will.

Ron said, "Annalisa would like the pleasure of your company for dinner tonight. She'd like to uh . . . discuss the terms of one of her upcoming projects."

"Why me?" Being a trial lawyer, he didn't specialize in divorce and entertainment law like Ron and Chad. "I've only worked on Dani's issues in case they went to court. Why wouldn't one of you look over Annalisa's projects?"

Ron's lips tilted into a smirk. "I doubt she wants to talk contracts. You're young, fairly handsome, recently single, and she likes men who work out. But she doesn't poach, so since I've been married to your mother, I haven't been able to help her in the way she might expect from you tonight. I want to be sure that you—Mr. Morality—understand that Annalisa is our largest, most profitable client, and whatever she wants she gets."

Michael stared into Ron's eyes for a long moment, trying to contain his rising temper. Michael had known Annalisa since he was a kid. She'd never want him that way. Would she? "I'll be happy to have dinner and discuss any legal matters she has on her mind."

"See, Dad." Chad snorted out a laugh. "I told you. It's no wonder his ex-wife turned to women." He swiveled toward Michael. "So that recent article in the *Journal* naming you as one of the top-ten eligible bachelors in town was just for show, wasn't it? Oh sure, you were the man at one time, going from Joe College Superstar to the Dallas Cowboys, but that little unfortunate accident brought an end to all of that, didn't it, sunshine? You date a lot of women, but you can't keep one happy for long, can you, Michael?"

He'd wanted to deck Chad for far too long, and here was his chance. Just as he clenched his fist to smash it into Chad's slimy face, their secretary's voice rang out. "Michael, your mother called. She's running late and wants you to meet her at the restaurant."

He lowered his fist to his side and let out a long breath. Chad wasn't worth it.

"Thanks." As he walked toward the hallway, Ron called out, "Tell your mother that despite our earlier . . . disagreement, I still expect her to host the dinner party tonight."

Michael shook his head as he punched the elevator button with his fist, wishing it were Chad's face.

When the doors parted in the empty elevator, he stepped inside and closed his eyes. His mother had sounded upset earlier when she'd invited him to lunch. She and Ron were obviously fighting again. He hated that Ron seemed to upset his mother almost daily lately.

A chime sounded and the doors opened again. Michael stepped into the lobby, determined to blow off the bad energy from the Chad and Ron meeting. After shoving the glass office doors open, he made his way to his mom's favorite restaurant a few blocks from his office.

The aroma of garlic and red sauce made him smile as he stepped inside the quiet Italian restaurant. He scanned the tables adorned with red-and-white checkered tablecloths. In the middle of each one sat a wine bottle with multicolored wax drippings decorating the sides.

His mother sat in a booth at the rear, her fair skin flushed and her green eyes lit with anger as she swiped at her shoulder-length dark-red hair. His mom appeared to be a delicate, beautiful woman on the outside, but she was Irish to the core, and her temper was nothing to scoff at.

He slipped into the booth across from her. "Should I go home and grab my helmet and pads? You look madder than hell."

Maeve's jaw clenched. "Ron's side dish got dumped and called to tell me all about it."

The news gut-punched him. "Ron's been cheating on you?"

"Yes." She closed her eyes, as if trying to regain her composure. "And it's not the first time."

"He's done it before? And you didn't tell me?" He wanted to beat the crap out of Ron—and his slimy kid, too.

"When I caught him the last time, you'd just found out about your wife and her . . . girlfriend. I didn't want to dump my problems on top of that. Heather was lucky I was engaged in my own battles, or I would have let her have it for the way you found out. She should have been honest with you."

The memory of that ugly incident a year and a half ago left him feeling as though he'd just been sucker punched—again. He'd tried to bury the betrayal he'd suffered but was still confused by it. He and Heather had usually had sex a few times a week the whole time they'd been married. They'd had two beautiful girls together, too. Carly and Amanda.

It had come as a complete shock when he'd arrived home early from a business trip and found her in bed with another woman. Heather had once hinted that she'd experimented with women in college, but she'd made it sound like a one-time deal. But since the divorce, he'd found out Heather had lied about a lot of things. "I still don't know how she kept something that big of a secret from me."

His mom waved her hand impatiently. "You didn't know because Heather is an extremely attractive bisexual woman who uses sex as a weapon. I'm not sure she knows what it is to truly love, and while I think that's sad, you couldn't have known something about her that she doesn't seem to understand about herself."

"Thank you, Dr. Laura, but it's still embarrassing."

"It's no reflection on you." His mom picked up her menu and studied it. "But the way you've been chasing anything in a skirt makes me wonder if you're trying to prove something to yourself. Serial dating isn't making you happy, honey."

He needed to change the subject. "I'm more interested in your problem. Ron doesn't deserve you. Let's find you a good divorce lawyer."

"I can't, Michael. Ron has all the money hidden away. When I threatened to leave him, he told me I'd never find it and I'd be left with nothing." She lifted her moist eyes and met his gaze. "He knows I can't afford to leave him. No one wants to hire a fifty-five-year-old woman whose only work experience was planning parties for a movie star years ago."

"You don't have to worry about money. I'll always take care of you, Mom." He hated that Ron had stolen his mother's self-esteem, turning her into his party-planning trophy wife.

He took her hand. "After Dad died, you did an incredible job of taking care of us. You're forgetting that you impressed Annalisa so much she offered you a great job, and she respected you enough to let us live in her guesthouse. You're one tough broad, and Ron doesn't have any idea who he's messing with."

"Thank you, sweetheart." Maeve narrowed her eyes. "But I didn't say I was giving up. I'm going to find that money, then take what's mine. Will you help me?"

"I'll start digging through his files this afternoon—assuming I can keep Annalisa's princess out of jail." He mentioned Dani because he hated to see his mother sad, and for some odd reason, the mention of Dani always brightened his mom's mood.

The creases in her forehead smoothed. "So, did you catch up with her at the courthouse?"

"Yeah. She's coming back to irritate me again this afternoon—that is, if she remembers our appointment." He took a long drink of water as the morning's events replayed in his mind. It probably wouldn't be a good idea to tell his mom about Dani's run-in with the lunatic. She'd just worry about her.

When his mom's eyes lit up, just as they always did right before she was going to butt into his life again, he nearly moaned.

She could barely contain her excitement as she leaned closer and said, "Speaking of Dani, you need to buy a house. Apartment life isn't good for your girls. They need a yard to play in. Why don't you ask her to help you?"

He choked on his water. "Are you serious? Dani would make the simple process of buying a house a disaster." He'd planned to buy a house for some time but had been so busy at work he hadn't gotten around to it.

"She's the daughter of one of your biggest clients. Annalisa would be upset if you used anyone else." His mother picked up her menu again and studied it, letting her words settle in.

"Look, while you find Dani—"

"Charming and irresistible?"

"I don't need her drama. What I need is order in my life now that the dust has settled from my divorce." He pretended to consider his menu, but his mom was right. He didn't want to piss off their largest client.

After running the problem around in his head for a few moments, he laid his menu down and glanced up in time to catch his mother trying to hide her smug smirk. "Okay. I'll ask her. But only because it'll be good for business."

"Good." His mom's smile bloomed. "Did she finally get Jake to sign the papers?"

"No. But she needs to. He's been nothing but trouble for her. Dani needs to find someone who's a grown-up rather than . . ." He trailed off and stared at his menu again. He wasn't going there.

His mother leaned across the table and whispered, "That's a whole lot of concern coming from a man who doesn't want Dani's drama. But until Jake signs the papers, you need to cool those jets, sweetheart."

"Believe me, there are no jets to cool here." Or at least none he was going to act on. He'd always been attracted to Dani, but she'd been the one to abruptly end their friendship before he could tell her how he felt about her, not him, and she'd cut his heart out. Then Heather, the only other woman he'd ever loved, betrayed him. Who needed it?

"Mmmm" was his mother's quiet response.

He shook his head and concentrated on the menu. It was futile to argue with his mother's all-knowing hum. "Oh, I almost forgot. Ron said he was still expecting you to host some party tonight?"

"Yeah. Like that's going to happen. Ron can go straight to hell."

Dani stepped into the master bedroom of Jake's latest crime scene, and her jaw dropped. As she scanned the humongous room, her eyes began to ache as badly as her face did. The curtains, bedspread, wallpaper, and even the carpet were all a shade of cotton-candy pink.

"You'd better hope the husband doesn't claim having to sleep in this room is grounds for an insanity plea. One look at this and no jury in the land would convict him," Dani said as she studied the nauseating decor. "This is more pink than a stomach-upset ad would feel justified using."

Jake shook his head and laughed. "I don't know any guy who'd put up with this shit."

When she walked into the equally pink bathroom, the chuckle died on her lips as an ice-cold chill ran up her spine. The blood splatter on the wall reminded her of the reason she was there. Drawing a deep breath, she moved toward the jet tub. She was just about to place her hands on the side, then stopped. "Do I need gloves?"

"No, we've already dusted that. Go ahead."

She laid her hands on the cool marble tub where the woman had died, closing her eyes and opening her mind for whatever the universe saw fit to fill it with. Still pictures began furiously slamming into her brain, like an out-of-control slide show.

Studying the images, trying to make them slow down, she saw a pair of male hands, a gun in the left one. "The wife was in the tub, painting her nails. I can see the bottle; it was called 'Pink Champagne.'" She took her hands off the edge of the tub, waiting for the images to stop. They were moving too fast and began to blur into fuzzy walls of color. After she cleared her mind, she laid her hands on the tub and tried again. "She had her eyes closed, lounging in the tub when he came in and shot her."

Her head seared fiercely with the familiar pain that always accompanied her visions, but she forced herself to continue to watch the gruesome scenes. Focusing on the details and not the poor woman, she asked, "Where's the nail polish? It's gone after he shoots her. Why would he take it?" She opened her eyes and met Jake's gaze.

He shook his head. "I don't know. There weren't any nail polish bottles on the tub or counters when we got here." He snapped on a pair of gloves and rifled through drawers and cabinets. He found a big plastic box under the sink containing multiple jars of polish. "Is it in here?"

Dani quickly scanned the collection of little colorful jars. She started to reach for the shade she recognized before Jake nudged her hand aside. He picked up the bottle she indicated with his gloved hand.

Checking the label, he showed it to her. When she nodded in recognition, he said, "She might've had a second bottle, but this one is half-full. Why would he take the time to put it back?"

Dani sighed and shook her head. "It's important Jake, but I don't know why, yet."

She was so tired it was hard to concentrate. But she closed her eyes again to regain her focus. A moving image of a pink bunny playing a bass drum appeared, but the beat wasn't right. "Jake, what's that movie whose theme goes *ba-dump . . . ba-dump . . . ba-dump ba-dump ba-dump ba-dump ba-duuuuump?*"

He frowned as he considered it. "*The Pink Panther?* God, honey, please don't tell me we're doing movie clues again? I'll never be able to watch another Julia Roberts flick after the last case."

Nothing was making any sense. She slumped onto the side of the tub in frustration.

Jake grasped her by the upper arms and pulled her back to her feet. "You're doing great. Then what, babe? Come on, you can do this."

She willed herself to see the rest and placed her palms on the tub again. "He laid his hand on her neck—to check her pulse."

Jake leaned down and whispered, "Did the hands have gloves?"

"Navy blue, but only the left. The right hand was bare."

"I knew it." Jake blew out a long slow breath. "The scumbag is left-handed." He pulled her closer. "Can you see the rest?"

"There's no more in here."

He tugged her toward the master closet. "How about in here?"

She scanned the monstrously large closet. It had endless rows of clothes, built-in shelves, mirrors, drawers, and even a dry-cleaning system on one wall. There was a pink, cushioned center island, and two other walls held a series of cubbies big enough for two hundred pairs of shoes. The last wall was cedar lined, sending off a pleasant aroma, and it held an array of evening gowns, most in shades of red or pink.

She closed her eyes, and the bunny started banging more loudly. He turned tight circles in the closet where they stood, but she didn't understand what it meant. "I'm not getting anything new in here, either. Still just the bunny in those battery commercials and the movie theme song."

Jake led her out of the master bedroom and down the hall to a smaller bedroom. They crossed to the bed that had been stripped of its mattress. Dani laid her hand on the headboard. It had so much energy it shocked her, and she jerked her hand off.

Unable to watch the horrid scene, she turned away. "He walked in here and pointed the gun at Jared's heart. The little boy's name was Jared, and he was awake. He knew he was going to be shot. Then the gloved finger squeezed the trigger." The little boy had big blue eyes and—oh God—it'd be a long while before she'd stop seeing the terror in them. "Who could do that, Jake? This guy's a monster." Dani's head roared with pain, her knees grew weak, and her whole body shook with repulsion. She had to stop; she couldn't take any more.

Jake moved next to her, running a soothing hand up and down her spine. "You and I are gonna lock that monster up forever. What happened next?"

Her mind went blank. Only the annoying theme song still whispered in her ears. "That's it. That's all there is. Sorry."

Jake led her out of the room. "How about I search online for all the *Pink Panther* movies while you have your meeting with the horny lawyer? Then we'll go back to your place, watch the movies, and try to figure this out. I'll pick up a bottle of Chianti, and we'll order a pizza."

Totally spent, Dani ignored his comment about Michael and sagged against him. "Okay."

Dammit, she'd just done it again. She'd promised herself she wouldn't get involved in another of Jake's cases. But how could she deny the family members of that poor little boy and his mother the one thing that might help heal their pain? To see the murderer sent to prison forever.

Jake checked the lock on the front door after they were outside. "Do you think the movie is the newer version or one of the classics?"

"I have no idea." Exhausted, Dani lifted her hands in confusion. "I hate those movies."

"Are you kidding? They're hilarious." He chuckled as he led her down the long driveway, quoting his favorite one-liners from the films. Thank God he'd run out of them by the time they'd finally reached the car.

"Hey, why don't I get us some microwave popcorn, too? It could be a long night." He gave her a quick eyebrow hitch as he opened the car door for her.

Dani fastened her seat belt and crossed her arms, waiting for him to slide in beside her. When he was settled, she said, "I want extra butter, and you're not spending the night."

"Man, you've gotten strict." Jake started the engine, then laid his arm across the back of the seat as he backed out of the driveway. His fingers snaked up, resting on the back of her neck, and gave her a light squeeze. "Why don't we wait and see what you say after we polish off that bottle of wine?"

Michael glanced up from his desk, suddenly forgetting all about the phone conversation he was having with a friend he had made plans with for the evening. Dani leaned against his doorjamb, her arms crossed, studying him with her exotic eyes. They were a mixture of gold, brown, and green, and he'd never seen any quite like them.

He tore his gaze from hers and noted the time. Three o'clock. Exactly. Would wonders never cease?

He motioned her inside as he continued his phone conversation.

His friend droned on about their teams' chances at the playoffs while Dani strolled around his office, examining the art hanging on the walls he'd bought from Dani's best friend, Zoe. Dani wore the same damaged clothes from earlier, her hair still a rat's nest of loose, wild curls, and her bruised face displayed a litany of color.

She'd never looked more beautiful.

Dani was the only woman he'd ever known who, while she was beautiful and always dressed nicely, had absolutely no vanity. She hadn't changed much from when they were ten, both of them running wild on her mother's estate and having the time of their lives.

When exactly had their relationship changed? They'd gone from being best buddies to arch enemies when they'd hit puberty, and he'd never figured out why.

His attention was drawn back to his phone call when his friend's voice buzzing in his ear had finally ceased. "A client just walked in, so I have to let you go. Sorry I had to bail on you tonight." He hung up and leaned back in his chair, waiting for Dani to finish her perusal.

She turned and assaulted him with a sexy smirk. "Breaking dates and hearts along the way, Mr. Most Eligible Bachelor in Town?"

Had everyone read that ridiculous article? He could've told her the truth; instead he shrugged. "Keeps me busy. But that's not nearly as interesting as the story must be about you scaling the mayor's wall while being chased by guard dogs."

She rolled her eyes and, ignoring him, gestured toward a picture on the wall. "You've got two of Zoe's paintings. I'm shocked. I thought your tastes were much too conservative for her style. I'd have thought a tedious country scene with hunting dogs would be more up your boring legal alley."

"You should be glad I'm not staring at guns all day. It's hard enough to resist using one on my most annoying client."

Her cocky smile disappeared.

He'd hit a nerve, so now he was duty bound to go for the kill. "Zoe's work has become more refined and mature with time. Maybe some of that will rub off on her best buddy, too, one day."

Her right brow shot up. "Good one, Michael. I'm impressed. I'll bet you've been saving that one up for weeks."

He smirked but hated to admit that it still stung a little that Zoe had taken his place as Dani's best friend when she'd dumped him, and they'd remained so. He'd always liked Zoe despite that, so he asked, "How is she?" and motioned his hand toward one of his guest chairs.

Dani winced as she slowly lowered herself onto the burgundy leather chair in front of his desk, sending a stab of guilt to his gut for his earlier joke about the gun. He'd have to take it a little easier on her—at least until she recovered from her parking lot attack.

When she was settled, Dani lifted her chin, her icy demeanor firmly back in place. "Zoe has a great husband, three kids, and is painting her heart out. She's absolutely content with her life. I've never known anyone else who could say that." The coolness fled from Dani's eyes, and the corners of her perfect cupid-bow upper lip tilted. "Remember how everyone couldn't believe she wasn't going to college after we graduated? All the teachers and counselors worried about her. They thought she'd end up a big hippie like her goofy parents."

"Yeah." He smiled at the memory. "She always knew what she wanted. She once said to me, after a few beers, 'Why do I need a college degree? I'm going to be a famous painter. Just ask Dani.' Was that, like, an inside joke or something?"

"Yeah, sort of." Dani shifted in her chair. "What do I need to sign?"

He pushed a stack of papers toward her. "First, Ron reprinted your divorce papers. You can sign them now, but I think I'd wait until you get Jake to sign. That way the signature dates won't be a year apart or more."

"You're just a riot these days, Mikey." She chuckled as she examined the stack before her. "Jake will sign them soon. He's coming around." She looked up and her smile faded. "It was more my fault than his that things didn't work out."

The misery in her eyes surprised him. He didn't think his ex-wife would admit something like that, even though she and the other girl were caught in the act. "Well, it's good you're still friends. Heather and I are struggling with that for our girls' sake." He pushed the divorce papers aside and replaced them with another stack of papers. "So, if you'll promise to give up wall climbing forever, sign these where indicated and give me a check for twenty-five hundred to cover the fine, your trespassing charge will miraculously disappear." He handed her his pen.

Dani's eyes widened. "Twenty-five hundred dollars?"

When he nodded, she said, "Um, okay. But I'll need a few days to come up with that much."

He knew her well enough to know he wasn't seeing evasion in her expression this time but absolute embarrassment. He didn't know why she wouldn't just ask her mother for the money, but then he'd never understood the relationship between Dani and Annalisa. "It needs to be paid this afternoon, or the deal is off. That's why I had to hunt you down at the courthouse. I can just bill your mother for it."

"No! You don't understand. I can't take . . ." Panic found a home in Dani's eyes as she trailed off. Her forehead crumpled, and it appeared she was about to go into some in-depth explanation he was sure he didn't want to hear.

"I'll pay this and then bill you later so we can file today. You can pay me back whenever you can, or we'll just take it out of your commission."

"Commission? What are you talking about?" Relief and confusion waltzed across her face as she quickly signed her name.

His conversation with Ron still gnawed at his gut. Surely Annalisa wasn't interested in him like that, but he wasn't taking any chances. "I need to buy a house. You're a Realtor now, evidently, so I thought maybe you'd like to help me out?"

"I guess I could tolerate being around you for more than ten minutes if a big, fat commission check is involved. What kind of price range are we—"

"That is, if you'll do me one favor." It looked like Dani was going to flip her lid. Might be fun to watch.

~

Dani's hopes for a huge commission check quickly faded as she frowned and crossed her arms. "I knew there'd be a catch."

There was always a catch with him.

Michael said, "Your mother has asked me to have dinner with her tonight, at her home, and I was hoping you could join us."

"Why?" A little alarm sounded in her head.

"No particular reason, other than it might make things more . . . comfortable."

Comfortable? That didn't make sense. Michael had known her mom since he was ten. He and Maeve had lived in the same guesthouse, which Dani currently occupied, for ten years. Something was definitely up. "Nope, not buying it. Spill it, Reilly."

He raised his hands in resignation. "Ron mentioned that . . . well, your mother and he . . . and she didn't poach but . . . now that I'm single, maybe she'd want more than that . . . like . . . sex?"

Yuck!

"Annalisa? And you? That'd just be . . . sick."

He blew out a breath. "Especially since you and I . . . just the one night, but there's a code of honor here. I'd never want you to feel like . . . so we agree, right? Ron's definitely mistaken."

Her stomach did a nasty flip at the thought of her mother with Michael. "God, I hope so."

He leaned forward, his voice rising on a panicked plea: "There's no way your mom would be interested in me like that? Would she?"

She was about to say no, before she realized her mother had, if you believed the tabloids, been with a few men recently who were about her and Michael's age. And she had to reluctantly admit that Michael was tall, dark-haired, and extremely good-looking. Just her mother's type.

Most every woman's type.

"I already have plans for dinner, but maybe I'd better join you for dessert." Or else Michael might end up being dessert.

"Yes. Please." Nodding like a bobble-head doll, he added, "Why don't you come over about eight thirty?"

"Okay. But if my mom's really serious about you, she'll just shoo me back to the guesthouse."

Michael's bobbing head stilled. He frowned and rubbed the back of his neck. "Maybe we could say I need to go back to your place and look at MLS listings because you're going to help me buy a house?"

That made sense, but they might need more. If her mom was thinking that way—and jeez, that'd be creepy—she'd just tell her they could do it later. No, she had no choice. She knew what they had to do. "If my mom thinks that you and I are, you know, interested in each other, she'd never . . . oh God, I can't even think about that. So, anyway, I'll come over about eight thirty and give you a little peck on the cheek, making you off-limits, and all should be well. Okay?"

Michael took her hand, stunning her when he gave it a friendly squeeze. "Thank you, Dani." His touch sent that stupid zing racing up her arm again, landing like a warm arrow in her heart.

His large hand was still wrapped around hers as she studied his grateful expression. Most men would jump at the chance to sleep with Annalisa Botelli, not caring if they'd slept with her daughter first, but not Michael. He was truly one of the good guys, always choosing the high road.

Michael had hurt her more deeply than anyone ever had, and he didn't even know it. She hardly could have told him she had to part ways with him because it had been too painful knowing he'd marry Heather and break her heart. Her damn dreams had ruined her relationship with the first boy she'd ever loved. And a few more after that.

She pushed away the bad memories and focused on the present. Even though she never let an opportunity pass to annoy Michael, she'd always respected him. So instead of sending him one of her typical acidic remarks, she tugged her hand out of his light grasp and gave him a genuine smile. "No problem. See you later."

Strangely, the prospect of seeing him later didn't fill her with the usual dread. That blow to her head earlier must've been harder than she'd thought.

Chapter Three

Michael pulled up in front of the massive front gates of Annalisa's compound and lowered his car's window. Dani's kidnapping as a child had prompted Annalisa to move from LA back to New Mexico and outfit her home with more gadgets than Fort Knox. While a tinny voice asked the nature of his business, a little camera whirled quietly in his direction. The tiny lens focused on his face. "Michael Reilly to see Annalisa." He knew the drill and held up his driver's license next to his chin.

When the large iron gates slowly parted for him, he drove up the long tree-lined drive. Annalisa's home resembled a massive English estate with its three-story stone walls and sweeping gardens. It was a stark contrast to the typical stuccoed mission-style homes of the Southwest.

Whenever he drove through the gates, warm memories always filled him of when he and his mother had lived in the guesthouse. And what fun times he and Dani had climbing trees and riding horses when they were kids.

The first time he'd seen the house, he'd judged the large, imposing structure as cold and intimidating, like a castle. He quickly learned that inside the solid masonry walls was a loud but warm and loving family.

Because Annalisa had never married, the quiet whispers told the tale that she had only ever truly loved one man—Dani's father. The tabloids often speculated who Dani's father was, ranging from plastic surgeons to men with ties to the mob. He and Dani had spent hours holed up in his bedroom in the guesthouse, playing detective. They were convinced they could figure out the mystery of her parentage, but never did, and eventually moved on to other pursuits. They used to spend so much time together they could practically read each other's thoughts. It had made Dani's sister jealous that he took so much of Dani's time and attention away from her.

Dani's younger sister, Sara, had something that Dani never had, though. A father. One who asked to be a part of her life. So, when Sara was whisked away by her dad for school breaks, Annalisa would slip her arm around Dani's slumping shoulders, and then around Michael's, and suggest they go on an adventure of their own. Often those jaunts included trips to Disney World, or sometimes they went to Europe, or Hawaii. Once, they'd even gone on an African picture safari. His passport overflowed with exotic stamps by the time he was sixteen, and he'd always been grateful to be included. To be made to feel a part of their family.

Dani had been the best friend he'd ever had. And eventually he'd developed romantic feelings for her but hadn't been sure how to change their dynamic. Dani had taken care of that out of the blue one day by ending their relationship for no apparent reason. And then they'd slept together the one time a few years later, which had only added to his overall confusion about her.

But how could he think of Annalisa as anything other than the woman who'd treated him as if he were her own child?

Ron had to be wrong. Annalisa had been motherly and kind to him. Well, as motherly as one of *People Magazine*'s "Sexiest Women Alive" could be.

He parked his car in front of the arched wooden doors and hopped out. He wasn't surprised when they opened before he could knock. Not looking forward to a potentially disastrous evening, he drew a steadying breath and followed the servant, clad in stern black, to the living room.

Annalisa held a wineglass, her expression pensive as she studied the fire in the massive stone hearth. Above it hung a larger-than-life-size portrait from when she was in her early twenties, at the peak of her beauty. Tonight, she wore something soft and silky that hugged her lush curves. He'd never seen her looking other than camera ready in all the years he'd known her.

She turned and, as if a switch had been thrown, beamed her infamous smile at him. The firelight bathed her in soft, complimentary tones. She'd truly earned her title as one of the most beautiful women on earth. Annalisa had the look of Sophia Loren and the body of a goddess, but, still, she was just Dani's mom. A woman who could be vain and demanding but loved her daughters more than any of the Oscars or Emmys that gleamed brightly atop the mantel at her back.

"Well, good evening, Michael. You're punctual, as always."

"Hello, Annalisa." He cleared the apprehension from his throat. "It's nice to see you again."

She crossed to the bar and poured him a glass of wine. "I know you value a fine wine as much as I do. I found this one at a small vineyard in Tuscany. I hope you'll appreciate it as much as I appreciate you being here tonight."

She handed him a glass and clinked her own against his, her eyes twinkling in the reflective firelight. As he stared back at her, his collar suddenly seemed two sizes too small. Surely, she wasn't flirting with him—just offering him a simple glass of wine. He needed to get a grip.

In the time he'd nursed one glass, Annalisa had polished off two, making him more uncomfortable by the moment. He still wasn't sure what he'd do if she made a pass at him. He'd keep his drinking to a minimum, though, to keep his wits about him.

By the time they sat for dinner, they'd discussed his mother, his daughters—now three and five years old—and then the conversation veered toward her latest movie. Mrs. Wilson, the chef, served all his favorite foods. She'd spoiled him rotten when he'd lived here, sneaking him cookies and regularly making his all-time favorite: chocolate molten cake. He'd have to go back to her private suite and thank her before leaving.

As he tried to enjoy the extravagant dinner, he did his best to keep up his end of the conversation. But he wasn't doing very well. Annalisa's tone, while friendly, was still just slightly flirtatious, and it caused ripples of anxiety in the pit of his stomach. Was he reading too much into her every word and glance? She had a reputation as a man-eater, and he hoped he wasn't on the evening's menu.

He wiped the sweat from his brow as dessert was served. Where the hell was Dani? She'd probably forgotten.

But even his anxiety couldn't suppress the ecstasy he felt when he lifted a forkful of chocolate decadence to his lips. The dessert was incredible, but he needed to stay focused. It was crunch time; he was down in the fourth quarter and needed a big Hail Mary. Dani was supposed to be part of the special teams, but she hadn't shown yet.

He was going to strangle her the next time he saw her. He grabbed his cell but then remembered she had phone issues.

"Michael," Annalisa purred with her sexy, movie star voice, "what's troubling you tonight?"

He looked up and met her gaze, forcing a bite of his dessert down his throat. "I'm sorry. Long day, I guess. Maybe I should just go?"

"Nonsense." She laid her hand on top of his. For a moment her eyes fixed intently on his, and she seemed to look right into his soul before a small chuckle escaped her lips. "I just realized that you and I have never had dinner alone." She gave his hand a light pat. "Let's have coffee in the den, and I'll tell you why I asked for you rather than Ron or Chad."

Oh, shit. Here it comes. "I was curious about that. I don't usually have much to do with your business dealings."

"That's true, but I wanted to talk to you about Dani. Ron and Chad don't know her like you do, and I hoped you could help me with something."

He blinked. So it wasn't a seduction after all? A huge wave of relief rushed through him, dropping his body temperature by a good twenty degrees. "I'll be happy to help you in any way I can, Annalisa," he said, scraping the dish for the last forkful of chocolate gooey delight. It was damn good, especially now that he could actually enjoy it.

When they were settled on opposite couches, safely separated by a large coffee table, Annalisa drew a deep breath. "Dani won't let me help her financially. She hasn't taken so much as a pair of shoes from me unless it was her birthday or Christmas." Annalisa stood and paced. Her Italian heritage showed in her dramatic hand waving. "It's ridiculous. She won't even go shopping with me anymore because she's always broke. And she spends all her time running people around to look at houses, which they rarely buy. Since she's getting divorced, she should be able to have her old life back. But she can't do it on her own. Dani's not like everyone else. She's . . . special."

Michael just barely curtailed his laugh at the word *special.* "Yeah. There's no one quite like Dani." But he was surprised, and a little impressed, to learn that Dani had actually cut the apron strings. He'd wondered if she took her Realtor job seriously, and now it appeared she did.

Annalisa threw her hands up. "She's not cut out for the business world. People will take advantage of her. Dani can't say no. She'd give someone the shirt off her back and then point them to her closet and ask if they'd like another. It hurts me to see her run ragged like this." She stopped pacing and her face turned stone-cold sober. "Michael, she's wearing clothes that are over two years old!" She added a dramatic shudder. "And that car she drives? It's a death trap on wheels. I need to find a way for her to accept money without her knowing it's coming from me. And that's why I need your help."

Helping with Dani's financial problems would probably mean spending even more time thinking about her after she'd sold him a house. The more he was around her, had reminders of her, the harder it was to remember how she'd hurt him so deeply in the past. But he couldn't refuse Annalisa; Ron would throw a fit. So, he'd have to keep his guard up and not let his former feelings for Dani seep back into his heart. But Annalisa's request presented the perfect opportunity to finally tell Dani's mother what he'd wanted to since they were both in middle school.

He plastered on his best stern-lawyer expression. "Let's look at the facts. Dani lives in your guesthouse, so she has a roof over her head. There's little chance of her starving to death with Mrs. Wilson, the best cook in the world, only a stone's throw away, so all the basics are covered. What I've never been able to understand is why you'd deny her the satisfaction of what you and I have both had."

Annalisa frowned, as much as the Botox injections would allow. "I have never denied Dani *anything*."

"That's exactly the point!" He hadn't meant to raise his voice but couldn't seem to restrain himself. "You and I have both worked hard and excelled in our given professions. You've won multiple Oscars, and are one of the most beloved actresses in the world. I've earned a Heisman Trophy and was a starting quarterback in the NFL. Dani's never been given the opportunity to work toward a goal and succeed, all by herself. You've never made her work for anything. If she wanted it, you made sure she had it." His heart pounded as he caught his breath. He should probably have stopped his rant, but he didn't want to. He'd kicked the door open and wasn't going to stop now.

"Dani needs to try, and maybe even fail, all on her own. Until she does, she'll never be truly happy. You're like the parent of an alcoholic who sneaks booze to her child rather than see her suffer through rehab."

Annalisa's head jerked back as if he'd slapped her.

He'd just given one of the most powerful women he knew a speech she hadn't asked for, then he'd ended it with an insulting remark that hadn't been called for.

No, that wasn't true. Someone needed to be honest with her, to tell her what Dani really needed. Dani was smart, beautiful, and deserved a real chance to make it on her own. She needed guidance and someone to believe she could do anything she put her mind to . . .

And where the hell had that come from? Dani was none of his concern anymore. She was just the daughter of one of his clients. Nothing more. He couldn't forget that. After his ex-wife had broken his heart, he couldn't take another blow from Dani.

When he met Annalisa's gaze again, she closed her eyes and sucked in a deep breath as if reeling in her infamous temper.

"Annalisa—"

She held up a hand to stop him, looking mad enough to call one of her many security guards and have him thrown out. But she'd asked for his advice, and now she'd damn well take it.

He crossed his arms and waited her out. He was right and Annalisa was wrong. Dead wrong. She shouldn't trick Dani into being reliant on anyone but herself.

Annalisa opened her eyes, staring intently into his. It was difficult to read what he saw in her expression, but it wasn't happiness.

She crossed her arms and paced the room, evidently having some sort of internal debate.

Finally, she circled around and stood directly in front of him. "I'll be damned, Michael. You might be right. Thank you for having the guts to tell me. Heaven knows, no one else around here ever stands up to me. With the exception of Dani, of course."

She paced away again. "I've never looked at the situation quite like that. After those bastards tried to kidnap her all those years ago, I think it made me a little overprotective." She sighed and shook her head. "Letting her founder won't be easy. It's torturous for me to watch, especially if she fails, but I honestly want to do what's best for her." She smiled and added, "You've somehow always known what Dani needed, even when you were just a boy. It's a valuable gift that I've always appreciated in you, Michael."

She sat on the couch next to him, then huffed out a breath. "But do you think there's *anything* we could do about that ridiculous car she drives?"

He laughed as the tension drained from him like water in a sieve. "Let me think on that a bit. Maybe we could come up with something." And it might prove to be a good opportunity to pay back the still-absent Dani. Maybe they were having a sale at the Buick dealership.

He'd find Dani—the lover of shiny, fast cars—the biggest granny boat he could find. Or worse, maybe a van. But how could he make sure she'd have to keep it? That'd take a little work, but he'd find a way.

"Michael." Annalisa grinned and laid her hand on the side of his face, giving it a gentle pat. "Be nice. I know you two enjoy your little games, but don't get cute."

How the hell had she guessed his plan? His face must've given it away.

~

Dani shook her head and threw buttery popcorn into her mouth as she and Jake watched the beginning of the third *Pink Panther* movie. Unfortunately, nothing was clicking in the clue department.

"Okay. Why is this funny? We all know that Cato guy is going to attack Detective Dumbshit shortly after he returns home. Every one of these movies starts this way."

Jake chuckled and snagged more popcorn from the bowl in her lap. "It's funny because we *do* know. And come on, you have to admit the stuff Cato comes up with is pretty damn good."

"I'd totally agree with you if I was a twelve-year-old boy, but because I'm not, it's still just stupid."

Jake wrapped his arm around her shoulder and drew her close, his breath hot against her cheek. "No one could ever mistake you for a twelve-year-old boy, sweetheart. You want to turn the movie off and go to bed?"

Dani leaned out of his embrace. Another two seconds of Jake's smooth whispers, and she'd be putty in his hands. But she was determined to keep her vow. He'd never sign the papers if she didn't. Worse, he'd never move on and find the woman he's meant to be with.

As she chomped another handful of popcorn, she had the overwhelming feeling that she was forgetting something important. "Oh crap, I'm late!"

After shoving the bowl into Jake's chest, Dani ran toward her mother's house, every pounding step sending more pain radiating to her still-throbbing face. Passing the pool and the tennis courts, she headed for the dining room's French doors and tried the handles. Locked.

She cupped her hands against the glass and peered inside. The room was empty, and the dishes had been cleared. She hoped she'd find them in the den and not her mom's bedroom.

Gross.

She tapped in her security code and walked through a side door.

When she entered the den, Annalisa was smiling at Michael and her hand lay on the side of his face. That couldn't be good. Her beautiful mother was like those sirens in fairy tales: just one glance and no man could resist her.

She needed to make her mom understand that Michael was off-limits. So after her mother dropped her hand, Dani marched up to Michael, sat on his lap, and tried to give him a quick peck on the cheek as they'd planned. But Michael turned his head and narrowed his eyes as his mouth slowly made its way toward hers. He was probably mad that she was late, but what the heck was he up to?

She narrowed her eyes right back. He better not.

He did.

Michael laid his soft lips against hers and took total advantage of the situation. Her first instinct was to lean away, but then the sweetness of chocolate and the tart notes of wine drew her in. Warm memories of him seeped into her heart, reminding her of how much they used to mean to each other. Of how much she used to love him.

Then he deepened the kiss, and the heat kicked in.

She hadn't been prepared for the belly-clenching kiss. She used to think his mouth should carry an R rating. In the years since their last kiss, he'd improved and would get nothing short of an X rating from her now.

He'd sucked all the air from her lungs and left her with about two working brain cells by the time she leaned back and blinked at him.

"You're late," he growled.

His gaze shot to her mouth again, and then to her eyes, as if asking permission this time. She couldn't muster a refusal. She should have, but she really didn't want to. She hadn't been kissed like that—ever.

Her head nodded all on its own.

Michael's lips were still tilted into a grin as he fused his mouth against hers again. His tongue slipped past her lips, taking a long, slow journey, exploring every crevasse of her mouth.

The bones in her body became hot and liquid goo. It was no wonder she'd lost all her abilities to say no to him that night during their senior year of high school.

When he finished their kiss, she stared into his eyes trying to figure out what the hell *that* had been all about. Not that she was complaining—just confused.

All the anger that had been etched on his face moments before was gone when he said, "Glad to see you, babe."

"Uhmm," she stammered, her mind refusing to provide the words she searched for.

Her mom cleared her throat. "This is a surprise, Dani. You hadn't mentioned that you and Michael were seeing each other."

Dani cringed. "Uh, yeah. We've been seeing a lot of each other lately." She turned and smiled at her mom, recognizing her error only seconds before her mother's eyes widened. She'd forgotten about her bruised face.

Annalisa quickly leaned closer, gently tilting Dani's chin. In a low, dangerous tone, she asked, "Who did this to you, baby?"

"It's nothing. I'm fine." She sent a look Michael's way, silently begging him not to tell.

Trying to distract her mother, Dani pulled Annalisa close and hugged her. Whispering in her ear, she pleaded, "Just let it go, please? It's no big deal."

She leaned back, studying her mother's expression. Too late.

Annalisa turned and smiled at Michael. "Would you excuse us, please? Dani and I need to discuss something in private."

Dani shook her head. "Michael and I have other plans."

"That can wait." Her mother's voice grew even louder.

Dammit. Recognizing that particular tone, she was in for quite the speech. Why her sister Sara never received that tone of voice, she'd never been able to figure out.

Michael cleared his throat as he stood. "Thank you for a wonderful meal, Annalisa. I'll be in touch." Then he turned toward Dani. "Since you don't have a phone or a car, how about I pick you up at three thirty tomorrow to look at houses? I'll jot down my requirements. And you forgot your divorce papers in my office today. Should I leave them both in the guesthouse?"

"That'd be great." Dani wished she could leave, too. "Jake's there, so maybe you could try to get him to sign the papers." She would have laughed at the pained expression Michael sent her before walking out the door if her stomach hadn't been tied up in knots.

She felt like a kid in high school, caught smoking in the bathroom, about to face the principal. Her mother often treated her like a child, unable to let her live her own life, always eager to share her helpful suggestions.

Her friends' mothers were not nearly as involved in their daughter's lives. But she and her mom had their special abilities in common. And so did her grandmother.

That kind of bond was hard to break.

There wasn't anyone, besides her grandmother, who understood the burden of living with a secret that, if she was careless, could affect her mother's career. Not to mention the fact that everyone would know what a freak show she was. Outside of her family, only Zoe and Jake knew her secret.

But every time she thought she was making progress at gaining her mother's respect, she always seemed to screw something up, and her mom would have to jump in to save the day. Maybe in the new life she was forging she wouldn't need as much rescuing. At least she hoped not.

Dani turned, prepared for her mother's lecture, but Annalisa wasn't there. She'd crossed the room and was pouring two glasses of wine. Were they going to have a quiet, rational discussion over a drink? That had never happened before.

When her mother held a glass out without uttering a single word, she didn't know what to do.

She accepted the wine, took a sip, and waited for her mother's rant.

It never came. The silence stretched.

Was she supposed to say something? Beg her mother to give her a tongue-lashing?

Dani couldn't stand the pressure any longer and blurted out the whole story. She'd even admitted that she'd just signed up to help Jake with another of his crimes, even though she'd sworn she'd stop helping him.

After another long uncomfortable moment, her mom finally spoke. "You've helped Jake save lives and put criminals behind bars, and that's an admirable thing. And except for the recent mayor trespassing situation, it's all gone fairly smoothly."

"Are you forgetting that you asked me to help you with that? You were the one who had that particular dream, not me."

Nodding, her mom said, "Yes, but scaling the mayor's wall and getting caught wasn't what I had in mind. However, you undoubtedly saved his political career by deleting those e-mails and transferring the money back where it belonged. And you and I are the only ones who will ever know that. I'm just not sure how you're going to keep fighting crime and hold down a full-time job, honey. If you want to continue helping Jake, that's up to you, but I don't want to see you hurt. Where is the man who hit you, and how can we be sure he won't come after you again?"

How many glasses of wine had her mother had? She was way too mellow about the situation. Maybe it was a trick. "He's in jail. Jake offered to help keep me safe when he gets out on Friday."

"If you don't mind, I'd like to speak to Jake about that myself tomorrow."

"Uh, sure. That'd be fine." She was totally confused. Her momer never asked for permission; she normally just did what she pleased.

Before she could respond, her mother wrapped an arm around her shoulder, giving her a light squeeze before she kissed her forehead. "I was going to ask if you'd like to come with me to LA tomorrow. I need to reshoot a few scenes from my last movie. I'd only be busy in the mornings, so I was hoping we could get together with your sister, put on our wigs and dark glasses, and then lose ourselves on Rodeo Drive. But I guess you've committed to helping Michael find a house and need to stay here?"

God, she missed their covert trips to Rodeo Drive. It had been forever since she'd been able to shop to her heart's content and eat lunch at her favorite restaurants. It was tempting, but her mother was right; she'd committed to Michael, and she really needed to pick up her commission check on Friday. And then there was that other thing: she was supposed to be acting like a responsible adult.

Wait a minute. Since when had her mom taken her job as a Realtor seriously? "Okay, that's it. What's going on? Why are you being so reasonable?"

"Nothing's going on. But I think someone who calls themselves a Realtor would need to remember to pay her cell phone bill and have a working car."

"The car wasn't my fault." She crossed her arms. "And I didn't forget to pay my phone bill. I just couldn't afford to pay it on time. That will all change on Friday." Suddenly a thought struck her. "Are you mad at me because I put a damper on your seduction plans with Michael?"

"Oh, for God's sake, Dani." Annalisa morphed back into her normal self. "How could you have thought, for even a moment, that I'd be interested in Michael that way?"

Now this was the kind of argument she could deal with. Yelling and screaming made sense. "Because Ron put that theory into Michael's head, and Michael put it into mine. So, you haven't been dating Shaun Winters or Ryan Matthews like the tabloids said? Because I looked up their ages on the Internet this afternoon, and they're both younger than me."

Annalisa rolled her eyes toward the ceiling as if praying for patience before sitting on the couch and striking one of her "I'm an important star" poses. "Their agents cut at least five years off their ages, and I'm not dating them. I've just slept with them." Her mom waved an impatient hand. "That's entirely different."

Dani was still trying to understand the difference when her mother added, "Ron has a big mouth. I slept with the man once, and look what it got me. Lawyers. Nothing but grief."

"Yeah. Tell me about it," Dani muttered, thinking of her one night with Michael and the complicated kisses they'd just shared.

Back in high school their encounter had started out as a party game. Chance, or maybe fate, partnered them together to share a kiss in private after not speaking to each other for almost two years. But when they'd kissed, as required by the game, things heated up too fast, and she'd let things go too far. She'd known better that he'd end up with another woman, but her heart begged her to put that aside and just feel what it was like to be with him. She'd wanted her first time to be with someone she loved. But making love to him had made her heart ache even worse afterward, knowing he'd end up with someone else.

"I almost forgot." Her mother pointed a perfectly manicured, accusing finger at her. "Michael was the first boy you ever slept with. You know I'd *never* sleep with a man you've been with."

"How did you know about that?" Dani slammed her wineglass on the coffee table. Her mother must've felt all the mixed emotions she'd been struggling with back then. Or maybe she'd had a dream confirming it.

Her mother gave a testy shrug before finishing off her wine. "I knew the minute I saw the expression on your face the next morning. And you didn't do so well hiding your feelings when you were kissing him a few moments ago, either, sweetheart. The little moan spoke volumes."

She'd moaned?

Dammit.

"There were no feelings involved. That was . . . oh, I don't know. He's just good at it, that's all."

Her mom smirked and raised a brow.

That silent routine wouldn't work a second time. And Dani was definitely going to make another trip to see her grandmother and beg for more tips to deal with her mother.

"I have to go." She gave her mom a quick hug. "I need to get back to the guesthouse before Michael and Jake come to blows. Have fun in LA."

Dani turned and was walking toward the door when her mother called out, "Any daughter of mine would act on those sparks Michael generated and be sure he was still there in the morning."

Without turning around, Dani replied, "Why should I settle for just Michael? Maybe I'll invite both Jake *and* Michael to stay over." It was impossible to shock her mother, but it was fun to try. And she'd gotten the last word in, too. No easy task when sparring with her mom.

As she slipped out the doorway, Annalisa said, "FYI. Threesomes aren't all they're made out to be. I love you, Dani. Sweet dreams."

Dani's quick grin sent a fresh stab of pain to her throbbing face. Her mother's quiet chuckle confirmed the threesome comment had been a joke, but as frustrating and confusing as Annalisa Botelli could be, there was never any doubt about the love between them. "I love you, too. Good night, Mrs. Robinson."

Dani shook her head and walked to the guesthouse. When she opened the door, she saw Michael sitting on the couch with his suit coat off, sleeves rolled up, tie loose, and his feet propped on top of a pile of books on the coffee table. He was laughing at the movie and scarfing down her popcorn.

She nudged his leg with her knee so she could pass by. After he pulled his feet off the table and sat up, she said, "Please, make yourself at home." She scooped the bowl of popcorn off his lap.

Exhausted, she stepped over his big feet and flopped beside him on the couch.

With his eyes still riveted to the screen, Michael reached into the bowl on her lap, then tossed back more popcorn. "I love these movies. They're hilarious."

It had to be a guy thing.

He'd just eaten the last of the popcorn, so she set the bowl aside and closed her eyes, resting her head against the back of the big, comfy leather couch. "Where's Jake? Did he sign the papers?"

Michael snickered at a dumb joke. "When I mentioned the papers, he suddenly remembered he had a crime to solve."

"Figures," she said and gave into a yawn.

Michael's shoulder warmed hers when he leaned close and whispered, "You look beat, Dani. You should go to bed."

She opened one eye. "Can't. I have a pesky guest who won't leave."

"Okay, I'm outta here." He dug a piece of paper from his pocket. "I made a list of requirements for my new home."

She tapped her hand against her yawning mouth. "Of course you did." Dani held her hand out to accept the page, then scanned the detailed list. "This sounds just like the house you used to live in, except for the guesthouse. Why do you want a guesthouse?"

"For my mom." He stood and shrugged into his suit coat. "She's going to leave Ron soon, and I want her to feel comfortable living with me and the girls." He glanced around. "Something like this would be nice. I like the two bedrooms, but we'd need more bookcases so she wouldn't feel compelled to leave her books stacked everywhere. That hasn't changed about you."

She was so tired she let a smile bloom before she could stop it. She'd forgotten what a big smartass Michael could be and she kind of missed it. And him. "I'm sorry about your mom's marriage, but I've always known she could do better than Ron."

"Yeah. Maybe you and I will make better choices the next time, too." When he grinned, she wondered if he was thinking about their kisses.

She certainly was.

As extremely hot as those kisses were, Michael needed to know nothing more was going to happen between them. She had her dream man in her future. He was the one she was supposed to be with, not Michael.

When he turned to leave, she grabbed his arm and pulled him back down beside her.

Curiosity knotted his brow.

How was she going to put it? "Michael, although Jake and I agreed we could, I haven't seen anyone since I've been separated. It just doesn't seem right until he signs the papers. And I'm not planning on seeing anyone for a while, because I want to focus on my job and on putting my life back in order. So, do we need to talk about what happened earlier in the den?" She couldn't quite bring herself to refer to the mind-blowing kisses directly.

Michael leaned close, gently tracing a finger along her jaw, just under her bruise.

She barely restrained her shiver at his light touch.

He whispered, "We probably should. Right after we talk about what we've never spoken of for over twelve years. What happened that night at the party." He laid a soft kiss on her aching cheek, then stood to leave. "Feel better. See you tomorrow."

After the door shut behind him, she moaned. There was no way she wanted to discuss the night they'd both temporarily lost their minds and slept together.

She was exhausted, so she closed her eyes to rest them for just a bit before she mustered the energy to get her butt off the couch and to bed.

A flash of light illuminated her closed lids, revealing her destined man with the scar. When it looked as though he might turn around so she could finally see his face, her stomach lurched in anticipation. But then, the stupid bunny banging his loud drum filled her mind. She tried to conjure Elmer Fudd to shoot the damn thing, but instead, the Pink Panther showed up and grinned at her. He held up a sign that said, "If you talk to Michael about *that* night, I'll tell you where the gun is."

She blinked her eyes open and forced herself awake. Lord, now she was negotiating with cartoon characters? She really needed to go to bed.

Or the nearest psych ward.

Chapter Four

Dani rolled out of bed, awoken at seven fifteen by the ringing of a cell phone. She yawned as she made her way toward the living room, intent on squelching the offending sound. Maybe she'd just toss it into the pool, then go back to bed.

Since she didn't have a working phone at the moment, Jake or Michael must've forgotten theirs. When she spotted a shiny new phone lying on the coffee table, her eyes widened. It was the one she'd wanted but couldn't afford. It was especially great because it could double as a lockbox key and had access to MLS listings.

She leaned down and picked it up, but it was too late; the call went to voice mail. A yellow sticky note attached declared, "You can feed a hungry man or you can teach him to fish—or some such thing. This is a tool to help you succeed as I know you will."

Recognizing her mom's handwriting, Dani grinned. That her mom was finally taking her attempt to be independent seriously made her smile linger.

Studying the complicated phone, she finally figured out how to retrieve her voice mail. She had twenty-five messages after not having cell service for almost a week, so she chose the most recent. Her mother's voice rang out: "I bet most of the other Realtors in town are out of bed by now. I hope this is the phone you wanted. Be happy this wasn't a car, and don't you dare try to return it. *Ciao, bella.*"

Ignoring her workaholic mother's dig about still being in bed, Dani pushed the "Delete" button and dialed her mom's number. When Annalisa answered, Dani said, "Thank you for the phone, Mom. Would I be totally off base to think that you probably didn't just pay my outstanding bill?"

"One of my assistants told me they had a special if I paid for a full year, and you know I can't pass up a good deal. So, you're welcome."

Yeah, like her mother ever looked at the price of anything before she bought it. And there was no such thing as paying for a whole year. Her mom must've told them to bill her directly. She was sparing her pride, and Dani had to love her mom a little more for that one. "I appreciate it. Say hi to Sara for me when you see her today, will you? Tell her I miss my little sister, and why doesn't she come here for a change."

"I will. Gotta run, I have ten more calls to make before I land. Stay safe."

"That's the plan. Break a leg or whatever." Dani disconnected the call and crossed to the kitchen, shaking her head at her mother's disregard for the rules. She always used her cell when she flew. Her mom said it was just one of the perks of owning her own plane. That and setting new records in the mile-high club, which had been way too much information.

Dani switched the coffee maker on as she listened to her voice mails. There were calls from the office, Jake, her friend Zoe, and then there were Michael's messages. She smiled at the way his voice grew more and more irritated with each one.

Michael hadn't changed a bit. Always the responsible sort.

She'd had a long night, thinking about their kisses and how they'd rocked her to the core. She'd told Michael she wasn't interested, and her mind agreed with that theory, but her body wasn't buying it. After mulling the idea over, she came to the conclusion that she just hadn't had sex in a while and that was what was behind her attraction to him, nothing more.

When she played one of the messages from an unknown number, Dani's heart stuttered. A male voice growled, "If you wanna live to see your next birthday, you'd better not testify against my brother tomorrow." Carlos, the car beater. He'd probably gotten her number from her listing signs around town.

Then the next message said, "I see you walking into the courtroom. I'm gonna hurt you if you say one bad word against my brother, bitch!"

She swallowed hard and then retrieved the third. "You're messin' with the wrong people, lady. I'm gonna track you down and kill you."

She'd gotten in way over her head this time. That wasn't a man who was having a temper tantrum, soon to forget about her. The guy was serious.

Now where was that gun Jake had given her? Running toward her closet, she dialed Jake's number. It went straight to voice mail, so she said, "Jake, I need bullets for my gun. I may have to shoot someone. And if I don't get my car back soon, it might be you." She punched the "End" button, then flung her closet doors open. After tossing shoeboxes and purses aside, she finally found the .22-caliber weapon Jake had taught her to shoot. Though empty, she'd feel better having it.

Not that she had to worry when she was home—she lived in an impenetrable fortress staffed with 24-7 armed guards—but maybe she'd carry the big black Coach purse today and keep her new friend tucked inside, just in case. Jake said he'd let her know when the Carlos person was released, and he hadn't been yet, but the gun was staying with her. Carlos might have friends she'd have to be ready for.

She plopped the gun into her purse and then spotted the perfect shoes to match. Then she spied a short black skirt and a jade-green silk shirt that would look fabulous together. Amazing how a wardrobe could be built around a gun.

She laid it all out on her bed, studying it. The outfit was killer, combining both fun and business.

Being a Realtor hadn't been a walk in the park like she thought it'd be. Looking at houses and seeing the latest and greatest designs were fun, but there was much more to it, and the work involved was brutal. Competing with other agents for listings, hours spent researching on the computer, clients pretending to be serious but who were really just looking for decorating ideas, and being expected to be a marriage counselor when the couples disagreed on their version of the perfect house were all just part of the job. The amazing thing was that she enjoyed matching the right people with just the right house in just the right neighborhood, and she was finally getting the hang of it. It'd be nice if she got paid a little more regularly, but, hopefully, that would come in time.

It really sucked being poor. She'd taken her former lifestyle for granted, but not anymore. Now she couldn't even afford to go to happy hour in her nice outfits and get . . . happy. But she was on the road to independence, determined to succeed on her own.

Before she showered and dressed, she needed to input Michael's requirements into the MLS system and find boring, nonimaginative homes with guesthouses. She was going to do as he asked, then she was going to run some of her own ideas through the system. It'd be fun to see which home he ended up with. She poured herself a cup of coffee, then got to work.

Just as she booted up her computer, she winced at a searing flash of pain as that stupid bunny with his bass drum began marching around in her aching head again. What could that mean? He was pink, like the master bedroom at Jake's crime scene. But that wasn't it. Did he depict a toy in the boy's bedroom? Something that could record the event? That probably wasn't right; the rabbit seemed most at home in the master closet. How about batteries? That was what it represented, but what would batteries have to do with that guy killing his wife? And why wouldn't that bunny stop playing that awful *Pink Panther* theme song?

Dani dropped her head in her hands and tried to force the images away. She had to concentrate on work. The only way to stop the images from bombarding her brain was to keep her mind occupied. Her grandmother had been the one to suggest reading books when unwanted visions started forming in her brain. She could usually stop them, at least for a while, by reading intently. That technique had resulted in four college degrees and had stopped the random visions about people she didn't even know from sneaking in.

Most of the time.

If only she could be like her mom and use her extra abilities only when she needed them, she'd be able to hold on to her new job.

She glanced up and concentrated on the listings displayed on the computer screen, forcing the beat of the drum in her ears to slowly fade away.

Michael was reluctantly impressed as he drove away from the fourth house Dani had showed him, all of which had been within his specifications. Maybe the pampered princess did know what she was doing after all.

He glanced in her direction, and memories of kissing her flooded back again. He'd thought about it all night and still couldn't find an explanation for his ridiculous behavior. They didn't even like each other—anymore. Nobody kissed someone they didn't care for like that. Did they?

At least she hadn't brought it up again. Maybe she'd blown it off just as he should. "So, that last house was pretty good, huh? It had a little more room for the girls to play, and the school is nearby and therefore their friends, too. And it had the largest bedrooms of any of them so far."

"Yeah," she replied then yawned widely.

"Am I boring you?"

"No more than usual." She rolled her head lazily in his direction. "The only interesting thing I saw today is how much you miss your kids. You seem like a good dad. I didn't think anyone as stuffy as you could be. When do Carly and Amanda get back from Heather's mother's house?"

So she'd actually been listening earlier when he went on about his kids. He never meant to overshare about them, but he loved his girls more than he'd ever thought possible. "Sunday. That is, if Heather doesn't decide to keep them away longer just to irritate me." When they stopped at a light, he turned and faced her. "Because you're new to the business world, I feel compelled to share some advice."

She raised a brow in her snotty rich-girl way. "I'm all aflutter that someone as important as you would stoop so low as to help little ol' me. Do tell."

Dani was the only woman he'd ever known who made him want to throw her across his knee and give her the spanking she deserved. That urge was almost as strong as the one to kiss her again. "It's difficult to get repeat customers when you tell them that they bore you. If you don't learn to curtail those comments, you'll have nothing to do but spend your days at the spa, being pampered. Sometimes adults have to make concessions to actually earn a living."

She yawned again, then added a long, luxurious stretch of her arms over her head. The clingy material of her shirt tightened over her ample breasts, outlining the possibilities he refused to let enter his mind.

"You're right, Mikey. Who'd want to go to a fun spa rather than spend a fascinating afternoon looking at boring, nondescript houses with a cranky lawyer?"

"Nondescript houses? Is that your underhanded way to get me to look at more expensive homes to increase your commission?"

The lazy cat finding its bit of sunshine on the thick carpet instantly disappeared, and Dani's claws came out. "I'm not like that, Michael, and you know it."

He did, and guilt twisted his gut.

She was right. He'd been out of sorts all afternoon. Looking at all those kids' cheery bedrooms made him miss his daughters and the life he used to share with them. For the past year and a half, he'd only had them a few days each week and every other weekend. It wasn't enough.

He glanced at Dani, who was still fuming like a semiactive volcano. "Sorry. That was out of line. I'd like to hear your thoughts about the houses we've seen."

Dani narrowed her eyes as if deciding whether or not he was being sarcastic. "Why would you want to buy a house, for this much money, that's just pretty good? Oh, wait, let me guess. Your last house, the one that Heather picked out, you looked at for ten minutes, and when she begged you to buy it, you did. Am I right?"

"Maybe." He turned his attention back to the road. She was exactly right, and it annoyed him.

"See, I knew that, because Heather was always so concerned about fitting in and never standing out. She'd want a house built by the same builder as her friends, one in the right neighborhood, with the right neighbors and the right schools. So what if the house was built entirely of spit and toilet paper with granite countertops thrown in? Just that it was the trendy new place to live."

Dani had pegged his ex-wife perfectly. He said, "I forgot. You and Heather were in drama together in high school, weren't you? What happened between you guys? Heather would never talk about it when I'd ask."

"Girl stuff." Dani crossed her arms tightly against her chest and frowned. "You know, the usual. Jealousy, talking behind each other's backs, being in love with the same boys—you don't want to know."

The miserable look on her face told she wasn't telling him every-thing, but he probably didn't want to know. "Okay. So I suppose now that you've placated me and shown me my poor choices, you'd like to show me what I'd really like? Even though I have no idea what that is?"

"Yep. I'd like to show you some older homes, completely remod-eled, so you can still have your granite, but the lot sizes will be twice as large, you'll have huge trees, spacious floor plans with big bedrooms, and there'll even be room for horses. We used to go riding almost every afternoon, remember? Your girls would love that."

He grinned at the memory. Horseback riding was the only sport Dani had been better at than him, and yet he never minded because they'd always had fun. His girls probably would love riding as much as he and Dani had. They were too young now. But later, it might be something he and the girls could do together. "Yeah, that sounds good, but I still need to be close to Heather so it'll be easier on the girls to go back and forth to school and visits."

"I've got that covered, too. Come on, Michael, you need to bust out. Take a walk on the wild side for a change."

He scowled for form's sake, but Dani was right. The homes they'd seen were a little vanilla. There really wasn't anything special about them.

"Okay, I'll have a look at some tomorrow. I'm starving. Want to grab some dinner?" When she gnawed her lower lip, as she always did when she was thinking, he added, "I'll even buy."

She narrowed her eyes again. "Why?"

He loved that she was suspicious of his motives. They'd always had a fun, teasing relationship, so why stop now? "Because when I'm hungry, I can't think straight. Like right now, I'm feeling a strange sense of remorse over my earlier remark about you bumping up your com-mission. I'm hoping it'll go away after I've had dinner. Otherwise, I'd have made you pay for dinner with your most important client. Me. That's how you should make them all feel, by the way. Like they are your only client."

Her face lit with a false enthusiasm that meant she was about to give it to him with both barrels.

He looked forward to the battle.

She said, "This must be my lucky day. Another helpful hint all rolled up in a dinner invitation?" She reached out and gave his arm a viselike squeeze, her touch sending a blow to his already shaky defenses against her. "Then I should probably return the favor by ordering the most expensive thing on the menu. That way you'll be able to forgive yourself a whole lot easier."

Typical Dani logic.

He had to hold back the chuckle that threatened to escape, while tamping down the heat her hand on his arm ignited within him. "I'd forgotten how considerate you are. Where would you like to go?"

"Anything's fine with me." Her grin turned mischievous. "But the Skyline Club is always a safe bet."

And it was one of the most expensive restaurants in town, but he loved the food there, and as much as he hated to admit it, it could be fun. "Then it's a date."

A sudden and familiar sadness settled over him as it had so many times since his divorce. Had he asked Dani to dinner because it was better than going home to his quiet apartment alone and nuking something? He hated to acknowledge that he was lonely.

The women he'd dated since the breakup of his marriage seemed more interested in his time in the NFL rather than hearing about his kids. At least he could share a meal with Dani and know she couldn't care less about his past. She wasn't interested in fame or notoriety. She hated that, having grown up the daughter of a famous actress.

She was the only one who ever truly seemed to understand him.

At the same time, Dani could annoy the hell out of him, but he got the most perverse satisfaction out of sparring with her.

He should probably see a shrink.

~

As Michael headed for her favorite restaurant, a quiet chime sounded from Dani's phone, so she dug it out of her purse and studied the screen.

"Jake forwarded an e-mail that says my car is ready. They want it off the lot by six. He'll try to meet us there, but he might be a little late. That's nothing new. Jake was late for our wedding and hasn't been on time since. It's at a place called Gabe's Garage." Like she'd know where that was. She quickly google-mapped it.

Man, she loved her new phone with superfast Internet.

Michael said, "It's five forty now. Where's it at?"

"Downtown." She gave him directions, and they were off.

At two minutes to six, they rolled up in front of a graffiti-covered body shop in the sketchiest part of town. A chain-link fence with barbed wire on the top surrounded a bunch of cars, and hers, with a shiny new windshield, stood just inside the fence. The "Die Bitx" was still there, so the department must not have had the budget for a new hood. She'd have to figure something out later.

The sign in the office window said they were closed already, and the hours on the door said they closed at five. Maybe someone was inside waiting for them?

She reached for the door handle, but Michael's warm hand covered hers and stopped her. "I'll get it. Stay in the car and lock the doors after me."

She wasn't going to argue with that.

As soon as Michael's door closed, she popped down all the locks. She peered through the windshield, admiring Michael's big, broad shoulders and fine ass in his expensive suit. But it wasn't only his nice build that she enjoyed. She'd forgotten how his smile could make her feel all warm and gooey inside. And how cute his face was when it lit with excitement whenever he spoke of his girls. They'd had a fun day even while giving each other a hard time. She'd missed having fun with Michael.

He reached for the shop's door just as a loud explosion sounded from inside. The big glass window blew out, and a fiery ball lit up the sky.

Her teeth rattled, along with all the windows and doors, while the force of the explosion hit Michael square in the chest. With his arms and legs extended out in front of him, his body flew backward against the hood of his car, slamming into it with a sickening thud. Debris poured down like an out-of-control hailstorm as Michael's body limply rolled off the hood and onto the hard pavement below.

Michael was hurt. She had to help him.

The fear for Michael and adrenaline racing up Dani's spine spurred her into action. She fumbled with the locks and then finally threw her door open. She jumped out, then heard someone down the street shouting to call 9-1-1 as she made her way to the other side of the car. The heat from the flames warmed the right side of her body as she struggled to comprehend what was happening. The office was closed. Was it an explosion from chemicals inside the shop? Or a setup? Was that a bomb meant for her? All she knew for sure was that she was afraid for Michael. She couldn't bear the thought of him being injured. He had two little girls to raise who needed their father.

Glass crunched under her stilettos as she rounded the hood. When she spotted Michael lying on the pavement with blood seeping from his forehead, tears filled her eyes.

Please don't let Michael be dead.

She crouched beside him. When he opened his eyes, she could finally breathe again. He was alive.

Thank goodness.

"Don't move, Michael." She checked his head wound. It didn't appear too deep, but there was a lot of blood. They needed something to stop the steady flow from his forehead. She wrenched the driver's door open and dived across the seats, hopeful he'd have something in the glove box she could use. She grabbed a handful of napkins, then dabbed his wound as the blare of sirens grew louder.

Michael's eyes focused on hers as she put light pressure on his forehead. Warm blood seeped along the edges of the paper, staining her fingers.

He blinked a few times before he said, "What the hell was that?"

"I don't know. But what else hurts?" She ran her hand through his hair, checking for other head wounds. His suit was a bit dirty, but he seemed intact otherwise. Her heart ached at the thought of what might have happened to him if they'd arrived just a minute earlier and he'd made it all the way inside the office.

Michael winced as he sat up. "I'm fine, Dani. I took harder sacks than that in the NFL." He took control of the napkins, then leaned against the tire. "Come here. You're shaking."

Firemen spilled out of a hook and ladder while the screams of multiple approaching sirens became deafening.

Michael tugged her onto his lap and wrapped his free arm around her shoulders, holding her tight while hoses sprayed water over the fiery building. "We're fine, Dani."

After the adrenaline settled down a fraction, she heard people talking about a bomb, and the shaking started right back up again.

She wrapped her arms around Michael and whispered, "I'm glad you're okay. I was so afraid that you'd—"

"What?" Michael put a finger under her chin and tilted it up. "If I didn't know better, I'd think you still care about me."

In that split second, when she didn't know if Michael was dead or alive, it had become crystal clear she still cared. A lot.

"I never stopped caring about you, Michael. And I miss you." She hadn't meant to say that—it must've been the shock—but there was no taking it back once it was out there.

He blinked at her, clearly confused by what she was saying.

She quickly added, "I was a hormonal teenage girl when we parted ways before. I made a big mistake. And I'm sorry." All true. She couldn't tell him the most important reason: that she was a freak who could see into his future.

A fireman approached them and looked Michael up and down. "How are you feeling, sir?"

Michael lifted the napkin from his forehead. "Just a cut. I'm fine."

The fireman leaned closer to examine the wound and nodded, then turned his gaze toward her. "Ma'am, that's a nasty bruise. How'd that happen?"

"Oh, this?" Dani lifted her hand to her face. "I'm fine. That happened yesterday." She'd thought she'd done a better job of covering the bruise with makeup earlier.

When the fireman's eyes cut to Michael, glaring with unsaid accusations about her handprint bruise, she quickly added, "The guy who hit me is in jail."

"Good." The fireman nodded. "Paramedics are on the way. Hang tight." He stepped back to give them some privacy.

Michael whispered, "Last night you said you didn't want to be involved with anyone right now."

"That's how I honestly felt . . . until you kissed me. I still don't want anything serious—my life is a mess at the moment." And there was the dream guy and his scar that she was still uncertain about. Was he the one for her or not?

Maybe it was time to live in the moment for a change, rather than worrying about the future so much. Could she be more like her mom and sister and have a casual fling with a man who made her toes curl when he kissed her? A guy who she honestly enjoyed spending time with? She'd just be careful to make sure her heart didn't get attached. "Maybe we can start by being friends again?" She sent him a weak smile. "With maybe some occasional benefits thrown in?"

"The benefits are tempting." The corners of his mouth tilted. "But I don't think you're over Jake."

"He's the one who can't let go. I'm definitely over Jake."

"I don't know, Dani. We're obviously still attracted to each other, but—"

Fear that he was about to say no to her offer made her kiss him. To *show* him how much she'd missed him. And how much she cared for him.

When he groaned and slid a hand to the back of her head, tilting her mouth to just where he wanted it, taking the kiss to a deeper level, she sighed with relief and sank into the kiss.

She snuggled closer and gingerly ran her hands through his thick hair, in case he was more hurt than she knew. Their bodies fit together as if they were custom-made, just for each other.

Whenever they kissed, it filled her with a kind of elation in a way no one else ever had. Even better then shopping sprees on Rodeo Drive. Or driving her Porsche over a hundred miles an hour.

And that was saying a lot.

The firefighter who stood nearby must've had enough, because he cleared his throat—loudly—reminding them that they were in the parking lot, not her bedroom. He said, "The paramedics are here."

Michael broke the kiss and helped her stand. "As nice as that was, let's take this one step at a time. Friends?"

"Yes. Friends." It was a step in the right direction, and she'd take it.

Chapter Five

After the fire was put out, and the paramedics had finished up with Michael, Dani studied her car sitting behind the chain-link fence. It was still ugly, even with a new windshield, but she couldn't get to it behind the locked gate. "This bites. The last thing I want to do is come back here to crazy land to get my car."

Michael's arm tightened around her waist, and he moved her out of the way of a busy bomb squad worker. "Ask Jake to pick up the car. There's nothing more we can do now, so let's go."

She looked up at Michael's bandaged forehead, and her gut lurched again at how close a call that had been. "Okay."

Michael took her hand and was tugging her toward his car when Jake showed up and stepped in front of them.

Jake wrapped his arms around her and pulled her against his chest. "God, I'm so sorry, babe. Are you okay?" After he was done hugging her, he held her at arm's length and checked her out from head to toe. "This was my fault. That was meant for me. Your car was checked in under my name. I've been having some problems with an ex-con who got out last month. Luckily, it was an amateur job or it could have been worse."

Jake had put more people behind bars than any other detective in his squad. Thanks in part to her woo-woo abilities. "Are you sure it wasn't Carlos?"

"Yeah. Carlos is right where he's supposed to be, with no Internet or phone access. Until Friday, anyway."

She blew out a long breath. "Okay. Can we go, then?"

Jake nodded and pulled her away from Michael. "I'll clean up here." When they were out of Michael's earshot, Jake laid a soft kiss on her cheek and whispered, "Don't know what I would've done if you'd been hurt because of me, Dani. I'd never forgive myself."

When he actually showed her compassion, it always made her heart go soft for him. She stared into his eyes, wishing Jake could have been the right one for her, but sadly, he just wasn't.

"But why the hell were you with *him*?" Jake asked, ruining their tender moment.

She sighed and crossed her arms. "We were on our way to dinner."

"Like a date?" His jaw clenched.

She didn't want to hurt him, so she laid a hand on his arm and gave a gentle squeeze. "It's none of your business anymore, Jake, but no. It wasn't a date. We'd been out looking at houses and got hungry." She'd keep the part about wanting to be Michael's friend with benies to herself for the moment.

"Whatever." Jake scowled in Michael's direction. "I didn't get those bullets you asked for earlier because usually you and bullets don't mix. But it's time to get armed, babe." He held his hand out in the direction of the smoldering building. "That's what can happen when someone hates your guts. Carlos told me today he hates yours and mine. I'll talk to your mom about beefing up the security at home by Friday."

"'Kay." But if she saw Carlos anywhere near her home, she'd shoot first and ask questions later. Probably better not to mention that to her law-abiding almost ex-husband, though.

Jake walked her back to Michael's car. When they got close, both Jake and Michael reached to open the car door for her, but Michael was quicker. When Jake's eyes narrowed, she quickly slipped between them and into her seat. "Thanks, Jake. I'll call you tomorrow."

Jake glanced at Michael and then back at her. "Be careful, babe." Then he backed away so Michael could close her door. She wasn't sure if Jake's warning was about Michael, Carlos Watts, or both.

As they headed out of slumsville toward the freeway, Michael's hand slipped over hers. "You okay?"

"Yeah." She glanced at his forehead. "Are you?"

Michael's phone rang before he could answer. His warm hand left hers to pull his cell out from his suit coat. "It's Ron. He's called three times. I'd better take this."

While Michael talked to his stepfather, Dani stared out the window, reliving the scary moment when she wondered if Michael was dead or alive. It was her punishment for helping Jake with his damned cases. She needed to remember the terror that filled her when Michael went flying through the air and just say no the next time Jake asked for her help. It was the only way she'd be able to start living a normal life.

Well, a little more normal anyway. No one could ever accuse her of having a normal life. Being Annalisa's daughter had guaranteed that from moment one.

After Michael hung up, he asked, "Do you mind if we stop by my office for a minute? Ron says he has a problem only I can solve."

"No, that's fine." She wasn't sure her stomach had calmed down enough to eat anything yet.

When they pulled up in front of Michael's office, Dani was tempted to just sit in his new BMW and breathe in the long-forgotten aroma of luxury and leather seats she'd once had. But she really had to use the ladies room, so she let Michael open her door and help her out. His hand on her lower back as he led her up the steps made her all tingly inside again.

Yeah, Jake needed to hurry up and sign those papers.

After she was done in the restroom, she followed the sounds of raised voices and a bawling child down a softly lit hall. Peeking into Ron's office, she saw a little girl with blonde hair lying on the floor, throwing a temper tantrum. Ron sat behind his desk, holding his head in his hands, and Chad paced back and forth, while Michael knelt beside the child, trying to sooth her. Before she could say anything, the little girl raised her head, locked gazes with her, then raced toward her. She didn't know what to do but brace for the impact.

When a set of little arms wrapped around her legs and held on like a rat aboard a drowning ship, Dani tried to hold her panic in check. Little kids terrified her. Especially ones who were crying at the top of their lungs.

"What's going on?" she asked Michael, who stood and dusted off his slacks.

Michael's face was red with fury as he waved a hand in Ron's direction. "I'm sure Ron's just dying to explain this one."

While Dani awkwardly patted the kid's back, she glanced at Ron, who rubbed his temples as if he had a headache. He spoke loudly, trying to be heard over the crying kid. "The child's mother dropped her off and informed my secretary that this little girl is my daughter. The woman said she had to leave for a while and to take care of her."

Chad added, "Don't forget the part about 'and it's your fault I have to hide.'"

Michael looked like a pit bull straining against a chain about to break.

"So who's the mother, Ron?" she asked.

He shook his head. "I don't know. There've been a few women who might qualify."

Michael let out a low growl, then grabbed Ron's lapels, pulling him out of his big leather chair. "The kid appears to be about two. Add another nine months and look it up!"

After Michael released him, dropping him back into his big leather chair, Ron frantically dug through his phone for clues.

Meanwhile, the little girl's whimpering became softer. Dani pried the little arms from her knees, then picked her up. The child's legs automatically clamped around Dani's waist, and the toddler's arms tightened around her neck, cutting off her air supply. The kid snuggled her face against Dani's neck, soaking her collar with tears and snot.

She'd rather face Carlos, the crazy car-bashing lunatic who'd threatened to kill her, than do this. At least she could point her gun at him and make him go away.

Dani sort of rubbed and patted the kid's back as Chad and Ron discussed all the women Ron had been seeing over the years.

With each new name thrown out, Michael seethed harder. She felt awful for him. He adored his mom, and that had to hurt.

While the child squirmed in her arms, she tried to think of something to say that might calm her, and then wondered if the kid was old enough to know her own name. She leaned closer and whispered, "Uh, hi? My name's Dani. What's yours?"

The little girl swallowed her tears, leaned back to face her, and made a sound like "Mah."

What kind of name was that?

Before Dani could ask for clarification, the little girl laid her hands on either side of Dani's face. "Owie." She leaned forward and laid a kiss on Dani's bruised cheek as gently as Michael had done the night before. Then the kid lifted a finger wrapped in a cartoon bandage. "Mah owie."

Touched by the child's concern for her face, Dani grinned and figured she should probably kiss the kid's finger in return. So she did. When the little girl beamed a sweet smile as a reward, Dani was certain she'd done the right thing, although she was fighting the urge to spit out the adhesive flavor lingering on her lips.

This was obviously a child who'd been loved. But what could make a woman so scared she'd dump off a kid with a man who knew nothing of her existence? Or maybe Ron did and hadn't stepped up to the plate?

The fear in the little girl's eyes was gut-wrenching. She was surrounded by strangers and must have wanted her mother. The intense emotions radiating from the kid made it impossible for Dani to get any sort of reading from her. Not even a color, which was odd.

Dani knew just how the girl felt, recalling how frightened she'd been during her kidnapping. She'd been just a little older than this child, and her heart ached for the kid.

As Ron continued to grumble and rustle around on his computer for clues, Dani crossed to the couch where a car seat, a backpack, and a diaper bag lay. At the beginning of every school year, her friend Zoe wrote her kids' names on everything they owned. This child was probably too young for school, but maybe she went to day care. Sitting down with the girl in her lap, she opened the backpack and peeked inside. She wasn't disappointed. "Ron, your daughter's name is Emma Anderson. Does that last name sound familiar?"

Chad stared at Dani, surprise lighting his face as if she'd just found the cure for cancer instead of using simple logic. But, oh yeah, she forgot: they all thought she was a total dingbat.

After repeating the last name, Chad turned to Ron, "Isn't that the last name of one of our accountants, Dad? The blonde, good-looking one?"

Ron's eyes grew wide. "Uh, yes it was. We have new ones now. But without a DNA test, I'm not conceding this child is my daughter. What am I going to do with the kid until I get the test results?" He turned to Michael. "You're the only one with any recent experience with children, so you need to take her."

Michael crossed his big arms, ignoring Ron's plea. "Why would our firm's ex-accountant feel the need to hide out?"

Chad piped up. "Who cares about that? We need to call social services. They'll send someone over and place her in foster care until this whole mess is settled." Chad quickly googled the number on his phone.

Ron nodded enthusiastically. "That's a great idea."

For ten minutes, Michael argued some lawyer gobbledygook about how Ron shouldn't do that, especially because he could be the father, but Ron wasn't buying it.

Chad finally blew out a sigh. "Found it."

"Give it to me." Ron's hand flew toward the phone on his desk.

Dani glanced into Emma's tear-filled blue eyes. Worry crumpled her little forehead.

A kid that came from a caring home that bought cartoon bandages for her owies would be frightened and absolutely miserable in foster care. "Ron, stop. You can't do this to the poor kid."

Ron waved her comment away with a sweep of his hand. "Dani, the last person I'd take advice from is a spoiled rich kid whose mother bails her out of trouble on a regular basis. Go do your nails or something."

"Don't talk to her like that," Michael snapped.

"You know your mother's temper, Michael." Ron lifted his hands. "I'd rather take a bullet than walk through the door with a kid from one of my affairs."

Dani asked, "Is a bullet what it'll take for you to grow a heart, Ron?" Hot anger seared her belly as she marched toward her purse. Ron was a cheating bastard and a heartless pig. He deserved everything he was about to get. If he wouldn't listen to reason, then maybe it was time to be unreasonable. For Emma's sake.

She plunged her hand inside her purse and pulled out her unloaded gun. Dani pushed Emma's face into her neck—the kid probably shouldn't see what she was about to do—and then pointed the gun at Ron. "Put that phone down right now. You are *not* sending this poor child into the foster care system. She's probably your own flesh and blood, you moron."

Ron slowly placed the phone back onto his desk, his eyes wide, his breathing suddenly shallow. "Hold on, Dani. There's no need for that. Let's just stay calm."

Dani heard Michael's quiet curse but didn't dare look at him, afraid she'd lose her battle to maintain her composure. The fear on Ron's and Chad's faces was hilarious and extremely gratifying. She might have to carry the gun more often.

She pulled herself back together. "What is your ex-accountant's first name?"

"It's . . . Julia," Ron stammered, "Julia Anderson."

Dani held the kid with one hand and her gun in the other. How was she going to use the phone? Gesturing with the gun in Ron's direction, she said, "Punch the 'Speaker' button and dial this number."

After Ron entered in the numbers she'd called out, Jake's voice filled the room. "Detective Morris."

"Jake, will you please run the name Julia Anderson and see if anything comes up? I'll wait."

He grunted. "You'll wait? Dani what the hell have you—"

"Please, Jake." She cut him off. "I'm on speaker phone, and I need this information quickly."

He let out a long-suffering sigh. "I'll put you on hold. Ander*son* or Ander*sen*?"

"Son," Dani replied.

As the police department's sappy on-hold music filled the air, Emma let out a long breath, snuggled deeper into Dani's neck, and closed her eyes.

Thank God.

But did snot come out of silk?

She motioned to Michael to come take the kid, but when he tried to lift Emma, she woke and started whimpering.

Resigned to ruining another of her favorite pieces of clothing, Dani hugged Emma tightly against her chest, tossed the gun in the direction of her purse, and flopped into one of the chairs in front of Ron's desk. Who knew how much a little kid could weigh?

When relief flashed across Ron and Chad's faces, she laughed. "You guys didn't really think that gun was loaded, did you? I'm not that irresponsible. Jeez."

Michael dropped into the chair next to her and whispered, "Nice work, Rambo."

Finally, Jake's voice sounded, instead of the offensive excuse for music. "You still there?"

She spoke quietly, trying not to wake the sleeping time bomb drooling on her chest. "Yes, what have you got?"

"Ms. Anderson has the IRS hot on her tail for some clients' overdue tax payments. Someone local is looking at her and her business partner regarding money laundering. If you know where she is, I need to know, or else you're harboring a suspected criminal."

Dani leaned closer to the phone. "I don't know where she is, but I've got her kid slobbering all over me. Do you have any information on next of kin?"

"Hang on." The sound of shuffling papers filled the air. "Maybe. The report shows a woman who might be Ms. Anderson's mother living up north, near Taos. We think her name is Martha Anderson, but she doesn't answer her phone. We haven't been able to confirm yet. Hey, your grandmother lives in that area. Maybe she could use her woo—"

"Uh, yeah." Dani cut Jake off again. "My grandmother may be of help to you. She seems to know everyone in Taos. Maybe you should call her and then let me know? Thanks, Jake." Dani motioned to Ron to disconnect the call.

After he did, Ron stared intently into Dani's eyes. "Please. Won't you take the child? She seems comfortable with you. I don't want to bring her home and upset Maeve."

Oh, she could learn to hate Ron. Maeve, the woman she loved as much as her own mother, did not deserve to have an illegitimate child shoved into her face. Maeve had always been there for her when her mom couldn't be, even after she'd stopped working for Annalisa. She was one tough lady, never afraid to stand up to the powerful Annalisa Botelli, and Dani had always admired her for it.

Before she could answer, Michael jumped out of his chair. "This is your problem, Ron, not Dani's."

He tugged on Dani's arm and helped her stand while balancing the kid. When Michael reached for Emma, Ron's eyes widened with panic. "I'll pay you, Dani. Name your price."

Michael's gaze met hers for a moment, silently asking if she was interested. She gave him a quick eyebrow hitch then turned toward Ron.

She was going to make up a sum so outrageous he'd never agree to it. "I've got a very hot client on the line right now, and a kid isn't going to help me sell any homes. I stand to lose a lot, so if you want me to babysit, I'm gonna have to charge you a thousand dollars a day."

Take that, you cheater.

"Done," Ron said without hesitation. He stood and held out his hand for her to shake. "Let me know what Jake comes up with for next of kin, will you?"

"Uh, well," Dani stammered, trying to realign her train of thought as she shook his hand. She should have asked for more, apparently. "I'll need three days in advance. If it takes any more time than that, we'll have to renegotiate. And if we find a solution sooner, you get no refunds."

Undeterred by any of her desperate attempts to get out of babysitting, Ron quickly reached for his checkbook and filled in the amount. He ripped the check out and handed it to her. "The child will need to have a DNA test tomorrow. I'll call you with the details."

Suddenly, the enormity of their transaction hit her. She had been so intent on making Ron pay for being such a jerk that she forgot that she knew absolutely nothing about children and now was stuck with one for three days. Worse, she might have a raving lunatic after her when he was released from jail in a couple of days. She couldn't endanger Emma's life.

Holy crap, what had she just done?

∽

Michael gently strapped the sleeping Emma into his daughter's car seat because it was easier than trying to install Emma's in the dark, and then he slipped behind the wheel. "Dani, are you the only human being on this planet who doesn't know you can go to jail for pointing guns at people?" He tried to keep his voice low but was losing the battle.

"Shhhh. You'll wake the kid. And it wasn't loaded, so it hardly counts." Dani frowned and crossed her arms. "Besides, Ron was so thrilled to be rid of his parental responsibilities he's probably forgotten all about it by now."

It was like banging his head against a brick wall trying to break through her version of logic. "Please refrain from doing that ever again. At least in my presence. But thanks for taking Emma. Ron got off too easy."

He would've taken Emma before he'd let her go with child services, but he would've made Ron beg. He wanted to spare his mother more heartache, but the child was obviously happier with Dani.

A smile tugged at his mouth when he recalled how she'd stood up for the poor kid. He didn't care for her guerrilla tactics but had to admit she'd gotten the job done.

Dani just kept surprising him.

She turned toward him with a deer-in-the-headlight look. "I can't believe I just did that. I have no idea what to do with a kid. We need to find her family right away."

"I'll help you with Emma, and I want to know about her mother as much as you do. My mom told me Ron has hidden all their money. He's making it difficult for her to divorce him, and I haven't had any luck digging through his office files. I'm thinking Emma's mom, Ron's ex-accountant, might know where that money is."

Dani frowned. "That is if we can find her."

"Yeah, and there's probably a reason Julia didn't leave her kid with the grandmother, because Ron couldn't be the best choice unless he was the last one."

"You're right, we're going to have to find Emma's mom." She stared out the window for a moment, then pointed to an ATM. "Hey, pull over, will you? I need some cash, and I want to get this check deposited before Ron changes his mind."

When Dani hopped out of the car to deal with the ATM, he glanced over his shoulder to check on Emma. She was a cute kid. Blonde, with an angelic face, and her little blue eyes were staring into his. She smiled and pointed out the window. "Mic Dee's!"

He turned and saw the fast-food joint that his daughters loved, too. "You're hungry, huh? What would you like?"

Emma sputtered, "Nuggeeees."

"Want a chicken nugget kids' meal?"

"Peeezzz," Emma said, nodding enthusiastically.

"Well, since you asked so nicely, nuggets it is. I'm not sure Quick Draw Dani will be as happy, though."

Emma clapped her hands. "Yay nuggeeees!"

Dani returned, then snapped her seat belt into place. "Now I can pay you back the twenty-five hundred you lent me. And thanks to Ron, I'm buying dinner tonight."

"Thank you." He pulled out and crossed the street, slipping into the drive-through. "Emma mentioned she'd like to partake of this fine cuisine instead of the boring adult food at the Skyline Club."

A bright grin lit Dani's face. "She said she wanted this? That's pretty good for a kid her age, isn't it?" She turned and smiled at Emma, who was bouncing up and down in the car seat. "I guess we have a little genius on our hands, huh, Em?"

Dani didn't protest even a little? He didn't know too many rich girls who made a habit of eating at fast-food joints.

At the happy sounds coming from the back seat, he glanced in his rearview mirror. He hoped the poor kid would have a place to live when her mother was sent to jail.

After they'd gotten their meal to go, Michael pulled into Annalisa's estate and parked beside Dani's eyesore of a car. Annalisa was right. Dani needed a new one.

They carted Emma, her diaper bag, and their food inside and found Jake reclining on the couch, watching a movie.

The smug look Jake sent Michael was a familiar one, but he stood and managed a "Hey," before he turned to Dani and beamed a smile at her. "Well, looky here, two gorgeous women for the price of one. How'd I get so lucky?" He reached out for Emma, who was snuggled against Dani's chest.

Starry-eyed, Emma went willingly into Jake's arms and smiled and cooed right back at him.

Dani took Jake's chin in her hand. "Em, when you get bigger and meet a boy who has a grin like this, run the other way. He'll just be trouble." She laid a quick kiss on Jake's cheek, then opened their dinner bags. "I would have gotten you a burger if I'd known you were coming over, but you can have half of mine if you'd like."

Michael watched Jake closely as he settled on the couch with Emma and her food. Dani and Jake's friendly relationship confused him. They were supposed to be getting a divorce, but sometimes they looked downright domestic. All that friendliness was annoying.

When Michael had kissed Dani in Annalisa's den, it'd been motivated by his irritation with her, but then she'd kissed him back, igniting the flame that had always smoldered for her. And then, after spending the afternoon with her, time that had nothing to do with her usual convoluted legal problems, he couldn't quite shake the feeling that he might be starting to care for her again.

It was like being sucked into a black hole. He didn't want to but couldn't help it. Even when he reminded himself of how Dani had betrayed him, abruptly ending their friendship when they were in high school, with no explanations.

That had cut him deep.

His father had just died when he'd met Dani, and she'd helped him heal, always there for him when he wanted her to be but careful to keep her distance when he needed to grieve alone. When she'd abandoned him, a part of his heart had grown cold. He'd felt a similar pain after his divorce last year. "Jake can have my burger. I've got to go."

Dani whirled around, her eyes wide. "You can't go. I don't know what to do with the"—she glanced at Emma, who was sitting on Jake's lap, chowing down chicken nuggets and sharing every other fry with him—"k-i-d."

"Jake's here. *Again.* Let him help. See you tomorrow." He hadn't meant to let his annoyance with Jake show. But clearly those two weren't all the way over, and he wasn't about to be a damn third wheel.

～

Dani panicked at the thought of being left alone with the kid. Michael seemed upset with her, so Dani tugged him aside and whispered, "Please? I really need your help, Michael."

His face tightened. "What do you need me for?"

"For, like, how to change a diaper, and what about a bath? Is she old enough to eat most foods, or are certain things off-limits? What time does she have to go to bed? That kind of stuff. Jake's good at flirting with and charming anything female, but believe me, when it comes to the messy details, he'll bolt."

Shaking his head, Michael sat down next to Jake and unwrapped his burger. He hadn't promised to help, but she was encouraged that he hadn't left.

She cut her burger in half and offered it along with her fries to Jake. Her pants had been getting a little tight anyway. She didn't need the extra calories.

When they were done eating, Michael ran her through all the particulars of taking care of a little girl. There were so many details she was afraid she'd forget some of them and was tempted to take notes.

Michael's cell rang, and he left to take the call, leaving her with the task of brushing Emma's teeth.

Jake took advantage of Michael's absence and squeezed into the bathroom behind her, leaning over her shoulder, feigning interest in the process. He nibbled on the back of her neck and whispered, "God, you're sexy when you act like a mommy."

"Knock it off, Jake." She threw an elbow to his gut.

He chuckled and pulled her closer. "Have my children, Dani. You're a natural."

She turned and pointed toward the living room. "Out!"

He sent her one of his slow, sexy grins. "What? That time of the month?"

"No. And if you ever say that to me again, I'll knee you." She was tempted to knee him anyway. Couldn't he see how hard this was for her? He knew she didn't know anything about kids. If it weren't for time running out for the search warrant in the pink house, she'd throw him out on his ear. "Go watch the damn movie for clues."

Jake let his grin bloom before he eased out of the bathroom, nearly running into Michael. "Counselor, if I were you, I'd get the hell out while you still can. She's ovulating or something in there."

Dani threw a wet, balled-up washcloth at Jake's smirking face, but he was too quick and caught it before it made contact. "See, you still love me, or you would've thrown the hair dryer."

A strange sense of guilt at Jake's "still love me" remark had Dani's eyes zipping to meet Michael's.

His brow lifted, silently asking her if she still did.

Well, she didn't. Not like that anyway. She needed to focus on her task, not the two annoying men in her house.

As she carefully executed all of Michael's instructions, she didn't miss the little half grin on his face that proved he was enjoying her ineptitude. He was probably thinking it was karma paying her back for that gun move she'd made earlier at his office.

After the bath and hair washing were done, she wrestled the kid into a pair of footed pajamas they found in her diaper bag. Dani wiped the sweat from her brow, then slid the long zipper up to the neck, completing the task. When she stepped back to admire her good work, Emma raised her hands high and said, "Ta-da!"

She and Michael laughed at what must have been a regular routine the child and her mother shared each night. "You're a big ol' ham, Em. I'll bet you're going to be a famous actor when you grow up, just like my mom."

At the mention of the word *mom*, Emma's bright expression faded, and she began to cry, "Wan Momma!"

Dani exchanged a glance with Michael. "I really suck at this." She scooped Emma up. "Hey, let's go find Jake."

When Emma and Jake were snuggled up in front of the movie, Michael gathered his things and started for the door without saying a word. Was he still mad at her?

She caught up and laid her hand on his arm to stop his hasty retreat. "Hey, what's the rush? Do you want to stay for a while? You seem to like these dumb movies."

Michael slipped into his suit coat. "You'll be fine now. Just put Emma to bed when she falls asleep on *Jake's* lap."

He was definitely mad at her about Jake. Something inside of her couldn't stand for him to be angry with her. Annoyed was fine, but not angry.

He stalked toward his car, so she trotted after him. "Michael, wait up."

His jaw was set when he turned and faced her. "What?"

She sent him her sweetest smile. "Thank you for asking me to help you find a house, for the loan, and for giving me a crash course in babysitting. I appreciate it." She wrapped her arms around his big shoulders and gave him a hug. When he didn't hug her back, she quickly released him.

His reaction hurt, but she forced the smile plastered on her face to remain, then started back toward her house.

"Dani?"

"Yeah?" She turned and walked back to his car, hopeful that his mood had lightened.

"How's Jake getting home?" He crossed his arms and frowned at her again. "Does he need a ride, or is he spending the night?"

She hadn't even thought about it. Jake must've driven her car home for her, hoping to spend the night. "I don't know. But he's not spending the night. I'll just have my mom's driver take him home."

He seemed satisfied with that and reached down to open the car door. On an impulse, she laid a hand over his to stop him.

Trying to keep the anxiety from her voice because he might reject her, she cleared her throat. "Have you thought any more about us? I don't know about you, Michael, but I had fun today. It isn't every day I get to pull a gun on a roomful of lawyers, you know." She gave his hand a quick squeeze, hoping he'd make the next move.

He didn't disappoint her.

Michael moved his hand to the side of her face, gently avoiding her still-tender bruise. He lifted her chin, then kissed her, taking his sweet time about it. When he pulled her more firmly against his hard body, taking the kiss to a deeper level, her heart thudded in her chest, matching the rhythm of his. Desire zinged through her veins as she snuggled closer, running her hands through his thick hair, careful to avoid the bandage on his forehead. They were both a bit banged up, but that didn't dampen the power of their kiss.

Disappointment filled her when his lips slowly lifted from hers. She could have gladly kissed him for hours. Maybe days.

Staring deeply into her eyes, he whispered, "Get Jake to sign the papers, Dani."

The buzz still sizzling through her body made her want that more than he'd ever know. "I'm on it."

Chapter Six

Dani stepped into the guesthouse, with Michael's hot kiss still lingering on her lips. She sat beside Jake, who had a sleeping Emma snuggled against his chest, intending to get serious about asking him to sign the papers.

He glanced her way. "So, I don't want to be pushy or anything, but I have to let the scumbag back into his house soon. What are we thinking about the clues?"

"Oh, so now that Michael's gone, it's back to business, huh? That whole scene in the bathroom was just some male territory-marking thing, wasn't it?"

"I have no idea what you're talking about." He smiled and tapped a finger against her forehead. "Any good woo-woo vibes going on in there?"

She closed her eyes, ordered her eager hormones to cool their jets about sleeping with Michael, and cleared her mind. Jake—and the poor woman and her son—needed an answer. "The closet has something to do with it." And then she saw a vision of the bunny shining a light at the Pink Panther, who was dancing on puffy pink clouds of insulation.

A bunny playing a bass drum, a flashlight, insulation, and the Pink Panther. What did the four things have in common?

Dani bolted straight up. "Wait! The *Pink Panther* movies weren't the key. It was television."

"What do you mean?"

"The bunny has to do with batteries, right? And what does every home have that needs batteries?"

"A vibrator?"

"No, you pervert." Dani smacked his arm. "A flashlight. The gun is somewhere dark. And the Pink Panther was a television spokesperson for insulation a few years ago, remember? It's in the attic, Jake."

He shook his head. "We've looked everywhere in the attic, Dani. And you're forgetting the nail polish. You said that was important, too, remember?"

"You've checked the whole attic? A home like that with a complicated roofline can have more than one scuttle."

He handed Emma to her. "Maybe it was there, but not anymore. Or maybe it's in an attic in a public place. Why don't you put her down and I'll cue up the next movie? The answer has to be here somewhere."

So sure she'd found the gun's resting place in the attic, she was filled with frustration over her cryptic clues as she carried Emma into the spare bedroom. Dani pulled the covers back in the darkened room, but then stopped. What if Emma awoke in the night? She'd probably be afraid if she was alone. Changing her mind, Dani took Em to her own bedroom and pulled the covers back. After carefully laying her down and tucking her in, she inched back from the bed and tiptoed out of the room. Before she got to the door, Emma began crying for her mother again.

It could be a long three days.

Not knowing what else to do, she slid beside Emma and pulled the child against her. She gently ran her fingers through Emma's soft, baby shampoo–scented hair. Dani had always liked it when her mom had done that with her.

After a few minutes, Emma settled down, and her breathing became more regular. Dani closed her eyes as the events of the long day began to catch up with her, trying to work through the bunny clues again. She'd just give it another ten minutes before she snuck out.

Dani blinked her eyes open after waking from a disturbing dream about bunnies and panthers, then squinted at the clock. It was after one in the morning. She'd fallen asleep for hours.

Very gently, she eased out of bed, then went to the living room to turn off the television. The movie was over, and the main menu flashed on the screen, belting out the dreaded theme song. She searched for the remote and found it on Jake's chest. He was sound asleep on the couch.

Pulling a blanket over him, she laid a kiss on his forehead, then turned out the lights. Looked like he was spending the night after all.

Michael slammed his hand against the steering wheel in frustration. He was going to be late for court because he had to make a stop at Dani's first. During breakfast, he remembered Dani couldn't take Emma anywhere without her car seat, and she needed to get her to the lab for her DNA test. He would have had plenty of time to transfer Emma's car seat from the back of his car and install it in Dani's if it weren't for the road construction on the freeway. She probably wouldn't know how to strap it in correctly and safely, so he'd have to swap keys with Dani and drive like a bat out of hell. That is if her car could go over fifty-five miles an hour.

He tore up Annalisa's drive, parked next to the ugly green car, and headed for Dani's front door. He rapped hard, hoping she was up, then wishing he'd thought to call her first.

Dani answered the door in a short, silky red robe that clung to her curves and highlighted her long, slim legs. "Hi there. What's up?" she asked as she opened the door wider in invitation and stepped back.

When he finally forced himself to take his eyes off her curvy body, he glanced toward the kitchen. Emma sat at the table eating a yellow cream-filled snack cake.

"You can't feed a kid junk food for breakfast."

Dani shrugged. "She wouldn't eat anything else. I tried cereal, a banana, an apple, a granola bar, and then this was all I had left. It won't kill her, and it can't be any worse than some of that sugary cereal kids normally eat."

"You still eat that snack food crap?"

"What? Don't you?"

When she smiled, the anxiety of being late was forgotten for a moment. "No, and we'll have a nice chat about our bodies being made of what we eat later." He didn't have time to explain to her about kids and sugar rushes. She'd have to figure that one out for herself. "I'm late. Please give me your car keys, and here are mine. You need a car seat to take Emma anywhere today. I'll call you later after I get out of court, and we can swap cars before we look at houses."

When Dani turned to retrieve her purse, Jake strolled into the living room with only a towel around his waist. "Dani, this razor's dull. Do you have another?" Jake pulled up short when he noticed Michael and grinned. "Well good morning, Counselor. What brings you by so early?"

Dani's eyes grew wide, and she muttered, "Oh, shit!" as she rushed forward, holding out the keys. "Michael, this isn't—"

"Don't bother." He snatched the keys from Dani's hand and walked out the door, not interested in her lame excuses.

After tossing and turning all night, trying to figure out what to do about his growing feelings for her, his answer was clear. She'd insisted Jake wasn't spending the night. But she'd lied.

He shook his head as he started her car and headed for the main gate. Dani was obviously still sleeping with him, so that was that. He'd had enough of women lying to him. She could be his damn Realtor and help him find Emma's mom, helping his own mother in the process, but that was it. He'd just file those hot kisses away right along with his memories of their one night, and forget about wanting more.

Unfortunately, every time he looked at Dani he wanted more.

~

Dani sipped coffee as she pondered a way to fix things with Michael. She should probably give him a few hours to cool off, then she'd call and explain why Jake had still been there in the morning. When she glanced up from her mug, she caught Jake, who was sitting at the table in the nook, staring at her. "What?"

"You aren't going to like this, but your mother and I discussed your safety options earlier. She hired a bodyguard for you. His name is Jerry, and where you go, he goes, until this is settled. Is that clear?"

She stared at Jake as anger slowly welled within her. Her mother and Jake had planned her whole safety routine without consulting her? She'd had bodyguards from the time of the kidnapping until she'd turned eighteen, when she finally had the power to insist her mother stop hiring them.

She hated having a tail but was actually pretty good at losing them. Her mom had insisted she take defensive-driving lessons, not realizing that Dani was using those new skills to evade her own protection squad. It had become a game when she was younger. It'd be fun to see how long old Jerry lasted.

Then she glanced at Emma, who was sitting on the floor playing with a stuffed blue rabbit named Wilbur. It was the only toy Dani had kept from her childhood. She'd had the bunny with her when she'd been taken by the kidnappers. Wilbur had given her comfort during the ordeal, and she'd never been able to part with him.

As much as she despised being followed, if Emma was going to be with her, then she'd just have to deal with it. She really needed to find

Em's mother before Friday, when crazy Carlos was going to be released. Otherwise, Em was going to have to stay home in the fortified compound with Mrs. Wilson or one of her mom's assistants.

"Okay. I can live with that."

"Good. Then I have one more question for you."

"What?" The gravity of his tone alarmed her.

"Do you want Michael as much as he wants you?"

She met his gaze, surprised by the sudden tears burning her eyes. She'd never lied to him and wasn't going to start now. "I think I might. We used to be best friends and . . ." She trailed off, not knowing how to explain how much she'd always loved Michael without hurting Jake. She'd never do that on purpose.

He nodded sharply. "I'll get the papers."

Jake crossed the room and picked up the bundle off the kitchen counter, then brought them back to the table. He lifted a pen to sign his name, then stopped. "Here's my last offer. What if I let you wear shoes while you're pregnant with our *one* child? And instead of having a hot meal waiting for me each night, I'll give you a break and pick up a pizza one night a week?" His forced grin gave away that he was trying to lighten the mood, but he couldn't quite manage it.

"Sorry, no deal." She laid her hand on his arm. "But we'll always be friends, right, Jake?" She swiped furiously at the tears that rolled freely down her cheeks. "Please promise me that."

He nodded as he flipped the pages, signing his name ten times. When he was done, he met her gaze, his eyes moist, too. "I know we need to do this, but I'll always love you, Dani. I've never had a better friend, and I'm afraid I might never have another like you again." He cleared the huskiness from his throat. "So you can tell Michael he'd better get used to the fact that I'll always be there for you and will always care about you, no matter what."

God, he could be so sweet sometimes. But they both needed to move on. So she needed to pull herself together.

"Same here, Jake." She leaned forward and kissed him lightly on the cheek. "And now that you've signed these, I feel obligated to tell you that Darlene, the dispatcher at your station, thinks you're incredibly hot. She's a nice woman, and you should give her a call."

Boy, that hurt to tell him that, but she wanted Jake to be happy. She'd always known Darlene was attracted to Jake and used to laugh it off while she and Jake were married. She couldn't blame the woman. Jake was damn cute.

He wiped his eyes and grinned. "How long have you known?"

"Awhile."

"And you didn't tell me until now . . . because?"

Sighing, she reached for his hand. "I wasn't ready to let her have you quite yet."

～

Dani was holding on to her sanity by a thread as she parked Michael's car in front of Zoe's house. Emma had bawled in the back seat, asking for her mother ever since their visit to the doctor for her DNA test, while Jerry the bodyguard trailed close behind. Worse, she was wired. Jerry had *commanded* her to wear a homing device along with an earpiece like the FBI used, so she could communicate with him as he followed her in his car. The guy was bossy and rude. And he wouldn't even let her stop for some ice cream for Emma because it was a public place.

She lifted her wrist to her mouth. "I'm going inside to visit my friend. You are not invited." Dani hopped out of the car to get Emma and nearly ran into Jerry. She lifted her chin and met his hard stare. He looked like Rocky, and of all the bodyguards she'd had over the years, he was the worst. The guy was a real hard-ass, and she was quickly growing tired of him. "What?" she asked as she broke their staring competition and leaned in to get Emma out of the car seat before Dani's eardrums practically ruptured from the crying.

He crossed his massive arms. "You need an attitude adjustment, lady. I'm in charge of your safety, and your mother's paying me. Not you. You don't give the commands. *I do!*"

Dani thrust Emma into his arms and leaned back inside for Wilbur and the diaper bag. "Fine. Do what you like but hurry up about it." She didn't give him a chance to argue and stormed to Zoe's front door.

As if she were a ticking time bomb, Jerry held Emma as far away from his body as he could manage. She couldn't blame him. Emma wasn't smelling so good.

When Zoe opened the door, Jerry thrust Emma at her. Then he sneered at Dani. "I'll secure the perimeter. Don't leave the house without informing me." He turned and beat a fast retreat.

"A bodyguard? This is just like old times, huh, Dan?" Zoe laughed as she tucked Emma against her hip. "Come on in. I was just about to feed Lindsey some lunch. My other two monsters are in school."

Zoe wiped Emma's tears with a Kleenex that appeared out of nowhere. "This must be the gorgeous Miss Emma I've heard all about. What's the matter? Has the mean old Dani forgotten to feed you today? I'll bet you'd like to meet Lindsey and have some mac and cheese, wouldn't you?"

When Emma sniffed pathetically and nodded, Dani wanted to pull her own hair out by the roots. "I didn't forget to feed her today. We had snack cakes for breakfast." Suddenly, she felt a little foolish.

Zoe glanced over her shoulder, staring at Dani with a very Annalisa-like expression. "Emma's diaper needs to be changed, too."

"That just happened a few blocks away." Dani caught up with Zoe and wrapped her arm around her shoulder. "Because you're my very best friend, I was hoping you'd want to give me a break and offer to change her. She's never had a diaper smell quite so . . . pungent before. I figured you must be immune to that by now, and I'm afraid I might pass out."

"Maybe you should rethink what you feed her for breakfast," Zoe said, but took mercy on her and carried Emma into Lindsey's bedroom.

In the time it took an Indy race car team to change a tire, Zoe strode into the kitchen and plopped Emma into a high chair right alongside Lindsey's. "There. All better now."

Dani sank into a chair in the cozy nook and waited while Zoe washed her hands, doled out globs of mac and cheese into two bowls, and placed them in front of the kids.

Zoe wore her usual uniform when painting, of ripped jeans and an old football jersey splattered with twenty-five different hues of paint. The temperature had dropped a bit now that October had finally arrived, so Zoe actually had a pair of sneakers on, but without socks. Her feet were usually bare from March to the end of September. She used to say it was because she spent half her childhood in a nudist colony while growing up with her hippie parents.

As scraggly as Zoe's clothes were, her beauty still shone through. Zoe's long, jet-black hair framed a face with fierce cheekbones and a wide mouth with full lips most women could only achieve with injections. She was half-Cherokee, half-Hispanic and was the most exotic-looking person Dani had ever met. Men stopped and stared at her when she walked down the street. And what she took most pride in wasn't her appearance, her successful painting career, or even her solid marriage, but being a mother. That was something Dani could never picture for herself.

Zoe secured the bibs in place, then beamed her perfect smile at the girls. "Okay, ladies, dig in."

Emma squealed with delight as both girls, ignoring their rubberized forks, ate with their hands. After about thirty seconds their faces were covered in yellow slime.

Dani sighed, enjoying her few moments of peace without any kid responsibilities, before Zoe joined her holding two plates with turkey sandwiches and chips.

Dani took a bite and grinned. "You know what? You're incredible. I never knew how much work a kid could be, and you have three."

"You just aren't trained." Zoe waved a hand in dismissal. "Don't worry, you'll get the hang of it."

Zoe took a bite of her sandwich, then took a swig of iced tea that Dani hadn't even seen her put in front of them. "Now, after your earlier call, I'm still a little confused. So what else is wrong, other than the fact that you've got a very big handprint bruise on your face, you're stuck with someone else's kid, and a crazy guy is after you, which probably explains the bodyguard?"

"Jake finally signed the divorce papers, and I kissed Michael. Three times."

Zoe laid her sandwich down and leaned closer. "I'm sorry about Jake, but you both know it needed to be done. And which Michael did you kiss?"

Before Dani could answer, the girls threw their bowls and forks on the floor, laughing like loons. "Hold that thought." Zoe rose to clean up the mess.

After the girls were tucked away in the nearby playroom, she sat across from Dani again. "Okay, now which Michael are we talking about?"

Dani pushed the plate that held her half-eaten sandwich away and whispered, "Michael Reilly."

Zoe's brows jumped to life. "*That* Michael? He's not married anymore?"

"No, he and Heather got a divorce about a year and a half ago."

Zoe's grin grew mischievous. "Then I'm guessing your celibate streak is about to end. We both know you have trouble saying no to Michael."

"Tell me about it." She laid her head on the table and moaned. "He's not the one with the scar from my dream, and yet I really want to sleep with him. I've turned into a slut."

Chuckling, Zoe ran a soothing hand down Dani's back. "I'm sorry to be the one to break it to you, but technically speaking, any thirty-year-old woman who has only slept with three men in her entire life and is contemplating sleeping with the first one again can't qualify for slut status. Sleeping with Michael won't even increase the number of men you've been with. I think you'll have to settle for the title of 'Horny Woman.'"

Dani snorted out a laugh. "God, that's pathetic. It's only been three and a half weeks. I should be stronger than this."

"Oh, stop." Zoe stood and cleared their dishes away. "You know you've always liked Michael even when you were insulting him. Especially then, because he's one of the few people who truly challenges you. Michael's smart, nice, and damn good-looking. If I weren't married and still madly in love with Will, I'd jump his bones in a heartbeat. Just sleep with him, Dani, and enjoy it."

Dani's heart warmed as her lips tilted into a grin. Zoe always got to the root of the matter, cutting through the flack, making her feel better. "He's really annoyed with me at the moment, which is nothing new, so I don't think the sleeping together is imminent. Just inevitable."

Lindsey ran into the room and tugged on Zoe's shirt. "Wan appa juu, peezz."

"Okay, but you need to have it in sippy cups so we don't have any spills in the playroom."

Dani quickly sat up. "Wait. You understood that? That sounds just like the noise that comes out of Emma's mouth."

Zoe handed Lindsey two cups of apple juice with goofy lids on top, and she ran back to the playroom. "Again, you're just not trained."

"I wish Em was old enough to talk properly. I need some clues to find her mother so I can give her back. And what's weird is, when I touch Em, I don't get any visions, or even colors in my mind. Everyone I touch has a color." Dani explained the whole Ron situation.

"Maybe kids have to be a certain age before the wacky Botelli women can do their thing?" Zoe frowned and sat beside Dani again.

"I'll bet your grandmother could *talk* to Em. You said just last week that you'd been meaning to go see her. Here's your excuse."

Maybe it *was* time to visit her grandmother in Taos. She could go the next day and be out of town when the crazy, scary Carlos person was released from jail. Her grandmother could sort through Emma's limited vocabulary to see if it held any clues, then maybe she could track down Julia's mother. She'd have to call Jake and see if he'd found out if her grandmother knew Emma's grandmother.

She felt better now that she had a plan. One that kept her out of Carlos's reach.

Dani hopped up from her seat. "Thanks for lunch. I have to go." She wrapped her friend up in a tight hug. "Call you later."

When she headed for the door, Zoe called out, "Dan? Aren't you forgetting something?"

"What?"

"Emma?"

"Oh yeah. Man, I really suck at this." Dani walked toward the playroom, where Emma and Lindsey were having a tea party with colorful rag dolls. Their game was so sweet that Dani leaned against the doorjamb to enjoy it. For just a bit.

After watching them for a few moments, she called out, "Hey, Em? Want to hit the road?"

Emma's little blue eyes turned toward Dani's, and then she waved at her new friend. "Bye-bye. Go Daaaani." Emma picked up the rabbit and tucked it under her pudgy little arm. When she grinned and held out her free hand, Dani took it and led her toward the front door where Emma's diaper bag lay. She smiled at the absolute trust Emma had in her. If the poor kid only knew she'd been stuck with the absolute worst babysitter on earth.

∽

Michael threw his briefcase in the direction of his desk, then picked up the phone to dial Dani's number. He needed to tell her about the new problem with her car. He wasn't looking forward to her reaction.

As the phone rang in his ear, he glanced at his mother, who sat across from him. He'd reconsidered and told her about Emma. Just in case his mom got cold feet and needed another reason to go through with the divorce from Ron. The good thing was she'd taken it like the trooper she'd always been. Then for some unknown reason, he'd spilled his guts about his confusing feelings for Dani. He'd left out the part about finding Jake at her house that morning, though.

He'd hoped his mother would talk some sense into him, but she only laughed and said it was about time he'd figured out how much he still cared for her.

What the hell was wrong with him? That Dani had lied about Jake spending the night meant he should bury the feelings he still had for her. And he really shouldn't be discussing them with his mother.

He hated that it felt as if his life was spinning out of control again. Like when his world had been turned upside down after his father's death, after Dani had suddenly abandoned their friendship, after the accident that ended his NFL career, and then by his divorce. Dani would surely have something to do with the next disaster in his life.

Worse, he and Dani were supposed to look at houses later. And the thought of seeing her again was already heating his blood.

When Dani answered her phone, she saved the niceties. "Are we still on for four o'clock?"

How should he break the bad news? Direct was probably best. "Yes, but your car threw a rod this morning about three blocks from the courthouse. I had it towed to a garage."

"Oh." Dani hesitated for a moment. "And?"

"The guy said the engine was a total loss. I'm not sure we can save it from the junkyard this time."

He expected her to scream and throw a fit, but she only sighed.

"I always hated that car. Maybe I can sell it for scraps. Where are you? Do you need a ride?"

She was being calm and reasonable after learning news like that? Had he been transported to a parallel universe? One where Dani had finally grown up? "I'm at my office. My mom gave me a ride."

"Oh good, is she still there? Why don't I pick you guys up? If she's going to be living with you, she may as well have a say in the house you choose." Then she quickly added, "Wait. She doesn't know about Emma. That might not be such a good idea."

"She knows. I told her." Michael slumped back into his chair, rubbing at the pain radiating behind his forehead. "What about Carlos? Maybe we should hold off looking for houses until that's all settled."

"No worries. Jake is on it. Carlos is still locked down. And to be extra safe, per my mother's requirements, I now have Jerry the bodyguard tailing me. He'll kill anyone dead who tries to hurt us. I'll be there in ten minutes." His phone went silent.

He met his mother's amused gaze. "Do you want to look at houses with us this afternoon?"

His mom picked up her purse. "I wouldn't miss it for the world, honey."

Chapter Seven

Dani pulled up in front of Ron's swanky office building, where Maeve and Michael stood at the curb waiting for her. Her ear still hurt from the dressing down she'd just received from Jerry for not using her blinker at a four-way stop. She'd been the only car in the intersection, for goodness' sake. The man needed to take a chill pill.

She hit a few buttons, finally finding the right one, and the window whirred down. "Hi, you guys, hop in."

Michael yanked open the door. "I'll drive. You can ride in the back." Then he glanced at Maeve. "Mom, why don't you take shotgun?"

Dani gave him a testy shrug, then slipped into the back seat next to Emma. He was obviously still angry with her.

Her bodyguard's voice shouted in her earpiece, "I'm glad you let him take over. You drive like shit!"

To show Jerry what she thought of his opinion, she lifted her hand behind Emma's car seat and flipped him off.

"Oh jeez, now you've gone and hurt my feelings."

"Butthead," Dani muttered before she gave Michael directions. After he pulled away from the curb, silence enveloped the car.

Emma must've felt the tension and, trying to be helpful, took the opportunity to show off the new word she'd learned that morning. With a big grin, she proclaimed, "Shit!" clear as a bell.

The look on Emma's face was so hopeful. It was as if she'd just learned a new color, and it took all Dani could do to curtail the laugh that bubbled inside of her. That is, until she noticed Michael's emerald-green eyes staring at her in the rearview mirror.

She smiled at his reflection. "That was your fault, you know."

"You're the one who used profanity in front of a child. Not me." Michael shifted his focus back to the road.

"Yeah, but I knew you'd jump to the wrong conclusion. You're just so . . ."—she glanced in Emma's direction, censoring her words—"tightly wound when it comes to Jake. There's a perfectly reasonable explanation for what happened."

"Can we do this later?" Michael said with a sigh. "I don't think my mother is interested in hearing about how you spent your morning."

Maeve grinned. "On the contrary, Michael. This is fascinating."

He sent his mom a sideways glance that included a heavy-duty scowl. "So what conclusion was I supposed to draw when I saw Jake strolling around in nothing but a towel?"

"That he'd just had a shower?" Dani replied and crossed her arms.

He met her gaze again in the mirror. "Alone?"

"Yes, alone. I was busy feeding Emma her nutritious breakfast, remember?"

"You kissed him," Michael snapped back, "and in my world, it's only proper to kiss one person at a time."

"Wait a minute. You kissed *me* last night, remember?"

His eyes narrowed in the mirror.

"Okay, I definitely participated in our kiss, but I didn't kiss Jake yesterday." Then she remembered she had. More than once, but all on the cheek. "Oh, wait. I guess I did. But those kisses weren't like ours. They were just . . ." How was she going to get out of the hole she was digging herself deeper into?

Maeve turned around and offered, "Like a peck?"

"Yeah. Thank you, Maeve. Those were just a peck, like you'd give a brother or something."

"Jake's not your brother." Michael turned up the radio to end the conversation.

Maeve switched it off. "Wait a minute you two. Time out. I'm not sure I understand this. So, Michael, you surprised Dani with an early-morning visit, and Jake was there?"

Dani called out, "Maeve, you've lived at Annalisa's and know that no one gets in without being announced. He didn't surprise me. The guard called and told me Michael was on his way. If something was going on that shouldn't have been, I had fair warning and would have had plenty of opportunity to hide the truth."

Maeve turned and faced Michael. "She has a point, sweetheart."

"Whose side are you on?" he asked his mother.

"She's on the side of justice, and you, being a lawyer, should be, too. Turn right at the next stop sign."

Silence fell over the car again, and after a few moments Emma enunciated perfectly, "Butthead."

"You got that right, girlfriend." Dani raised her hand for a high five.

Emma grinned and slapped Dani's hand.

When they pulled up in front of the vacant house, Dani released Emma from her car seat, then tucked her onto her hip. Jerry instantly appeared at her side.

He said, "I'll go in first. Stay behind me at all times."

She rolled her eyes as she dealt with the lockbox to retrieve the key. "Carlos's friends couldn't possibly know I was going to show this particular house this afternoon. You're such a drama queen."

Jerry's jaw clenched. For half a second it looked as if he was going to take out his gun and shoot her himself, saving Carlos Watts the trouble. But she must've made her point, because he shook his head and moved aside. "It's your life, lady. Why do I always get stuck with the smartasses?"

Dani sent him a smug grin. "Just lucky, I guess." She unlocked the door and swung it open. "Why don't you just stand right there till we're done? And if a nefarious character carrying a bundle of envelopes tries to put them in that little box right there, shoot him. It's probably a bad guy dressed as the mailman."

When Jerry's hand inched toward his gun, Dani figured she'd pushed him far enough for one day, and her work was done. She followed Michael and Maeve into the house and then set Emma down. "The owners had to relocate due to a job change, so I'll bet they're eager to sell."

While Jerry stood guard outside as the rest of them toured the interior, Emma latched onto Maeve, holding her hand and babbling about something only the two of them seemed to understand.

It was a testament to Maeve that she could put aside the fact that Emma had been sired by her husband's infidelity. Michael had an awesome mom.

Michael, on the other hand, was driving her nuts by giving her one-word answers since they'd gotten out of the car. He'd had every right to jump to the wrong conclusion, but she'd explained what happened. He just wasn't buying it for some reason. It took every last ounce of restraint not to smack some sense upside his hard head.

When they passed the master-bedroom closet, she couldn't stand it any longer and yanked on his perfectly knotted tie, pulling him inside with her. After slamming the door behind them, she slapped the light switch. They were going to clear things up between them once and for all. "You said you wanted to talk about 'that night' back in high school, Michael, so talk."

He whispered, "After that night, you avoided me, wouldn't take my calls, or even read the notes I asked people to give you. All I wanted was to tell you I was sorry I let that happen."

Apologize for the best sex she'd ever had? Clearly, she still had more feelings for him than he did for her. It'd make having a casual fling easy on his part; she'd just have to put her feelings aside for the sake of great sex.

Shouldn't be so hard to do. She'd buried her feelings for him for the past twelve years just fine.

"Apology accepted. So let's talk about last night. I slept with Emma, Jake fell asleep on the couch, and then he signed our divorce papers this morning." Not waiting for his response, she took his face in her hands and kissed him.

It didn't take long for his pursed lips to soften and match her frenzied pace.

What was it about him? The heat from their joining seeped into her body, warming every part of her, especially the good ones.

With his lips never leaving hers, he flipped their positions, backing her against the door. One of his big thighs ended up between her legs, and his large hands slid down her body in one long, slow stroke, leaving every place he touched burning for more. His kiss was so hot it turned her legs to mush. She feared they wouldn't hold her up much longer.

His eager mouth left hers just in time for her to draw a breath before she passed out, and then his lips trailed down the side of her neck. She finally found the strength to open her eyes, and behind Michael, a small door stood open that led to a storage room in the attic.

In a flash, searing pain, along with a vision, filled her mind. The Pink Panther held up a sign with a big red arrow pointing to the rafters.

She knew where the gun was that Jake was looking for. That damned panther had told her if she talked with Michael about "that night" he'd show her the answer. She hated that something so pink and sneaky held that much power over her mind.

She ran a hand through Michael's thick hair and whispered, "Can we take a little time-out for just a second? I need to tell Jake something."

"What?" Michael's head shot up. "You lay a kiss on me like that and then ask me to wait while you talk to your . . . to Jake? You were thinking about him while you were kissing me?"

That sounded really bad when he put it like that. "No, I wasn't thinking about Jake. I was thinking about the closet. Wait. I mean of course I was thinking about you, until I opened my eyes and saw what I needed to tell Jake." She held up her hand. "That came out wrong, too. Let me try again."

Through gritted teeth, he growled, "Just call him."

She quickly dug her cell from her purse. "I would've waited, but Jake's got a deadline, so I'll just be a second and then I'll remind you where we were."

Michael stood with his arms crossed, staring at her while she dialed Jake's number. When he answered, she turned away and lowered her voice to just above a whisper. "It's behind that cedar wall in the master closet. It slides open. Go inside the storage room and shine a flashlight toward the rafters. When you see the shimmer of pink nail polish, you'll find where the guy marked the spot so he could retrieve it later. The thing in question is tucked between the beams behind the metal nail plate."

Jake blew out a long breath. "Good job, babe. Thanks."

She put her phone back and turned around, but Michael was gone. She cursed under her breath, because apparently she wasn't allowed to cuss out loud as long as she was living with a little mynah bird, and caught up with everyone in the kitchen. When Michael opened the French doors and led Emma to the backyard, Maeve grabbed her arm and held her in place.

"By the scowl on Michael's face, I'm gonna guess there wasn't much kissing and making up going on in that closet?"

"We did the kissing part, and that went well, but the making up didn't happen. Michael is a little sensitive about Jake."

Maeve wrapped her arm around Dani's shoulder. "You have to admit you and Jake are probably the friendliest almost-divorced couple most have ever met."

"Jake and I don't hate each other. We just weren't meant to be married. I had to make a phone call to Jake and told Michael it'd only take a minute. He didn't even let me explain afterward. Maybe Michael and I were better off when we weren't speaking to each other unless we had to."

Maeve pulled Dani into a hard hug, then ran a comforting hand up and down her back. "I think you both could have handled the Jake situation this morning a little better, honey."

Maeve had a point. Michael was hearing her say she was over Jake, but the way she was still so involved in his cases could come off as confusing. "I still need to talk to Jake until my Carlos Watts problem is solved, but you're right. I shouldn't have kissed Jake on the cheek. It's an old habit I need to break."

"That sounds like a good place to start." Maeve sighed. "Listen. Michael's heart was just as broken as yours was back in high school, Dani. I know you were in love with him, but I don't think he understood how much he cared for you until you stopped talking to him. I'm sure he doesn't want to be hurt like that again if you still have feelings for Jake."

Dani's stomach took a dive. "You knew I was in love with Michael? I never told anyone that."

She nodded. "You were a sixteen-year-old, starry-eyed girl, who looked at Michael like he invented chocolate cake. It used to melt my heart. And he was a typical oblivious boy. It was hard to watch two people who cared for each other so deeply hurting that much. So please don't give up on Michael until you get what you want."

"We may not want the same things, then what?" She rested her head against Maeve's shoulder. It was always a comfortable spot.

"You might be surprised to learn that we don't always know what we want in life until we end up with it."

Dani conjured up her dream man again. She should probably ask her grandmother's opinion about why he was walking away in her vision. Maybe her mom was right; maybe he wasn't the one for her, but were she and Michael meant to be together?

～

After dropping his mom off, Michael headed for Annalisa's compound. He checked the rearview mirror to be sure Jerry was still close on their tail and caught Em's reflection in the back seat. Her head was cocked sideways in her car seat, and she was sound asleep. "Did you give Emma a nap today before you picked me up?"

Dani threw a thumb over her shoulder. "Sleep is sleep, right. Doesn't that count?"

Why he bothered to leave Dani detailed childcare instructions was beyond him. She generally made up her own rules as she went along anyway. "If Emma naps this late in the day, it might be hard to get her to go to bed at a decent hour."

Dani shrugged. "Well, then I guess us girls will be watching late-night movies tonight."

He shook his head but let it go. She'd just have to figure it out on her own.

Dani laid a soft hand over his on the console between them. "You've been awfully quiet all afternoon. What did you think of the homes we saw?" He refused to let her thumb rubbing slowly back and forth on the back of his hand distract him.

"I liked them. But I'd like to look at a few more like those before I make up my mind." And while they were talking about making decisions, it was probably as good a time as any to share the one he'd made about him and Dani. "And I think it'd be best to stop whatever this thing is between us before it goes any further. Why don't you stick to being my Realtor, and we'll just forget the rest?"

"Michael, I'm sorry about the closet." Her fingers laced with his. "It's over between me and Jake. I swear. I shouldn't have kissed him. You were right."

Her cell rang, so she gave his hand a gentle squeeze before she dug her phone from her purse.

She read the screen and cringed. "Okay. This is Jake. I should probably answer in case it's about Carlos, but I won't if it'll make you angry."

Of course it was Jake. He was like a rash that wouldn't go away. "Answer it."

He blew out a long breath as he studied the road ahead. Jake was trying to protect Dani. They were going to have to talk. Maybe Michael needed to take her at her word that they were really over. But trusting Dani, letting his heart get potentially stomped on again wasn't something he was sure he wanted to do.

After Dani answered, she listened for a moment before a smile bloomed. "Yes. We'll be there in like ten minutes. Please wait for us. Bye."

She tucked her phone away. "So Jake says the FBI just finished confiscating Julia's electronics. Because they suspected wire fraud, they got a warrant, and Jake tagged along. He asked if we wanted to grab anything of Em's before he locks up."

"Does Emma need something?"

"I told Jake that I'm taking Emma up north to Taos tomorrow to visit my grandmother. And hopefully find Julia's mother. Em needs some warmer clothes, but mostly I want a chance to snoop around Julia's stuff for myself."

He turned and met her eager gaze. "You think you're going to find clues that the FBI missed?"

"Um, yeah." She chewed her bottom lip while she pondered. "Like, maybe something only a woman would notice?"

"News flash. They have women agents, too. But if Em needs warmer things, then fine."

He would have liked to get his hands on Julia's computers before the FBI took them, but maybe there'd be old paper files lying around that the FBI wouldn't have been interested in, from when Julia worked for Ron. Then maybe he'd find what he needed to help his mom, choose a house, and then remove himself from Dani's life again.

∽

Dani chose to remain quiet the rest of the way to Julia's house. First, because Em obviously needed her beauty rest in the back, and she feared there'd be yelling if she brought up the closet and Jake again, and second, because the look on Michael's face was not a pleasant one. She'd get him to reconsider their relationship after he had some time to cool off. If he didn't want to sleep with her, that she could live with. But she didn't realize how much she'd missed having Michael as a friend until recently. She needed *one* normal person in her life.

When they pulled into Julia's driveway, Jake stood waiting for them with a big smile on his face. He even opened her door for her. Would've been nice if he'd done that while they'd been married. He was clearly doing it to irritate Michael.

He said, "Hey, babe. Let's make this quick."

Michael lifted a semi-asleep Emily from her car seat and waited for Jerry to join them; then everyone trooped toward the front porch.

Jake said, "Hey there, Counselor. Long time no see."

Michael's lifted brow was his only response.

Yeah, that's all they needed. More reminders for Michael about how the day started with Jake in nothing but a towel.

Then Jake turned and beamed a big smile at the still-sleepy Emily. "Hey there, cute stuff." He reached out to take Emily from Michael, but she shook her head and snuggled her face into the crook of Michael's neck. Bright girl. It was one of Dani's favorite places, too.

Jerry took his post in front of the house while they went inside. When Michael put Emma down, she let out a little happy squeal and then ran through the house shouting, "Momma?"

Oh, crap.

Dani looked up at Michael. "My bad. Again."

He shook his head. "I didn't think of it, either, dammit. I should have."

When Emma reappeared with tears and confusion on her face, it made Dani's heart hurt. Em looked up at Michael and lifted her little hands. "No momma?"

"No. I'm sorry, Em." He picked her up again and gave her a hug. "But we're going to find her. I promise."

Michael sounded so sure that Dani totally believed him, too.

She swallowed the lump in her throat. "I should probably go find some warmer clothes for her."

"I'll pack her a bag. Why don't you guys look around?" Michael seemed happy to make his escape from Jake.

And her.

Jake took her arm and led her toward the master bedroom. "I want to show you something in here." Once inside he whispered, "I can't figure out how to open that cedar panel in casa de pink. You need to come back with me and help. Time's running out."

The last thing she needed was for Michael to find out she was spending time in a closet with Jake. But there was no way she'd let that guy get away with a double murder.

"Okay. I'll take Em home, let her meet Mrs. Wilson, then I'll have Jerry run me over there. Don't say anything in front of Michael. He's already mad at me because of you."

"Can't say I'm sorry to hear that." Jake's grin turned mischievous. "What's Mrs. Wilson making for dinner? Please tell me it's her famous pot roast."

"Doesn't matter. We're going to find that damn gun, and you'll be busy all night processing the scumbag."

"True. But I love me some leftovers."

Ignoring him, Dani headed for Julia's closet. Mrs. Wilson's leftovers were just one more thing he wasn't getting anymore.

She stepped into the closet and pulled up short. "Boy, Julia's a neat one."

"Yeah, unlike you." He threw an arm around her shoulder.

He was right. She'd never had the need to have shoes lined up perfectly, or have belts and accessories organized in little cubbies. She always found what she needed; it just took her a while sometimes.

She sloughed off Jake's arm and moved to the bedroom, quickly riffling through Julia's things inside the nightstands, then in her dresser, but nothing popped for her, so they headed to the kitchen.

In the nook, Dani found a notepad that looked promising but got a big bunch of nada from touching that, too. Then she spotted a pile of opened mail neatly stacked on a little desk in the corner. She shuffled through the envelopes.

When Michael and Em reappeared, he leaned over Dani's shoulder. "Find anything?"

"Nope. Just that Julia is scary neat and has a ton of past-due bills."

She picked up a stack of coupons to move aside and out slipped a flyer. It was a slick postcard advertising a grand opening special for a casino in Las Vegas. The rooms were only twenty dollars a night, and it boasted the best odds on the strip.

Dani picked up the ad to stack with the other junk mail, and a bolt of pain seared through her head. Her mind saw a flashy magician on a stage pulling giant rabbits from a huge hat. The image shook her so badly she lost her balance and stumbled against the desk.

"What's wrong, Dani?" Michael wrapped his hand around her arm to steady her.

She turned over the advertisement, and her heart gave a quick thud. "Do you remember when we had all those snow days that winter in the seventh grade and were stuck at home? We were so bored we decided to try to figure out who my father is?" Through the rags and her mom's old appointment books, they'd narrowed it down to a plastic surgeon and the man smiling up from the postcard. Mario Giovanni. The flyer told that he'd just opened another new casino on the strip in Las Vegas. He'd owned many over the years, and Dani had always wondered if that was the real reason her mother had always forbidden her to go to Vegas.

She couldn't tell if the energy she felt from the card was because the guy was her father or because it had something to do with Julia's whereabouts.

Great.

Michael shifted Emily to his other hip and then leaned down to inspect the back of the flyer. "That's the mob guy."

No one had ever proven the guy was in the mob, but members of his family had gone to jail for some very bad things.

Michael's forehead furrowed as he gave her a hug with his free arm. "We thought it was the plastic surgeon back then, remember?"

After losing his dad from cancer way too early, Michael always hated that she had a father somewhere in the world she didn't know.

"Yeah. Probably." Her mom had vowed to never tell who her father was, so it didn't really matter. Much.

Jake had his back to them and was talking on his cell, so she opened her purse to slip the casino ad inside. It was definitely important; she could feel it. It might be just the excuse she'd need to hide out in Vegas to avoid Carlos, and at the same time check the Mario guy out. She'd need to wait until they found Em's grandmother in Taos, though, first. Maybe she could drop Em off with her grandma and avoid lugging a kid to Vegas.

"Nope." Michael tugged the ad from her grasp. Then he laid it back on the desk. "There's an active investigation happening. You need to leave things as they are."

"Fine." She really didn't need it anyway. She knew the name of the casino now, and that was enough.

Michael pulled her close by his side. Probably because he still felt sorry for her about her father. Or he wanted to be sure she didn't take anything else.

But the hug felt nice. Maybe there was hope that she could still change his mind about them having a casual friends-with-benefits relationship.

Jake ended his call. "If you guys are done, let's lock up and go." He stared into her eyes and hitched his brows, probably silently reminding her that they needed to get their butts in gear and over to the pink palace.

In the car, on the way back to Annalisa's house, Michael glanced her way. "I'm going with you to Taos tomorrow to find Julia's mother. I think Julia is the key to finding Ron's hidden money. But I have something I have to take care of in the morning. We'll go after lunch."

She opened her mouth to tell him he had some nerve—just assuming he'd be invited and putting her on *his* timetable—but stopped. She really didn't want to hunt for Julia's grandmother alone, and he wanted answers for his mom's sake as much as Dani did.

"Fine. I have to stop by a title company and pick up a commission check in the morning anyway. But Carlos gets out of jail late tomorrow afternoon, so I want to be out of here by two."

"Have Jerry drop you guys off at my office at one, and we'll go from there."

"Sounds like a plan."

About an hour later, Jerry and Dani rushed up the stairs to join Jake amid the nauseating pink master bedroom crime scene. The search warrant was only good for another few minutes, so they'd have to hurry. When they hit the door, Jerry stopped dead in his tracks. "Holy shit!"

"No kidding." You'd think the shock of so much pink would have worn off after seeing it once before, but nope.

Jake leaned his head out of the closet. "What the hell took you so long?"

Dani squeezed past Jake and made her way toward the cedar wall. "Don't yell at me. I've had enough screaming and bawling today. I snuck out of the kitchen while Mrs. Wilson distracted Em with making cookies, but I could hear the kid crying at the top of her lungs as we drove away." It had sent an arrow to Dani's heart, but she wasn't sharing that part.

"Sorry." Jake ran a hand up and down her back in apology. "I've tried everything. The damn thing won't open."

Laying her hands on the wall, she closed her eyes and concentrated. Nothing happened. Not even a low hum of energy she'd expect to get. Now was not the time for her spotty visions to fail her. Maybe she'd used up her quota for the day with the casino ad earlier. "Have you looked for a button or a switch of some sort?"

Jake nodded. "I've looked everywhere."

She ran her hands over all the walls and then pulled a pair of shoes from its cubby. "Maybe it's hidden in the back of one of these." There must've been two hundred little posh shoe hotels.

Jake helped, and they were tossing shoes over their shoulders when Jerry said, "What the heck is this wacky thing anyway?"

Dani said, "It's a combo steamer and dry cleaning system. We could use a hand over here, pal."

"Not my job, lady." Jerry flipped some switches, and steam poured from the nozzle. "Cool."

The man was more immature than Emma.

Dani continued throwing $500 shoes behind her as she searched as fast as she could. She knew the gun was behind that wall. She could feel it. "Jake, can we bust the panel down?"

"I could be in some deep shit if I did, but if we don't find something quick, I might have to risk it."

Jerry tilted his head. "Weird. I wonder what this does?" He flipped up a pink square handle, and the cedar wall began to slide open.

She could have kissed Jerry on the lips—if he weren't Jerry.

Dani grabbed the flashlight from Jake's back pocket and went first into the unfinished room behind the panel. When she flipped a light switch on the wall, a stingy bulb barely illuminated a secret wood-lined storage area. The beams above were at least ten feet high. Maybe more. Math had never been her strong point.

Shining the light into the rafters, she finally spotted it. The pink nail polish painted on the wood, shimmering along with the dust motes. "There, see it?"

A slow grin stretched Jake's lips. "You were right. But how are we going to get it?"

Jake and Dani both searched through the junk stacked up around the room, but there wasn't anything sturdy enough to stand on. Crap. They'd have to improvise.

She figured Jerry was a good six feet four, Jake was six, and she was five nine. Jake would be too heavy for Jerry, so tag, she was it.

Maybe if she could stand on Jerry's shoulders, she'd be able to reach behind the nail plate that was a foot or so above the beam. "Jerry, get in here!"

He squeezed his massive body beside her and Jake. "Is *please* not in your vocabulary, lady?"

"My name is Dani. Not lady. Maybe when you can get that right, I can say *please*. Lean down. I need a boost."

Jerry wrapped his big paws around her waist and then hefted her butt onto his shoulder. She tossed the flashlight to Jake, then grabbed on to some conduit along the wall for balance until she could get her feet under her.

"Wait. You need these." Jake tossed her a pair of latex gloves. Dani's hands were so sweaty with nerves she struggled to get them on.

Jake growled, "We've got less than twenty minutes, Dani. Hurry." Then he tossed up the flashlight.

She switched it on, but she wasn't quite high enough to see over the joists, so she let the flashlight fall to the floor. She was going to have to feel around for the gun.

She slipped her hand behind the metal nail plate and—nothing. Her stomach dropped to her toes. That couldn't be right. Did the guy get there first and remove it? Why else would there have been pink nail polish on the rafter?

She stood on her tiptoes. "Jerry, stand on your tiptoes. I can't reach all the way."

"What's the magic word, *Dani*?"

She tapped the side of his head with her sneaker—lightly—before Jake shouted, "Knock it off, you two. We're almost out of time."

Jerry lifted her up another few inches, and she swept her fingers back and forth. Still nothing but wood.

She stretched her arm as far as she could, the rough beam scratching her skin, drawing blood as she pressed against it, and then finally her fingers connected with . . . something. Through the gloves, she couldn't be sure what it was, but it was just out of her reach.

So she took ahold of the rafters with both hands and pulled herself higher, off Jerry entirely, and wrapped an arm around one of the beams. Her right arm shook as she struggled to hold on. She stretched as far as she could, until her other hand landed on something hard—the gun. Thank God.

"Got it!"

"Good job, babe." Jake beamed a big smile. "Hand it down. I have to call this in."

She stretched again to place the gun in Jake's gloved hand, then he ran out of the room.

Jerry looked up at her with his hands on his hips. A lethal grin lit up his smug face. "So how ya getting down, Einstein?"

Both her arms were shaking so badly she'd probably fall down any second. She hated what she'd have to do, but the alternative was going to hurt a lot worse. "Okay, dammit! *Please*?"

"Please what?"

"*Please* will you help me, Jerry?"

Smiling, he moved under her. "I'm only doing this because you might survive the fall, then tell your mom. I want my bonus." He lifted up both of his hands. "Lower yourself as far as you can—"

Too late. She was no gym rat. Her arms gave out. All she could do was close her eyes and hope.

Jerry's loud grunt and the pain in her butt—not Jerry, the actual pain in her rear end—indicated she'd landed in one piece. It hadn't been so bad. For her, anyway.

Jerry made a good crash pad.

After rolling off, she slowly stood upright. It appeared she was all in working order, so she leaned down and whispered in Jerry's ear, "I guess you're too hurt to look after me anymore. Can you ask your boss to be sure your replacement is nicer than you? And can catch better?"

When Jerry's lips curled with the scariest sneer she'd ever seen, that was her clue to run.

Chapter Eight

Michael unlocked the door to his apartment and let Dani and Emma step inside before him. He crossed the room and laid their purchases on the couch. He wasn't letting Dani go to Taos without him. He wanted to find Emma's mother as badly as Dani did, even if that meant driving her and Emma there with Jerry trailing behind.

The girls had just gone to a title company and picked up Dani's commission check and then to babyGap.

After paying him back for the trespassing fine, Dani had spent most of the remaining money Ron had given her on Emma.

Dani was the most frustrating woman he knew, but she'd always been generous and kindhearted. He found it difficult to stay mad at her for long when she kept doing nice things. Like standing up to Ron on Emma's behalf or buying Emma new clothes. She'd even splurged on a ridiculous purse so Emma could carry her new crayons and little cardboard books with her, using money that she must've desperately needed now that she was supporting herself. It couldn't be cheap to be Dani. The yearly bail money she must have to come up with for herself alone had to be staggering.

But then the closet incident, when Dani stopped kissing him to call Jake, was all it took to put his guard back in place. He'd do his best to avoid any more kissing. Dani hadn't resolved her feelings for Jake, and besides that, she was just too much work.

As Dani wandered around his apartment, being nosy, picking up knickknacks and examining the art, he led Emma into his daughters' bedroom to set her up with some toys. Emma squealed with delight when she spotted a two-story dollhouse. She started to cross the room, then stopped. She turned and wrapped his legs up in a tight hug.

He lifted her up to his eye level and met her grin with one of his own. When she wrapped her little arms around his neck, his heart melted just as it did every time his daughters did that. "Have fun, sweetheart. You deserve it."

After a quick hug, he put her down so she could explore the room. She ran from toy to toy as if it were Christmas morning, babbling with delight. Satisfied she'd be fine on her own, he went to his bedroom, then to his closet to pack for their trip. After a few minutes, Dani appeared and leaned against the doorframe.

"Michael, you are a scary neat housekeeper."

"Just the opposite of you. One more reason we should go our separate ways after I buy a house." He tossed a duffel bag at her to pack Emma's extra things.

She caught the bag, then let it fall to her feet. "I disagree. Opposites make for the best couples sometimes." Stepping over the duffel, she moved closer and wrapped her arms around his shoulders. "I'll apologize one more time for the closet scene. It had nothing to do with Jake, just the crime he wanted to solve." She snuggled her curvy, hot body against his and hugged him tighter. "And look, we're in a closet again. Let's pick up where we left off."

His mind shouted, *Don't do it! Step away.* But his mouth wouldn't listen. He kissed her.

Dani was like a euphoric drug to an addict. He couldn't say no. He'd never wanted a woman so badly.

It was a wonder he could command his feet to move with his mind so muddled from her intoxicating kiss, but after they tripped over a pair of shoes and then the duffel on the floor, he somehow managed to back her out of the closet. Cracking just one eye open, he found his target. With his body still pressed tightly against her sexy, soft one, he slowly guided her to where he wanted her. In his bed and underneath him. When Dani's knees finally hit the edge of the bed, he pressed her down onto it.

He'd just covered her supple body with his when Emma yelled out, "Dani?"

Her eyes popped opened. "Don't move, I'll be right back," and then she wiggled out from under him, leaving him even more aroused.

He rolled over and stared at the apartment's stark white ceiling. He wasn't a seventeen-year-old horny teenager and should be able to show more restraint.

But he wasn't going anywhere until she got back.

When she appeared again, she held Emma in her arms. "Sorry." Dani wrinkled her nose. "She was scared when she couldn't find us."

He rolled off the bed and went back into his closet. "We shouldn't have done that again anyway."

"Why not?" She followed him, then picked up the duffel bag. "I thought we were both on the same page here. We've both just ended a marriage and aren't looking for a serious relationship, so we'll just have a casual fling."

He turned and met her gaze. "Have you ever had a casual fling?"

"Well, no." She shrugged. "But, I don't see why it has to be so difficult."

He wasn't sure he could have a casual fling with her. Not when he obviously had no restraint when it came to her. But maybe if they slept together and put the initial fire out, the rest of the need in him would flash and burn, too. Then they could just have a simple, fun relationship like they used to have.

Who was he kidding? A relationship with Dani could never be a simple one.

"Let's get packed and go." He shoved jeans, shirts, and sweaters into his bag.

Dani opened her mouth like she was going to argue but then snapped it shut. She turned and marched out of the closet with her aristocratic chin held high. "Come on, Em. Let's pack these cute new clothes we picked out. All the other babies are going to drool over your new look." Dani poked Emma in the ribs.

When Emma giggled, Dani said in a stage whisper, "Yeah, I thought the drool joke was a good one. The 'old Michael' would have laughed, too."

He closed his eyes and ran his hands down his face. What had he gotten himself into with her?

Shaking his head, he scooped up his bag and followed behind Dani, helping her pack Em's bag, supplementing it with a few of his daughters' things as they went. After they locked up, all three trooped down to the parking lot where Jerry waited for them in his car.

Michael opened his SUV's rear hatch, then threw in his bag. When he turned to accept Emma, Dani lifted her wrist to her mouth to speak to the bodyguard. "Okay, listen up. When we get to my grandmother's house, if she shoots at you, you will not fire back. Is that clear?"

Michael whipped his head toward her. "What? Why would your grandmother shoot at us?"

She held up a finger to hold him off as she listened to Jerry's response in her earpiece. "Hey, look, you big baby, she rarely hits what she's aiming for, so it just wouldn't be fair. Besides, she's your employer's mother. I think shooting grandma might put a dent in the old Christmas bonus, don't you?"

Dani disconnected and laughed as she handed her bag to him. "Jerry's going to be pissed off the whole way up now, and I love it."

It could be a very long day.

~

Dani was starving, so she'd asked Michael to pull over at a gas station. They were almost to her grandmother's house and she needed to stock up on a few things.

After a quick shopping spree, she shifted the bags of groceries in her arms and climbed back into Michael's car. "Okay, all set."

He frowned at the bags. "Aren't we just spending one night?"

"Yes. But it's always better to pack in our own food. You'll see."

"I imagine I'll see more than I want to. How far is it?"

"Fifteen minutes. And I got you a treat for being such a good sport today."

Michael had been extremely quiet the whole trip, despite her attempts to lighten his mood. She'd been able to tease a few grins from him, though, so she still held out a little hope that she could fix their relationship. She was pretty good at getting her way when she put her mind to it.

She dug through the bag, then thrust a snack cake in his direction. "My grandmother is a terrible cook, so I got you something just in case she won't let me make dinner."

When it looked as though he were about to protest, she laughed. "Oh, wait, that's mine. I got you a very healthy granola bar." She reached into the bag, then tossed the bar to him. Then she unwrapped Em's snack. "And for you, Little Miss Emma, I got peanut butter crackers and a juice box."

"Thank you," Michael murmured as he watched her open her cream-filled chocolate cake. "You aren't really going to eat that, are you? Do you know what kind of crap that's made of?"

She took a huge bite and, with her mouth full, mumbled, "Good crap."

He stared into her eyes for a moment before he lost the battle, and a smile lit his gorgeous face as he pulled out onto the main road. "Now Emma can add talking with her mouth full to all the other decadent things she's learned while living with you."

She took a normal-size bite of her gooey chocolate delight and smiled. "I didn't have to teach her that one. She's already pretty good at it." She turned and faced Emma. "Aren't you?"

Emma sent her a big crumb-filled grin. "Yuuuumm."

Dani finished off her treat, then reached for her cell phone. "I'm going to try to reach my grandmother one more time. I really wanted to avoid being shot at."

"You were serious about that?"

Nodding, she listened as the phone continued to ring in her ear. After ten rings, she gave up.

Tilting her wrist up so their tail could hear, she didn't speak directly into the microphone but said loudly, "Okay, I think what we'll do is send Jerry in first, let him get shot, and then we'll get a new bodyguard who isn't so obnoxious."

Jerry's voice sounded in her ear. "Funny, but I'm onto you. I checked out this shooting problem with your mother a while ago."

Damn. Her mom had probably ruined all the fun.

Michael looked as if he might pop a vein, so she had mercy on him. "I was just playing with the bodyguard. She does shoot at trespassers but won't aim at anyone directly. Her eyesight has been fading in the last few years, so she shoots high. We'll just get close, then I'll call out. Thankfully, there's nothing wrong with her hearing."

Michael grunted. "So this is why I've never met her. She's nuts like you."

"Yeah, pretty much, but she's lovable."

A slow-growing grin formed as he turned to meet her gaze. "You can be, too. Sometimes." His hand found hers, and he gave it a quick squeeze.

After enduring his quiet brooding all day, his sweet gesture sent a wave of warmth rushing through her. Leaning close, she whispered in his ear. "Does this mean I'm forgiven?"

"For now. I can't make any promises until after we make it through the shooting gallery."

"I'll take it." She sat back in her seat and couldn't help her silly grin. It was like sculpting with granite. It'd take one little chunk at a time to win over his hardened heart.

~

Michael drove slowly over the bumpy one-lane road that led to Dani's grandmother's house, with Jerry trailing behind. Piñon trees and low scrub brush lined the edges of the gravel drive. The sun was fading quickly, and the trees and vegetation grew denser with each passing minute.

He'd tried talking himself out of a relationship with Dani for the full three hours their trip had taken but couldn't do it. He wanted her—more than was reasonable. There was no denying it.

It didn't help that she'd been great with Emma. The kid had snoozed on and off during the long drive, but the minute she awoke, Dani entertained her and made them all laugh with the ridiculous road games she'd made up. It reminded him of how much fun he and Dani used to have together. She could always make him laugh, no matter how dire the circumstance seemed at the time.

So, he'd do his best to keep things simple, as she wanted. And now that the decision was made, he hoped they could start as soon as possible.

But first, they had to face the threat of being shot by a crazy old woman. "It's just occurred to me to ask if your grandmother has indoor plumbing and electricity."

Dani nodded. "It's remote, but she has the basics. And since my grandmother won't leave Taos anymore, my mom has to come here to visit her and sleep in a twin bed or on a pullout couch. You know Annalisa, so you can imagine how well that goes over. Mom never stays long. But I like it up here, and my grandmother gets me, so I always enjoy visiting. And I usually lose a few pounds because the food's so bad, so that works, too."

That her grandmother wouldn't leave Taos must be why he'd never met her when they were kids.

As they rounded a bend, a porch light shone through the trees. He slowed the car and crept closer, stopping just in front of a cedar cabin with a bright-blue tin roof. Dani reached over and beeped the horn in a long-short-long pattern, then hopped out of the car. Walking slowly toward the porch, Dani called out, "Grandma? It's Dani."

He got out too and then freed Emma from her car seat but held her behind the protection of the car, just in case. He worried about Dani's safety as well, although she didn't seem at all concerned.

Not sure what to expect, he hoped Dani's gun-toting grandma wouldn't have wild hair, missing teeth, and a face that would scare Emma.

When grandma stepped onto the porch, the only part he'd gotten right had been the shotgun.

It became apparent where Annalisa's and Dani's incredible looks came from. Dani's grandmother didn't look a day over fifty, had shoulder-length, lightly curly brown hair just like Dani's, and her jeans and turquoise V-neck sweater showed off fit curves.

She raised the gun before Dani could call out to her again. "Whoever you are, I didn't invite you, so go away or I'll shoot!"

Jerry jumped in front of Dani with his gun drawn.

Dani leaned around Jerry's massive shoulders. "Hold your fire, Annie Oakley, it's Dani."

Her grandmother squinted and stepped closer. "Dani? What are you and your smart mouth doing sneaking up here in the middle of the night? And who's the thug?"

"Middle of the night?" Dani glanced at her watch. "It's only six thirty."

"I know honey, but tomorrow's date night. I've got a live one who won't let me get much sleep afterward, so I need to rest up. I'm getting too old for all-nighters."

Dani groaned. "Okay, that was too much information. But if you really want to shoot someone"—she leaned back and waved a hand in Jerry's direction—"you can shoot the thug. I'll promise not to tell."

Her grandmother chuckled as she leaned her gun against the porch rail. "Your mama put a bodyguard on you again, huh?" After giving Dani a hard hug, she patted Jerry's cheek. "Poor man. Dani can be a handful, can't she?"

Jerry grunted. "You got that right, lady."

Then Dani's grandmother walked over to where Michael was standing and scooped the whimpering Emma out of his arms. She stared into his eyes. "Hmmm, you're no thug. And you're not Jake, so he must've signed the papers. Dani's always had good taste in men. My name is Eva, by the way."

"Nice to meet you. Michael Reilly." He shook her outstretched hand.

How was he supposed to respond to the part about Dani's men?

Before he could think of something to say, Eva smiled at Emma. "I'm sorry if I scared you when I yelled, honey. Why don't you come inside, and we'll see if we can find you a cookie?"

Dani grabbed his arm and tugged. "Good idea. It's freezing. Let's all go inside." Then she turned to Eva. "I've got cookies, Grandma. I also brought all the fixings for grilled cheese sandwiches and tomato soup so we wouldn't put you to any trouble."

Michael stepped across the threshold, bracing for what he'd find in the remote cabin, but was pleasantly surprised. Eva had a recently remodeled kitchen, and the cozy living room with comfortable-looking furniture had a huge flat-screen television and an equally nice computer set up in the corner. The cable box near the television brought hope that they'd have the essentials: ESPN and the Internet.

Even more interesting were the portraits that hung on every available wall. There were some of Dani and Sara at various ages, many of Annalisa, and the most incredible one of all hung above the fireplace. It was of all the Botelli women—Annalisa, Dani, Sara, and Eva, and it was stunning. He moved closer, studying it. Eva's name, scrawled in the lower right-hand corner in bold red, surprised him.

Then it occurred to him that the painting that hung over the fireplace in Annalisa's living room must have been done by Eva as well. She was truly talented, if not a bit odd.

He wandered to the computer. A pair of glasses lay next to the mouse. The screen revealed Dani's grandmother had just been in a chat room. Grandma's screen name was hotty69.

Dani slipped beside him and wrapped her arm around his waist. "Would you mind grabbing the diaper bag from the car? I talked my grandmother into changing Emma in hopes of distracting her from helping me in the kitchen. And because I hate changing diapers."

"Sure." He pointed to the glasses. "So your grandmother, an accomplished artist, is only blind when she doesn't wear her glasses, and please tell me the sixty-nine in her screen name is referring to her age?"

Dani leaned closer and scrolled up the thread, reading the previous entries. "She used to make her living painting portraits until she either got tired of it or because she had to start wearing glasses. We've never really been sure which it was. She's vain and only uses them when she's alone, so I'm guessing the glasses are why she quit."

As she continued to read, Dani frowned at the screen. "Grandma is sixty-nine, so that must be what it refers to. It couldn't be . . ." Then she let out a low chuckle, and after reading one of the risqué entries aloud, she said, "Maybe not. I knew my grandmother paired with the Internet was going to be a mistake."

∼

After Dani put the last dinner plates in the dishwasher, her grandmother announced what the sleeping arrangements would be, then headed for her bedroom. Dani and Emma were taking the pullout couch in the living room, and Michael and Jerry were taking the spare bedroom with the twin beds.

Emma was snoozing against Michael's chest with Wilbur the bunny tucked under her chin while Jerry and Michael both stared like zombies at a sports program, so Dani slipped away to talk to her grandmother.

She knocked softly on the bedroom door. "Grandma?"

Her grandmother opened the door and grinned. "I was wondering how long it was going to be before you came to find me. You've got a ton of worries, don't you, sweetheart? Including a very handsome one named Michael."

Dani closed the door behind her. "Keep your nose out of that part, and let's get to the rest. What did you figure out about Emma's grandmother?"

"Well, the chances of your babysitting gig being over don't look so hot."

"Great."

Not what she wanted to hear. What now?

Chapter Nine

Dani flopped onto her grandmother's bed, preparing to hear about Emma's grandmother, while Eva crossed to the bathroom to remove her makeup. Grandma said, "Martha Anderson is a drinker, or at least she was the last I heard. She lives off the road that leads to Angel Fire in a little run-down cabin, rarely leaving her house. Used to be she held a job at the post office, but rumor has it they let her go after two trips to rehab didn't stick. But who knows. People can change. I haven't seen her in years. She might be on the wagon now."

Dani's hopes of an adult-only trip to Vegas quickly shattered. "Well, that might explain why Julia left Emma with Ron. We'll pay Martha a visit tomorrow and see if she's heard from her daughter. Would you mind keeping Emma while Michael and I talk to her? I don't want Martha to see Emma and start making noises about keeping her. There's no way I'm leaving Em with a drunk."

"Do I detect protectiveness from a woman who insists she doesn't like children?" Eva walked back into the room and sat beside Dani on the bed. "Because it's pretty apparent the way Emma never lets you out of her sight for long that you are her hero."

Dani lay back and stared at the ceiling rather than meet her grandmother's curious gaze. Emma's fear of being left behind was apparent to Dani, too. It tugged at her heart. But, her hero? That was a huge responsibility she wasn't sure she wanted. "It isn't that I don't like kids, exactly. They just scare me. Or they used to. Emma kind of grew on me, and she's a pretty tough little kid. I guess I've always been afraid to like children because I don't want to be tempted to have my own. I wouldn't pass the 'gift' on to anyone else on purpose. It makes my life a living hell sometimes."

"I know, sweetheart." Eva gave Dani's thigh a pat. "Your mother and I had those same thoughts. But because I took the chance, I've got a wonderful daughter and two terrific granddaughters who I wouldn't trade for the world."

Her grandmother stood and picked up a jar of night cream. She slathered it on her lightly lined face. "The reason I live so far away from people is I'm tired of the noise they put into my head, especially now that I'm advancing in years. You and I don't have your mother's ability, or maybe it's her sheer will, to block it all out, and we tend to get sucked into other's problems. It can wear you out, or you can learn to deal with it."

"Tell me about it." Dani groaned.

Her grandmother crossed the room and sat on the bed again. "Your mom had the same fears of having children as you do. But she took one look at you after you were born and told me she'd done the right thing by having you."

"Yeah." Dani blew out a long breath. "She's always told me that."

She rolled over and faced her grandmother. "I've had this over-whelming feeling that the guy in my dream is the one I'm supposed to be with. And have children with. I was trying not to think about the kid part, but do you think that man is the one for me, or is he walking away from me and breaking my heart, like mom says? Should I pursue another relationship with someone else?"

Eva laid her hand on the side of Dani's face. "You're wondering if you should sleep with Michael."

"No," she said with a laugh. "I'm definitely going to sleep with him. But I don't want to start something, then hurt him or me, like I did with Jake. So we're going to keep it casual."

"Casual? Good luck with that Miss I've-only-slept-with-three-men." Her grandmother chuckled before she kissed Dani's forehead. "But back to Jake. He helped you grow up and see the need for independence from your mom. He was just what you needed at the time, and you'll always have a dear friend in him. What's so wrong with that? All you need to do now is get Michael naked. Then you'll have your answer."

"What is it with you and mom wanting me to sleep with Michael?" She rolled off the bed. "Thanks for having us. We'll be out of your way before your date tomorrow night, hotty69."

Grandma snorted out a laugh. "You're just jealous because I'm getting more action than you are. But before you go, what about this Carlos person who's after you?"

Dani opened the door, then turned and faced her. "I talked to Jake earlier. He said there's a guy outside mom's gate staking out the place, but they don't know where Carlos is. Jake doesn't think they know where I am, but until they find Carlos, I'm stuck with that damn bodyguard."

"You could do worse." Eva wiggled her brows. "He's kinda cute in an Italian stallion sort of way."

"Oh my God. You're attracted to the thug?"

When grandma rolled her eyes, Dani caught a clue. Grams was just pulling her chain. Feeling a little foolish, she crossed the room and laid a kiss on Eva's cheek. "Now I know where my smartass genes come from. Good night, Grandma."

"Good night, honey. Sweet dreams."

Dani ignored the snickering coming from behind Eva's closed door and got ready for bed. She slipped as quietly as she could beside Em on the pullout couch that Michael must've set up for them. Her mind was full of unanswered questions about Emma's missing mother and Maeve's hidden money. But mostly she'd hoped that by leaving town, they'd thrown Carlos Watts off her trail. She flipped over to her side and recited the alphabet backward, then forward, then backward again, forcing her mind to quiet and let her sleep.

Then the loud, sharp pop of a gun going off made her sit straight up in bed. It was close. From inside the house. Had Carlos Watts found them?

She needed to get Em somewhere safe.

Heart pounding, she scooped up the now wide-eyed Emma and held her close as Jerry ran past them in the living room with his gun drawn. Dani leaned down and grabbed the gun from her purse, hoping she really had the guts to use it now that Jerry had given her bullets for it.

The little red alarm light was still lit, proving the security system was still activated.

As Jerry headed toward Grandma's bedroom where the shot came from, Michael rushed in and grabbed her hand. "Too many windows." He dragged them into the hall bath. "Stay here."

He slammed the door in their faces.

Dani turned on the light and hugged the whimpering Em tighter as they tried to listen through the locked door. Muffled voices sounded, but no more gunshots, thankfully. She strained to hear but couldn't make out what they were saying. Finally, Grandma shouted, "There. He's right there!"

Panic set in again. Dani would never forgive herself if her grandmother was hurt because of her.

Another gunshot rang out, and her blood ran cold.

Then, there was nothing but silence. Her heartbeat pounded in her ears. She and Em were sitting ducks if someone was in the house. But where should they hide?

When the knob on the bathroom door wiggled, she tried to convince herself that she could shoot to kill. If not for herself, then for Emma.

Dani unlocked the door and raised her gun, ready to defend them. A hand curled around the wood as the door opened wider.

Sweat beaded on her forehead.

"Dani? You okay?" It was just Michael with a big grin on his face.

"You scared the crap out of me! What the hell is so funny?" Dani lower the gun and tried to steady her shaking hands. But Michael's smile had to mean her grandmother was okay.

Relief washed through her and calmed her just enough to notice Michael was wearing a beer T-shirt and silk boxers.

He owned beer T-shirts?

He said, "Seems your grandmother has been having some trouble with a rat. She shot at it and missed. But Jerry got it."

Oh. My. God.

Jerry walked by holding a bag she assumed had the corpse in it. He said, "Are all you Botelli women crazy? Jeez."

Evidently.

Safe from marauding rats once more, they all went back to bed.

Dani had just fallen asleep again when Michael's voice whispered in her ear, "Scoot over."

"Why?"

"It's not safe for you guys out here alone." When he lifted the covers, cold air raised goose bumps on her back.

As Michael snuggled close, he whispered, "And Jerry snores."

"Behave." She slid closer to Emma, who was laid out all akimbo.

"I'll try, but you're one hot woman, Ms. Botelli," he whispered as he cozied up beside her again.

Michael's body was the subject of every woman's sweaty dreams, but with a kid in the bed, it might not be the best time to share that thought with him. "Good night, Mr. Reilly," she replied with her best stern-schoolteacher tone.

He laid a chaste kiss on her cheek. "'Night, Dani."

A while later she awoke with Michael spooned against her back, his big arm around her waist and Emma curled up against her chest. It was like being the warm, gooey center of a grilled cheese sandwich.

So Michael liked to cuddle? That was kind of nice. If Jake's hands were on her, it was to convince her to have sex with him. He'd never been one for snuggling.

Content, she fell back asleep.

When her eyes opened next, the morning light shone through the living room windows as the aromas of coffee, overcooked bacon, and burned toast filled the air. Michael's hand, under her T-shirt, was kneading her breast while his thumb did things that made her girls stand at full attention. She glanced around, relieved to hear Emma's voice in the kitchen, and whispered, "What are you doing?"

He wriggled closer. "Feeling you up."

She flipped over and faced him. "Yeah, that part I figured out on my own. We're in the middle of my grandmother's living room, Michael."

"To my undying regret." His face lit with an incredibly charming grin. "Morning, Dani." And then he kissed her.

She slid her hands under his T-shirt. His hard muscles bunched under her caress as he continued doing wonderful things under the covers to her breasts.

They really needed to quit before things got out of control, and she was doing her best to stop kissing him. But it felt so good, so right.

She'd break the kiss any minute now.

When one of Michael's hands strayed south toward her panties, it drew her out of her happy little haze. She'd never be able to stop if he was as good at that part as he was at kissing. Then she remembered their one time together and knew just how good he was.

Dani captured his hand to stop him, then lifted her mouth from his. He was awfully cute, all mussed up and scruffy, in the morning. It made her smile. "Good morning to you, too, Michael."

Jerry appeared in the doorway. "Hey, horndogs. Grandma says breakfast is almost ready, so get your hands off each other and get in here." He laughed as he went back to the kitchen.

Dani moaned and rolled onto her back. "I'm convinced he's the devil."

Michael wrapped his arm around her waist, pulling her beside him again, then laid his head on her chest. "And he snores like a freight train."

"You probably just made up the snoring so you could cop a free feel." She tugged, none too gently, on a lock of his thick black hair. "Yesterday you were questioning the wisdom of our fling, remember?"

He tightened his hold on her. "I blame it on those secret powers you have."

Secret powers? Her stomach clenched. "What do you mean?"

"Irresistible charm and beauty. No mere mortal can defend against it. So if you can find us some alone time, I'll make it worth your while."

She let out the breath she was holding. Of course he couldn't have known her secret.

"I'll have to see what I can arrange."

Alone time? Oh yeah, she was definitely going to work on that. She just had to figure out how to get Emma back to her mother for that to happen. Hopefully, Emma's grandmother knew something to speed up the process.

She really needed to get up and get busy on that but was feeling lazy and content, happy to be Michael's pillow.

Because his head was right there, she ran her fingers through his dense hair. While she lightly scraped her nails against his scalp, he made happy little sounds until they were interrupted by the ringing of her cell phone.

It was probably Jake checking up on her. If she didn't answer, he'd worry. If she did, Michael would be angry with her.

He murmured against her chest, "Aren't you going to get that?"

"Um, maybe I'll let the voice mail get it rather than ruin this nice little moment?"

Michael rolled off her and headed for the shower. "Say hello to Jake for me."

"Dammit," she muttered as she reached for her phone. "Hello?"

"Hi, babe. Everything all right?"

She needed to ask Jake to stop calling her babe, at least when other people, like Michael, might hear and get the wrong impression. "Everything's fine here. Anything new there?"

"Uhhh," he hesitated in a familiar way. Jake always made that sound before he gave her bad news.

"What? Is it about Carlos Watts?"

"No, we still don't know where he is, and a different guy relieved the last one on stakeout duty outside your mom's place. Maybe Carlos is taking the restraining order seriously and letting his friends tail you."

"Did I file a restraining order? I don't remember doing that."

"I filed it for you, along with the battery report, and forged your signature. Carlos is not allowed to be within a hundred feet of you, or we can toss him back into a cage."

"Good. What else is up?"

He cleared his throat. "I asked Darlene for a date tonight. She said yes, and now I'm wondering if it was the right thing to do."

"I think that's a great idea. Just don't sleep with her on the first date. She'll think you're cheap."

"I am cheap. But what if she asks me first?"

"Then all bets are off. But she might not respect you in the morning—you slut." She blinked at the unexpected tears blurring her vision and struggled with the big lump forming in her throat. Clearing it away she barely croaked out, "I have to go. I'll call you after we see Emma's grandmother and let you know what's going on, okay?"

"Okay . . . thanks." He was quiet for a long moment. "Be careful, babe." Then he quickly hung up.

She rolled onto her back, squeezing her teary eyes shut. It was just weird to encourage the man she used to be in love with to see, and sleep with, someone else. But she'd done the right thing, and now Jake was going to start dating again. He'd be happier in the long run, and so would she.

She threw the covers back to get ready for the big day.

～

After what only her grandmother could term breakfast, Dani and Michael waved good-bye to Em and Grandma on the front porch.

Emma wailed, straining to free herself from Eva's tight grasp as Dani and Michael walked toward the car on their way to visit Martha Anderson. It was better for Em if she didn't go. What if her drunkard grandmother pulled rank and demanded to keep her?

Dani looked over her shoulder again. The betrayal in Emma's eyes sent a dagger to Dani's heart.

"Okay, you can come, Em." She walked back to the porch and took Emma from her grandmother's arms. "Would you mind coming along so you can sit with her in the car while we talk to Martha?"

Her grandmother shook her head, murmuring as she walked toward the car, "She's got your number, you softie. She would've been fine ten minutes after you left."

Emma grinned, and her tears instantly dried up. The little stink bomb had been playing her, but Dani couldn't help but let her. She'd begun to care for Emma, and what was so wrong with that? Anyone with a heart couldn't resist that cute little smile.

"Go, Daaani. Wan Bur."

Dani snapped Emma's car seat straps into place. "Bur?" She glanced at her grandmother for help with the translation.

"The blue bunny she's been carrying around with her everywhere she goes. His name is Wilbur, right?"

Michael piped up. "I'll get it." He grabbed her arm and stopped her from opening her car door before he whispered in her ear, "So does this mean we can't stop for breakfast? I dumped mine out when Eva's back was turned."

She'd done the same.

"I guess not, but I have snack cakes in my coat pocket." She added with an evil grin, "And for the right price, one could be yours."

He laid a smacking kiss on her lips. "Slip me one now so I can eat it before I get back with the bunny."

She snuck one into his outstretched hand. "But you know they're full of crap, and we are what we eat, right?"

"Shut up, Dani."

Still smiling, she strapped in, waiting for him to return.

The drive to Martha's house was stunning. Her home was located in a pass, east of town. The narrow road curved beside a little stream that was visible occasionally through breaks in the pine trees. At a bend in the road, a wide valley spread out before them. Deer and cattle quietly grazed on the dry winter grass, and small cabins with puffing chimneys dotted the countryside. Dani turned to point the animals out to Emma, but she was sound asleep in her car seat. Driving more than twenty minutes always seemed to give Emma instant narcolepsy, but that was probably a good thing. Or maybe she wasn't giving Em enough naps.

Turning back to the view out her window, Dani drew a deep breath and then sighed at the beauty. She'd always felt a connection with the area but wasn't sure she could deal with the slower pace. The quiet was what her grandmother craved, and she understood that. Especially after the week she'd had.

She wasn't doing so well with her vow to stay out of harm's way for more than a day or two at a time, or at making money at her new job. That was hard to do on the run from a crazy guy, but at least Jake had signed the papers. That was a little progress. It'd just have to be enough for now.

Eva's voice broke through her musings. "It's the next road on your right, Michael."

Martha's little cabin stood a few feet off a dirt road. The weathered wood cried out for a coat of varnish, and the front porch sagged badly. The metal roof was rusted and bent, and a few of the windows were boarded up. No, Emma would never have to live here, not as long as Dani had something to say about it.

They got out, and Jerry slipped beside them. Dani grabbed Michael's hand as they approached, unsure of what they were going to find. She was pretty certain it wouldn't be good. Michael gave her hand a quick, reassuring squeeze before he knocked.

After a few moments, a woman with mousy brown hair streaked with gray opened the door. She was tiny and dressed in a tattered robe. Her face was gaunt and pale, and she looked seriously ill, or maybe hungover. Blinking a few times, as if the light hurt her eyes after emerging from her darkened home, she said, "Hello?"

Michael introduced them as Julia's friends and asked if they could come in. Martha hesitated for a moment, then opened the door wider. Jerry waited outside.

"I'm sorry everything's such a mess, but after my chemo sessions I don't have the strength to clean up after myself."

While the outside of the home was in dire need of repair, the inside was dated but tidy and neat. The only things out of place were the blankets she must've been huddled under to stay warm while she watched television on the couch. It couldn't have been more than fifty degrees inside.

Dani was prepared to dislike the woman, but instead her heart bled for her. She lived alone in a little cabin in the woods, freezing and barely able to care for herself. Dani would tell her grandmother. Eva would rally the locals and be sure Martha got help.

Dani didn't want to waste any time, so she took a chance that her hunch about the postcard they'd found in Julia's kitchen had been right. "We're here to help Julia. We know she's in Vegas, but she didn't have time to fill us in on the rest of the story. She said to ask you."

Martha rung her hands together. "Julia told me I was the only one who knew where to find her. And that I shouldn't discuss her whereabouts with anyone."

"I know." Dani nodded and pasted on her best reassuring smile. "But think about it. How else would we know where to find you if Julia hadn't told us?"

"I suppose that's true. She must trust you if she told you where I live. Come in and sit down." Martha moved the blankets out of the way.

Michael shot Dani a confused glance but, luckily, didn't comment.

After they were all seated, Martha said, "Julia is just desperate. She's in Vegas with the last ten thousand that was left after her business partner stole hundreds of thousands from their clients."

Michael asked, "If her partner stole the money, why didn't she go to the police?"

"Because he went to the police first and made it look like *she* stole the money, that bastard. Julia went to Vegas to hide until she could figure out what her partner had done. She couldn't do that from a jail cell. And she hoped she might get lucky enough to at least earn back enough to get the IRS off their backs." Tears welled in Martha's eyes.

Dani laid a hand on her frail leg. "Do you need anything, Martha? Can I get you something to drink?"

"Oh, well, if you don't mind, I'd like another glass of water." She waved a hand in the direction of the kitchen. "My mouth gets dry from the chemicals they pump into me."

Michael volunteered and disappeared into the small kitchen, as was Dani's hope. He was always polite, and she was sure he'd offer, but she had to act quickly before he returned. "We want to help Julia get the money back so she can clear her name. Which casino is she staying at?"

Dani needed to double-check because she still wasn't sure if the reaction she'd had to the ad at Julia's house was because of Mr. Giovanni, Julia, or both.

"I can't remember the name." Martha blinked like a confused owl as she appeared to search her memory. Michael returned with a glass of water and held it out to her.

"Thank you, Michael." Martha took a long drink, then said, "It's a new casino, and they had a special. And the best odds on the strip, evidently. I wrote down the name of the casino and the room number over there, on the pad by the phone. So, do you think you can help her?"

Michael retrieved the pad and scanned the information, sending her a nod, silently confirming it was Mario's casino from the ad.

While Michael typed the information into his phone, Dani reached out for Martha's hand. "Yes, I think we can help her. And we have Emma with us. Would you like to see her?"

"Oh yes, please. She's just a little angel, isn't she?" Tears welled up in Martha's eyes all over again.

It took every ounce of will not to cry right along with her. "I'm sure Emma will be excited to see you, too."

"I'll go get her, Dani." While Michael left to retrieve Emma, Dani wandered over to a side table that held groupings of family photos. They needed to recognize Julia if they were going to find her in a busy casino. It looked like Julia might have sisters or cousins, because there were three blonde women who might qualify. They must've lived out of state, or surely Julia would have let Emma stay with one of them.

She'd told Martha she was a friend of Julia's so how was she supposed to ask which one she was? "Uh, Martha, is there a recent picture of Julia we could take along? I'll get it back to you. I thought Emma might find some comfort in having a picture of her mom until we reunite them." Wow, where had that idea materialized from? It might just work.

Martha frowned and pointed toward the table. "Oh, you can have any of them, just take your pick."

Crap.

Okay, so she'd have to give back her self-appointed genius title. She leaned closer and sorted through the photos. She was just about to give up when Martha said, "Oh, wait a minute. I have a new one that isn't framed. I think it's just over there." She struggled to get up, then crossed to a little, battered corner desk. Opening a drawer, she pulled out a picture, then turned and hobbled back to the couch. Dani helped Martha settle back in and accepted the photo.

It was of Julia and Emma and must've been taken only months before. Perfect. "I'm sure Emma will enjoy having this, thank you."

Martha squeezed Dani's hand. "Thank you for being such a good friend to Julia and for taking care of Emma."

Guilt swamped Dani as she patted the woman's frail hand, hoping Martha would still say that after Julia told her the whole story later.

~

Eva, Dani, Michael, Jerry, and Emma all huddled around her grandmother's kitchen table, devising a plan of attack. Well, Emma, who was seated on Dani's lap, was more interested in her frosted animal crackers but seemed happy to be included in the group.

"We have to go to Vegas. There's no other option," Dani said. "It's about a ten-and-a-half-hour drive from here. I googled it. If we leave soon, that'll put us in Vegas around eleven o'clock tonight, just when the action starts."

Michael frowned. "Why? We could just call the police and have her picked up. After we hear the whole story, I might offer to represent her."

She couldn't tell Michael her plan because it involved helping Julia win enough money to keep the IRS happy while they figured out the rest. Jake had told her the IRS was just looking for Julia to make a payment on behalf of her clients, and no charges had been filed regarding the stolen money because they didn't have enough evidence yet. They just wanted her for questioning. So if the IRS money was cleared up, Julia would be free, and Emma could go home.

Winning a lot in Vegas was easy when she could use her extra insights. She'd only been to Vegas once with her friends when she'd turned twenty-one. She'd been so determined to look up Mario but had chickened out. The good part had been that she'd won enough money to pay for her and her three girlfriends' whole trip, plus she financed a complete shopping spree for them all in the best designer shops in town.

When she'd returned home, her mom had blown a gasket. She forbade her to ever return to Las Vegas, or anywhere that gambling occurred, vowing to cut her off completely if she ever did. She was appalled that Dani would "steal" like that, when she gave her anything her heart desired. Her mother then proceeded to lecture on the responsibilities of her extra abilities, blah, blah, blah.

It had taken months for her mom to get over that indiscretion, but Julia, if she was telling Martha the truth, needed help, so Dani wanted to try. And it was the fastest way for Emma to have her mother back. And if Dani figured out who her father was at the same time, it'd be a complete win-win.

She wouldn't keep a dime more than was necessary and would work out a way for Julia to return the money to the casino. She wasn't sure how, but they'd worry about that later.

Her grandmother caught her hand under the table and whispered, "Are you sure about this, honey? I'll hear your momma screaming at you all the way up here if she gets wind of this. You could just ask her for the money. Lord knows she has more than she can spend."

"I can't, Grandma. I've made a promise to myself to make it on my own. I'm not asking mom for money. This will work."

Eva nodded, then turned to Michael. "I think Dani's plan's a good one. This way you might be able to talk Julia into turning herself in. Won't that look better for her, Michael?"

He rubbed the back of his neck as he considered. "Maybe. But what if we drive all the way out there, and she refuses to come back with us? It would be a complete waste of time."

"Oh, come on, Michael, it's Vegas. We'll have a great time even if we don't get her to come back. And maybe if we can find Julia, we can have some alone time." When she sent him a quick eyebrow hitch, he grinned.

Jerry, who hadn't said much, looked a little pale. "Uh, I think I like Michael's plan better. It makes more sense, and we can stay out of her problems. You have enough of your own, Dani."

Dani shot back. "What about insane Carlos Watts? No one knows where he is. This will give Jake a little more time to find him so they can keep an eye on him. I'll be much safer in Vegas than at home." Take that Rocky. Argue with that logic.

Michael ran a hand down his face. "Dani, you should have been a lawyer. You can BS your way around anything." He turned to Jerry. "So what do you say? Want to go to Vegas?"

"Well . . . uh," Jerry stammered, "I have this problem."

Before he could finish, Eva laid her hand on top of Jerry's. A sympathetic expression formed on her face. "Any chance you're addicted to gambling?"

Jerry blinked in confusion. "Yeah. How'd you know?"

Dani sent Eva a sharp elbow jab. Sometimes her grandmother forgot to hide her secret abilities. Eva was the nosiest sensitive in the world.

Dani quickly added, "If that's that case, why don't you call your agency, and we'll have someone else go with us?"

That might work out great. She'd finally be rid of the hard-assed bodyguard. Surely the next one wouldn't be as strict.

Jerry stared at Dani for a full minute before he said, "You'd just love that, wouldn't you? No way, princess. Your mother hired the best, and that's what she's going to get. I can handle it. Let's roll."

Chapter Ten

As Michael drove down the brightly lit, congested strip in Las Vegas, Emma and Dani snoozed. When he stopped at a red light, he glanced at Dani, studying her. Sleeping, she looked as innocent as she had in high school, and memories of "that night" filled his head.

The alcohol had flown freely that evening, and someone at the party suggested playing an old middle-school game. But since they were all seniors, the stakes were higher. The game involved spinning something, and whichever couple was chosen got twenty minutes in the dark laundry room of their host's basement to do whatever they wanted. The only rule was that the couple had to kiss at least once.

When it had been his turn and the bottle landed on Dani, she'd sent him a frown, but she stood to play along. All of his buddies cheered and made crude comments under their breaths as they slapped him on the back, wishing him luck.

Every guy there wanted to be paired with Dani. She was the prettiest girl in school. But they all knew she didn't sleep around.

Taking her hand, he'd pulled her into the laundry room, figuring after the one kiss they'd just talk until their time was up. He was so sure he wasn't getting anything more than a kiss he'd even flipped on the light switch instead of leaving them in total darkness. He'd looked forward to catching up with her because she hadn't had a real conversation with him for years. He'd planned to ask her why.

But when he'd started to ask what had happened between them, she laid her soft fingers on his lips to stop him. Then she'd stood on her tiptoes and kissed him. It had shocked him at first, but it hadn't taken long for him to catch up.

There was something different about kissing Dani he didn't understand at the time. He'd never felt so many different feelings all at once. And there was a warmth in his chest he'd never felt before. When she'd ended the kiss, it felt like he was being deprived of air. So he kissed her again, prepared to stop if she protested. Instead, she'd plastered her curvy body against his and wrapped her arms around his neck, giving him the green light. He'd wanted to kiss Dani since they were fourteen but never did because he was afraid to ruin their friendship. He'd always known he'd loved her as a friend, but at that moment, with Dani wrapped up in his arms eagerly kissing him back, it became clear that he'd been a fool not to act on his feelings.

While his hands roamed the soft curves of her body, Dani quickly unbuttoned his shirt. She slowly parted it and pulled it from his shoulders; then she got busy on the zipper of his jeans. He lifted her shirt over her head, and when her hands moved behind her back, and she released the clasp on her bra, letting it fall to the floor, it was like getting sucker punched in the gut. Dani was the most beautiful woman he'd ever seen, and it made him wish they weren't in a laundry room. He'd have liked their first time together to be somewhere nice. He'd started to suggest a change of venue, but she just shook her head and kissed him again. He couldn't think about anything but her after that.

He'd grabbed a condom from his wallet and then stepped out of his jeans and boxers. Glancing around the small room, he found a folded towel in a laundry basket. After he'd laid it out on top of the dryer, he slowly lifted Dani on top. Then he'd moved between her legs and kissed her again. He'd tried to go slow, to take his time with her, but when she breathed out his name—something that hadn't passed Dani's lips in almost two years, and something he missed more than he'd realized until that very moment—it was like a switched flipped inside of him. He wanted her so badly.

But he needed to be sure she was ready. Dani nuzzled her face in the crook of his neck and kissed him while she eagerly rocked against his hand. When he used his thumb to stimulate her while his fingers plunged inside of her, she'd groaned. It made him rock hard.

He took as much time as he could to please her, but he couldn't last much longer, so he slipped inside her tight body. It took all his will-power not to just pump away all his pent-up lust for her, but he went slowly at first, taking long strokes. It had felt so damned good, so right to be inside of her, that he couldn't hold back any longer. So he lifted Dani's mouth to his because he'd wanted to kiss her while they came together. To show her how much he still cared for her.

Dani had eagerly kissed him back, her hands exploring his body as he made love to her. When she'd moaned his name against his lips and let herself go, he was certain he'd pleased her as much as she'd pleasured him, so he finally allowed himself the release he so badly needed.

They were still wrapped together, trying to catch their breath, when she buried her face into his neck again. Like she couldn't look at him.

Alarmed, he leaned back and faced her. "Did I hurt you?"

She slowly shook her head. "It was amazing."

"Dani, I didn't plan for that to happen. I just thought we'd—"

She laid her fingers against his lips again. "Please don't tell anyone. I couldn't bear if you told all the guys on the team. They'd all think I was a . . . but this was my first time."

He stared into her eyes for what felt like an eternity, trying to figure out what to say, what to do. If he hadn't been in such a hurry, and thinking clearly, he would have known she hadn't had sex before. He couldn't believe he'd just treated a virgin that way. He should have asked, gone slower. He'd probably been too rough with her and hated himself for it. "I won't tell anyone, Dani. I swear."

"Thanks." She quickly buttoned her shirt and slipped off the dryer. "Goodbye, Michael. Have a nice life."

"What? Wait, Dani." He caught her hand before she made it all the way to the door. "Can't we talk about this? About us? I've missed you."

She stood on her tiptoes and laid a soft kiss on his cheek. "We aren't meant to be together, Michael. I'll always wish you well. And I look forward to watching you play for the Cowboys soon." Then she walked out of the laundry room without looking back.

In the next few weeks, he had tried to talk to her, but she never took his calls and avoided him the remainder of the school year. Then they'd both gone off to college and moved on with the rest of their lives.

The light turned green, pulling him back to the present, and they continued at a snail's pace toward the hotel. Dani lay in the seat next to him, her kissable lips still slightly parted in sleep. He'd never told anyone about them, as he'd promised, but he'd wanted to make that night up to her ever since.

Were they making a mistake by starting something? Dani talked big about casual affairs, but she wasn't the type to have them, no matter how hard she wanted to convince herself she was. He'd had his share, particularly since his divorce, but what if she wanted more? What if he got in too deep, and they both got hurt?

Dani was the opposite of the type he'd decided to date. He wanted to find a woman interested in having an easygoing, mature relationship, with no ties, no obligations, and no complications. He was a father first and doubted he'd get serious about another woman until his girls were older. In the meantime, he planned to look for a woman intent on her career, with or without kids, who didn't need or want a commitment.

So what was he doing driving to Las Vegas with a woman who still ate junk food, had a bodyguard because a psychopath was after her, was possibly still in love with her ex-husband, was babysitting a child his stepfather had sired while married to his mother, and was at times the most frustrating woman on earth?

He might as well get a baseball bat and knock himself upside the head, because a relationship with Dani was bound to do just as much damage. She confused him, irritated him, and . . . he smiled every time he thought of her.

That was happening more than was good for him lately.

When she yawned and stretched her arms over her head, he turned and faced her.

She beamed a sweet smile at him. "For a minute there it looked like you were pondering the fate of the world. Then you got a really goofy grin on your face. What were you thinking about?"

No way would he ever confess his thoughts. That would be suicide. "I was thinking I'm happy we're almost there and that I'm hoping we find Emma's mother so I can get some of that alone time."

"Hmm. That explains the goofy grin, but not the rest." She pointed out window. "Oh, there it is, we're here. Sorry, I didn't mean to sleep so long."

"That's okay." As he moved forward, finally able to change lanes, he glanced up at their hotel. "I looked this place up on Eva's computer before we left. One of the original casinos was blasted to make room for this one. It has an old Chicago gangster theme. Should be interesting." But the man who owned it was one of many men speculated to be Dani's father. Dani always hated the idea that she might have mobster blood running through her veins and, instead, had chosen to believe the plastic surgeon was her dad.

He and Jerry handed the valet parking attendant their keys; then they all walked through the sliding glass doors and into mayhem. The flashing lights, loud electronic beeps, shrill sirens, and clanking of coins in the winner's slots bombarded them. Emma's eyes widened as she snuggled tighter against Dani while they walked through the lobby. He'd been tired after the long drive, but only a few moments inside the brightly lit casino made him feel like it was midday again. All his senses were on high alert. A slick trick.

He turned to ask Dani what she wanted to do about the room arrangement and caught sight of Jerry, whose eyes had begun to glaze over. He moved beside the bodyguard and slapped him on the back, none too lightly. "Hey, buddy, snap out of it. You have a job to do, remember?"

Jerry wiped the sweat from his upper lip. "Yeah, I can handle it. Let's check in. We need rooms that connect."

Michael had his doubts about the guy holding out for very long and turned to Dani, who was scanning the casino floor. He leaned close and whispered, "Are we sharing?"

She tore her gaze from the busy casino floor and assaulted him with a sexy smirk. "Yeah. I'll pay half."

"That's okay. I think I can handle twenty dollars a night." He couldn't fight his grin as he laid his credit card down to begin the process. Emma and Dani would share one of the beds, and he'd be alone, at least until they found Julia. But surely he could talk her into some shower games after Emma fell asleep.

As soon as they were inside their brand-new, spacious hotel room decorated with thick carpet, old-fashioned tasseled lamps, and fake-antique furniture from the 1930s, Dani picked up the phone and dialed Julia's room number. No answer.

She glanced at Michael. "Let's just hope she stayed here to gamble, or we won't catch her until tomorrow."

"So, what are we going to do with you know who"—he nodded toward Emma—"while we look for Julia?"

"I've got that all worked out. Just give us girls twenty minutes, and we'll be set."

While Michael got busy checking his e-mail on his phone, Dani started Emma's bedtime routine. Amazingly, Dani was getting pretty good at it.

Emma, all ready for bed and snuggled into her footed pj's, looked like a sleepy Botticelli angel, a surprise after snoozing so much during the long drive. Her heavy-lidded eyes met Dani's, and instead of her usual enthusiastic "ta-da," she yawned, pulled the bunny closer, and asked, "Nigh nigh?"

"Yep, sweet dreams, kiddo." Dani tucked Emma under the covers, then lay beside her, running her fingers through her hair to help her fall asleep. Emma wasn't acting like her normal bedtime self, filled with sweet giggles and grins. Was the stress of being without her mom catching up with her? She hoped the poor kid wouldn't be scarred for life after spending a few days with her incompetent babysitter.

Emma snuggled closer and whispered, "Luff ew."

Dani gazed into a set of little blue eyes that were so full of adoration that no translation was needed for that one.

So maybe she wasn't the best babysitter, but the kid didn't seem to notice. She hugged Emma tight and whispered, "Me too, Em. And everything's going to be all right. I promise."

It wasn't five minutes before Emma was sound asleep. So Dani gingerly slipped off the bed and went to the bathroom to cover her bruised face with makeup.

After she was done, the gross yellow-and-green handprint was just barely visible. A little lipstick and blush, and she was ready to go.

She yanked open the hotel room door where Jerry stood outside in the hall like a sentinel. She tugged on his collar, pulling him into their room. "Okay, baboon, here's the deal. Your new job is to watch Emma while Michael and I look for her mother tonight. Got it?"

He paled. "No way. I'm not watching a kid. You're bad enough. I'm not going there."

"She's out for the night." Dani shoved the remote into his hand. "Just sit over there and watch television until we come back. If I feel threatened, I'll call you on this handy-dandy device I'm hooked up to, and you can grab Emma, then come save me. If she wakes up, talk to me. It's not that hard."

Jerry glared at her. "I'm supposed to be watching you, not a kid."

"I won't leave the casino downstairs. They must have a gazillion security cameras, and I've also got big, strong Michael with me. I don't think I could be any safer anywhere else without you."

He pondered her words for a moment, then shrugged. "Yeah, okay. But do not leave this hotel." He settled into one of the chairs. "And if the kid even whimpers, you'd better get your ass back here, pronto."

Dani shot him her most evil smile. "Of course. But wouldn't it be too bad if the noise level in the casino made it impossible for me to hear your sweet nothings murmuring in my ear?"

Jerry flipped her off.

She blew him a kiss.

Michael held the door for her, and then they were off to find Julia downstairs in the casino before Jerry could change his mind.

After they stepped inside the empty elevator, Michael pulled her against him and whispered in her ear, "You need to give Jerry a break."

"I fought with him on purpose so he'd still feel manly after being put on babysitting patrol. I know he's struggling, and I thought keeping him away from the temptation made the most sense."

He smiled. "You may be compulsive, crazy, and impetuous, but you can also be very kind, in your own puzzling way." Then he kissed her.

Dani sighed, savoring the slow, tender pace he set.

She was all wrong for him. Michael was structured, goal-oriented, responsible, successful, and—she just wasn't. But there was something about him she couldn't resist. Every time he kissed her, she forgot all the reasons they'd never have a real relationship, because he'd never be happy with a woman like her. She had to remind herself that they were just going to have some sex, hang out occasionally, and that'd be it. She assumed that's how it'd work, anyway.

Spending time with him over the past few days, though, had her wishing for something more than just being his occasional sex partner. Beyond her physical attraction to him, she respected him more than any other man she'd ever known.

Because Maeve had always kept her up-to-date on Michael's activities, she'd found out he never took his natural talent for football for granted. He'd worked hard in college, even knowing he had a starting NFL quarterback position waiting for him, and earned straight As. He never took chances, and in his case, it had paid off.

He was the most down-to-earth, reliable, steady person she'd ever known. The type every mother wanted her daughter to marry. She probably wasn't good enough for him, but something about him made her want to try to be. Maybe if she worked a little harder at her new life plans, he'd see that she could change.

Michael ended their kiss, then leaned back and smiled. When his dimples appeared, it gave her heart a quick palpitation. He said, "So, what's the plan if we find her?"

She hadn't worked out all the details on that yet, but Michael was way too practical to go along easily with her gambling scheme. "Well, I think we'll listen to her side of the story, then go from there. But the number one goal is to keep her out of jail so Emma doesn't have to live with Ron."

"Okay." He nodded as the elevator doors parted, and they were assaulted by a tsunami of noise again. "I want to ask her what she knows about Ron's hidden money, too."

Dani took his hand, tugging him toward the blackjack tables. "That's definitely on the agenda. And if it were me, when we find the money, I'd take all of it and make Ron beg for his half, but then I'm not as nice as your mom."

"Good idea. We'll talk her into that when we find it."

The loud casino was packed with people trying to win their fortunes. The vintage music playing overhead added to the din. It was a large place, one of the biggest in Vegas according to the ad in Julia's kitchen. And in keeping with the gangster motif, the male workers wore fedoras, pinstriped vests, and spats on their shoes. The women's uniforms consisted of gray pinstriped super-short skirts, three-inch black heels, garter belts, and low-cut, filmy white tops.

A cocktail waitress with exceptionally large breasts batted her eyes at Michael, leaned close enough for him to get a nice view of her assets, and asked if he'd like a drink. Her name tag read "Bunny." Like that was her real name.

When Michael declined, she sent him a little pout, then turned to Dani. "You want somethin'?"

Yeah, she wanted something. She wanted to smack the sneer right off the woman's overly made-up face, but instead just shook her head, hoping the pit bull would go find some other woman's man to sniff.

After the waitress flounced away, Dani glanced at her sweater and jeans, suddenly feeling underdressed and definitely not looking her best. Not that there weren't others dressed casually, but she'd only packed clothes for the cooler weather in Taos, not for an evening in a casino. If she was going to play the part of a high-stakes gambler, she'd have to have a better outfit. But, first things first, they needed to find Julia; then maybe she'd go check out the boutique.

Michael's hand slipped around her waist, pulling her next to him. "You're the most beautiful woman in the room, Dani, no matter what you're wearing."

Was she that transparent? "I'm thinking it was more about how much that waitress hoped you liked what she was *serving*. But you probably didn't even notice all the silicone on the menu, did you?"

He chuckled and pulled her deeper into the crowd. "Do you think they were fake? Thanks for clearing that up for me. Now I won't have to wonder about her chest all night."

"Keep it up, and you're sleeping with the snoring freight train again." She elbowed him in the ribs. It was like smashing her arm into a brick wall. It probably hurt her more than him.

"That was a lame jab. We really need to work on your upper-body strength. It's probably due to your poor diet." He tugged her closer. "And for the record, I could never be attracted to a woman like that. She looked like a hooker." He laid a soft kiss just in front of her ear that made her knees go weak. "Those fat-filled treats you're so fond of seem to be making you cranky, and they're sucking away all of your sense of humor."

She stopped walking and gazed into his amused eyes. He was right, and that was strange. Not that he was right, especially about her love of snack cakes, but that she was jealous. She'd never been the jealous type.

She stood on her tiptoes and planted a quick kiss on his lips. "I guess I can't blame that woman for trying. You are kinda cute. Let's find Emma's mom." She slipped her arm through his, then added, "And I have plenty of upper-body strength. I was just taking it easy on you earlier because you're such a wimpy lawyer. I didn't want to hurt you."

His low chuckle warmed all her good parts again. They seriously needed to find some alone time.

But first they needed to find Julia.

After they'd made two complete rounds of the casino with no luck, they sat down at a bar near the main bank of elevators to have a drink. Maybe they'd catch Julia when she came back from wherever she'd gone.

While they sipped their drinks, a small group of people walked toward them. In the middle was an attractive man, probably in his midfifties. Beautiful, scantily clad women hung all over the other men in the group, but the one in the middle didn't have a partner. The outer ring of people consisted of muscled men who looked like they'd be Jerry's best friends.

As they passed by, a gap formed in the ring of people, giving her a better view. The man in the middle met Dani's gaze and held it.

When his eyes locked with hers, it sent a punch straight to her gut.

It was Mario. He was tall, had light-brown hair with a touch of sophisticated gray at the temples, olive skin, and reminded her of an Italian don, but that was par for the course in the hotel. He nodded at her, and then one of the women he was with stole his attention. "Mr. Giovanni, you've done such wonderful things here. You're a genius."

Mario continued walking, but after a few paces stopped, excused himself from the group, then returned to their table. He held his hand out. "Excuse me, Ms. Botelli, but we haven't formally met. I'm a friend of your mother's. My name is Mario Giovanni. Welcome to my humble establishment."

Dani took his outstretched hand and shook it, stunned that he knew who she was. Her mother was so beloved that, after Dani's kidnapping, her mom's pleas to the press to never photograph or buy pictures of her daughters had been heeded for the most part. But there were the occasional cell phone pix that caught them around Albuquerque without their disguises, so it was possible. "Hello, Mr. Giovanni, it's nice to meet you. This is an amazing place." She lifted her free hand toward Michael. "This is my friend, Michael Reilly."

Dani tried to tug her hand free, but Mario wouldn't let go. He stared intently in her eyes so long it made her squirm. *Was* the guy her father?

Finally, he released her hand and held his out to Michael. "Mr. Reilly, it's a pleasure to meet any friend of Daniella's. How long will you be staying with us?"

"That depends, but probably a night or two at the most." Michael slipped his hand around her shoulder, pulling her close.

Mr. Giovanni nodded as he reached inside his suit coat pocket. Panic filled her for a brief second, and she almost expected a gun to appear, but it was just a little card. He handed it to Michael. "Please, use this to eat and drink to your delight during your visit. Your room will be on the house as well." Then he turned to her. "I would venture your mother doesn't know you're here. I'm sure she would have let me know. When you see her next, please say hello for me, won't you?"

The way he frowned slightly as he studied her face again made her feel like a bug squashed onto a microscope slide.

Finally, his features morphed into a friendly grin. "You are as beautiful as your mother, Daniella. I'm glad to have finally met you."

"Thank you, Mr. Giovanni. And thank you for your generosity. We appreciate it. I'll be sure to give your regards to my mother." How she would do that without her mother knowing she was in Vegas was going to be a trick, though.

He smiled politely, then quickly turned and walked away, leaving Dani with the oddest sensation in her belly. No one ever called her Daniella except for her mother.

Michael waited until Mr. Giovanni was out of earshot before he said, "Are you all right?"

"Yeah. Just a little freaked out, I guess."

Jerry's voice screamed into her ear. "Get your butt up here now. The kid's awake and bawling her brains out for you."

She sighed and grabbed Michael's arm. "Em's awake. We have to go."

They hurried upstairs to their floor again, and Emma's wails could be heard down the long hallway. When Michael opened the door, the noise was louder than the slots downstairs.

Dani quickly scooped Emma from the bed, and Jerry ran into the hall to stand guard. She held Emma in her arms, rocking and pacing, but was unable to calm her. Somehow Emma still managed to cry while sticking her fingers in her mouth, chewing on them and slobbering up a storm. Her forehead felt warm, and her cheeks were flushed.

She glanced at Michael for help. "She was acting strange when I put her to bed, too. Do we need a doctor?"

He took Emma from her and, after a minor struggle, convinced her to let him see inside her mouth. "She's getting her molars. Maybe

155

her mom packed some pain meds." He dug through her diaper bag and found an almost empty bottle of red liquid. There wasn't enough left for a full dose. But he dug some more and came up with a teething ring that he handed over. Emma immediately put it into her mouth and bit on it, seeming to find some relief.

Michael said, "I'll run out and find a drugstore. Be right back."

"Thanks." Dani took Emma from Michael and walked her around the room, trying to soothe her. Jerry came back inside after Michael left and flopped into a chair, picked up the remote, and flipped through channels, staring at the television screen, sweating like a crazed drug addict going through withdrawal.

It was obvious he was in dire straits and jonesing for the casino in a bad way.

As much as she didn't care for his bossy ways, she hated to see any-one suffer, and he clearly was. She worried that as soon as everyone was in bed, Jerry'd slip down to the casino.

As she paced the room, cuddling Em, she pondered what she could do to distract him. She could call Michael on his cell and ask him to pick up some booze to let Jerry drink himself to sleep, but that probably wasn't the best idea. The alcohol would probably just lower his inhibi-tions and willpower even more.

What else would distract him? Television obviously wasn't working.

"Jerry, are you on any of those dating sites? The ones where people who travel can find a dinner date at the last minute by the location on your phone?"

He grunted. "How long have you been off the market? Those are hookup sites, Dani. Dinner is completely optional. But that's not a bad idea." Jerry dug his phone from his pocket.

"Really? You mean people just meet up with nearby strangers to have sex and then say, 'See ya'?"

"Try not to blush, Little Miss Innocent." Jerry chuckled while he swiped his thumb across the screen.

Her hand flew to her face. Was she blushing? No, he was just teasing her. But yuck.

She leaned over his shoulder. Jerry's profile showed him clad in leather from head to toe, sporting a big smile. She didn't even know he knew how to smile.

Em seemed content gnawing on her chew toy like a puppy, so Dani plopped down beside Jerry and settled Emma onto her lap. He was flipping through women so fast it was hard to keep up. "What kind of woman are you looking for?"

"One with big tits. I'm not too picky about the rest."

"Ah. So pretty eyes or a nice smile are all wasted on a guy like you, huh?"

"Pretty much." He continued flipping through women at warp speed while she watched.

"Wait." She pointed to the screen. "That redhead is really pretty. Let's see what her profile says."

"Nope. Redheads remind me of my kindergarten teacher. Ruins all the fun."

"I suppose it would. Wait. Stop. Back up one. I think I recognize her." The woman who flashed by looked just like the big-boobed cocktail waitress who had flirted with Michael earlier. "If her name is Bunny, I think she's perfect for you."

Jerry's forehead crumpled as he studied her profile information. "You're right. These other pictures on here show off the assets better. And her name *is* Bunny. It says she's located less than a half mile away. How'd you know that?"

"Michael and I ran into her downstairs. She works here." Odd that someone who met that many men would need to be on a dating site, but maybe they had rules about dating guests at the casino or something. "Why don't you see what time she gets off work?"

"I will. But it's always best to have a backup option on these sites." Jerry tapped in his message and then went right back to swiping.

A minute later his phone chimed. Jerry read the message and sighed. "She said she'd love to meet up, but she has to work until three a.m., if I can wait. Too bad." He went back on the hunt, swiping the screen.

Bunny did seem just what Jerry was looking for. "Wait. The man who owns this place is a good friend of my mom's. Maybe we can see if she can take a little break. You probably don't need more than ten minutes for this kind of dating, right?" Dani sent him a smirk.

"Ten minutes?" Jerry's hand flew to his chest. "That's insulting, Dani. I'm a gentleman in the sack who aims to please. I'd need a minimum of twenty minutes. Gotta let them finish one drink first, right?"

"Of course. What was I thinking?" She shook her head and rose to pick up the phone. He was just kidding again. She hoped.

Whenever her mother wanted something done for her while staying in a hotel, she called the concierge. Dani picked up the phone and dialed.

A smooth voice answered. "Hello, my name is Ben. How may I be of assistance this evening?"

The nice man was just dying to help her. "Hi, Ben. I was wondering if Mr. Giovanni is available?"

"I've been given orders by Mr. Giovanni himself to see that all of your needs are fulfilled, Ms. Botelli, so I'd be happy to help you."

"Great. There's a cocktail waitress who works here named Bunny, and I wondered if you could arrange an extended break for her? Like maybe an hour?" She glanced at Jerry to see if that was enough time for him to be gentlemanly. When he nodded, she said, "Bunny said she'd like to meet my friend. Here in the hotel. Upstairs."

Ben cleared his throat. "Ms. Botelli, if it's a paid companion your *friend* is looking for, I can arrange for that. Is there a particular type of woman your friend prefers?"

Crap. He thought the hookup was for her. "It's not for me. It's for the guy in the connecting room."

"I see."

No he didn't. "No really, it's for the guy next door. They used one of those app things to meet."

She tilted the phone toward Jerry so Ben could hear and called out, "Jerry, tell Ben what attracted you to Bunny."

Jerry cocked a brow. "Her pretty smile?"

She rolled her eyes as Ben struggled to stifle his laugh. "Yes, Bunny has a lovely smile, among other things. So we'll direct her to room twenty-five nineteen instead of yours for her date."

Thankfully, her reputation as a heterosexual was still intact. She had no trouble with whomever people loved, but she could imagine Ben selling the story of Annalisa's daughter's sexual preferences to the tabloids. Worse, if that happened, then her mom would know where she was.

"Could you send up a good bottle of champagne for them, too?" If Bunny was only getting one drink, it should at least be a good one.

Ben agreed to let Bunny have the rest of the night off and then quoted the price of the bottle. Nice champagne didn't come cheap. But their rooms and all of their meals were going to be free, so she could probably swing it.

"That sounds good. Send her up as soon as you can!"

Michael pulled his pillow over his head but it didn't block out the sounds of the thumping headboard in the next room. You'd think in a newer hotel it would've been a little more secure.

Emma had settled down after the pain killer kicked in but wouldn't let Dani leave her side, so they were in the other bed, and he was alone.

Dani couldn't possibly be asleep with the tribal beat filling the air, so he threw his spare pillow at her. "Bright idea, Botelli. Jerry's getting some, we're not, and we have to hear all about it."

"I was just trying to help." When the banging paused for a moment and then began in a whole new beat, she snickered. "It certainly seems to be distracting him."

"How long do we have to listen to this?"

"It's Jerry, so probably not too much longer." She tucked the pillow he'd thrown at her under her head. "I wonder if Julia's the type to stay out all night and sleep all day. I'm surprised she wasn't back when I called a few minutes ago. It's after one."

Sighing in frustration, he focused on their conversation rather than the activity in the next room. "Yeah, maybe we should pay Julia a visit very early in the morning."

"Good idea." She snuggled into her pillows and closed her eyes.

She was quiet for a few minutes while Jerry's orgy of two raged on, then she said, "I almost asked earlier if you were on a hookup dating site like Jerry, but you aren't."

Intrigued, he rose to his elbow and propped his head on his hand. "What makes you so sure?"

"Because you'd want to talk to a woman first, get to know her before you slept with her. I'm not saying you wouldn't sleep with her on the first date, but if you did, you'd buy her dinner first, or breakfast if she let you stay over, or make sure she had a ride home. You respect women."

"You know how my mom wasn't always treated right by men after my dad died. I swore I would never be that kind of guy." He shrugged. "But you don't sleep with many men *because* of your mom. Every time she would bring around a guy she was dating, you'd plaster on this really big fake grin while you shook his hand. I could always tell how much you loathed them based on how high your right brow rose."

"Really? I didn't realize I did that." Her lips slowly morphed into a sad grin. "It's weird how well we can read each other, isn't it? I used to think of you and me like yin and yang. Opposites in so many ways, but we still fit together at the core."

"Yeah. It's probably why we get such perverse pleasure in teasing each other. But we both know not to cross the line. Poke at the real scars on our hearts." It had been the best part about being Dani's friend. They trusted each other with their every thought and feeling, knowing the other would never break the promise to keep things only between them.

Dani whispered, "It makes it safe—and fun—to spar with you. I never had that deep connection with Jake. It made me sad."

He nodded. "I kept waiting for that to happen with Heather, too. I realized on our sixth wedding anniversary it never would." Knowing what he and Dani once had made that night with Heather even harder. It was the night he'd known his marriage was over, but he wanted his girls to have a cohesive family more than he'd wanted to make himself happy.

"What happened?" Dani sat up and propped her pillows against her headboard.

He'd never told anyone about that horrible day. But Dani would understand better than anyone. "I had just signed my second NFL contract, which came with a large bonus. Heather told me she'd like a necklace for our upcoming anniversary that weekend that cost almost half a million dollars. She said being married to a football player who was always gone or at the gym entitled her to it."

Dani smiled. "And you said no, not because of the money but because it isn't safe to walk around with that kind of jewelry, right? Even my mom only wears the good stuff to the Oscars."

"Exactly." Dani did know him well. "Heather pouted for a few days but then seemed to get over it. She'd told me not to worry about our anniversary plans because she'd taken care of everything, so I bought her some really nice diamond studs and looked forward to whatever surprise she had for us. Turns out she'd decided to throw us a black-tie party at a country club and had invited two hundred people. One of the few times I was able to talk to her that night, she pointed out the other players' wives and how much their jewelry cost. And that I had embarrassed her by not buying her the necklace, and she hoped I was happy."

"Ouch." Dani got out of her bed and joined him in his. She snuggled against his side and wrapped an arm around his waist. "Seems she got caught up in the glitz and glamour of pro sports. I'm sure it's easy to do."

"I think it's the only reason she married me. She'd always wanted that lifestyle. She stopped even pretending to be happy after I was forced to quit playing."

Dani gave him a quick squeeze. "If she really knew you, she would have arranged for a horseback ride into the woods for just the two of you. And she would have packed a picnic basket with fancy cheeses, healthy little turkey-and-avocado sandwiches with the crust removed, of course, and something chocolate for dessert, like truffles. And a very nice bottle of wine. Am I right so far?"

He ran his fingers up and down the soft skin on her arm. "Sounds perfect. What next?"

"You'd stop in a secluded place, lay a blanket down by a lake or stream, and seductively feed each other grapes. And after a few glasses of wine, you'd make sweet love to her on that soft blanket."

Dani saw clear into his heart, the same one that had just flipped over in his chest. There was no doubt now that he still loved her. And that they could still trust the other with their deepest secrets. "But if it was *your* perfect anniversary, the scenario would be a bit different. You'd still love a ride into the woods, but you'd want to make it a race."

She shrugged. "Of course. That'd make it more fun."

He laid a quick kiss on the top of her head. "Stop interrupting. You're ruining the mood."

"Fine. Go on."

"You'd pack your picnic basket with the things you said before, but then you'd add snack cakes, fat-filled meatball subs, the fixings for ice-cream sundaes on ice, and you'd make it two bottles of the good wine.

The loser of the race, which you'd already know wouldn't be you, would have to eat the other's favorite foods. You'd seductively feed each other the cherries from on top of your sundaes, because that would be much more fun than healthy fruit. Then after maybe three or four glasses of wine, you'd be so impatient to have your way with your date you'd rip off his clothes, draw him in the lake, and ravish him. He'd be the happiest guy in the world."

She laughed. "I especially like that last part with the ravishing and the happy guy." She lifted her chin up and laid a soft kiss on his lips. "Any chance the happy guy could be you in this scenario?"

"I'd like it to be. I've been thinking I might need a little more yin in my life."

Dani sighed. "And I've been working on having more of your yang. God knows if anyone needs more yang, it's me."

He wrapped her up and rolled onto his back, settling her on top of him. "I'm happy for you, Dani. Cutting the apron strings is going to be hard, but you can do it. And maybe you'll even be able to finally find out who your father is, or isn't, this weekend. You pretend it doesn't bother you, but I know it does."

"Yeah." She scrunched her nose. "Did you notice Mario's eyes?"

He had. They were the same exotic mix of brown, gold, and green that hers were. If he blocked out the rest, it was like staring into Dani's. "Yes. But he's Italian, and so are you. Maybe it's a common-trait thing?"

She drew a deep breath, then slowly blew it out. "Yeah, that's probably it."

Dani didn't sound any more convinced than he was. He was pretty sure she'd just met her father. Maybe he'd just ask Mr. Giovanni. That way Dani would know for sure, since her mom wouldn't tell. It wasn't fair to Dani. She had a right to know who her father was and the opportunity to have a relationship with him, if Mr. Giovanni wanted that, too.

He'd give anything to have his father back, and it was the least he could do for Dani.

Yeah. He'd ask the next time he saw Mario.

When the headboard banging stopped, Dani snuggled closer. "Finally. But you know I'll be dreaming about ravishing you in that lake all night now. Thanks for the added frustration."

"My pleasure. I'm glad we can finally go to sleep now so we both can get the dream started." And then, as if on cue, the banging next door started up again.

"It has to be male enhancement pills." Dani moaned. "That's the only explanation. Maybe you can borrow some for tomorrow so we can make up for lost time."

He tucked her head under his chin and settled in for the night. "After twelve years without you, there will be no pills required. Brace yourself, Ethel."

Dani's shoulders shook with laughter as she buried her face in the crook of his neck. "Can't wait. But for tonight, it's nice to snuggle."

As much as he wanted Dani, sleeping beside her and just being with her were infinitely better than what Jerry was doing next door with a stranger. But tomorrow couldn't come fast enough.

Chapter Eleven

At 6:20 a.m., Dani rapped on Julia's hotel room door and then placed Emma in front of the peep. Michael and Jerry stood off to the side, out of sight.

After a few more knocks, the door swung open. Julia's forehead crumpled in confusion as she reached out and took Emma. "Who the hell are you? And why do you have my daughter?" Julia planted a kiss on Em's forehead. "Hi, baby." Then she tucked Em onto her hip. "What's going on?"

Dani started to answer, but Emma was squealing in delight, making it hard to be heard. Dani had to bite back the acerbic remark that lay on the tip of her tongue regarding abandoning children. "Your mother sent us to help you get the money back." After Dani made the introductions, Julia reluctantly opened the door wider and let them all in.

Julia was a pretty woman, a grown-up version of Emma with strikingly bright-blue eyes, blonde hair, and full porn-star lips. Her gaping robe had Jerry ogling her nicely formed bust, which, as everyone now knew, was his favorite part of the female form.

She shut the door behind them. Julia adjusted Emma and then, thankfully, her robe. "My mother sent you? That doesn't make any sense, and why do *you* have Emma instead of Ron?"

Before Dani could reply, Emma wrapped her body tightly against her mother and proclaimed loudly, "Bad Momma! Emah go, too!"

Way to go kiddo; that's telling her.

But when Julia's head bowed and fresh tears sprung from her eyes, Dani softened. Julia appeared to be closing in on desperation when she replied, "I'm sorry, baby. I didn't have any choice."

After they cleared up the details on how they came to be in possession of Emma, Julia explained that her partner had stolen the money electronically from some of their bigger clients' accounts, and most didn't know until they went to make their payroll tax deposits. She'd confronted her partner, Greg, and he'd told her everything was going to be fine because he'd invested the money in some offshore "sure bets," and not to worry.

The next thing she knew, their clients were receiving nonpayment notices from the IRS. After she was caught snooping in Greg's computer files, he went to the police and pointed an accusing finger at Julia to buy himself some more time. Then he disappeared.

Michael asked, "What did you mean when you dropped Emma off with Ron? That it was his fault that you had to hide?"

Julia shook her head and pulled Emma tighter against her chest. "I just said that to scare him into keeping Emma. Ron is her father, but I never told him because I don't want anything from that heartless jerk. But none of my other relatives are in a position to take her. I didn't have any other choice but to leave Emma with him on such short notice."

Julia dropped down on the side of the bed. "He'd asked me to help him take advantage of some questionable loopholes in the tax code while we were seeing each other. I wouldn't have recommended any clients do what he wanted to do—it definitely falls into the 'gray area' of tax accounting—but I was madly and stupidly in love with him, totally believing his song and dance about leaving his wife, so I helped him shelter large amounts of money."

"Is the IRS after you for Ron's accounts?" Michael asked.

"No, I don't think so. As I said, it's questionable, not illegal, but now with them going through our files, I'm sure I'm going to have to defend that move as well as the truly illegal ones of my business partner. I know gambling what's left was stupid, but I'm desperate. Greg left a paper trail leading straight to me, and I had nothing to do with any of it. You have to believe me. I can't go to jail and leave Emma."

"We'll work it all out." Dani laid her hand on Julia's arm and closed her eyes. A calm blue light filled Dani's mind. In that instant, she knew Julia was telling the truth. It looked like the worst thing she was guilty of was helping Ron hide the money they could surely retrieve. "I'll help you win the money back if you'll help us find Ron's hidden money. How much of the ten thousand is left?"

Julia's eyes filled with tears again. "Five hundred dollars."

That was going to make things a whole lot harder. She'd hoped for at least five thousand, so she could make it up playing poker, but it looked like they were going to have to start off smaller. Slots would probably be the best bet.

Michael asked, "How much do you need to keep the IRS at bay?"

Julia's brow furrowed. "I need a hundred. It's impossible. I'm screwed."

Dani gulped. "A hundred thousand dollars?"

"Yeah, and that's after taxes, which the casino will automatically withhold, so I'd need closer to a hundred and thirty thousand."

Michael's eyes narrowed. "What are you thinking, Dani? No one can win that much money with a lousy five hundred bucks. That's insane."

She met Michael's hard gaze, then glanced back at Julia. "I'm actually a very good gambler. The way I play is sort of like your 'gray area' accounting, so if I win this money, you have to promise to find a way to pay the casino back when all of this is settled. If nothing else, you can bring it here and purposely lose it." Dani held out her hand for a shake. "Deal?"

"Deal." Julia pumped Dani's hand.

She checked Julia out, calculating they were similar in size, except Dani's bust was a little smaller. "So, do you have an outfit I can borrow? One that will make me look like a bimbo with too much money to blow?"

Julia's face lit with a slow grin. "Oh yeah." She turned toward her closet and pulled out a skimpy red dress, then leaned down to pick up a pair of matching three-inch stilettos.

Dani trotted into the bathroom, stripped to just her panties, and slipped into the dress and then the shoes. The dress was so tight she had to lose her panties, too. When she opened the door and modeled the dress for everyone, Emma clapped and Julia hummed in appreciation.

With widened eyes, Michael uttered a single word. "No!"

Dani laughed and met Julia's amused gaze. "Well, now we know it works." She turned and faced the mirror. How Julia's larger breasts didn't spill right out of the skimpy halter top was a mystery. As it was, Dani's were displayed in a barely legal manner. The hem line was short enough she'd have to be careful not to flash anyone Britney Spears style when she sat down.

It was just the look she wanted. She needed the men at the poker tables to look at her body, not her expressions. She was a terrible liar and didn't have much of a poker face. Boobs and curves she had in spades, so why not use them?

Michael slid behind her and growled in her ear, "Dani, this is crazy. You're not leaving the room dressed like that."

She took his chin and planted a quick kiss on his lips. "Quit acting like my mother and listen for a minute. It's all part of the distraction plan so I can bluff in poker. You're welcome to accompany me and defend my honor while I'm out there. In fact, I'd like that very much."

Before he could respond, Jerry called out, "Hey, Dani?"

When she turned and faced him, he held up his phone and took a picture.

"What are you doing?" She slammed her hands on her hips.

"The next time you refuse to do what I want, I'm gonna send this picture to your mom." Jerry laughed as he tucked his phone into his pocket.

She sent him the stink eye before she turned to Michael for support. He crossed his arms and shook his head. "Don't look at me. I wish I'd thought of it first."

Dani was insane. Michael had half a mind to jump into his car and leave her and Jerry to fend for themselves. How she could parade herself around the casino in that hooker dress was beyond him. And he was pretty sure she was buck naked under there but didn't really want to know the truth.

Pacing back and forth in their hotel room, he stopped to gaze out at the Las Vegas skyline. In the daylight, the town looked almost as tacky as Dani's dress.

And her plan was just nuts. No one could turn $500 into $130,000.

He wanted to give Emma back, grab a little of that alone time with Dani, then be sure Julia turned herself in. He'd probably have Julia in and out of custody within a few hours since they didn't have enough to charge her with anything yet. That is, if she was telling the truth about not being involved with the money scam. How could Dani be so sure Julia was innocent? No one's gut instincts were that good.

Dani was putting her makeup on in the bathroom, so he crossed the room, intent on talking her out of her latest Lucy Ricardo scheme.

Taking a deep breath for patience, he leaned against the doorjamb and folded his arms, watching as Dani applied thick layers of war paint to cover her bruised face. She was prettier to him without any makeup at all.

She looked up and met his gaze in the mirror's reflection. "What?"

He ran a hand down his face, still struggling for composure. "Why are you doing this?"

"Because she's innocent and needs a break." Dani pumped her mascara wand a few times. "I really am an incredible gambler, Michael. You'll see."

"No one is that good. And I don't want men thinking you're a hooker. Let's just talk Julia into going home with us."

She was about to apply a layer of lipstick, then stopped and laid the tube on the counter. Crossing to him, Dani snuggled against him and whispered in his ear, "It's sweet of you to care about how other men look at me, but I'm more interested in what goes through your mind when you see me."

Things he had no business confessing were threatening to escape, so instead of answering, he kissed her. It was either that or tie her up, throw her over his shoulder, and take her home.

When he leaned back, she stared into his eyes and grinned. "Thank you. I'll get this over as quickly as possible, and then I'll show you what I think of when I see you."

He was thinking he should just leave. Nothing good could come of her ridiculous plan, but as he stared into those witchy, beautiful eyes, his resolved weakened.

Damn her.

Their alone time better make her silly scheme worth it.

"All right. You win. Let's go."

~

Dani led Michael by the hand to the slot machines first. They needed enough money so she could bet big at the poker table. The clanging of the coins hitting the metal trays and the flashing lights threatened to give her a migraine. That was the last thing she needed when she was already going to have a raging headache from what she was about to do. Visions didn't come to her for free. They hurt.

But she was happy to be free of her bodyguard for a few hours. Jerry was with Em and Julia shopping on the strip. He was reluctant to go at first, but after a phone call to the head of the hotel's security to be sure she'd be watched on camera at all times, Jerry finally agreed to cooperate.

Dani hoped they could win the money fast enough so that she and Michael could find some alone time before everyone got back. The lust in Michael's eyes as he looked at her made her want to keep Julia's hooker dress forever.

"Here's half the money, Michael. Play the max bet each time." She laid her hand on the machine in front of them, and a vision of a calm lake appeared in her mind.

"That plan should have us broke and done with this in under ten minutes." He started to sit down, but she grabbed his arm and stopped him.

"Not that one. It's not ready to pay."

"And you'd know this how?"

Whoops. She was so busy thinking about that lake, she almost slipped up. "It's that instinct thing I was talking about, remember?"

He looked at her like she'd lost her last brain cell. "So, are you like those people who place bets on the winner of the Super Bowl based on the color of the uniforms?" He leaned against the stool with the money in his fist, as she continued down the row, touching machines.

She shrugged. "You could put it that way." She laid her hand on a machine a few feet away from Michael, and a clown appeared in her mind. Clowns were just creepy, so she moved on. The next machine created a vision of a parade with confetti falling. "This one's it. Play the maximum bet."

Michael sat down and slipped a twenty in the slot. "So I'm playing this one because it's girly and pink?"

If he only knew how much she'd come to loathe the color pink. "Let's just see if it pays."

After a few more tries and some really weird visions, she found a machine opposite Michael that gave off fireworks, so she sat down and started feeding all her bills into it. Before she could press the button to place her first bet, Michael's machine came to life, the red light flashing and alarm blaring for the attendant because it was such a big payout.

"I won twenty-five hundred dollars." Michael whipped his head toward her. "Has to be a coincidence."

"Probably." She withheld her smug grin and hit her button while they waited for an attendant to pay off his jackpot.

On her fifth try, her machine made all kinds of noise, and she won $1,000. The tired-looking attendant in her pinstriped skirt shook her head as she crossed to Dani and read the screen. "This must be your lucky day. For you both to win that big is rare." She counted out the bills into Dani's outstretched hand.

"Thanks." Dani handed the attendant a hundred-dollar bill as a tip. "Have a great day."

"You too. Good luck." She tucked the bill into her top and walked away.

Because it might raise suspicions if they won another jackpot so soon, it was probably time to take their winnings and go. "Let's find the poker tables."

Michael slung his arm around her shoulder as they headed across the busy, loud casino, weaving in and out of people. "Maybe we should quit while we're ahead?"

"Nope." Dani shook her head. "I'm on a roll. It'd be a crime to shut down a hot streak like the one I'm on."

"Right." Michael handed her his share of the winnings. "But you'd have better odds playing craps rather than poker."

"Craps? Really?" She'd never played before, but how hard could it be?

"Yeah. But stay away from the sucker bets in the middle of the table. Your best odds are the pass or come lines. I looked it up while you were in the shower." Michael dug out his phone and pulled up the rules.

Leave it to practical Michael to do his research.

After she'd read the quick guide to winning, she changed her mind about poker. Craps could be a whole lot faster. And she wouldn't have to worry about her poker face. "Let's do it!"

"I'll wait for you right there." He pointed to a nearby row of poker machines. "I can't stand to watch money be thrown away."

"Such a cynic." She stood on her tiptoes, leaned her chest against his, and whispered, "After I win and prove you wrong, I know just what I want as a reward."

His eyes darkened with desire. "What's that?"

"You. Naked, in my bed." She laid her mouth on his and kissed him.

He kissed her back so deeply she was tempted to give up her mission and drag him upstairs right then and there.

He slowly ended their kiss. "I think we should both get naked, win or lose. You're barely dressed anyway."

"Very funny. Be back in a few." Dani drew a deep breath to compose herself, and then got serious about picking a table.

She wished Michael would've mentioned craps earlier. Her feet were killing her in Julia's heels. Not that she'd ever admit it to him, but she'd give anything to be wearing her comfy jeans and sneakers at the moment.

She glanced around the pit area, intent on picking a lucky table. There were only three active, so she headed for the busiest, loudest one.

After finding an open spot, she nodded to the four casino workers who manned the table, and then checked out her gambling mates.

The man to her immediate left, who was dressed in designer wear from head to toe and loaded down with gold jewelry, had his arm around the man next to him. He sent her a friendly smile.

Next to the men was a fiftyish, pleasant-looking blonde woman who stood by a cute but slightly chubby man who was seriously into checking out Dani's chest.

A younger, well-dressed man and woman stood next to the older couple. They were awfully tan for October. Maybe they'd just returned from a cruise. Or by the way they were making googly eyes at each other, maybe their honeymoon. It was sweet.

Dani laid her cash down and called out, "Change please," like the guide had said to do, while she waited for her chance to hop in and place a bet. She'd make smaller bets until it was her turn to throw the dice.

After everyone placed their bets, the stickman asked the younger lady to Dani's right to choose which dice she wanted of the five before her. She shook her head, and the choice went to her husband. The guy picked up two dice, had his wife blow on them for luck—like that was going to help, the amateurs—and then he tossed them across the table. Shouts of "seven" and "eleven" rang out as everyone watched the dice settle in.

He rolled snake eyes and crapped out. Thankfully, she'd only bet twenty bucks. And even better, it was her turn to throw the dice. When the dice appeared before her to choose two from, she laid a finger on the first die and got nothing. The second die was the same. Zilch.

Panic began to set in. She couldn't make the money she needed on her own, dammit. Beginners luck could only hold out for so long.

When she moved her finger to the third die, the color green filled her mind. Hopefully that meant money. The next die gave off nothing, but luckily the last one gave off a green hue as well. The guide said she should place bets on the pass line, but not being certain the color green in her vision was a good thing, she laid down only two thousand. Then she let the dice fly.

Everyone around the table shouted out numbers, while Dani concentrated as hard as she could on the number seven. When the dice settled, it was a six and a five. Eleven. Still a winner!

She'd just doubled her bet. Cheers went up as the dealers paid off the players who bet with her, and then the same two dice appeared before her again. Thinking back to the instructions she'd just read, she didn't want to roll a seven going forward or she'd lose, and the dice would pass to the shooter on her left. So she picked up the dice, getting the same green hue in her mind, and tossed them against the side again. They added up to six. The new number to roll before a seven came up, or she'd lose.

The older couple laid some bets in the middle while everyone else pretty much played the safer ones. They all looked at her in gleeful anticipation, calling out the numbers they wanted to see. Dani leaned over the table, careful to keep the girls inside her slutty top, and tossed the dice to the other end. After bouncing off the far wall, the dice added up to six. Another win! She left her winnings on the table and added the fifteen hundred she'd held back the first time.

The cheers became louder, and the betting got hotter for the next round. Dani left the full $9,500 on the table, earning her a raised brow from the boxman, who watched her intently. Then she scooped up the dice.

When a red haze filled her mind, her stomach clenched. She'd just bet all the money on bad dice.

The instructions on Michael's phone said new dice were handed out only for the first throw. She had no choice but to hope for the best and maybe some of that beginner's luck.

She leaned forward to throw the dice, and one of her stilettos slipped right out from underneath her. The dice in her hand flew in the air, nearly hitting the stickman in the head. As she caught herself on the table's edge, he quickly leaned out of the way. The dice landed on the floor behind him.

"Whoops." She got herself upright again and adjusted her halter top, which threatened to give everyone a peep show. "Sorry. I'll get them."

Both of the dealers and the boxman said, "No!" in unison. The stickman leaned down and picked up the dice, tossing them to his boss. After they were inspected, five dice were placed in front of her again.

Maybe Julia's stilettos were bringing Dani some much-needed luck.

After finding two dice that gave off a green aura, she let them fly. When they landed, they added up to seven, thank goodness. It made her winnings total about nineteen grand. Her table mates cheered her on so loudly that a crowd began to form around them.

Just as Dani was about to toss the dice again, the older lady across from her asked, "You look a little familiar. Have we met?"

Dani's stomach took a quick dive. She didn't want to be recognized as Annalisa's daughter. If the lady posted something online, her mom would know she'd been in Vegas.

Plastering a smile on her face, Dani said, "No, I don't think so." Then she let the dice fly and won again, distracting the nosy woman, who quickly doubled up on her bets before Dani's next throw.

But then the woman frowned and tilted her head. "I never forget a face. It'll come to me."

The fancily dressed man next to Dani looked her up and down. "You do look a little familiar."

That's because she looked an awful lot like her mother. She hesitated for a moment, considering. Maybe she should move on to another table. But she was on a winning streak she didn't want to break.

Screw it. She'd have to take the chance while she had it. Her heart pounded with anticipation, and fear.

Please don't let me roll seven and lose it all now.

She pulled back half of her $38,000 in winnings, just in case. And because it'd make conservative Michael proud of her.

She turned and searched for him. He was pacing back and forth nearby like an expectant father. When their eyes met, he patted his heart and sent her a wide smile.

He wasn't the only one who nearly had a heart attack on that last throw. Or maybe he was sending her his love? Smiling, she turned her attention back to the game.

A large hand landed on her shoulder, and Mr. Giovanni said, "Ms. Botelli, may I have a word with you, please?"

The blonde woman across from her proclaimed, "I knew it! You're Annalisa Botelli's daughter. You were the one kidnapped when you were a kid."

As Dani glanced around the table, recognition had them all nodding their heads. The man next to her took out his cell phone.

Mr. Giovanni moved between the phone and Dani, saying, "I think it's time to take a break. Won't you join me?" His tight grasp on her arm left her no choice but to follow.

She glanced over her shoulder at her chips, and he said, "Don't worry. They'll be there when we return." Mario sent a nod to the box-man, then tugged her away from the table.

Michael stepped in front of them, his brows raised in question. "What's going on?"

Mr. Giovanni held up a hand to ward Michael off. "We'll be right back, Michael. I just need a word with Daniella. No more than ten minutes, I promise."

Michael's eyes met hers, and she gave a nod, so he stepped out of their way. "I'll go watch your chips until you get back."

"Thanks." Dani struggled to swallow the fear rising in her throat. She was being dragged off by a mob guy. One who probably wasn't happy about losing $38,000.

Mr. Giovanni took out a key fob from his pocket, and a door slid open as they approached. When it closed behind them, eerie silence washed over them. They entered a long, deserted hallway. No one in the loud casino would hear her if she screamed for help. Terror had her heart pumping triple time.

He released her and crossed his arms. "Your mother wouldn't appreciate you gambling. Out of my deep loyalties to her, I feel compelled to ask you to contact her right now."

Crap, crap, crap! She'd rather take her chances with the mob guy standing before her than endure her mother's Italian temper. But then, his stern expression sent all sorts of images from every gangster movie she'd ever seen into her head. She didn't want to die swimming with the fishes.

Her mother's wrath it had to be.

"Sure. No problem." With shaking hands, she dug her phone from her little purse that was strapped across her body and slowly dialed her mom's number. She dreaded the conversation they were about to have. Turning her back to Mario, she took a few steps away for some privacy.

Her mother answered, "It's not a good time, honey."

She whisper-screamed, "Mario Giovanni asked me to call you." She glanced over her shoulder and sent a fake smile his way. "Or rather, he made me call you."

"You're in Vegas?" Her mom was silent for a beat. "What the *hell* are you—"

Dani quickly summarized the situation. "Is he . . . dangerous? Will he hurt me?"

Her mom moaned. "Mario would never hurt you. But you need to give him back every dime and walk away. I wouldn't blame him if he threw you out!"

"Do you think he knows I'm cheating . . . sort of?"

"Sort of? Dani, I'm too angry to speak to you right now. Give the money back and go home!" Annalisa cut their connection.

Dani turned around and forced another smile. "So, mom says, hey. And she suggested I return all the chips and tell you I was just having a little fun and wouldn't dream of keeping my winnings."

His grim expression gave nothing away. He was probably a killer poker player. He was probably a killer *killer*, too!

After a long, uncomfortable moment, he said, "Why don't we make it interesting?"

"What did you have in mind?" She was really afraid of whatever his answer was going to be.

He wrapped his arm around her shoulder as companionably as Zoe would have done and led her back to the sliding door. "How about I let you roll the dice just one more time? Then win or lose, your gambling here will cease immediately."

Dani's shoulders slumped in disappointment. She'd come too far to lose everything in one toss of the dice, but what choice did she have? "Okay. But can I pick my dice?"

He laughed as the panel slid open and loud noise blasted them in the face again. "That'd be stacking the odds unfairly in your favor, wouldn't it, Daniella? We'll use mine." His hand dipped into his suit coat pocket and he pulled out two dice.

He couldn't possibly know about her "hunches." Could he?

When they got back to the table, a larger crowd had formed. Mr. Giovanni announced Dani's intention of playing for a single pot worth almost $230,000, and a cheer went up from the excited people surrounding them.

Mr. Giovanni sure knew how to work a room. He was probably doing it for the publicity it'd generate for his new hotel. She hoped her luck held just one last time.

Every other person watching had their cell phones out, snapping pictures or taking video. It made her desperately regret her clothing choice.

Michael leaned close to be heard over the noise. "Are you okay?"

Nodding, and fighting her anxiety, she whispered in his ear, "Cross your fingers for me. I need all the help I can get here."

When the people watching quieted, Mr. Giovanni laid the dice from his pocket on the table in front of her. Then he instructed one of the dealers to put all her chips on the seven in the middle of the felt top. It paid five-to-one odds. He was making her place a sucker bet, dammit.

Nice trick, Mob Man.

As the crowd yelled encouragement for a seven, Dani picked up the dice. Her hand shook as she waited for an aura. She got black. She had no idea what that meant, but it didn't bode well.

She glanced at Michael, who held up both hands with crossed fingers.

Dread washed over her. She didn't want to let Julia and Emma down, but the odds just weren't in her favor anymore.

"Here goes nothing." Sucking in a deep breath, she flung the dice across the table. The action seemed to turn into slow motion as everyone's heads turned and tracked the progress of the dice as they hit the side and bounced to the table. The first die landed with a solid thump on a five. Then the second die landed on its edge, teetering between a one and a two.

Please land on the two.

She couldn't watch anymore, so she closed her eyes. When excited shouts filled the air, she slowly cracked just one eye open. She'd rolled a seven.

Thank God!

As she let out the breath she'd held, Mario quickly scooped up the dice and returned them to his pocket. A set of arms surrounded her, and then Michael's mouth landed on hers. After he'd kissed her, he whispered, "I should've known if anyone could do this, it'd be you. You're like a cat with nine lives, Dani."

Yeah. If only he knew the truth.

She glanced at Mario to gauge just how angry he was about losing that much money and was surprised when he winked and patted his suit coat. Were those dice rigged? And had he let her win?

Mario leaned close and whispered, "Congratulations, Daniella. The next time you come to Vegas, please stay with me . . . but gamble somewhere else." He grabbed her hand, held it over her head, and shouted to the crowd, "Ms. Botelli wins."

Mario nodded to the boxman, and with her hand still in his, he led her and Michael to an office suite on the second floor. After Dani explained all about helping Julia, Mario instructed an older woman who looked like Betty White to transfer money to the various accounts that Julia had e-mailed to Michael's phone. As Dani sat quietly, watching the remaining balance of her winnings grow smaller and smaller, her cell rang. It was her mother, so Dani rose to take the call in the outer office so everyone wouldn't hear her getting her ass chewed up and spit back out.

When Dani answered, her mom's angry voice blasted out, "Why are your breasts plastered all over the Internet?"

"Are the ones you're referring to in a bright-red halter-top dress?"

"Now the whole world has a practically naked picture of you. Didn't being kidnapped teach you anything about keeping a low profile? And worse, you look like a common streetwalker. If you can't afford a decent dress, then you'll need to get a better job or start accepting help from me."

"Mom, I didn't mean—"

"You never mean to do dumb things, Dani, but you just can't seem to help it, can you? Why can't you be more like your sister? At least when she screws up, she has the sense to call so we can start damage control!"

Ouch.

It wouldn't do any good to remind her mother that she was thirty years old, not sixteen, and could dress however she liked. Since they were old enough to walk on their own, she and her sister had been lectured on "acceptable public behavior."

Her mother fiercely protected her public persona, carefully planning her every move, and always dressed as if there were going to be reporters waiting. Appearances meant more to her mother than the Oscars she'd won. All the cell phone cameras at the craps table should have reminded Dani that warning her mom *would* have been a good idea.

Having a famous mother sucked. Why couldn't her mom be more like her grandmother, who didn't give a damn what anyone thought of her?

The stress of the day left her unable to put up any semblance of a decent fight, so she whispered, "I'm sorry, Mom. I'd never embarrass you on purpose."

The lack of challenge in her words must've thrown Annalisa completely off-balance, because her voice softened by ten decibels when she replied, "When are you coming home?"

It was approaching three o'clock on Sunday afternoon, too late for the long drive home. She and Michael had decided to stay the night and leave in the morning. "Tomorrow."

Dani pondered the question that burned to escape. Why not? Her mother was already pissed off, and all she could do was refuse to answer again. "Is Mr. Giovanni my father?"

"I promised your father I would never reveal his identity . . . to anyone!" Those ten decibels were back and rose by twenty.

Her mother's curt reply launched a missile that landed directly in the center of Dani's already bruised heart. Feeling utterly betrayed, she said, "Well, of course. Because he's much more important than me. It was *dumb* of me to have asked!" She ended the call and fought her sudden urge to cry.

Drawing a deep breath, she threw her shoulders back and joined the others again.

Mr. Giovanni smiled and said, "All we need now is your account for the rest, Dani."

"My account? Oh, no thank you. Please keep the money, Mr. Giovanni. I don't want it." As badly as she could use the money, there was no way she was taking any for herself. *That* would feel like cheating.

Her phone dinged with a text from her mom. Dani, I'm sorry. I was upset. I didn't mean to hurt you.

Whatever. Dani hit "Send," tucked her phone away, and turned her attention back to Mr. Giovanni.

With a raised brow, he asked, "Are you certain? Your mother mentioned something about your substandard transportation."

Her mother was quite the Chatty Cathy when it came to Mr. Giovanni, wasn't she? "Yeah, well, my mother doesn't know it yet, but that car is down for the count, so I'll be acquiring a new one with my latest commission check. Maybe the next car won't be such a great embarrassment to her. Like I am."

With tears burning her eyes, Dani rose and headed for the door. She'd had about all she could handle for one day. She called out, "Thank you for all your help, Mr. Giovanni, I appreciate it."

Michael appeared beside her as the office door swung closed behind them.

Mr. Giovanni's angry voice called to his assistant. "Get Annalisa on the phone. And don't take no for an answer."

Great. Now what had she gone and done?

Chapter Twelve

Michael considered it a wise move to remain silent, lengthening his stride to keep up with Dani's angry ones, as they headed toward the bank of elevators. In all the excitement, he'd forgotten to ask Mario if he was Dani's father.

He wouldn't leave Vegas without asking.

Dani had become upset about something while they were in the accounting office, but he didn't have a clue what it could be. And why would she turn down all that money when she needed it so badly?

Maybe because it came from Mr. Giovanni? Had he told her he was her father during their earlier chat, or had he threatened her? Daring a glance her way, he noted her trembling bottom lip. Not only was she angry, but she was fighting against tears as well.

Mr. Giovanni had treated her nicely in the office, even as he watched his $130,000 being dispersed. Michael doubted he'd missed anything that could have passed between them.

As they waited for the elevator doors to open, he stepped closer and slipped his arm around her shoulder, pulling her against his side.

Dani leaned her head on his shoulder. "I'm sorry I wore this dress when you asked me not to. One of these days maybe I'll learn to listen to the voice of reason."

Voice of reason? Something was definitely wrong for Dani to admit that. Should he ask or just let it go?

He laid a kiss on the top of her head. "What's wrong, Dani? Can I help?"

She turned and slipped her arms around his neck, staring intently into his eyes. "Yes. You can promise you won't yell at me when you see my chest plastered on your Internet homepage, because I'm afraid you will."

"I already have. It was the top story a few minutes ago. They were all excited about it because it's so rare to dig up any news about you and Sara. But I've been looking at your chest all day, and the last thing I want to do is yell at you." He leaned down and kissed the silky, soft skin just in front of her ear. "I want to make love to you, Dani."

When she responded with a low, sexy hum, he whispered all the things he intended to do to her lovely, now-famous chest.

To his great relief, she leaned back and smiled. The wicked gleam in her eyes suggested he'd made just the right move to help her forget her troubles.

"Since this dress inspires such creativity in you, maybe I should ask Julia to let me keep it?"

He pulled her firmly against him as desire heated his blood. He leaned down as if to kiss her, stopping a breath away from her parted lips. "Over my dead body."

When he closed the gap and kissed her, Dani's lips curved into a grin under his.

The elevator doors parted, and he led Dani inside, squeezing between the other five passengers already aboard.

When the doors swooshed open on their floor, he took her arm and led her toward their room.

"Hey, Mario Andretti, slow down. I'm wearing heels here," Dani said as she struggled to keep up.

He checked his stride and, after slipping a hand under her knees, picked her up. "This will be quicker."

When they were in front of their door, she nibbled on his ear as he tried to swipe the card in the lock. Distracted, he tried three times to get the little light to turn green. With his path finally clear, he kicked the door open, stepped inside, and dropped Dani to her feet.

Backing her up against the closed door, he released the clasp that held the top of her dress up, intent on making good on his earlier promises.

Just as his hands filled with her soft, warm flesh, Jerry's voice boomed out, "Jeez, horndogs, get a grip. There's a little kid in the room."

He instantly dropped his hands to his sides as Dani fastened her top. Seriously? They couldn't catch a break.

Dani leaned her head around his shoulder. "Jerry? What's Emma doing here?"

Michael glanced down, checking to see if Dani was covered enough to move aside. When it looked like they could earn a G—no, with that dress they'd get no less than an R rating—he turned around.

When Emma spotted Dani, she screeched with pleasure, crossed the room, and launched herself at her as Jerry replied, "What do you mean? Julia said you knew."

Dani picked Emma up, then laid a quick kiss on her puckered lips. "Hi, Em."

"Hi, Daaani." She turned and beamed a sweet smile at him. "Hi, My Coal."

As disappointed as he was to be interrupted, he couldn't help his grin. It was the first time she'd ever said his name. "Hey, Emma."

Dani turned her attention back to Jerry. "What were we supposed to know?"

"She got a tip from one of Greg's relatives and left to find that scumbag in Arizona. She said she'd pick up Emma on Wednesday, or Thursday the latest. Oh, and she said Emma had her last dose of Tylenol for her teeth at two o'clock." He lifted his hands. "Guess you're back on babysitting duty."

Dani's head whipped around, and she met Michael's gaze. She muttered the same word his mind was screaming.

"Dammit!"

~

While Michael checked his e-mail, sitting up against the headboard in the other bed, Dani tucked the sleepy Emma under the covers and kissed her forehead. They'd had a busy evening, going to dinner with Mr. Giovanni at one of the restaurants in his casino that had an entertaining Teppan chef, then to a magic show playing in his opulent theater.

Completely charmed by Emma at dinner, Mr. Giovanni had joined them for the show, scoring them front-row seats, and arranged for Emma to help with one of the tricks. The crowd roared with laughter when she gave them a perfectly timed "ta-da!" The kid was definitely a ham, with a real future in show business.

Emma had babbled about the show long after it was over, especially about the animals. Doves had soared above their heads, and live bunnies hopped around the stage, but it was late, and her little eyelids couldn't stay open another minute.

After attending the show, Dani understood the weird magic-hat vision she'd had a few days earlier in Julia's kitchen when she found that postcard advertising the hotel.

Emma pulled Wilbur under her chin. "Nigh, nigh, Bur. Nigh nigh, Daaani." Her little eyelids slowly drifted closed.

Satisfied Emma was asleep, Dani rose and tossed Jerry the bottle of meds she'd picked up from the gift shop. "Take these, and don't argue. We leave in the morning."

He studied the bottle in his hand. "What? Are these sleeping pills?"

She nodded and crossed her arms. "Very mild but effective. Mr. Giovanni said he'd station men outside our rooms, so you can sleep. Come on, Jerry, you can do this. It's our last night. Julia would be proud of you for resisting temptation."

"Ya think?"

The stupid grin on his face moved her. She probably had the same expression every time she looked at Michael. Jerry was clearly smitten with Julia. Or maybe just her boobs, but still. "Yeah. Women like strong men who can resist temptation. I'll be sure to tell her."

He glanced up and met her gaze. "Thanks, Dani. And just so you know, I didn't send that picture of you in the dress to your mom. I was just playing with ya."

"Thanks. But I still think you're a pain in the ass."

Chuckling, he nodded and headed for the door that connected their rooms. "You're a bigger one. Good night."

Afraid she wouldn't be able to behave herself, Dani kissed Michael good night, turned out the lights, and crawled beside Emma instead of Michael. She'd promised him a good time when they got home, where Emma could be tucked into a separate bedroom.

She stared at the ceiling, sexually frustrated and madder than hell that Julia had taken off again, when her phone dinged with a text.

It was her mom. Dani? Are you still up?

She was tempted to ignore her, but just couldn't do it. Yes. What?

I know you're angry with me, but could you please come up to the penthouse? Mario and I would like to have a word with you.

Her heart skipped a beat at the mention of Mario and her mother in the same sentence. Her mom must've flown in from California. Why?

Please, Dani? It's important.

Oh, all right.

She threw the covers back and slipped her sweater and jeans over her tank top and gym shorts.

Michael raised his head. "What are you doing?"

She leaned down and whispered in his ear. "My mom and Mario want to talk to me."

"I didn't hear the phone."

"My mom texted me."

"I'll go with you." He threw back his covers and started to rise, but she laid a hand on his hard chest to stop him.

"Jerry's drugged up and sound asleep next door. You need to stay with Em." She kissed his stubbly cheek. "I'll be right back."

Yawning, he settled back in, mumbling, "'Kay."

Michael was so cute in his silk boxers and beer T-shirt. Who would have thought *GQ* Michael would ever own a Corona T-shirt? Smiling, she searched the dressers and nightstands, finally finding her key. After pulling the door shut behind her, she found a third thug like Jerry waiting for her. The other two nodded as they sat outside their doors in the hallway.

Thug number three said, "Hello, Ms. Botelli. I'll take you up."

She followed him into the elevator. The man slipped a card into a slot she'd never noticed before that illuminated a large bright-blue capital *P* on the electronic menu. Once the doors had closed, the elevator took off like a rocket, and after only a few seconds, the doors silently opened, revealing a dark living room framed by large windows that highlighted the Las Vegas skyline. As soon as she stepped into the room, the elevator doors softly whooshed closed behind her.

City lights sparkled in every direction, and it took her eyes a moment to focus on two people in silhouette, their arms crossed, nose to nose, in the middle of a full-blown fight.

Fascinated, Dani sat on the arm of a plush couch to watch.

Mario was growling. "You are the most stubborn woman on earth. Look at the whole picture. You're too narrow-minded and treat her like a child."

"Oh, and now you're going to give me parenting lessons?" Her mother's eyes grew wide, and she poked him in the chest with her index finger. "You've got a hell of a lot of nerve, buddy!"

Dani had never seen any man elicit that much emotion from her mother, and she thoroughly enjoyed the show. But when Mario glanced in Dani's direction, his hand shot up, instantly shutting her mother up.

That hand move was impressive. The two of them obviously had some sort of intimate relationship.

"Hello, Dani. Thank you for joining us," he said pleasantly.

Huffing out a breath, her mom turned and plastered on a smile. "Hi, honey." Then she crossed the room and, in a comforting familiar way, tilted Dani's face up and laid a kiss on her forehead. "I'm sorry it's so late. Thank you for coming."

"I couldn't help overhearing your . . . discussion, but didn't want to interrupt."

Her mom let out a sorrowful moan.

"Sorry." Mario smiled. "We didn't see you there." Then he raised a brow and faced her mom. "Annalisa, I think you should start."

Her mom sent a lethal stare his way, then turned and faced her. "Mario and I were just discussing our differing opinions about your earlier gambling spree. While he finds your behavior noble, helping your friend out, I forbade you to gamble, and I meant it. He and I will never agree on that, but I want to apologize for the way I handled your question about your father. I did make a promise to him"—her eyes narrowed at Mario—"and as a result, I made you feel as though you were less important to me than him, and that was not my intent."

Dani shrugged. "Okay. Apology accepted." Her mom had always made her feel that way when it came to her father. Nothing had changed. And it was late. She turned to leave.

"Wait. One more thing. Mario also made me aware that I've given you another inaccurate impression. You are not and have *never* been an embarrassment to me, Dani. I love you." She wrapped her arm around

Dani's shoulders and pulled her close. Whispering in her ear, she murmured, "You and Sara mean more to me than anything in the world, and I'm sorry I hurt you, sweetheart."

Dani returned the hug, relieved their feud was over. "I should have called, so I'm sorry, too, Mom."

Annalisa released her and then crossed her arms. "Now it's your turn, buddy."

Mario joined them and then cupped her mother's face in his hands.

Dani cringed. She hoped he knew what he was doing, because when her mother had that expression on her face, no one was safe.

He whispered, "Well done, my love." After laying a lingering kiss on her lips, one that left her mom with a slight grin on hers, he turned to Dani. "Why don't we all sit down?"

She'd seen her mother kiss other men, but never one who made her knees go weak.

Dani shook her head in wonderment at the way Mario handled her mother, too, as she settled into the cloud-soft sofa. She'd never have believed it if she hadn't witnessed it.

Her mom sat next to her and took her hand, as if the news he was about to share was going to be bad. Dani braced for the worst and dearly hoped her mother hadn't talked him into asking for the money back. For Emma's sake. She needed her mother.

Mario took a seat on the couch across from them. "Dani, I was born into a family that made their living in a questionable manner. In my early twenties I'd had enough, and because I'd met your beautiful mother, I wanted to be a legitimate businessman, for her sake and mine. My grandfather was the romantic sort, not to mention a huge fan of Annalisa's, so he sympathized with my plight. He released me from my family obligations and gave Annalisa and me permission to marry. But, not long after I was released, my grandfather died, and my father did something that made our marriage impossible."

Mario stood, then walked away toward the large wall of windows. Staring out at the skyline with his hands folded behind his back, he continued. "My father wanted me back in the business and threatened to kill Annalisa, who was pregnant at the time, if I didn't continue his dirty work. I was heartbroken, but knew his threats weren't idle ones. So I went back to work for my family, and your mother and I staged a very public breakup. I couldn't risk her life or"—he turned and faced them—"yours, Daniella."

Her mom tightened her grip on Dani's hand. She felt the squeeze, but the rest of her body went numb. It wasn't a shock to hear that Mario was her father—she somehow knew the first time she met him. It should have been a relief or maybe even made her angry, but it left her feeling slightly ill. The same ruthless blood that ran through Mario's father's veins ran through hers as well, and it sickened her. Sure, she'd done a few things that could have gotten her thrown in jail, but they were always to help others. She'd never intentionally steal or, for God's sake, kill someone. Had Mario killed anyone?

Did she really want to know?

She met his hopeful gaze. What did he want her to say? What should she say? It takes time to develop feelings for someone, and while she was grateful for the way he'd handled her gambling, and he seemed like a nice man, she felt nothing more than a mild fondness for him.

A sudden urge to flee came over her. Slowly rising from the couch, she said, "Well, thanks for telling me. I don't understand why you kept it a secret this long, especially because now I know you've obviously been seeing each other, so you must've worked things out. But, at least I know now, and that's something. I need to get back in case Emma wakes up. Good night."

Finding it hard to draw a deep breath, Dani turned and started toward the elevator. Her mom could've told her. She'd kept her mother's secret about her dreams her whole life. Why would this secret be all that different? Her mother's lack of trust in her still hurt.

She was searching for a button to summon the elevator when Mario appeared beside her. "After I returned to the family business, your mother and I saw each other on the sly. I continued arranging for my freedom, but my father found out and had you kidnapped as a warning to me. After that, I thought it best you never knew who I was. Annalisa and I didn't see each other for over twenty years out of fear of my father and what he might do to you. When he died last year, he left the family business in the hands of my brother, who released me because he knows how much I love your mom. I'm no longer involved, and it's important to me that you understand this casino is a legitimate business venture."

She was still trying to wrap her head around her own family kidnapping her when he laid a hand on her arm and turned her toward him. "I love you, Dani, but I don't expect you to reciprocate. I regret not being a part of your life until now, but I couldn't tell you of my existence until I was sure it was safe, and that's only happened recently."

So that's why they'd never told her. Made a lot more sense after hearing all of that.

Her mom joined them, circling her arm around Mario's waist. "I've asked Mario to marry me, but he won't. He's afraid it would damage my career if anyone dug too deeply into his past. He might be right, but my publicist tells me he could spin it in my favor. So for now, I have to settle for seeing him whenever our schedules allow."

Her mom slipped her other arm around Dani's waist and pulled her close, making a tight triangle among the three of them. "I've tried making Mario jealous by making it look like I was sleeping with younger men—which you noticed, and I'm sorry for that, too, by the way. But I wasn't. I hoped he'd see what a mistake he was making by not marrying me, but it didn't work. It just pissed him off instead of motivating him, because Mario knows I love him. You get your stubborn streak from him."

She'd always figured she'd gotten her stubborn streak from her obstinate mother. But at least that explained her mom's recent attraction to younger men. She'd hated the thought of her mother acting like those desperate, aging celebrities who tried to hang on to their youth by being with people half their age. Her mom would always be a great legend no matter what and could afford to age gracefully—with the help of Botox and plastic surgery, of course.

To her surprise, Dani gave into her urge, giving her father a quick, sympathetic hug. "Any man who has the guts to take on a Botelli woman has to be stubborn and have the patience of Job. I'll wish you luck, Mario."

"Thank you." He grinned as he slowly released her. "Please come back and see me again, Dani. But I stand by my requirement that you gamble somewhere else. I'd be happy to provide you the names of my biggest competitors." He pushed the elevator button.

"Okay, but maybe you'd like to come to New Mexico? Thanksgiving's coming up." She blinked back her tears as the elevator doors slid open, and she stepped inside, where the same guard waited for her.

Mario said, "I'll be there."

When the doors closed, she sighed. She finally knew for sure who her father was. Maybe since Mario had gone to so much trouble to be with her mom, he'd been serious about cleaning up his act and really was a legit businessman. Maybe he'd turn out to be an okay guy. Especially because it was obvious how much her mother loved him. She'd never seen her mom so googly-eyed about a man. It warmed her bruised heart.

When the doors parted again, she walked to her room, waved to the guards, and then quietly let herself in. She didn't want to wake Michael but had an overwhelming need for him.

She wanted to be held, safely wrapped in his strong arms until the world righted itself again.

Stripping down to her pj's, she checked on Emma, then lifted the covers on Michael's bed and slid beside him.

Mumbling something unrecognizable, he wrapped his arms around her, pulling her close. She molded her body against his warm one and laid a soft kiss on his pouty lips.

He blinked his eyes open and grinned. "Hey." Then his hold on her tightened, and he tucked her head under his chin. "So what was that about?"

"They wanted to tell me that Mario is my father. They couldn't tell me until recently because of Mario's family. They really are what we'd thought. Mobsters of some sort, I guess. It's so weird to think I have relatives who are criminals. I've always hated that thought."

He shrugged. "Every family has black sheep. Some are just darker than others, I guess."

"Dark enough to have me kidnapped?" That crossed too many lines to count. It made her shudder again just thinking about how evil her grandfather must have been to do something like that.

Michael lifted his head. "Seriously? That's who kidnapped you? Your own family?"

She nodded. "I suppose that's why I wasn't hurt. It was just a warning to Mario. But now I can finally understand why my mom never married—she'd been waiting for Mario—and why she was always so protective of me and Sara."

Michael let out a long breath. "If there's one thing I know for certain, it's that your mom loves you, Dani. And I love you, too. I never stopped."

Never stopped?

She'd assumed he'd never loved her like she'd loved him. It was the only way she could make sense of her painful dream. The one in which she'd watched him marry someone who wasn't her.

She sat up and took Michael's face in her hands. "Then why did you marry Heather?"

He laid his hands over hers and smiled weakly. "Because you'd removed yourself from my life, and she was the opposite of you in most every way. I didn't want the painful reminders. You, Dani Botelli, are one of a kind, and no one could ever take your place in my heart." He pulled her close and kissed her.

It was the first kiss they'd shared that wasn't filled with urgency and lust. Instead, it was patient and sweet. Like a salve to her already tender heart.

It was disturbing to find out who her father was, and it hurt a little, but at the same time it was a strange relief. But hearing Michael say he'd always loved her made everything right in her world again.

When his lips left hers, he whispered, "I know this has been a tough night for you, but when a guy spills his guts, it's torture to leave him hanging."

"Oh, sorry!" She leaned her forehead against his and smiled at the uncertainty in a pair of eyes that rarely were. "I love you, too, Michael. Always have." She lay down beside him and snuggled against his side. Had that dream forced her to create her own fate? If she hadn't parted ways with Michael in high school, would he have still married Heather?

It was all too much to think about for one night. The important thing was that Michael loved *her*.

"So, are you okay?"

"Yeah." She closed her eyes and smiled. "I am now."

~

Michael awoke with his arms filled with a curvy, sexy woman. Dani was wrapped around him like a stray vine, and he wanted her so bad it hurt. His desire to make love to her consumed him, but he still worried about the rest. Dani was a complicated package and would never be easy, but wasn't that what made her so different from any other woman he'd ever known?

He lifted his head to check on Emma, dismayed when her blue eyes stared into his from the opposite bed. When she grinned sweetly, he was swamped with guilt over his frustration that he couldn't have Dani because of Em's presence.

But he could fix that, or at least he hoped so, and he gently slid out of Dani's embrace. After Emma was dressed, her hair combed, and teeth freshly brushed, he knocked on Jerry's door. Dani had slipped into the shower, unaware of his big plans for her.

When the door opened, Michael tugged his wallet from his back pocket and held out two twenties. "Would you take Emma down to the corner and grab us all some breakfast?"

Jerry frowned and shook his head. "That's not in my job description, dude."

"I need you guys to disappear for forty-five minutes or so. I want to be alone with Dani. *Comprende?*"

Jerry snagged the bills from Michael's hand. "Okay. I'll try to keep her away as long as possible, but the kid gets itchy when Dani's not around." Jerry leaned down and scooped Emma up. "Hey, kid. Want to go to Mickey Dee's?"

After spending time with Jerry the day before, Emma seemed more comfortable with him, so Michael held his breath and hoped she'd agree.

Emma clapped her hands and grinned. "Yay, Mic Dee's!"

When the door slapped closed behind them, Michael grabbed a condom and jogged toward the bathroom, wrestling his shirt off on the way. He opened the door, letting billowing steam escape, and stepped inside. Tossing his shirt aside and stripping to the skin, he called out, "Dani, can I join you?"

She must not have heard him over the din of the water, so he yanked on the shower door and leaned in.

The sight of her was like getting hit in the gut with a two-by-four. Dani was stunning. Her head was tilted back, eyes closed, as she rinsed the shampoo out of her long, silky hair. His heart stuttered as he gazed at her goddesslike body. She had exceptional, soft curves, and his hands ached to caress each one.

When her left eye popped opened, he waited for her to throw him out or invite him in. A grin tilted her lips, and his hopes soared right along with the heat in his veins. She finished rinsing the suds from her hair, then turned around. "It's not a lake, but there seems to be plenty of water. Want to do my hard-to-reach places?"

"I could do that." He stepped inside and closed the door behind him, reminding himself to take it slow. He owed her that. He wanted to make up for their last time together. It'd just be an added bonus if he could make her beg for him in the process.

Reaching for the soap she held out, he slicked the bar across her soft shoulders as he nibbled on her long neck. She tasted faintly of flowers from her shampoo, and when he'd had his fill, he trailed his soapy hands lower, along her back toward her tight butt. Using both hands, he kneaded her firm, slick, heart-shaped rear, pleased by her low groan of pleasure when he dropped to the floor, taking extra time at the back of her knees When he reached her calves, he turned her around and started up the front.

Her legs were so long and sexy it was no hardship to take his time, but he nearly lost it when her muscles quivered as he slowly made his way past her thighs toward the heat in the center.

When he replaced the soap with his mouth, she writhed as his tongue laved, stroked, and teased her. She let out a strangled "Oh God," so he slipped his fingers inside her and moved in a rhythm her hips instantly matched. He was rock hard, barely able to tolerate the need building inside, but refused to stop until she came.

Her hands slapped the sides of the shower as she strained against him. She let out a low moan just before she tightened around his fingers with a viselike grip, and her head fell back. "Michael, I can't—"

Then she let go. That tempted him to plunge inside of her so he could join in the intensity of her orgasm. But he'd made a promise to himself, so he held back and waited for her to still again; then he rose and slipped his hands up her slick, supple body until they found her full breasts.

While nibbling on her ear, he whispered, "You're so damn beautiful, Dani."

~

Dani felt she should say something back, like "So are you" or something, because God knows he was. But her mind was mush. He was doing things to her body that made her weak. His big hands gave her such intense pleasure, and he'd made it all about her. Not asking for anything in return.

She was finally able to whisper in his ear, "I haven't held up my end of the deal." Her hands slid down his muscled chest past his narrow waist and found him hard and ready. She slowly stroked him, wanting him even more when he let out a low sensual moan.

He stopped her hand. "I didn't treat you as gently as I should have the last time. I'll always be sorry for that. Please let me make it up to you."

She met his gaze as memories of that night filled her thoughts. It was the most unbelievable night of her life, making love to a man she loved. She'd turned down so many boys, but didn't feel a bit of guilt about being with Michael. She'd meant to put a stop to things, but deep down, she hated to admit that she hadn't wanted to. She'd always vowed to wait until she was married, and because she couldn't—or because it wouldn't be Michael—she hadn't wanted to. "I loved that you were my first. It was incredible."

His mouth twitched into a grin. "For me, too. But let me show you how I wanted to treat you the last time but was too young and stupid to know better. Please?"

She leaned her head back as his large hands covered her breasts. His tone was so serious she felt the need to lighten his mood. "Well, okay. If you insist. I don't want to be difficult."

A laugh rumbled deep within his chest before he kissed her. After he'd stolen every rational thought from her brain again, he whispered, "Difficult is exactly what you are."

He was doing magical things to her breasts again that were taking her to the edge of reason, so she'd just let him take over and go with the flow.

Michael's thumbs found her nipples, which were hard and standing at full attention. He leaned down and laid his mouth on one, teasing and sucking until she made low whimpering noises.

When she couldn't take another minute of his sweet torture, she said, "Now. Please."

"Almost there, baby." He slipped his hands around her waist and lifted her up, leaning her back against the stone wall. She wrapped her legs around him, and after grabbing the condom from the soap dish and wrestling it on, he kissed her. Then he grabbed ahold of her butt and slipped inside her. The onslaught of sweet sensations stole her breath.

As his tongue caressed and teased her mouth, her body tightened around him, inviting him to venture deeper. Her hands moved of their own accord, clamping onto his hard ass, and she pulled him against her, silently begging him to take her harder and faster.

But then he slowed the tempo, switching to long, slow strokes, pushing deeper and deeper with each one. Dani groaned as her body pulsed harder around him.

When he picked up the pace, she couldn't hold back any longer and closed her eyes. Bright lights burst inside her lids as she came again.

After one last groan, Michael pumped furiously inside her until they both found glorious relief.

Dani struggled to draw the steamy air into her lungs as she slowly ran her fingers through Michael's wet hair. Hot water poured over them while she was still wrapped around him. She was probably heavy, but moving just yet wasn't an option. Her legs felt like rubber bands.

Michael had certainly been thorough, and she had to give him extra points for that. It was as if he'd thrown open the door to a hot furnace she never knew burned inside her. She'd never experienced such deep, intense desire for any man. She hoped he was feeling the same way about her.

She opened her mouth to say so when Michael, whose face was still buried in her hair, whispered, "That was even better than the last time. I didn't think that was possible."

She felt equal measures of smugness and relief that it had been good for him, too. "Me neither. I don't think I'll ever think of a shower in quite the same way." She grabbed a handful of his thick hair and tugged his head back so she could kiss him. "You're still just as pretty as you were in high school, Michael."

He snorted out a laugh and settled his head in the crook of her neck again as he caught his breath, too.

He nibbled on her neck and made his way up to her ear. "I'm afraid if I don't put you down soon, I'm going to embarrass myself when I drop you."

"Sorry." She loosened her legs and slid down his slick body, eliciting another deep groan from him.

"If I thought we had enough time, I'd show you a few other tricks I've learned since high school. But Jerry and Emma will be back soon." He dipped his head under the hot water and grabbed the shampoo.

Dani popped the shower door open. Cool air stung her cheeks as she reached for towels from the nearby heated rack. "I never even asked where they were. I took one look at you naked and completely forgot about them. Thanks for sending them wherever you did." When she turned, water and soap slithered along all the hard dips and curves of Michael's beautiful chest. Desire heated her belly all over again.

"They went to grab breakfast." He turned off the tap, then accepted the towel she held out.

Ignoring her primal needs, Dani trapped her soggy hair on top of her head with a quick twist, then wrapped a second towel around her body while he told her about Emma and Jerry's mission and how he hoped he'd ordered her what she wanted.

She crossed to the sink and wiped a circle in the foggy mirror with her hand, not caring a bit about what he'd ordered for breakfast. She was still in a lovely, dreamy haze, already plotting how they could arrange some more alone time.

When the mirror cleared, Michael's back was framed in the reflection as he bent over to tug on his pants. Dani's eyes grew wide. There was a squiggly scar snaking its way down his shoulder blade—same as the one from her dream.

Whipping around, she crossed to him, then grabbed his shoulders. "Where did that scar come from?"

Panic stole her breath, and her heart banged inside her chest, but not in the pleasant way it had only moments before in the shower.

He couldn't be the man in her dream. Because if her mother was right, he'd hurt her like no other man ever had. After spending the last few days with him, the possibility of parting ways forever made her heart ache.

"From my car accident." He glanced over his shoulder. "The roof support gave way and tore my shoulder up. I know it's not pretty, but I guess I should have warned you, because you're as white as a sheet."

She slowly shook her head as she struggled to absorb the idea. "No, I'm sorry, it's not so bad to look at, I just . . ." What? She couldn't tell him. Pulling herself together, she said, "It just looks like it must've been so painful. I hate to think about that time when we were all waiting for you to wake up in Dallas."

His brows knit in confusion before he leaned down and laid a quick kiss on her lips. "Thank you, but I'm fine now. It rarely hurts anymore."

He slipped his shirt on, then turned and wrapped her up in a tight hug. "Dani, I wanted to talk to you about that time in the hospital. To thank you—"

His cell phone rang in the other room. "Sorry, it's probably my office." He kissed her again, then quickly walked out of the bathroom, giving her some blessed alone time to think.

What else could go wrong? In a matter of a week her car had died for good, crazy Carlos Watts was waiting back home to kill her, Jake had signed the divorce papers and had his first date, and Emma had lost, then found, then lost her mother again. Her bosom had become famous across the land, and in becoming so had angered her mother. And just last night she'd learned who her father was and now knew she was descended from a long line of gangsters.

But Michael, being the man in her dream, took the prize.

Chapter Thirteen

As her mind reeled from her discovery about Michael, Dani quickly dressed and dried her hair while he dealt with a problem from his office via e-mail. They needed to hurry and get on the road so they both could get back to work.

After they ate, Dani called the penthouse to thank Mario for their stay, but he wasn't in. She said goodbye to her mom, then they gathered their things and headed downstairs to the lobby.

Dani smiled as she handed over their electronic keys. The man helping her had a nametag that read "Ben," with the title of concierge below it. "Hi, Ben. Is Mr. Giovanni around?"

His face lit with a knowing grin. "I don't know, Ms. Botelli, but I'm sure he'll want to see you. Can you wait here for just a moment? I'll see if I can find him."

"Sure." Emma was heavy, so she plopped her on the counter while Jerry and Michael discussed the fastest route home.

Ben reappeared a few minutes later. "I'm so sorry, Ms. Botelli, but I couldn't locate him. Shall I take a message?"

"No, thanks. I'll just call him later. Thanks for all your help."

"Anytime. Oh, and just so you know, we had a strange computer glitch. That special charge for your friend's champagne was lost." e winked at her. He sent her a knowing wink. "Have a safe trip home."

"Thanks, Ben. You're awesome. I'll see you again soon." She hitched Emma on her hip and started for the doors.

"I'll look forward to it, Ms. Botelli. You're a most interesting woman."

That probably wasn't a compliment.

As they approached the sliding doors to retrieve their cars from the valet parking, Jerry's hand snaked out and grabbed her arm. "Wait. I want to make sure things are cool out front. Stay here in the lobby until I get back. Your whereabouts are hardly a secret after your dress was plastered all over the Internet yesterday."

Dani and Michael stopped, letting Jerry go ahead. She hadn't thought about that, but he was right. If he didn't know before, Carlos Watts definitely knew where she was now. That was another stupid move on her part.

Just as their cars drove up, Mario called out her name. Michael took Emma from her arms. "I'll strap her in. Take your time."

Dani turned and greeted Mario. "I wanted to say thank you again for our stay and for helping with the money. In all the confusion, I forgot to tell you I made Julia promise to give it back when everything is settled."

"I wish I had your refreshing optimism, Dani, but I won't hold my breath." He grinned. "However, if she shows up on my doorstep with the loot, I wouldn't turn it down."

He slipped his arm around her shoulder and walked her to the car. Jerry appeared at her opposite side. "Have a safe trip. I'll see you next month."

Just as Mario opened her car door, a sharp pop rang out.

Someone yelled, "Gun!" and her heart nearly stopped.

Had Carlos found them? She couldn't breathe. But she needed to do something.

She started to dive into the car beside Michael, but Jerry slammed the door shut and pulled her to the ground, covering her with his body. From her sideways viewpoint, crushed under Jerry's weight, she watched

Mario lift his pant leg at the ankle and pull out a gun. The sight of his gun sent another wave of panic through her veins. She hoped that Michael and Em were safe in the car above her. That they'd *all* stay safe. God, she didn't want to die. Especially now that she'd finally reconnected with the man she'd always loved.

People shouted, and more gunshots rang out as her heart raced triple time. Jerry's heft made it difficult to draw a full breath, and her head felt light. Mario shouted to the security team when they arrived. "Over there, in the dark Jeep. Stop them."

The next thing Dani heard were shouts, more gunfire, then squealing tires. After a few moments of silence, the car door above her opened. Michael handed Emma to a guard, and then he was escorted out by the security team.

Thank God they were safe. She thought they were all going to die. Because of her.

Her legs were weak and could barely hold her as Jerry and two other men helped her up and surrounded her. They ran back into the lobby and into a waiting elevator. When the doors closed, Mario slipped his card in the slot, and the large *P* showed up on the screen. Then he turned and wrapped her up in a hard hug. "Are you okay?"

Dani blinked back her tears and nodded. After a few moments, she released him, then reached out for Emma, who was wailing with fear. She drew Emma against her chest, then looked up at Michael as her own fear got the best of her. She couldn't stop shaking as hot tears slipped down her cheeks. "I'm so sorry. I don't know what I would've done if you guys had been hurt. This was all my fault."

Michael leaned down and brushed a soft kiss against her forehead. "We're fine, Dani."

When the doors parted to the penthouse, Mario stepped out first, reaching for his cell phone. "We'll take you out through the underground with your mother. We do it all the time when she visits. You'll be safe. You can all fly home with her."

He turned to Michael and Jerry. "I'll have my people drive your cars home for you. Maybe Carlos's men will make another move, and this time they'll get more than they bargained for."

Dani didn't even want to know what that meant, but she had a good idea it wouldn't be pretty.

～

While Dani stared out at the white puffy clouds floating in the deep-blue sky, Jerry sat up front in the cabin of her mother's jet, snoring. On the couch, Emma sat on Annalisa's lap, listening intently as Annalisa read a script to her.

A smile tugged at Dani's lips as she recalled doing the same thing with her mom. Her mother could read a dictionary and make it sound exciting.

Dani closed her eyes and sighed. That had been entirely too close, and they all could have been killed. She wasn't letting Emma off her mother's estate until Julia got back to claim her. There was no way she'd risk Emma's or Michael's lives again.

She should break things off with Michael, for his own safety, but didn't want to. Especially after just learning he was the man from her vision. Her stomach ached at the thought of him leaving her. Maybe her mother was wrong about that.

Dani turned and stared into Michael's pretty green eyes, surprised he'd been watching her. "You must be so angry with me. If I hadn't been so stupid—"

"Beating yourself up isn't going to solve anything." He gave her a quick kiss, then leaned back. "I need your undivided attention, because we have to go over the rules."

"What rules?"

He unlatched her seat belt, then scooped her into his arms, placing her on his lap. "Rule number one. No more kissing Jake. Or anyone else."

She blinked in confusion. He was talking about rules for them? Part of her feared—and hoped for his own good—that he'd run the other way as soon as they landed. But he needed to come back for her after Carlos Watts was in jail. "I told you. Those weren't real kisses, Michael. They were just—"

"Real or not, no more kissing him, Dani."

"Fine. And the only man I plan to do anything else with is you."

"Good." He nodded sharply. "Rule number two—"

"Wait a minute. I thought we were having a casual fling. Isn't the point of that type of relationship that there are no rules?"

"After this morning"—he leaned close and whispered so her mom couldn't hear—"I want more."

Her heavy heart soared. "Okay, if you insist. But you've gotten awful bossy all of a sudden."

His expression remained deadly serious. "Rule number two. No more hooker dresses."

"That's a given," she said with a sigh. "What's rule number three?"

"My girls have to come first. Heather plays games and calls me at the last minute, interrupting my plans, claiming I've forgotten some event or scheduled visit." He tapped the phone in his pocket. "Everything goes in here, but she likes to make my life difficult. Therefore, she's bound to make ours difficult as well. But, I'll drop whatever I'm doing for my kids."

"No problem. You're a great dad."

"I try. Rule number four." He lowered his voice again. "I'm in charge in the bedroom."

She leaned away from him and crossed her arms. "What? No way am I agreeing to that. As a matter of fact, I want to be in charge. You have to do whatever my little heart desires or the whole deal is off." She nipped his bottom lip to send her point home.

"Done." His mouth tilted in a mischievous grin.

"You were just pulling my chain, you sneaky lawyer."

He pulled her close, hugging her tight. "I was just making sure you were paying attention."

"Okay. Then we need to discuss rule number five. That's the one where, when you overhear me talking with Zoe about intimate details of our relationship, you can't complain."

His forehead crumpled. "How intimate?"

"Every detail."

"That was to pay me back for rule number four?"

"Yep."

He nodded. "I should probably expect that kind of behavior from a sneaky Realtor."

She grinned as she snuggled against him and closed her eyes. But very soon, she was going to have to tell him about rule number six—that he needed to keep his distance from her until the Carlos Watts problem was solved. She wouldn't risk his life again.

When they arrived home, Michael carried a sleepy Emma to the guesthouse for her. In front of it, a deep-blue Lexus hybrid SUV with a big red bow stood gleaming in the afternoon sun.

Dani dialed her mother. "Mom, how many times do I have to tell you? I'm not accepting gifts like this anymore."

"It's not from me. It's from your father. Read the card, Dani."

She tugged the envelope from under the windshield wiper and opened it.

Daniella,
I've been deprived the privilege of acknowledging thirty Christmases and birthdays for my only child. Please accept this from me. It would give me great pleasure to know you're driving a safe and environmentally friendly car.
And the windows are bulletproof.
Love,
Mario

She shook her head and tucked the card back inside the envelope. She said to Michael, "Mario is appealing to my sense of environmental consciousness, and not doing a bad job in the guilt department, either. Do you think I should keep it?"

Michael passed the sleeping Emma to her and popped the hood. He smiled as he studied the engine. "Sweet. I wonder if you can tell when it's running on batteries or gas? And yes, you should keep it. He wants to be your dad, so let him." He slammed the hood closed. "Can I borrow it? I haven't seen my kids in over a week, and I don't have a car."

"Sure." She grabbed his shirt, pulled him against her, and kissed him. When she'd had her fill, she reluctantly released him. "So, I guess I'll see you when I see you?"

"You'll see me later tonight. I don't have my girls again until the weekend."

Good. Then she'd have a little time to come up with the right way to tell Michael he wasn't welcome in her life—for now.

Later that night, Michael tossed the bag that contained his suit for the next day on a chair before slipping out of his jeans and T-shirt, relieved that Emma was in Dani's other bedroom.

He slid beside Dani, and when she turned and sent him a sleepy grin, everything aligned in his world. "Heather had a meltdown I had to deal with. Sorry I'm so late."

"'Kay . . ." Her voice slowly trailed off as she fell back asleep.

That wasn't the reception he'd hoped for, but he couldn't blame her. It was late. Resigned to no sex, he banked his need for her and snuggled closer. "Night, Dani."

It was probably for the best. After fighting with Heather and putting up with her irrational demands, it showed him how different

Dani was from his ex-wife. While Dani was complicated in her own way, she never whined or carried on, like Heather did with regularity.

He wanted to tell Dani what a refreshing change she was and how he looked forward to seeing her whenever they were apart, but that probably wouldn't have been wise at this point. He loved her, but they still needed to take things slowly, let their past relationship mistakes fade and give their hearts time to heal. And he needed to be sure she wouldn't hurt him again.

He'd always loved Dani, but he wouldn't have his heart stomped on twice, so he'd just keep his thoughts about wanting to marry her and be with her the rest of his life to himself for now.

Suddenly, Dani bolted straight up. "You're here. Sorry." Her hand reached out, and soft lamplight spilled over them. She was wearing something silky that just barely covered her, and his belly clenched with desire.

"I must've fallen back asleep after the guard told me you were on the way." She rubbed her eyes. "I need to give you this."

He accepted the slip of paper she held out. "What is it?"

"I'm invoking rule number four. It's a list of what I'd like you to do to me tonight."

He grinned as he read it, and by the time he'd reached the end of the list, he was unbearably hard. "In exactly this order?"

Her eyes lit with mischief. "Uh-huh."

"No problem. But what's the 'rule number six discussion' mean?"

"Let's see if you survive all the other items first, then we'll talk about that." She turned off the lamp, tugged the paper from his hand, and straddled him. "Oh, I see you've started without me."

He flipped her onto her back and settled between her legs.

She moaned with pleasure as he engaged in item number one.

~

The next morning, the shrill alarm of Michael's phone drove home the fact that they had been up entirely too late the evening before, but, holy shit, what a night it was. Dani really knew how to put together a list.

His hand searched for the screaming device buried in the pile of clothes beside the bed. After finally finding it, he switched it off and rolled over to find her staring into his eyes. "Morning." He'd set the alarm a few minutes early in hopes of getting a little action before work, and now that she was awake, odds appeared to be in his favor.

"Morning. Are you ready to finish the list?"

Had he forgotten a step? God, he hoped so. "Absolutely. Which item needs to be taken care of?"

He reached for her, but she evaded and sat up. Then she leaned her back against the headboard and wrapped her arms around her bent knees. "Someone fell asleep, and we didn't get to the last one. Rule number six?"

"Hey, it's tough being a sex slave. You wore me out." When she didn't seem to find the humor in his comment, he sat up and leaned back against the headboard, too. In an attempt to lighten her sudden dark mood, he added, "I'm hoping item six involves mandatory morning sex. But if not, maybe you could cut to the chase and just give me the executive summary. Then we'll have time for both?"

Her lips tilted slightly, but the determined gleam in her eyes didn't fade. She rose and slipped into her robe. After tying the knot, she huffed out a breath. "I think we need to take a break."

His stomach took a hard, fast dive. A brief flash of the last time she'd dumped him slammed in his mind. He'd been a damn fool to open his heart up to her again. She could hurt him like no one else—and she just had. "I should have known you'd do it again."

Her brows knit. "Do what again? After what happened in Vegas, I think—"

"It doesn't matter. If you're done, then so am I." He rolled out of bed, then gathered his things. He wasn't going to be made a fool of twice. He'd leave her before he'd give her the knife to stab him in the heart again.

Dani crossed the room in two long strides and wrapped her arms around his waist. "I want you safe until Carlos Watts is in jail. I don't want this, either, but we have no choice."

He stared into her pleading eyes. As the red haze of anger slowly faded, her intentions became clear. She was trying to protect him, not dump him. What she'd done in the past had clouded his thinking.

Her arms wrapped tighter around him, drawing him closer. "I couldn't bear it if you were hurt because of me." She stood on her tiptoes and kissed him. The warmth from her lips spread through his chest, easing the fist that clutched his heart.

Stepping back so he could think clearly, he quickly prepared his defense. "Let's discuss this rationally. First, you have no idea how long this problem is going to last. It could take weeks for Jake to put him behind bars for good. Second, what kind of a man would I be to leave you alone when a lunatic is after you?"

Dani crossed her arms and lifted her stubborn chin. "Yes, it could take some time, but it's not your job to protect me. I have a bodyguard for that, someone who is detached from the situation and isn't going to let personal feelings cloud his judgment."

She was no pushover. He'd have to find her weak spot.

He dumped his clothes on the bed, then slipped his arms around her stiff shoulders. "After last night, how could you suggest this?"

Her pursed lips softened for a brief moment. "You do follow directions very well, but it's for your own good, Michael."

"I'm a grown man who can take care of myself, as well as make my own choices. You've made your concerns known, so if I choose not to heed them and anything happens to me, it's my own fault.

Not yours. You show me no respect by trying to take this decision out of my hands."

Her mouth opened, but nothing but a hiss of air escaped. When her forehead wrinkled as she stared at him, he knew he'd won.

She lifted her hands in resignation, then turned and marched out of the bedroom, mumbling, "Damn lawyer!"

He smiled at his victory as he scooped up his clothes and headed to the shower.

Michael was still smiling when he stepped into the living room, but his grin quickly faded when he noticed the concern etched on Dani's face as she lowered her cell from her ear. "What's wrong?"

"That was Jake. He called to tell you that your car will require a few repairs. The good news is the men who shot at us are either dead or behind bars. Mr. Giovanni's men were very thorough."

"Was Carlos Watts one of them?" Michael asked, hoping Dani's nightmare would be over.

"No. But one of the surviving men is willing to testify, for a lighter sentence, that it was Carlos Watts who hired him. So now they can lock Carlos up for years . . . if they can find him.

"They will. Let's let Jake worry about that part."

"I'm trying." Dani circled her free arm around him and pulled him toward the door. "Come on, let's go eat." She smiled down at Emma. "And I bet you'd like to bake cookies with Mrs. Wilson. I'm going to talk her into watching you for a little bit today while I run to the office."

～

After they were all settled around the table in the massive kitchen, Mrs. Wilson's face glowed while she filled Dani's plate with gooey, rich French toast. "It's been too long since you've let me feed you, sweetheart."

Dani took a huge bite and moaned. "I'm a fool. Why do I bother cooking for myself when I can come over here and have one of your incredible meals?"

Mrs. Wilson snaked a soft arm around Dani's shoulder, pulling her against her ample bosom. "You're not a fool. What you are is an excellent cook. I know because I taught you myself. But you're stubborn as two mules and only cook when you feel like it."

"You've been talking to Jake again, haven't you?"

"He may have mentioned a thing or two about that the last time he came begging for dinner." Mrs. Wilson chuckled and shook her head. "He's a charmer, that one."

Michael cleared his throat and sent her an irritated look.

It was probably a good time to change the subject.

She didn't have to, though, because her mom swept into the room, looking ready for a *Vogue* photo shoot. "Well, good morning all. What a pleasant surprise."

"Hi!" Emma beamed a sweet smile and held out a piece of French toast dripping with syrup. After the plane ride, Emma thought Annalisa was better than fruit snacks.

When her mom leaned down and actually let Emma stick the gooey bread into her mouth, Dani nearly fell off her chair.

"Yuumm?" Emma asked with a hopeful grin.

Her mom nodded. "Double yum." She tilted Emma's face and kissed her forehead, one of the few places that was still clean. "Thank you, honey."

Then Annalisa reached for Dani's face and kissed her forehead, too. "Good morning, sweetheart. You're keeping the car?"

The triumphant gleam in her mother's eyes made her wonder whose idea the car really was—hers or Mario's. "Yes, and I've already called and thanked him. But what's up? Any more fairy dust and we'll all be enchanted."

"Mario is rethinking the idea of marriage. Thanks to *you*. He said he'd like to be a more active part of our family."

Dani's heart turned a little gooey with the idea that her mom might finally have the chance to be with the only man she'd ever loved. But her mom had fought for things in the past, and once the battle was won, quickly lost interest in them. "That'd be good, right?"

"That'd be very good." She hugged Dani before she turned to Michael. "Well, I suppose I better kiss you, too. I wouldn't want you to feel left out."

She kissed the top of Michael's head. Then her eyes found Dani's. She sent her a sly wink, obviously figuring out he'd spent the night.

Mrs. Wilson slipped beside them, holding Annalisa's extra-large mug of coffee, and tapped her cheek. "What about me? I'm definitely feeling left out here."

Her mom chuckled before she kissed Mrs. Wilson's cheek with such an exaggerated smack it made Emma giggle. Then she snatched the mug. "*Damn* employees, always demanding more. You can never keep them happy." Then her mother took a long drink and sighed. "This is the best coffee in the world. I guess I'll keep you around for a while longer."

Dani smiled and dug into her French toast. Mrs. Wilson had been with them for as long as she could remember. Her mom loved Mrs. Wilson as much as she and Sara did.

After another long drink from her mug, her mom said, "So, Michael, I hear your car is going to be in the shop for a while. We seem to have a surplus around here. Why don't you choose one to drive?"

He glanced at Dani and raised a questioning brow.

"It'd be no trouble. Mom's bought me three cars that I wouldn't accept, and they're all sitting there begging to be driven. There's a Porsche, a BMW, and a Mercedes."

Michael turned and grinned at Annalisa. "Thank you. If you wouldn't mind, I'd like to borrow one with a back seat. For my girls?"

Her mom smirked and slid a glance Dani's way. "Then you'll want the perfect-for-a-Realtor-to-show-homes-with Mercedes."

Dani sent her mom an eye roll in acknowledgment of her smartass comment, then turned her attention back to her succulent French toast.

Her mom said, "I'd love to stay and visit, but I'm late. Have a safe day, everyone." She took a step away, then stopped dead in her tracks. "I almost forgot." She leaned down and whispered in Dani's ear. "You're going to have to fight for him, baby. Just remember that he loves you." With one last squeeze, she released her and walked away.

Dani tucked into her meal rather than meet Michael's curious gaze. Her mom must've had another dream.

Just as Michael opened his mouth to speak, Mrs. Wilson laid two more pieces of French toast on his plate, then laid a hand on his shoulder. "Don't let all this talk of Jake bother you. Charming isn't what lasts, you know. It's steady, reliable, and good that makes it through the long haul." She gave his shoulder a pat, then turned and stared into Dani's eyes. "Some women just take a little longer to figure that out, that's all."

Dani closed her eyes, barely suppressing her groan. She was being assaulted from all sides. "Look, Jake has signed the papers and now he's just a—"

"Butthead!" Emma said with pride.

Michael struggled to hide his smirk as he finished off his breakfast.

After they were done eating, and while Emma was still in the kitchen, happily playing in cookie dough with Mrs. Wilson, Dani walked Michael out to the garage. She was still a little upset that he'd ignored her request to stay away but let it go because she hadn't come up with a good comeback for that stupid "you show me no respect" line of his. Who did he think he was? The Godfather?

"You were awfully quiet during breakfast, Michael."

He shrugged. "Talking about Jake doesn't interest me."

She pulled him close, enjoying the way his big arms slipped around her, almost instinctively. "Then we won't." She playfully nibbled on his lower lip, then leaned back and smiled when his eyes darkened with desire for her. That was something she'd never tire of.

His dimples deepened with his grin. "When can we look at those other two houses you were so excited to show me?"

She didn't want him anywhere near her outside her mother's compound. "Um, I have to work at the office from twelve to three today. I hate to ask Mrs. Wilson to watch Emma longer than that, so maybe another time?"

His grin faded, and she feared her plan was a little too obvious.

"I'm not going to stop seeing you, and I need to buy a house." His big hand gave her butt a sharp pat. "Stop by my office when you're done."

"Okay, but will you be extra careful today? Hey, maybe we should have my mom hire a bodyguard for you, too?"

He narrowed his eyes at her.

Michael wasn't budging on this one. "It was just a suggestion."

"A bad one." He leaned down and kissed her in that slow, patient way of his that always left her a little weak. When he was done, he asked, "But Jerry's going to be with *you* all day, right?"

"He's going to meet me here at eleven thirty. I still don't know how I'll explain him if anyone walks into the office needing to see a house, though."

"You'll figure it out. See you later."

Yeah, she'd already figured it out earlier when she'd spoken to Jake on the phone. She didn't have floor duty exactly, but she was still going to work. She was going to meet with Jake and her broker to figure out a way to flush out Carlos. Using herself as bait in one of her office's empty houses seemed to make the most sense, but she'd keep that part from Michael until Carlos was in jail for good.

Hopefully, they'd be able to put the final touches on the "Catch Carlos Watts" plan so she could get back to living her life.

Chapter Fourteen

Dani sat next to Jake in the office of her broker, Susie, surrounded by oversize Texas furniture, complete with a tacky side table with cowboy boots for legs and pictures of beauty pageants with big-haired women on every wall. Susie was Miss Texas twenty-five years ago. In an attempt to retain her former beauty, she'd had so much plastic surgery she'd achieved clown status, according to Jake.

Susie had "surprised" big eyes and a weird perpetual smile, and thanks to Botox, the rest of her face stayed oddly frozen in place, making it hard to read her true reactions. As a result, she looked thrilled that Dani was being chased by a lunatic and needed her help. She twanged, "Oh my God, Dani. This is horrible. What can I do to help, honey?"

Jake stifled a grin. He was the one who'd put the clown idea into Dani's head, and she'd never been able to get it out. To pay him back for that, she gave him a discreet kick in the shin, before she said, "I was wondering if we could use one of the empty houses in our inventory to set up a fake open house? Something that's been on the market so long no one will actually come if I post it on my Realtor page."

Jake added, "It'd be great if it was a little remote and had some growth around to conceal my men."

Jerry, who stood in the rear of the office, said, "And near a highway for a fast getaway."

Susie slowly nodded. "Well, why don't we just take us a look-see then?" She tapped away on her computer with her perfectly manicured blood-red nails. "We do live in the high desert, gentlemen. Dense growth is going to take us outside of town, maybe the east mountains for some trees?"

Dani inspected her fingernails while pondering why people from Texas always seemed to end every sentence with a high-pitched question mark.

She noted that her own manicure sucked. She should get to that soon.

Susie finally called out, "Here we go now. This is just perfect, boys. It's been empty for three years. Everyone this side of Abilene has seen this piece of cow dung, and it's just off old sixty-six." Susie's printer whirred and then spit out the listing.

Maybe she was wrong. Not one question mark in that last ditty. But she wasn't a boy. Didn't she count, too? It was her life at stake.

Dani snatched the printout Susie held out before Jake could take it and read the deets.

Impatient as always, Jake snatched it back. "Thanks. I'll run out there and check things out. We'll shoot for day after tomorrow. That should give Carlos time to see your web page announcement for the open house, Dani. Give me your lockbox deal."

Damn Jake. When he'd used it before, she'd warned him it was punishable by huge fines, and she could even lose her Realtor's license for loaning out a lockbox key. Even if he was a cop.

Susie's scary face whipped in Dani's direction, and maybe Susie's eyes got a tad wider. Before Susie could chastise Dani—or fire her—Dani grabbed Jake's arm and stood. "See why I'm divorcing him? His sense of humor is so bizarre. We'll just go get a key from the back."

Susie slowly shook her head. "You exhaust me, darlin'. If it weren't for your mother . . . just don't go and get yourself dead, please. I don't have the patience to train someone new."

If it weren't for her mother? "What does my—"

"You ladies can chat later. Let's go." Jake tugged Dani along with him out into the hall.

"Let go. I want to ask what she meant by that."

"Just leave it. She's probably talking about using Annalisa's fame."

He was covering something up. She stopped in her tracks and crossed her arms. "I've never lied to you, Jake. I'd appreciate the same consideration."

"Dammit, Dani." He cringed and pulled her away from Jerry. "I don't lie to you . . . often. But if I do, it's always for yours or someone else's own good. Can't you just leave it?"

"No."

"Interesting that you've never lied to me, but you're lying your ass off to your new boy toy." He crossed his arms, too, and then turned all smug. "I'll tell you what Susie meant when you come clean with Michael. About the open house and about the woo-woo stuff, too. He has the right to know what he's getting himself into. It's a pretty damn big deal not everyone can handle."

A ball of guilt formed hard and fast in Dani's belly. He knew just how to push her buttons. "You can be such an ass, Jake."

She raised her hand, signaling for Jerry to stay put in the lobby area; then Dani turned and headed for the utility closet where they kept all the keys. Jake trailed a few steps behind. She'd never called him a name like that, so now she felt guilty for that, too.

While she searched for the key, Jake stood nearby with his hands stuffed into the front pockets of his jeans. He was being unusually quiet, but she counted that as a blessing.

Jake whispered, "I just meant that as someone who loves you, I'd be mad if you risked your life and didn't tell me. And I shouldn't have said the other thing."

True on both counts. Michael was going to know she'd done the bait and switch behind his back when it was over. Maybe she'd better come clean after all. No doubt it'd be an ugly battle. But the woo-woo statement was a low blow she never expected to come from Jake, making it hurt even worse.

She found the key and handed it over. "Now that we have a plan, I'm going to go see Michael and tell him about it. But it's too soon to tell him about the other part. I can't go around telling every man I date something that will affect not only me but possibly my mother's life and her precious reputation, too. So, spill."

"Fine." He ran a hand down his face. "After we separated and you were having trouble finding a job, your mom made a deal with Susie to throw some business your way now and again—for a fee."

So, all Dani thought she'd accomplished in her attempts to support herself weren't because of her own hard work? Wow. That hurt ten times worse than what Jake had just said about her woo-woo stuff. "How do you even know that?"

He shot her one of his charming smiles. "I'm a top-notch detective?"

She waited him out.

"Dani, you're . . . different. That makes things harder for you. I was worried your pride would get in the way and you'd suffer for it. I asked your mom to be sure you were taken care of when I couldn't be the one to do that anymore. We both knew you'd never accept any direct help. You can be a little hardheaded."

Code for Dani's not just a loser, but a stubborn loser on top of it? Great.

And ouch, again.

Well, at least she knew she had one legitimate client. Michael. And she was going to find him the perfect house, dammit, and prove them all wrong.

She sent Jake on his way and then sat down at her desk to find Michael the perfect home.

After two long hours of weeding through listing after listing, she finally found it. A home that fit all of his requirements, and some added ones she thought he'd really like, too. It even had a fabulous guesthouse for his mom. She couldn't wait to show him.

She hopped up from her desk, grabbed her purse, and called out to Susie as she ran by her office, "I'm off to sell a house. See you tomorrow. And thanks again."

Susie gave a little finger wave. "Well, I hope that's all true, darlin'. Good luck."

Jerry caught up with her as she headed out the glass doors. He asked, "Where do you think you're going? Your mother gave me strict orders. Work and home only."

"To Michael's office. Don't argue with me. It won't do any good. Besides, we'll be in my new bulletproof vehicle, so everything will be fine."

He grabbed the keys from her hand. "Yeah, but I want to get there in one piece, so I'm driving this time."

"Whatever." Dani smiled as she climbed into her new car. Since Jerry's car had been damaged in Vegas, they'd taken hers. It'd been fun to scare the crap out of him on the drive to her office.

While he drove, she posted her open house online. This could be the best thing she'd ever do, and they'd flush Carlos out—or the last thing she ever did if it all went wrong.

With the "winner, winner, chicken dinner" of MLS printouts in her hand and Jerry standing guard in the hall, Dani knocked on the frame of Michael's office door. He was hard at work at his desk. She was relieved to see he was in one piece and looking extremely healthy. And very yummy in his slick lawyer duds.

When he glanced up, a cute, slightly annoyed frown at being interrupted lingered but quickly got replaced by a grin. "Do you have an appointment, Miss?"

It seemed Michael was in the mood to play, feeding her a handy opening line. "Nope. But I was hoping you could be persuaded to allow me just a few moments of your valuable time."

He tossed his heavy pen on a stack of papers and leaned back in his chair. "Why don't you come over here and persuade me?"

She added a little extra hip action as she sauntered toward him. Better to get him all worked up and distracted before she started telling the truth about things.

She grabbed his chin and pulled him close. "I can be *very* persuasive."

"Prove it." He pulled her onto his lap.

Before she could, he beat her to it and laid his soft mouth on hers. Michael's kisses were even better than Mrs. Wilson's French toast. Yuuummmm.

But, oh yeah, she was there for a reason, so she slowly leaned away. "I've got good news and bad. Which do you want first?"

"The good."

She laid the MLS listing on his desk. "I found the most incredible house for you. And we should go see it this afternoon." Mostly because she might get killed soon while impersonating a sitting duck.

She held her breath as Michael studied the listing. She was getting better at the being-a-Realtor deal even if no one else thought so.

She hoped.

When Michael's lips slowly tilted at the corners, she could draw a full breath again. He says, Hhh

"Yep. This may be the one. I'm impressed, Dani."

Take that, former Miss Texas! "Then let's go."

She started to wriggle off his lap, but he held her in place. "I just got a text from Heather. She decided she needs an emergency mani-pedi, so I have to pick up the girls at four. Do you think we can make it back in time?"

She checked the time on her phone and did some quick math. "Easy peasy. Let's roll."

"Okay. But what's the bad news?"

She suddenly had no spit in her mouth. Probably better to just blurt it all out at once, like ripping off a bandage, in one stroke. "Jake and I have come up with a plan to flush Carlos Watts out. We're going to hold a fake open house. I posted the deets on my web page."

Michael's neck muscles began to bulge, but she forged on. "I'll be wired and in full riot gear, complete with helmet and bulletproof vest, but they'll never even get near me, because Jake will have a team hiding on the property. They'll ambush Carlos before he even gets out of the car."

Michael's eyes grew dark with anger, and his jaw clenched. "What if Carlos sends someone else to do his dirty work like he did in Vegas? You'd be risking your life for nothing, Dani. Don't do it."

"We figured Carlos has learned his lesson about sending someone else to do his job, and chances are he'll do it himself. I can't live like this, Michael. Waiting to be killed. I have to do something."

Michael rubbed the back of his neck and growled. "So your mind's all made up? And it doesn't matter what I think?"

Her stomach hurt. "That's why I'm telling you about it now instead of doing it behind your back—which was my original dumb plan so you wouldn't worry. But then I realized how betrayed you'd feel afterward. This really isn't all that different than you choosing to risk your life by being with me after I asked you not to, Michael."

"This is entirely different!"

No, it wasn't. But she didn't have a good rebuttal, so she waited as a thousand emotions clouded Michael's eyes while he stared deeply into hers.

After a two-minute stare-off, he finally closed his eyes and shook his head like he was going to give in.

Maybe dating a logical lawyer wouldn't be such a bad thing after all. "So, you get why I have to do this, Michael?"

"I think it's too risky. But I'd probably do the same thing if I were in your shoes. How about you text Jake and ask if he can meet us at a coffee shop or something nearby? I'll feel better if I can hear for myself what he's planned."

"Okay. But what about the house?" She sent a text to Jake. He responded right back and said he was nearby and wanted to talk anyway after he'd checked out the listed house. He'd meet them in the lobby in five minutes.

"The house can wait until after this is over. We need Carlos in jail so you're safe. *You* are all that matters to me right now."

Her heart did a happy jig in her chest. "Weird. That's how I feel about you, too. Maybe this you-and-me thing is going to work out well after all."

"Maybe." He pulled her against his chest. "Do you have any other secrets, Dani? Because if you're like Heather, hiding a huge secret, then I need to know now. I don't want to go through hell like that ever again."

The ache in her gut was back again. She couldn't tell him about her special stuff. It was too soon. He was way too black and white in his thinking to easily accept what she could do was even possible. It'd take time and a plan of some sort to ease him into accepting her powers.

"I'm an open book." Her heart split into a million pieces as she lied to him. "Let's go meet Jake."

She sucked.

Dani slipped off Michael's lap, and then Jerry followed behind as the three headed down the hallway to the elevator. She glanced at Michael as they stepped inside, and she could practically see the wheels spinning inside his skull as he processed her sitting-duck plan. Might be good to get Jake and Michael to work together for a common goal for a change. Maybe they could actually become friends.

After the elevator doors parted. Michael laid his hand on her lower back, and they walked into the lobby. Two men even bigger than Jerry appeared before them. And one of them was Carlos.

All the air whooshed from her lungs.

She glanced to the side for an escape route, but all she could see was the receptionist, her shoes peeking out from behind the desk. As if she was lying on her back.

Ice-cold fear shot up Dani's spine.

Please don't let the receptionist be dead because of me.

Carlos's lips tilted into a sneer. "Well, well, well. This must be my lucky day. I was just gonna kill you, Reilly, but looks like I got myself a twofer." When he and the other thug rushed forward, Michael pushed Dani behind him, and Jerry tackled the thug.

This wasn't going to end well.

Jerry and Michael wrestled with the men, but then a riot stick like the cops used connected with Jerry's head, and he went down with a thud.

Her mind screamed for her to run, but she couldn't move. Fear paralyzed her. That and she couldn't leave Michael to fight the men alone. But she'd forgotten to pack her gun that morning.

Carlos got a hand free and slammed the butt of his gun against Michael's temple, ending the battle in less than five seconds. Watching Michael's body crumple to the ground killed her worse than the thought that she was going to be next.

Jerry was out cold, and now Michael was, too. She'd tried so hard to keep Michael safe. His girls needed him. She had to do something to put a stop to it all. But what? Focus and logical thinking seemed impossible.

When Carlos's leg cocked back to kick Michael, she yelled, "Stop!" She met Carlos's hate-filled gaze. "It's me you want, not them."

Carlos slowly nodded. "You're right. I can finish him off later." He lifted his gun and pointed it at her chest.

Carlos's face turned wavy, so she blinked her eyes to bring him back in focus. The contempt in his eyes left no doubt. This was it. She was going to die.

Jake's voice called out. "Police. Drop your weapons or I'll shoot!"
Thank God.

The second thug dropped his gun and lifted his hands in the air. But Carlos kept his gun pointed at her.

Black dots appeared before her eyes. Maybe if she passed out first, she wouldn't feel the pain as the bullet sliced through her heart.

Jake eased his way toward her, his gun aimed at Carlos the whole time. "Drop it, Carlos. Or you're not walking away alive." Jake nodded to the other guy. "Down on your stomach. Hands behind your back."

Dani glanced at Michael, relieved to see he was trying to sit up. When his eyes locked with hers, the love and concern in his gaze brought fresh tears to her eyes. She held out a hand, motioning him to stay down, out of harm's way.

Carlos said, "Are you waving good-bye to lover boy, Dani?" A sick smile formed on Carlos's lips. "Because I'm not going to die here today for nothing. Bye-bye, bitch."

She closed her eyes and waited for the bullet to end it all. When a deafening shot rang out, something hit her like a sack of cement, and she flew to the ground. Then another shot sounded, and a loud thump sounded beside her.

It was hard to breathe with so much weight on top of her, and her shoulder hurt from hitting the floor, but she was definitely still alive. But was Jake?

When she blinked her eyes open, Jerry lay on top of her with a gun in his hand, his eyes closed, and his shoulder soaked with blood. He must've jumped in front of her and taken the bullet.

Carlos was on the ground a few feet away, his eyes fixed in a vacant stare, obviously dead.

Was it finally over?

She drew in a much-needed gulp of air, hoping to stave off the need to pass out.

Jerry, true to his promise, must've killed Carlos for her. But was Jerry going to be okay?

She wriggled out from under his weight while trying to regulate her breathing and slow her pounding heart.

She glanced to the side and saw Michael sitting up and holding his head, so that was one less concern for her rattled brain to deal with.

While Jake cuffed the second guy, she grabbed Jerry's wrist to see if she could find a pulse. "Jerry? Can you hear me?" Her teeth chattered so hard it was difficult to speak.

"Not in the mood to chat, okay?" He opened his eyes and grimaced.

He had a sense of humor, which had to be a good sign.

She blinked back her tears as the scream of approaching sirens filled the air. "Thank you for saving my life, Jerry. Maybe you're not such a pain in the ass after all."

He smiled weakly but kept his eyes closed. "You still are. I *hate* getting shot."

She let out a pent-up sob as a paramedic slipped beside them. Jake helped her up and pulled her close. "Are you all right?"

"I'm fine, but Michael's hurt. And the receptionist. Over there." When Jake took off to check on the girl, she gingerly moved to Michael's side and crumpled beside him on the floor. "God, I'm so glad you're alive." The swelling on the side of his head was concerning, though.

He took her hand and laid it over his heart. "You too."

Jake returned with a concerned frown. "Looks like she's going to be all right, too."

That everyone seemed okay was a huge relief.

When Michael's eyes fluttered and he swayed, Jake quickly knelt and helped him lie down. "Hang on there, Counselor. Let's let the paramedics have a look at you."

Dani moved out of the paramedic's way as she let the tears she'd been struggling to withhold fall. The concern and speed at which the paramedics worked on Michael told her he was hurt worse than she thought.

"Tears? You never cry." Jake slipped an arm around her tender shoulder. "I'm sure he'll be fine, Dani."

She shook her head. "It's just that I love him so much, Jake. It scares me to think of how much worse this could've turned out if they'd ambushed him in his office. He'd probably be dead." A new wave of tears overcame her.

Jake slowly nodded as he let his arm drop. "If that's how you feel about him, then you need to tell him, babe."

Jake was right. She couldn't do what Heather had done to him and withhold a huge secret about herself. As soon as he was better, she was going to have to tell him what she'd only told two other people outside of her family. She hoped he wouldn't walk away from her, like he'd been doing in her dream. "I will."

Jake started to leave to take care of business but then turned back and took her hand. "If he can't take the news, you'll still have me. I'll always love you, Dani. Just the way you are."

God, she hated the pain that radiated from his eyes. It seemed all she'd done lately was hurt the men she loved.

Michael opened his eyes at the sound of a familiar voice. Nurses had been fussing over him for two solid days. All he'd wanted was an hour of uninterrupted sleep, but Dani was always a welcome distraction.

She laid a soft kiss on his forehead. "Hey there. How're you doing?"

He sat up in the hard hospital bed, adjusting the uncomfortable gown. "Good, now that you're here. They're letting me go home this afternoon."

"That's awesome." She settled in beside him.

He wrapped his arm around her shoulder. "Being in the hospital again reminded me of something I never finished thanking you for the other day. My mom told me that after my car accident, you loaded her onto Annalisa's jet and flew her to Dallas. She said you made sure she ate and slept, and took turns with her beside my bed until I woke up."

"Yeah. The doctors didn't think you'd pull through. It was the longest six days of our lives."

He took her hand. "My mom said that on the sixth day, when the doctors were preparing Heather and you guys for the worst, you told them they were wrong, because you knew I was going to wake up. It wasn't a half hour later that I did. She said the first person I asked for was you. But then you went home as soon as I was fully conscious. Why?"

Dani stood and poured him a glass of water. "Heather was making it hard for me to be there."

"Was she mad because I said your name first?"

"Yeah. She asked me to leave." Dani chewed her lower lip and seemed to have some sort of marathon debate going on inside. Finally, she said, "But maybe this is a good time to tell you how I knew you were going to wake up."

That was a strange thing to say. "You hoped, like everyone else, right?"

She slowly shook her head. "No. I *knew*." She sat beside him again and laid her hand on his arm. "This is going to seem a little unusual, but I need for you to hear me out. Have an open mind. Promise you won't make any judgments until I finish. Please?"

The tears in her eyes filled him with uneasy dread. "Just spit it out, Dani. How bad can it be?"

"Well, it's not a bad thing, per se, but it's not normal." She drew a deep breath. "I have dreams that come true. And I see visions sometimes if I touch things. I'd had a dream that you'd wake up, and you did."

He rubbed his aching forehead. She wasn't making any sense. Maybe his brain wasn't firing on all cylinders yet. "Everyone has dreams. Some come true and some don't."

Dani stood and paced back and forth for a moment before she finally said, "I dreamed you'd marry Heather. Instead of me. It hurt so badly that I couldn't be around you anymore. That's why I stopped being your friend."

"But that makes no sense. Heather hadn't even moved to town yet by the time we parted ways."

"Right?" Dani nodded. "How else could I have known?"

No. Stuff like that wasn't real.

The ache in his belly began to match the one in his head. "What about the vision thing?"

Dani glanced around the room, then crossed to the other side and picked up a vase of flowers and closed her eyes. "These came from your secretary." She put the flowers down and then picked up a sudoku puzzle book. "This came from your daughter."

How the hell could she know that? "You probably read the card in the flowers."

She shoved the vase his way. "See any card?"

That's right. There wasn't one in the arrangement, because his mom had removed the cards from all the flowers and stacked them on the table the night before so he could take them home.

Holy crap, things were getting weird. "So what happens when you touch . . . people?"

She sat beside him on the bed again. "Depends. If I open my mind, sometimes I just get a color, like an aura, and other times still pictures will appear. It's all very annoying, actually."

He couldn't grasp the theory. It just didn't make any sense. There was no such thing as that kind of . . . power. People who claimed to have powers were charlatans who took advantage of people.

As his mind scrambled back in time, replaying things from their shared past, cold dread skittered up his spine. Looking back, it did make sense. The way Zoe had told him that she didn't need to go to college because Dani said Zoe was going to be a successful painter. She'd told him lots of things when they were kids that had since come true, too. He'd thought it was just another of the games they used to play, but there was no way anyone could have been that accurate by guessing. And the gambling. That's how she'd won all that money in Vegas and why she wouldn't take any for herself. And how she'd known he'd play on the Cowboys one day. There was no way anyone could have known which team he'd be drafted by.

So it was true. Dani must have some sort of strange intuitions.

As he processed the facts, a sick dread settled in his gut. It overwhelmed him to think that visions and dreams actually existed, but more so at how he didn't know something so huge about the best friend he'd ever had. The woman he loved. And who claimed to love him back, but did she really?

"Why didn't you tell me before now, Dani? Who else knows?"

She took his hand. "Zoe and Jake, Mom, Mario, Grandma, and Sara."

The fact that Zoe knew unraveled him completely. Why would she tell a friend rather than the person she claimed to love? He and Dani used to tell each other everything. Or so he'd thought. What else hadn't she told him?

"When did you tell Zoe?"

Dani frowned. "I think it was in the eleventh grade."

He tugged his hand free and crossed his arms. It hurt to touch her. It hurt to look at her. "Why didn't you tell *me*? We were best friends."

She lifted her hands, then let them fall. "My mother forbade me to tell anyone about our dreams, and I used to listen better when I was little. I was a belligerent teenager when I told Zoe."

"*Our* dreams?" No way could this be happening. "So your mom has prophetic dreams, too?"

"Yes. Remember my trespassing charge? My mom had a dream and figured out her friend, the mayor, had been embezzling government funds to feed his gambling habit. I snuck in and put the money back, from my mother's accounts, before anyone caught him. That family vacation they're on right now is really to the rehab place he's checked into."

"Dani, it's a federal offense to tamper with government funds. You and your mother could go to jail for doing that!"

"I know. But we did it for his own good. He'll get better, and no one will ever know. It's like how I've helped Jake solve so many crimes."

Jake again. Of course.

But it finally explained why she was always in court, testifying.

"And you and your mother commit crimes on a weekly basis? You're lucky that you're both my clients, or ethically I'd have no choice but to turn you in." How could he be with someone who broke laws on a regular basis? The same laws he'd promised he'd defend when he became a lawyer.

Annalisa had told him Dani had just been discreetly dropping off something private for her at the mayor's house and that the trespassing charge had just been a misunderstanding. Not a federal offense. So Annalisa was a liar, too.

Dani sighed. "I'm sorry, Michael. But our intentions are always good. We help people with our abilities, not hurt them."

He still couldn't come to terms with any of it. With the powers and the crime committing and the lying, Dani was breaking his heart—again. But it was the lying he couldn't forgive. She was no different from his ex-wife.

Maybe all women were liars.

As he stared into Dani's eyes, his fractured heart turned to stone. "You and my mother were the only two people in my life I trusted completely. You know trust doesn't come easy for me. By lying to me, you crossed that line. The one you and I swore we never would with each other. I think you'd better go."

She lifted her hands in frustration. "Michael, I love you. I just didn't know how to tell you. I know how black and white you are when it comes to the law, but I was just trying to help the mayor. Please don't shut me out."

Tears slid down Dani's cheeks, but he refused to be moved. He'd asked Dani directly if she'd had any secrets, and she'd said she was an open book. "Looks like that lying, cheating gangster blood runs in you, too. Just leave, please. We're done."

"Gangster blood? Really, Michael? For the record, you just crossed the line, too." She angrily wiped her tears away. "I'm still the same person you've known for twenty years. Nothing's changed. When you're ready to be reasonable, we'll talk again." She gave him her back as she turned to leave.

Reasonable? That was rich. He wasn't the one being unreasonable. Dani was being unreasonable to expect him to just overlook her playing Robin Hood on a regular basis. She'd done the same thing in Vegas, by using her skills to cheat. Just because her intentions were good didn't mean she wouldn't go to jail in the future if she were caught doing something like she'd done at the mayor's office. What if they'd gotten married and had kids like he'd wanted? Would he be taking them to see their mother in jail?

Worse, she'd lied right to his face. That was something he'd sworn he'd never tolerate again from a woman. He had his girls to think of. He'd never want to bring a dishonest person home to them.

He and Dani were through.

Chapter Fifteen

When she turned to leave, crushed by Michael's reaction, Dani nearly ran into a nurse who was staring at them with widened eyes. Had she heard the part about Annalisa and Dani committing a crime?

Panic stole Dani's breath as she stared into the nurse's eyes. The woman slowly backed away, then hurried out the door. Dani turned toward Michael, but he wouldn't meet her gaze. What had she done? Surely the woman would tell everyone she knew, and it'd be no time before the story broke. Any news about Annalisa was big news. Especially if the nurse thought she'd committed a crime.

Maybe they could just deny it.

She ran to Michael's bedside. He stared straight ahead as if she didn't exist. "You can't tell anyone, Michael. You have to promise me you won't confirm what that nurse says." Desperation drove her voice up two octaves. "Besides the possibility of jail, it could ruin my mother's career!"

His jaw clenched. "Maybe you should have thought about that before you broke into the mayor's house. Just go."

She laid her hand on his arm, and he shrugged it off, breaking her heart all over again. "If not for me, then for my mom? Please? Her reputation means more to her than anything else in the world. She's the one with the most to lose."

Michael finally met her gaze. His eyes held none of the warmth they had when she'd first entered the room. Now they reflected hurt, betrayal, and disgust. "She wasn't the only one to lose something today, Dani."

His words slammed into her like a Mack truck. "You and I don't have to lose anything, Michael. Nothing has to change."

He slowly shook his head and looked away. "It already has."

The finality in his voice made everything inside of her ache. With great effort, she managed to make it to the door and then the elevator. Once inside she broke down in tears.

She'd lost him.

Dani barely remembered driving home, but found herself standing in the doorway of her mother's study. Her mom, who was on the phone, met her gaze and hung up. She didn't even say good-bye. "What is it, honey?"

"I'm so sorry, Mom."

"About what?" Annalisa's eyes narrowed. "Tell me."

After she'd told her mom the whole ugly story, Dani slid into one of the chairs in front of the desk and waited for the blow that was sure to come. She didn't care. Nothing could be worse than Michael's reaction. She'd been careless and deserved every bit of her mother's wrath.

After a few moments Annalisa slapped her hands on the desk. "We have to get on top of this right away. It was only the one nurse, right?" Her mother picked up the phone and dialed. "It'll be our word against hers."

"I guess."

"Michael won't talk, will he? We can just say she misunderstood."

Dani met her mother's gaze and slowly shook her head. "Michael is so mad at me right now I don't know what he's going to do."

Her mom leaned across the desk. "If he confirms this, I'll hire the best lawyers to keep us out of jail, but I'll *never* work again, Dani! Who'll want to hire a suspected criminal to play the role of someone's beloved mother?" When her publicist answered, her mom spun around in her chair, giving Dani her back.

She couldn't think of a time she'd ever felt worse. She'd managed to ruin a relationship and career all in the matter of minutes. She had to be the biggest screwup of all time.

~

Michael stared at the hospital ceiling, longing for home. He needed to think, and after that eavesdropping nurse left, he hadn't had a moment's peace. Every other nurse in the place snuck in and asked him questions he refused to answer. Not because he was protecting Annalisa, but because he hadn't decided what he'd do.

When the door opened again, he closed his eyes, hoping whoever it was would think he was asleep and go away.

"Hey there, Counselor. Guess your hard head saved you once again."

Jake. Of course. Dani must've called him already.

He opened his eyes and noted Jake's cocky grin. "Are you here to gloat?"

"Gloat? Are those tiny brains cells of yours still a little scrambled?" Jake pulled a chair up beside the bed. "I was checking on a witness downstairs and figured that even though I don't like you, I probably owe you for trying to protect Dani. That took some brass balls to step in front of that armed asshole. Or, maybe you're just dumb. Either way, thanks, man."

So he didn't know yet, or he was just pretending he didn't. "How could you live with someone with such . . . weird abilities? Does she know your every thought?"

Jake's eyebrows shot up. "What?"

"Dani told me about her . . . whatever it is."

"No, she can't read thoughts." Jake glanced over his shoulder, checking to be sure they were alone. "I've had a harder time living without her than with her." He ran a hand down his face. "I knew what Dani was before we started seeing each other. She'd had a vision and tried to tell me about a kidnapping. I didn't take her seriously, figuring she was just another one of the nutcases we regularly deal with. But something made me check her story out anyway. Dani saved a kid's life. How do you not respect a person who risked her own secret to save a stranger's life?"

"It's not a matter of respect. It's a matter of . . . abiding by the law. And always telling the truth." Two things that Dani knew full well were the most important to him. It's probably why she'd lied to him, which just pissed him off all over again thinking about it. Although, saving the kid's life was the right thing to do.

Jake's jaw clenched. "You've known her longer than I have. Dani's honest to the point of brutal sometimes. She doesn't lie."

"She's lied to me for twenty years. So, congratulations, you win. Dani's all yours now." It killed him to say that. To let Jake have her back. But he just couldn't see a future with Dani anymore.

Jake shook his head and started for the door. "Why would I want a woman who is clearly in love with someone else?" Grasping the door handle, he turned and said, "Even if that someone else is a narrow-minded *prick*." Jake slammed the door behind him.

Later that evening, Dani was so devastated about losing Michael, and angry that he'd so quickly end things between them, that she could barely function. She counted all the ways she was sorry she'd ever lied to him as she packed all of Emma's things and placed them by the door. Julia had called and said she was back in town and was due any minute.

Dani slumped next to Emma on the couch as they watched cartoons together. Earlier she'd turned on the local, then national, news, dismayed when interviews with that damn nurse made all the headlines. The nurse claimed that she'd overheard that Annalisa and Dani had conspired with the mayor to commit a crime. The side note to make the story more sensational was that both Dani and Annalisa dabbled in the occult. The press was in a frenzy because no one was able to contact the mayor—he was on vacation with his family and had asked for some much-needed privacy for his wife, who'd been ill, before he left—and because her mom's publicist had told reporters that Annalisa and her daughters had left that morning for a holiday and were out of the country. Michael was the only chance for a story.

Thankfully, the mayor was in rehab and wouldn't be out for a few weeks, and they were all safe from the press at home.

Pictures of her in that stupid red dress from Vegas were just as prominent. Speculation ran rampant, and because there was no real news to report that day, all the news agencies were scrambling to get Michael's side of the story since no one else was talking.

Would he keep their secret?

Would he ever forgive her? Give her a second chance?

She'd finally switched to something less depressing. Not that Emma had complained about the news. It was as if she knew how sad Dani was, so she was being especially good. God, she was actually going to miss the kid. Who would've ever thought that?

Emma laughed at a prank a blue cat pulled, but Dani couldn't quite work up the energy to smile. She'd tried calling her mom to see how things were going, but her mother wouldn't talk to her, claiming she was too busy. It seemed she was persona non grata at the moment. And who knew how long that'd last?

When the phone rang, Dani sighed. As suspected, it was the guard announcing Julia's arrival. "Well, kiddo, your mom's here."

"Yay, Momma!" Emma beamed a sweet smile, hopped off the couch, and raced for the door. Dani opened it, and they both waited as

Julia's car approach. When her mother opened the door with her arms spread, Emma was there to hug her.

Dani's heart hurt with memories of waiting for her mom to come home after a long shoot, and of the sheer joy on Annalisa's face when she saw her and Sara. Now she wondered if her mom would ever speak to her again. Or if there'd ever be another film in her future.

Dani forced a welcoming smile. "Hey, Julia. Did you find your business partner?"

"Yeah, his mother told me about a houseboat they keep on Lake Havasu, and sure enough, there he was. The police arrested him this morning, and he gave a full confession."

"Congratulations. That's great." Dani leaned down and gathered Emma's things. "I still need the information on Ron's accounts. Can you e-mail that to me?"

"I'll do it first thing in the morning. I hope he hasn't changed his passwords, or you won't be able to access the money." Julia loaded the bags; then she turned and gave Dani a hard hug. "I don't know how I can ever thank you."

Dani grinned at Emma. "Maybe you could let me babysit occasionally." Her gaze zipped back to Julia's. "But only for a few hours at a time—not days."

Julia laughed. "That's a deal. Hey, do you know where Jerry is? He hasn't answered my calls. I'm a little worried."

"He's fine now, but at University Hospital, recovering from a gunshot wound. I saw him earlier today, and he's his usual cranky self. He asked about you guys."

"Really?" Julia's grin widened. "Maybe we'll stop by tonight."

Dani knelt down, determined not to cry, and wrapped Emma in a bear hug. She closed her eyes and drew a deep breath, memorizing Emma's scent. It was a combination of chocolate, because of the candy bar she'd sneaked her after dinner, mixed with baby powder. "Goodbye, you. I'm gonna miss ya."

Emma kissed Dani's cheek. "Bye-bye."

When Dani finally willed her arms to release Emma, the kid started toward the car and then stopped. Turning, she walked back with Wilbur held high. "Daaani's Bur."

She gazed into the rabbit's adorable face and then into Emma's and the dam burst. She couldn't stop her tears and didn't bother to try. That rabbit had once meant the world to her. Maybe Emma would find comfort from the bunny, just as she had. "I think Wilbur would be happier with you, Em. Want to keep him?"

"Yay!" Emma grinned and wrapped her arms around Dani's legs. "I luff Daaani."

She croaked out a whisper, "I love Emma, too."

Narrow-minded prick? Jake's words ate at him as Michael paced his living room. He hadn't had any more peace at home than at the hospital. When he'd finally been released the day before, reporters had shoved microphones in his face and followed him home. At least the security gates surrounding his apartment kept them confined to the parking lot.

The press wanted him to confirm the nurse's story. He crossed to the window and checked outside for an escape route. Maybe the vultures had tired and given up.

Nope. They'd camped out all day.

The doctors had advised him to stay home from work for a few days to be sure he recovered fully, but he was going crazy. He felt like a prisoner in his own home.

A friend who produced a local news show had called and asked for an interview. He'd said it'd stop the reporters from hounding him. But should he do it or just hide out until they got tired of waiting? His buddy said since it involved Annalisa, that could be a very long time.

He flopped onto the couch and turned on the television. A local reporter was talking about Annalisa, of course, and then the view switched to the police station. A woman asked Jake if it were true that his ex-wife and her mother had committed a crime and if they practiced any kind of occult or witchcraft.

Jake sent the reporter a wide smile. "I like to think everyone has a little woo-woo ability inside of them. It's just most people haven't tapped into theirs yet. I know my hunches are rarely wrong, and I use them to put scumbags behind bars." He turned and started to walk away, but the woman wouldn't give up.

"Don't you think Michael Reilly's refusal to acknowledge the eye-witness's statement is an admission to the crime in itself?"

Jake's features turned cold. "Mr. Reilly suffered a serious head injury. He needs time to recover. I'm sure he'll do the right thing when he's feeling better." Jake stared into the camera and it felt as if he were looking directly at him. Then Jake strode away.

"Do the right thing?" Michael pointed the remote at the screen and hit the "Off" button. "Yeah, and what is the right thing, Jake? Lying to someone you claim to love?"

His mood foul, he stood to pace again.

When he couldn't sleep the previous night, he'd searched online for information about psychics and people who claimed to have extra pow-ers, as Jake had said. After he'd gotten past the obvious fakes, he'd found studies and serious research that confirmed that people with exceptional powers do exist. Police forces around the world have used them from time to time. While it still made him uneasy to think Dani had those extra abilities, at least she used them in a positive way.

He glanced out the window again. The Mercedes Annalisa had loaned him had miraculously appeared and sat gleaming in his assigned parking space, the key in his mailbox. Maybe Annalisa was just trying to soften him up so he'd lie to the reporters.

A pang of guilt hit him in the heart. Annalisa had taken him on worldwide adventures and had always showed him nothing but love and respect. She'd offered the car out of kindness, and she'd probably had it moved for him for the same reason. It was Dani he was angry with.

He dropped his aching head into his hands and groaned.

What was he going to say to the reporters to make them go away, so he could have his life back again? He didn't want to lie. It'd be no better than what Dani had done to him.

But Dani's plea to keep her secret replayed in his mind. She was right: Annalisa's lawyers would probably find a way to get them off if they got charged for anything, and it'd be Annalisa's reputation he'd hurt more in the long run by telling the truth.

But he always told the truth.

Dani rolled over and blinked her heavy eyelids open. The morning sun, reflecting off the water from the pool, swayed in gentle patterns on the ceiling above her bed. She conjured up her schedule for the day, and her heart sank. Her work calendar was clear, unfortunately. She could've used the distraction, not to mention the money a sale would bring.

She didn't even have Emma to get dressed and fed. Strangely, that depressed her even more. Maybe she'd just pull the covers over her head and stay there all day.

No, that was the coward's way out. What she needed to do was talk to Mrs. Wilson. Surely, she'd seen the news by now and was probably feeling just as betrayed as Michael.

Not bothering to get dressed—because she seriously considered retreating back to bed if things didn't go well—Dani padded to the main house in the tank and boxers she'd slept in. She shuddered at the cool October air as the aroma of something sinful and delicious drew her to the kitchen.

Giving the swinging door a shove, Dani stuck her head inside. Mrs. Wilson was pulling a tray of chocolate chip cookies from the industrial oven.

A big lump formed in Dani's throat. Mrs. Wilson was baking them for her. Emma was gone, and her mom never ate cookies.

Mrs. Wilson turned and raised a brow. "I figured that'd lure you out of your cave."

When Dani only nodded, Mrs. Wilson slammed her hands on her ample hips. "Oh, wipe that sheepish look off your face. What? Do you think I don't love you anymore because you have some weird dreams? Did you really think a person can live in the same house with you two for twenty-five years and not figure it out?" She held her arms out wide in invitation.

Dani crossed the room, letting herself be wrapped into Mrs. Wilson's warm embrace. "You knew?"

"I overheard you explain to Sara how it all worked many years ago. That's when I fully understood. You were about nine then."

"You could've sold your story to the tabloids and been a million-aire." Dani snuggled closer, thankful not *everyone* she loved was angry with her.

A deep chuckle rumbled from Mrs. Wilson's chest. "Yeah, and that would have made me a lonely old woman with nothing to do but count her money. I'd rather be a part of this family and feel loved."

"You are." Dani gave her one last squeeze. "I wish Michael could be as understanding as you."

Mrs. Wilson turned and filled an oversize mug with coffee. "Give him time, honey. It was quite the shock when I figured it out. But it might not hurt to bust out some of those gourmet cooking skills you've been keeping to yourself. You know what they say. The way to a man's heart is through his stomach. My Arthur would've agreed."

She accepted a warm cookie and the mug Mrs. Wilson held out. "Arthur was lucky to have you. I'm not sure I could ever be as good a wife as you were. Thanks for the cookies." Dani took a bite of the warm, gooey treat. The decadent flavors filling her mouth almost made her smile.

"You can be any kind of wife you set out to be. You just have to decide what that is, young lady." She crossed her arms and narrowed her eyes. "The cookie was for you, but the coffee is for your mom. Take it up to her bedroom and, while you're at it, make up with her."

Dani started to refuse, but the steely gleam in Mrs. Wilson's eyes had her mouth snapping shut. With a deep breath for courage, she turned and made her way to the stairs. When she glanced up, it seemed like miles to the top.

As she walked toward her mother's bedroom, the aroma of coffee in one of her mom's favorite mugs made her feel like a kid again. On those Saturday mornings, when her mom was in town, she and Sara awoke as early as they could. They'd stop by the kitchen and get mugs of coffee—half-filled so they wouldn't spill—and tried to catch their mom sleeping. They never did. She was always up, reading scripts or talking on the phone. She'd see them in the doorway, push her half glasses atop her head, then throw the covers back in invitation.

They'd race across the room, slap the mugs down, then dive into the huge, comfy bed, where they'd snuggle with their mom while deciding what to do for the day. It was one of her favorite memories. Mostly because her mom was gone more than half of Dani's childhood, off shooting movies.

Dani reached her mom's bedroom door and quietly knocked. Maybe she'd get lucky and her mom would still be asleep. For once.

Her mother's quiet "Come in" made Dani cringe.

She slowly opened the door to what she used to call the fairytale room. The bedroom took up half of an entire floor. The walls were covered in soft fabrics, the carpet deep, the furniture gleaming dark antiques, and the four-poster looked like one you'd find Sleeping Beauty in.

Her mom was propped up against the headboard reading a script. She looked like a queen, dressed in lace and surrounded by silk. Even without makeup she was beautiful.

Without glancing from the papers in her hand, her mother threw the covers back, just as she'd done all those years ago. Dani's dread eased a bit before she laid the coffee down on the nightstand, then she slowly slid between the warm, silky sheets beside her mom. When her mother's arm slid around her shoulder and pulled her closer, Dani nearly sighed. "So, you're not angry with me anymore?"

Her mom tossed the script she was reading aside; then her glasses landed on top of it. "No. I'm not angry with you, Dani. Not anymore anyway." She waved a hand toward a pile of scripts. "I must be getting old. The only scripts I get these days want me to play someone's mother or colorful aunt. But the one I was just reading is a first. They want me to play a *grandmother*. The only way I'm playing someone's grandmother would be to my own grandchildren. You and Sara could help me out there, by the way."

Dani didn't think it wise to comment on the kid remark. She was already walking a thin line and didn't need another argument about why she wasn't having any of her own. Instead, she let out a low hum.

"I'd just like you to consider it, that's all."

"Um hum."

"Oh, never mind. God, you're as stubborn as your father." Her mom chuckled and laid a kiss on the top of her head. "Something just occurred to me. It probably hasn't been fair to ask you to keep my secret all these years. Maybe it'd be best to make a statement and let the chips fall where they may. Let them all believe I'm a criminal who dabbles in the occult. Who cares if I don't work again? I've got more money than I can ever spend. I suppose I could take up a hobby or something."

"A hobby?" Dani snorted in disbelief. "You'd miss all the attention, and it'd make you cranky. Then you'd be even more difficult to live with."

"You're a little brat and always have been." She gave Dani's rear end a sharp smack. "Speaking of cute little brats, where's Emma?"

Dani's throat tightened. "Julia picked her up last night." She blinked back her unexpected tears. "Is Em going to be okay?" Her mom had dreams much further in the future than Dani usually had.

"Yes. And I'm going to help her break into show business. That's assuming I'm not blacklisted. Speaking of which, have you heard from Michael?"

"No. I'm going to e-mail him Ron's account numbers after Julia sends them to me this morning. Maybe he'll have calmed down by then."

"He's upset and hurting. And so are you. I'm sorry for that, sweetheart." Her mother was quiet for a moment before she said, "I know this feels like the end of the world, but things tend to work out the way they're supposed to."

"Yeah. Maybe he'll be so happy to have Ron's account numbers to help his mom he'll give me another chance to explain."

"When you give him the account information, include a message from me, will you? Tell Michael to do what his conscience allows. I don't want to put any additional pressure on him."

Dani whipped her head toward her mom. "Do you really mean that? Or is that a trick to make him feel guilty?"

"No"—her mom slowly shook her head—"it's not a trick. Even when Michael was a boy he couldn't tell a lie. It's just the way he's put together. He's a lawyer because he truly believes in right and wrong. If he decides to give the press a statement, he'll suffer for it if I ask him to cover for me, and I don't want to put him in that position. I love him too much."

That was all true about Michael. It was why it hadn't been easy to keep her secret or lie to him when he'd asked if she had any secrets. She should have told him the truth when he'd asked. She'd made the biggest mistake of her life by lying to him. But had her mom thought through the consequences if Michael talked?

"Seriously, Mom? You'd want him to tell the whole truth? Even if it means risking your career?"

What career?" Her mom huffed out a breath. "I'd rather retire than play someone's *damn grandmother*." She added a dramatic shudder.

Dani smiled for the first time all day. "I think you'd be a great grandmother. Gotta go. Love you, Mom."

"I love you, too, even if you do have loose lips. There's a surprise waiting for you in the guesthouse. You're welcome, by the way."

Dani chuckled. "Thank you. I think."

She hurried back to the guesthouse, feeling slightly better, thankful her mom hadn't disowned her. When she opened the door, she was greeted with a loud screech, then a set of arms flew around her neck.

Her sister, Sara.

"Hey, you. What are you doing here?"

Sara, a pint-size copy of Dani, even though she was fully grown at twenty-five, rolled her eyes dramatically. "Mom's circling the wagons until this blows over. I was *commanded* to come home. I heard you really screwed up this time."

Leave it to Sara to get right to the point. "Yep. I probably set a new record."

"Oh, whatever. Mom always fixes it." Sara paused to read something on the cell phone in her hand, then her head popped up. "Since we're not allowed to leave the prison tonight, want to get shitfaced and complain about men?"

"Sure. Why not?"

Sara dropped onto the couch, her fingers moving with lightning-fast speed over the keys on her cell phone, sending a text. "Good, because I heard grandma's coming to town, too. She's always a good time, right?"

Even their grandmother had been summoned to the compound? Man, her mom must be worried.

Michael stared at his computer screen, debating. Should he open Dani's e-mail or delete it? She'd referenced Ron in the subject line, but surely that wasn't the only thing the message would contain.

Slowly, like the needle of a compass that couldn't help but point north, his hand moved to the mouse pad. He tapped the button to open the message, and Ron's account numbers instantly appeared at the top. That meant Julia must've finally come back.

It also meant Dani would be missing Emma.

But that wasn't his concern anymore.

He turned his attention back to the screen. She'd kept the message short.

> I hope this helps. Let me know if I can do any-
> thing else. Love, D.

Love? She sure had a twisted way of showing her love—lying to someone for years.

But it'd been nice of her to get the numbers from Julia. His mom would appreciate it. Dani had always loved his mom, and vice versa.

He'd wanted to get his mother's views on Dani's behavior, but not until he did the press conference. He'd decided in the middle of the night that he'd do it. To make everything just go away. He wouldn't share Dani's secret with his mother if he wasn't willing to tell the world. His gut burned with dread as he thought of it.

He'd considered just saying "No comment," but the press wouldn't give up that easily. Annalisa was always big news, and because her people were so good at spin, there was usually so little of it, and that just made it that more appealing to the pit-bull reporters clawing and scratching over each other's backs for the biggest celebrity story of the year.

He scrolled down to the end of the e-mail and found a postscript.

> BTW, my mom said do whatever your conscience tells you.

He closed his eyes and leaned back in his chair. She was making it easier on him to tell the press the truth. Dammit.

He reached for his phone. The sooner he got the news conference over, the better. Then he could wipe his hands clean of Dani and restore some blessed peace in his life.

After arranging to meet his friend at the television station, and trying to use the data Julia had sent via Dani, he sent a text message to Julia. I just tried the passwords. Ron must've changed them. We didn't find any financial info on Ron's computers at work or home. Ideas?

After a few moments, his phone chimed. His apartment?

Ron had an apartment? Actually, that made sense. When he was naming off all the women he'd seen, he'd have to have somewhere to take them. Address? Do you have a key?

He drummed his fingers on the desk, waiting for her response.

1519 Henderson. # 211 May still have key. I'll get back to you.

Good. It looked like they might just beat Ron at his own game, after all. Now he had to decide what he was going to say to the press.

It would've been easier if Annalisa had called him up and ranted and raved like she usually did if she was unhappy. Instead she'd treated him like she always had—like a son. How was he going to fix things and still be true to his word?

Chapter Sixteen

Dani and Sara sat on the couch in the guesthouse, chocolate sundaes in their hands, waiting for the six o'clock news. The station had sent out a teaser saying Michael was making a statement, and they had the exclusive story.

When Dani glanced down at her treat, her stomach roiled, so she set it on the coffee table without taking a bite. What was Michael going to do? It had been so stupid to tell him her secret in a public hospital, but the timing had seemed so right. She'd never make a mistake like that one again. And she'd never lie to him again. If he'd ever forgive her.

Now her mother's happiness lay in Michael's hands. And if Annalisa was unhappy, then *everyone* was going to be unhappy.

The front door opened, and her mom and grandmother breezed in. Her mother raised a brow. "Ice cream this close to dinner, ladies?"

"Dani said I could choose what we were having, so this *is* dinner. Want one?" Sara licked gooey chocolate from her spoon.

Eva chuckled and sat on the arm of the couch. "You bet."

Her mother slipped between Dani and Sara and let out a long sigh. "What the hell? This is probably the end of my career anyway. Make mine a double, honey."

"Woo-hoo! Mom's gonna eat carbs. I should video this." Sara raced to the kitchen.

Dani slid her sundae toward her grandmother. "You can have mine. I can't eat."

Eva's eyes lit up. "Well, I for one have an iron constitution, so I'll be happy to take it off your hands. Besides, I have confidence in that boy. He'll do right by you."

Her grandmother hadn't seen the way Michael had looked at her in the hospital or she'd never have been so sure.

When Michael's image appeared, Dani's heart broke a little more. He was so handsome, even with the big, ugly bruise over his right brow. But his green eyes were hooded and solemn, which probably wasn't a good sign.

Sara jogged into the living room and handed their mom a sundae just as Michael was introduced. "God, he's so frickin' hot. Why do you get all the best-looking ones, Dani?"

Dani shushed her, just as the anchorman asked Michael, "So, Mr. Reilly. Nurse Wright claims to have overheard a conversation between you and Ms. Botelli that indicated that she and her mother might have committed a crime on behalf of the mayor and that they have some sort of tie to the occult, or fortune-telling. Is that true?"

Dani held her breath, waiting for the ax to fall.

Michael cleared his throat and shifted in his seat. "Nurse Wright overheard a man high on painkillers having an argument with his girl-friend. It was a personal matter between Dani and myself that I'm not willing to discuss except to say that it was about a breach of trust. I'm sure Ms. Wright believes she's telling the truth, but she misinterpreted the meaning of our conversation."

The anchor frowned. "Mr. Reilly, let me ask you directly. Are Annalisa and Dani criminals?"

"Criminals?" Michael laughed and held up his hands. "Hey, I'm a lawyer and know the consequences of slanderous name-calling. I'd never call them that."

"Ms. Wright claims you both used the words *crime* and *special powers* multiple times in the portion of the conversation she overheard."

Michael laughed again, looking so confident that Dani grinned right along with him.

"John," he said and leaned closer to the anchor as if sharing a juicy secret. "I can assure you that I don't have any psychic powers, although I find most women expect men to have some of that. We're supposed to know what they're feeling and thinking all the time, and when we don't have a clue, they go ballistic."

The anchor nodded in agreement. "But what about the committing-a-crime part?"

"Dani and I were having a communication issue, so while I don't recall the exact context of our conversation, partly because of the pain pills, I do recall us talking about a crime. The whole conversation is still a bit fuzzy. I guess it's possible we were talking about her mother and a part in a movie?"

The anchor looked downright mad at losing out on the biggest scoop of his career. "If this is all as you say, then why haven't Dani or Annalisa made any attempt to clear the matter up?"

"I've read accounts that Annalisa is out of the country. I'm sure when she gets wind of the situation she'll have herself a good laugh. Besides, don't aging celebrities like Annalisa think any publicity is good publicity?"

"Ouch!" Annalisa slapped her sundae on the table. "I'm going to box his ears for that one—right after I give him a big kiss."

The anchor asked, "But what about Dani Botelli? Why hasn't she stepped up to put a stop to all the rumors about her? A statement through the publicist, at least, denying it."

Michael grew sullen. "I ended our relationship yesterday. I'm sure she's angry and upset with me—and the situation—not worried about some silly rumors."

That wiped the grin off Dani's face. He'd made it sound so permanent.

When the anchor opened his mouth, Michael raised a hand and cut him off. "That's all I'm going to say on the matter, and I'd like to ask the media to leave the Botellis and myself alone now. Thank you." Michael tugged off his microphone and stood, ending the interview.

Dani squeezed her eyes shut to stop the tears that threatened. Michael's statement should put an end to the rumors. The press had only an unsubstantiated statement from a nurse that had grown legs because it was a slow news day.

She was grateful for the way he'd handled it, but she wished she hadn't seen the anger and hurt in his eyes that only someone who knew him as well as she did could see. It didn't bode well for a future relationship with him. She'd always feared he'd be unable to accept her, let alone love her, if he ever found out the whole truth about her.

Annalisa sighed. "Well, he didn't lie exactly, but he didn't tell the whole truth, either. I'm glad he's one of my lawyers. He's damn good." Annalisa gave Dani a quick hug before she rose. "I've got to call my agent. Suddenly playing a colorful aunt has some appeal."

Sara jumped up and ran for her cell phone. "Awesome. This means I have a get-out-of-jail-free pass for tonight. Dani, let's do girls' night tomorrow. I've got a date. Mom and Grandma, are you guys in?"

"Sure," they said in unison. Her mom and grandmother exchanged a glance before her mom said to Eva, "I'm going be here to keep you in line, Mother, so get that unholy gleam out of your eyes. There are some things the girls need to learn about men all on their own."

Dani forced a smile and glanced at her watch. "Sara, you've been here for half a day and you already have a date?"

Her sister beamed a mischievous grin. "Remember geeky Rick Johnson who always had a crush on me?"

Dani conjured up a pimply kid with braces and glasses. "Yeah?"

"He grew out of the geeky part. He now owns his own software company, and he ditched the glasses. He's almost as cute as Michael."

She turned to their mother. "Hey, Mom. I saw a kick-ass Porsche in the garage. Can I borrow it? I'm supposed to meet Rick for drinks in an hour."

"You have to ask your sister. The Porsche belongs to her. But what happened to the days when young men picked young women up at their front door?"

Sara rolled her eyes. "What? Are you kidding? What guy wants to come here and have his mind read by some crime-committing aging celebrity fortune-teller?" Sara grinned and kissed Annalisa's cheek before their mother could reply.

Eva snorted out a laugh, and Annalisa turned on her. "They both get their bad attitudes from you. Now, if you'll all excuse me, I have to call my plastic surgeon, too. Sara has given me a complex." She marched out the door, and Sara turned her big puppy dog eyes on Dani. "So, can I use the car?"

"The car doesn't belong—oh, whatever. Yes, you can borrow it."

"Thanks, and don't wait up. Night, Grandma." Sara streaked out the door.

Her grandmother wrapped her arm around Dani's shoulder and remained silent while Dani sent a text message to Michael to thank him for the press conference.

After Dani laid the phone on the coffee table, Grandma said, "I wish I could tell you things between you and Michael will get better honey, but I can't."

Dani blinked back her tears. "Yeah. But you and mom must've known about Michael. Both of you practically shoved me into bed with him so I could see the scar."

"We only saw snippets of things we knew must've been slated to happen soon. But we were hoping." Her grandmother sighed. "I think it's supposed to be this way, sweetheart. I mean, there has to be a limit to how far in the future we can see. Who'd want to know on their wedding day that they'd be getting a divorce in a few years? Like you and Jake? Or worse, who'd want to know the day they were supposed to die? I think God made it all work this way on purpose, for those like us."

Dani glanced at the phone on the table, wishing for a response from Michael. "Probably."

But it sucked sometimes.

Her grandmother was quiet for a moment, seemingly deep in thought. "Well, I guess it's just you and me tonight, kiddo. Want to watch a movie with your old grandmother?"

"Yep. But we're not watching anything romantic and sappy. It'll just depress me more. I need some action. Maybe a classic like *Die Hard*, *Indiana Jones*, or *Rambo*?"

"Definitely *Rambo*. It reminds me of Jerry. Where is that hot bodyguard of yours anyway?"

Dani shook her head and flipped through her DVDs. "He's taken, hotty69. You'll have to settle for the movie."

Michael turned the six o'clock news off and walked to the kitchen, thankful the whole ordeal was finally behind him. Before he made it to the freezer to pick out his dinner selection for the evening, his phone chirped, indicating a text message. Maybe it'd be Julia, telling him she found the key to Ron's apartment.

Ron always played golf on Friday mornings, so Michael hoped they could go to the apartment, find the computer and passwords he used, and transfer the funds back to the new account his mom had just opened. And even more, he hoped he'd be around to see Ron's face when he figured it all out.

He opened the message, but it wasn't from Julia. It was from Dani, and it simply said, Thanks.

Before he could figure out how he felt about that, his phone chirped again. The new message was from Jake. I guess you're not a prick. Just narrow-minded.

He smiled. That was as close to an apology as he'd get from Jake.

Michael turned his attention to the freezer and chose a garlic chicken and pasta dinner. After programming the time into the microwave, he stared at his phone, pondering if he should reply to Dani's message.

Probably not.

The microwave beeped, pulling him out of his trance, and he quickly yanked his meal out, tossing it onto the counter before it could burn his fingers. He gingerly pulled the plastic off, careful to avoid the hot steam, and then poured himself a glass of milk. With nothing to do until his meal cooled off, he picked up his phone and replied to Dani's message. You're welcome. Take care.

Then he tossed his phone aside and stared at his uninviting meal.

He lifted his fork and forced himself to take a bite. The food tasted like crap, but he needed to eat something, so it'd have to do. Between the hospital food and his freezer, he hadn't had a decent meal all week. It wasn't hard to ignore the meal and let his mind wander back to Dani.

She'd told him it had hurt her to be around him when they were in their teens. It made sense. It'd be miserable to know someone you loved was going to marry someone else before it happened.

Shaking his head, he shoved another bite into his mouth, trying to block the sound of Dani's low, smoky voice telling him that she loved him. She'd loved him for over twenty years. But was it true? Could he trust her not to leave him again?

Once a liar, always a liar?

He was so deep in thought that when his phone chirped again, he jumped. This time it was Julia.

Found key. When do u want to go?

Michael smiled in anticipation. He felt like kicking someone's ass, and it might as well be Ron's. 9:00 a.m. tomorrow?

He finished off his dinner, looking forward to Julia's reply. When the phone sounded, he snatched it up.

Miss u.

The sender's name showed "Dani"—not that he hadn't figured that out already—and his stomach had sudden thoughts about rejecting his lousy dinner.

Nope, he wasn't going to do it. He'd leave things as they were and just ignore her. Ending things for good was best.

Another text came in, this time from Julia. Gr8, see u then.

After dinner, Michael tried to watch a movie, but Dani's message kept him from enjoying it. He spent the whole time convincing himself that it was right to make a clean break. And in time he'd forget about her and move on. Just as he'd done before.

He finally switched to a book on his e-reader, but then ended up tossing it aside. After a glance at his watch, he was thankful it was nearly nine thirty, and he could justify going to bed since he was supposed to be recovering.

After flopping from side to side in his tangled sheets for two hours, he stomped to his darkened kitchen and yanked his phone from the charger cord. When he pressed the keys, the light created a halo of blue around his hand, illuminating the keyboard as he replied to Dani's message.

It was a mistake, but his fingers typed the two lines his heart told him to write.

When he was done, he slid under the covers, instantly falling asleep.

≈

Dani was awoken by the ringing of her cell phone. She reached out to find it, hoping it'd be Michael, disappointed when it wasn't. "Hi, Julia."

"Hey, Dani. I saw that crap about you guys on the news last night. God, the press will report anything no matter how ridiculous it is, just to get ratings. But I'm sorry about you and Michael. I thought when Emma said, 'Dani cry,' she meant when we left, but she was talking about before that, wasn't she?"

Dani cleared the lump from her throat. Emma saw more that she let on, evidently. "Yeah. Michael and I had a misunderstanding."

"Well, it just so happens I'm supposed to meet Michael at nine at the apartment Ron meets all of his women. I'm going to let Michael in so he can check out Ron's computer and hopefully transfer the money back. Do you want to do it instead? Would it give you guys a chance to clear things up?"

She could have kissed Julia. "Thanks. That'd be great. Give me the address, and I'll meet you at eight forty-five."

Dani scribbled the address down, then hung up. As she was about to lay her phone down, she noticed a text message waiting. It was from Michael.

Her heart lurched before she pressed the button to summon it on the screen. Can't deal with this now. Then she read the next line. Maybe I'll call you in a few weeks and we'll talk.

Maybe? In a few weeks? That wasn't especially encouraging, but at least he hadn't ignored her completely. She was going to have to take the initiative and make the most of her time with him at Ron's apartment.

Something Mrs. Wilson said the day before had her racing to her mother's kitchen. One thing Dani could make better than anyone else, even Mrs. Wilson, was stuffed cinnamon rolls, and she had just enough time to make a batch. Hopefully, they'd still be warm when she met Michael.

They were his favorite, and while it might not do any good, she was desperate and willing to try anything.

As she grabbed the items from the pantry, thankful her secret ingredient was there, too, she mentally chose an outfit that would make any man with a pulse sit up and beg. If that didn't work, one thing was for certain: Michael always enjoyed a good fight, and she was going to give him one.

～

Michael's stomach sank when Dani strode across the parking lot at Ron's apartment with an overly bright smile, a silky shirt that showed an intriguing amount of cleavage, and a suspicious bag in her hand. "What are you doing here?"

Dani thrust the bag toward him. "It seems Julia has a matchmaker's heart. She wants us to make up."

He glanced at the bag but knew by the sweet aroma what was in it before he opened it. Memories of munching on the delectable treats he used to beg Dani to make for him rushed back and hit him in the gut. His hungry gut. Tearing the bag open, he took a huge bite of one of the decadent sweet rolls and moaned. "God, I used to love these."

"You used to love *me*, too," Dani murmured.

He studied her as he finished off the first roll, then plunged his hand into the bag for another. He wasn't going to be bought by a bag of rolls, no matter how damn good they were. And he wasn't going to be manipulated by two scheming women. "I appreciate the rolls, Dani, but do you have the key? I'm in a hurry."

Instead of handing it over, she ignored him and led the way to the stairs.

Resigned to the fact that she wasn't leaving, he followed her. He'd just ignore the sinful scent Dani's perfume left in her wake. And why the hell did she have to wear a tight skirt that made her ass look so tempting? If she was trying to kick his butt, she was doing a damn good job of it.

She obviously wanted to play games, and that was fine with him. He could give as good as he got. As she slid the key into the lock, he leaned close and whispered, "You look nice. Got a *hot* date later?"

Dani scowled at him before she violently kicked the door open. "No. Work." She lifted her chin in that snotty way of hers that he adored, then marched inside.

Score a point for him. "You really should've rung the doorbell. How did you know Ron wasn't here?"

She turned and crossed her arms under her impressive cleavage. "I'm a *freak*, remember?"

He'd been messing with her for showing up uninvited with a bribe; he hadn't meant to hurt her. "I don't think you're a freak, Dani. Let's get on with this."

Dani shook her head. "I called his secretary and found out he was playing golf."

"Yeah. He usually does on Fridays." They crossed through the living room, decorated in dark leathers and glass, toward the hallway. Dani followed close behind as he turned into a bedroom. It was the master, and it held an enormous bed with a mirrored ceiling above it. Across the room hung a huge flat screen television with a video camera perched along its side, presumably to make his own movies. Michael turned and met Dani's gaze.

She slowly shook her head. "He's a frickin' perv."

"Yep." Repulsed, especially on his mom's behalf, Michael turned and crossed the hall to the second bedroom. Dani didn't follow. The sounds of drawers opening and closing in the master drifted his way.

The second bedroom held file cabinets and a desk with a computer on it. He slid into the leather chair, hit the "Power" button on the computer, then called out, "Would you stop snooping and get in here? I might need help with these passwords."

After a few minutes, Dani appeared in the doorway. "Ron could open his own sex shop. I'm going to need my hand sanitizer after we leave. It's disgusting."

"Quit touching things and you'll be fine. We don't want to leave fingerprints and get busted for breaking and entering." With that thought, he abruptly raised his hands from the keyboard and rubbed the back of his stiff neck, contemplating. Maybe he shouldn't be doing this. Was it wrong to protect his mother from a man who played dirty?

Dani moved behind him, nudged his hand aside, and rubbed at the tension in his shoulders and neck. "We aren't doing anything wrong. Your mother asked you to help her move the money, not steal it. You're just putting it in an account so the lawyers can divvy it up fairly. Ron was the one who did your mother wrong by hiding it."

Trying his best to ignore her soothing touch, he turned and met her gaze. "Did touching me just now let you read my thoughts?"

"No." She rolled her eyes. "It was written all over your face. Unfortunately, I know you too well, Michael."

Dani whispered soft curses under her breath at him for jumping to conclusions about her as she continued kneading his sore shoulders. He nearly wept with joy when his muscles stopped burning and finally loosened. He hadn't realized how tense he was. But he had to fight a grin as she kept up the quiet muttering. It wasn't easy to make her *that* mad.

She gave his shoulders one last squeeze. "There, is that better?"

He rolled his head back and forth. His shoulders and neck were as pliant as putty. "Yeah, thanks."

"Good." She gave him a light smack upside the back of his head. "That was for the 'got a hot date' comment." Then she began digging through desk drawers.

"Hey, I'm recovering from a serious head injury here."

"Keep it up and I'll give you a more serious head injury, buddy."

He chuckled as he turned his attention to his phone and pulled up Ron's account numbers. As he searched the computer for financial sites, he clicked on the Internet connection and then tapped the "Down" arrow on the "Search" bar. A list of sites Ron had recently visited appeared.

He blew out a low whistle. "You think HotBabes.com is where I should start looking? Or perhaps WetHotandWild.com?"

Dani shook her head as she searched through the hanging files in the credenza behind the desk. "I guess his home movies aren't enough. Let's just hope he hasn't spent all of your mom's money on porn sites."

Michael slipped his hand inside the bag and grabbed another cinnamon roll as he scrolled through the long list of smut. Finally, he found a financial website that Julia had sent information about.

He finished off the roll and waited as a screen for an overseas banking institution loaded. Feeling full and content, he said, "Thanks for the rolls, Dani. And the shoulder thing. You could make a living as a chef or a masseuse if the Realtor thing doesn't work out."

"Or a gangster, right?"

He turned and stared into her eyes, hating the pain he'd put there. "I shouldn't have said that in the hospital. I was hurt and wanted to hurt you back. I apologize for that. But I was sincerely thanking you for the rolls, Dani."

She grunted, then slammed a file drawer shut. "You're welcome. Are you gonna share?"

"Sure, go ahead." He didn't miss the soft swell of breasts rising over black lace that appeared before him when her shirt gaped as she reached across the desk for the last roll.

She was definitely trying to kick his ass. And it was working.

As badly as he wanted to reach out and touch, he wouldn't. Instead, he turned his attention to the task at hand.

After he navigated to the home screen on the banking site, a screen appeared asking for an account number. He picked the one from Julia's list that matched the site and typed it in. Then he tabbed down to the next box and typed in the password. A loud beep announced the password was invalid.

"Damn. He changed it."

Dani leaned over his shoulder. "Try Studman10."

"That's sick."

"Just type it in."

He did, and the screen moved on to the next one.

Amazed, he turned and stared into her exotic eyes. "Did you do that with your power thing?"

"No." She held up a piece of paper. "I found a file marked 'Passwords.'"

He barked out a laugh before he snatched the paper from her hand. "You might've mentioned that fact earlier. Let's get this done and get out."

Michael transferred more than $500,000 from the first account. After he'd emptied it, a message appeared saying that a confirmation e-mail would be sent to the designated address. That meant Ron was going to figure out what had happened quickly.

He turned to Dani. "Ron's going to rupture an artery when he sees what we've done. While I finish up here, will you please call my mom and ask her to send an e-mail to Ron, explaining she hasn't spent the money but just moved it. And tell her to pack a bag. She needs to be out of the house when Ron gets home tonight. She can stay in my girls' room if she'd like."

While Dani called his mom, he finished emptying the other accounts. By the time he was done, he'd moved more than $5 million.

Dani tucked her phone into her purse. "Your mom just sent the e-mail, and she's packing as we speak. I invited her to my house for a girls' night tonight and told her she could stay with us or at your place. She'll let you know what her plans are when she decides."

"Girls' night? My mother doesn't—" The scrape of a key in the front door shot panic through him. "Shit. He's here." He quickly hit the "Power" button on the computer, snagged his things, then wrapped his arm around Dani's waist, pulling her along with him into the closet. He'd just barely pulled the door closed when Ron called out, "Make yourself at home, honey. I just need to check my e-mail. Hopefully, all's quiet at the office, and we'll have a little more time."

A sultry, young woman's voice said, "You're checking your e-mail? Now?"

Ron sounded distracted when he said, "It'll just take a—" He was cut off, and the desk chair groaned with what Michael could only guess was her added weight on Ron's lap.

He whispered to Dani, "Not again. Why do we always end up listening to other people having sex?"

Dani's warm breath tickled his ear as she moved closer. "That's what you get for being so mean to me. Text your mom and have her call him. That ought to break things up."

"Good idea. And I'm not being mean. We'll discuss it later." He grabbed his phone and furiously tapped in the message as the moans in the office got even louder. And more disgusting.

Dani hissed, "This is grossing me out."

"Let's just hope my mom gets the message. Soon."

He quoted football stats in his mind to block out the noise, praying his mother would hurry. He wasn't sure he could stand another minute without busting out of the closet and making a run for it.

When a phone rang, he and Dani glanced at each other in the dim light and grinned.

Ron said, "That's my wife's ringtone. I better take it."

"What? No. Call her back later."

Ron groaned. "I would, except she's busted me one too many times lately. I don't need any more complications. I'm supposed to be on the golf course, so I can't say I was in a meeting. I'll get rid of her."

"Fine. But hurry."

Ron said, "Hi, honey." There was a long pause, then the sound of tapping computer keys. "Why can't you just tell me what the e-mail says? Maeve—"

He let out a low curse. "She hung up on me. I'm supposed to read some e-mail." A few more keys tapped, and then he screamed, "What the hell? Oh my God. How the hell did she do this? Get off me." The sound of the girl's feet hitting the floor had Dani's hand whipping up to cover her mouth. Her shoulders shook with laughter beside him, and it was all Michael could do to contain his own.

"Hey! What was—" the girl complained, but Ron cut her off.

"Get out. I have to go to my office to deal with something. Now!"

"You're an asshole, Ron." The sound of the front door slamming sounded while Ron banged drawers open and shut. Finally, after a few minutes of muttered curses and plans to call his broker and accountant, the front door slammed again.

After five minutes of silence, Michael slid the door open and stepped out. He grabbed Dani's hand and pulled her along with him. "Let's go."

Dani laughed like a loon as he led her down the steps. When they were by her car, she finally managed to get herself under control. She said, "Ron's finally going to get what he deserves."

"Yeah." He studied his shoes for a moment, searching for the right words. Nothing profound popped into his mind, so he met her expectant gaze again. "Thanks, Dani."

He should do it now. Just end things so he could move on and find a sane woman. "I'll call you later. After I've had time to think."

So, he'd do it later. Or, even better, he'd do it on the phone, when he wasn't staring into those bewitching eyes. Her spell had already started casting wishes and wants into his mind again. But he wasn't going to cave.

Before he could step back, she stood on her tiptoes and laid her mouth on his.

The power and need in their kiss pulled him under fast and swift. His heart ached for her, and he had no choice but to drown in the sweet pain. If only for a few more moments.

How could he live the rest of his life knowing what this was like? To be pulled to someone like the tide to a rocky shore? Because rocky was what life with Dani would always be. It'd never be smooth sailing.

Did he want smooth sailing? Or did he want to feel the way that only Dani had ever made him feel? Content and . . . no, he needed to end the kiss.

He didn't have to, though, because Dani slowly lifted her lips from his. She stepped back and cocked a brow. "Think about *that*, Michael." Then she turned and pressed her car's remote.

She'd almost made him cave with that move, but he needed to be stronger than that. "Dani?"

"What?" Her eyes shone bright with unshed tears when she met his gaze.

"Come here." Dani wasn't the type to use her impressive cleavage to influence men and would never walk into her office looking like that on purpose. She'd made an exception for him.

Dani walked back to him, her chin tilted high as she met his steady stare.

He lifted his hands, letting just the back of his fingers gently brush against the deep V of her breasts before he slowly fastened two of the open buttons on her soft blouse. "This shirt was a nice move to show me what I'm missing, but it's not professional for the office. Have a pleasant day at work."

Her mouth gaped before a low growl emitted from deep within her. Defiantly, she yanked opened the top button, as he knew she would—that's why he'd buttoned two—and then she marched to her car. "Really? Professional advice after you just kissed me like that? Why

I love you is beyond me, Michael Reilly. You're such a—" Her curse was cut off by the slamming of her car door.

He sent her a wave as she backed out of her parking space, nearly taking his toes with her. She started toward the exit but suddenly slammed on her brakes and rolled her window down.

When she met his gaze with narrowed eyes, his stomach clenched with anticipation of her next move. It'd no doubt be a scathing tongue-lashing. He probably deserved it for kissing her back like that, encouraging her. But it couldn't be helped whenever he kissed Dani.

Instead, she shot him the finger and then tore out of the parking lot.

She'd gotten in the last word after all.

He smiled.

Did he want the drama that came along with Dani? The fun, the excitement, the way he felt whole when he was with her? Even though she came with a price, he'd felt alive again after many years of just going through the paces of life, because of her.

God, what was he going to do about Dani?

"He buttoned up your blouse?" Zoe rolled on the floor with laughter, nearly knocking over her drink. "Did he at least cop a feel while he was at it?"

Girls' night was in full bloom in Dani's living room, and they'd all had enough to drink to float a boat. "It's not funny. And of course he copped a feel. He's a guy." Dani turned to her mother for support. "He was being such a jerk."

Her mom shook her head. "I saw what you were wearing when you came home from work today. You weren't playing fair yourself, honey."

Dani shrugged a shoulder draped in a football jersey that just happened to be a replica of the one Michael had worn when he was on the Cowboys. "That's beside the point."

Sara rolled over and laid her head on Dani's shoulder. "I'm on your side, Dan. Even if they aren't."

"Thanks, kiddo." When Sara yawned and closed her eyes, Dani feared her sister was out for the night. She'd probably just have to leave her on the floor where she lay.

Then her grandmother said, "The cinnamon rolls were a nice touch. But where you really screwed up was when you were alone with him in that closet."

"Mother." Annalisa let out a small warning growl.

Grandma ignored her. "Seriously, you should have jumped his bones and shown him what's what."

Zoe snorted out a laugh and crawled next to Dani and Sara on the floor. "It really would have been perfect. You guys did it the first time in a laundry room, then a shower. Why not the closet?"

Dani sent Zoe the evil eye. "Remind me not to tell you this stuff anymore. You have a big mouth."

Sara's eye's fluttered open. "I've never done it in a laundry room. I'm gonna have to try that." Then her lids slammed shut again. Just when they all thought she was asleep, she said, "How about you, Grandma? Ever done it in a laundry room?"

"They didn't have laundry rooms when I was young enough for that nonsense. We did it in the basement. That's where we used to do laundry."

Zoe chuckled and took another hit from her glass. "How about you, Annalisa? Has a big, famous star like you ever done it on the washing machine during the spin cycle? That's the best way, you know. It adds a little extra punch."

Dani whipped her head toward Zoe, making herself dizzy. "What? You've never told me about that one. You've held out on me, and as your punishment, I'm gonna call your hubby right now and get the details." Not that she'd actually do it; she was just teasing her.

Zoe's husband always cringed whenever anyone talked about sex. He managed to be a macho hunk and incredibly sweet at the same time. Kind of like Michael, now that she thought of it.

To keep her threat real, she searched for her phone on the coffee table, digging around all the leftover snacks they'd grazed on. Suddenly she found herself pinned under Zoe's long body. "Don't you dare tell Will I told. He'll kill me." She grabbed Dani's phone and put it in her back pocket before she rolled off her. "It was that last daiquiri's fault I let that slip. So how about it, Annalisa? Ever done the washing machine boogie?"

Her mom's lips tilted into an evil grin. "Large appliances aren't nearly as effective as smaller ones in that department, ladies."

Zoe and Eva laughed hysterically while Dani groaned. "God, Mom. Have another drink, why don't you? Then you can really loosen up."

Sara suddenly sat up and joined the living again. "Hey, speaking of Mom, could I have a Porsche like Dani's, please?"

"No. Your sister earned hers. You haven't."

"Earned it? What does that mean?" Sara blinked in confusion.

Her mom leaned down and kissed Sara on the top of the head. "You need to get a job and become a responsible member of society, like your sister. Then you'll have earned a Porsche." Annalisa sent Dani a wink.

Her mom's comment, along with all the alcohol she'd consumed, made Dani feel warm and gooey inside. Maybe she'd finally earned a little of her mother's respect.

Sara frowned. "When did this new rule happen?"

"Yesterday, when I thought I was never going to work again. I think I just grew up, too." Her mom let out a long sigh, then drained her glass.

Before Sara could argue, a phone rang. Confusion creased Zoe's brow for a moment before she realized she still had Dani's phone in her back pocket. When she tugged it out and read the display, she grinned. "Well, speak of the devil. It's Michael."

Dani leaped for the phone, but Zoe held it high over her head. "Maybe I should tell him what I think about the way he's treating my best buddy?" Zoe sent her a mischievous grin. "You'll thank me for this later." She punched a button and said, "Hey, bonehead, how's it going?"

"Dani?" Zoe had hit the "Speaker" button so they all could hear.

She reached for the phone again, but Zoe had arms as long as a six-foot-three basketball player's, so Dani called out, "No, it's my inebriated ex–best friend."

Michael didn't miss a beat. "Oh, hey, Zoe. Is my mom there?"

Only because Zoe was so wasted and had let her guard down was Dani able to snatch the phone back. But she was too drunk to figure out how to turn the speaker off. "No, she called earlier and said she'd made other plans. Why?"

"I can't find her. I've called her cell, but it goes directly to voice mail. When she hadn't called to let me know what her plans were, I went to her house, but no one is home. I'm worried about her, Dani. What if Ron's done something rash?"

That sobered her up a bit. "Is her car there?"

"No. Both of their cars are gone, and Ron wasn't at the office when I drove by a while ago. Can you remember exactly what she said when she called earlier?"

Dani closed her eyes, begging her foggy, drunk mind to focus. "Um, just that she wasn't in the mood for fun, maybe next time, and that she was going away for a few days. She didn't tell me where."

He was quiet for a few beats. "Why wouldn't she have called me? I know she's distracted and upset about the divorce, but it doesn't make sense."

Annalisa called out, "Maybe we can help. We'll be right over, Michael."

"Dani, are any of you sober enough to drive?"

"No." They could barely walk, much less drive. "But my mom's an *aging* celebrity who loves any attention she can get, so she has a big, shiny chauffeur-driven car."

Michael groaned. "I was going to apologize for that. I just haven't gotten to it. Sorry, Annalisa."

Her mom was obviously way drunk because she just grinned stupidly before she slid off the couch. "I know you didn't mean it, honey. Don't worry, we'll be right there."

Chapter Seventeen

Michael paced back and forth in his mother's driveway as he waited for Dani. Finally, a long black limo pulled up, and three very drunk Botelli women stumbled out before their driver could open the door for them.

"Let me help you there, Eva." He grabbed Dani's grandmother's elbow before she landed on her ass. Then he turned to Annalisa. "Thanks for coming. I called the police, but they said without any signs of a struggle they couldn't do anything for forty-eight hours."

Dani weaved drunkenly to the front door. "That's because you're too stubborn to ask Jake for help."

He followed Dani, balancing Eva at his side. "I tried. But they said he was in the field and couldn't be reached."

Dani patted a few pockets, searching for something. When she spotted the phone in her hand, she laughed. "Oh, there it is."

She was totally shitfaced. That was all he needed.

Dani closed one eye to focus before she pecked at the keypad. Her phone was in speaker mode, and it rang a few times before Jake answered, "Hey, babe. What's up?"

Dani grimaced at the babe remark and stumbled out of earshot to talk to him.

Before Michael could follow her, Annalisa hooked her arm through his and, along with Eva, proceeded to walk him through all the rooms of the house, searching for clues. When they were in the kitchen, Annalisa closed her eyes. "The answer's in here."

Eva nodded and closed her eyes, too.

He didn't know what he was supposed to do, so he stood there holding them both up, feeling foolish.

Dani tripped through the door. "Jake's going to start the paperwork, and he's put an ADD—no, an APP? You know, one of those things on Maeve's and Ron's cars? We're supposed to call if we figure anything else out." Dani cocked her head. "What are you two doing?"

Annalisa opened an eye. "There's a vague signal here. Be quiet."

Dani rolled her eyes and began riffling through the paperwork on the little desk by the phone. She lifted the receiver. "Let's see who Maeve called last." Dani hit "Redial" and giggled. "Oh, it was me. That doesn't help."

"Quiet!" Eva and Annalisa both said in unison.

Dani lifted both hands in defense before she started snooping again. She picked up a pad of paper triumphantly. "It has something to do with this! I can practically feel the energy calling my name." Dani closed her eyes and winced before she opened them and stared at him. "I'm getting a purple dinosaur. Does that mean anything to you, Michael?"

He shook his head, totally baffled. "No."

Annalisa crossed the room and held the pad in her hands. She was quiet for a moment before she announced, "I'm getting pine trees and a stream."

Eva huffed out a breath and snatched up the pad. "Amateurs, both of you. Give it here." She did the same routine as the others, then a smile tilted her lips. "Michael, your mother is at their cabin in the woods. It has a red tin roof and a big wraparound porch, right?"

The vision thing was weird but useful. He'd forgotten about that place. His mom and Ron had owned it for less than a year, and he'd only been there once. "Yes, that's right. I think I can remember how to get there. It's about an hour and a half away. They never installed a phone, as far as I know, and there's no cell service. I'll go check it out."

Dani crossed her arms. "We'll all go in case you can't find it. If you can get us close enough, we'll be able to help you find her."

He didn't want to be trapped in a car with three drunken women, but Dani was right. He might need their help. "Okay, let's go. I'll drive."

"Just like a guy. Why do men always have to drive?" Dani muttered as she slipped in the seat beside him while Eva and Annalisa settled in the back.

"First of all, if any of you three drove right now, you'd get a DUI. Second, I don't want to attract the unwanted attention that big limo might."

She shrugged. "I guess that kinda makes sense." Then Dani crossed her arms and stared out the opposite window.

It was going to be a long, painful journey.

Michael wasn't worth talking to at the moment, and besides, Dani wasn't entirely sure she wasn't slurring her words. She did her best to ignore him as they entered the freeway heading west. After a few minutes, his voice broke into her buzzed brain. "What did you do with Zoe?"

Dani turned and sent him her best death stare. She was *not* making small talk with a man who had the gall to button up her blouse.

After a long, uncomfortable moment, her mom answered from the back seat. "She and Sara are passed out at Dani's house."

"Oh." His lips tilted into a slow grin before he whispered, "Nice shirt, *babe*."

Dani glanced down and grimaced. Her jacket was unzipped, displaying his jersey. She'd forgotten she'd had it on. He probably thought she'd been wearing it while she pined for him.

Which was true—and totally embarrassing. "Thanks. I found it at the bottom of the bargain bin. They were having a sale on it because the guy is a jerk and no one else wanted it."

He chuckled as he stared at the long road ahead.

Michael was so weird that way. He should retaliate. Instead, he seemed to enjoy her comeback as much as she loved to zing it at him. He didn't fight like anyone she'd ever known, and *that* was annoying, too.

She was still trying to gauge his mood when he whispered, e was wewird that way. he seemed o He"Can we please call a truce, Drunk Girl? At least until we find my mom?"

Drunk Girl?

Good one. Now he was fighting properly.

"No. What we need to do is settle this. I find it interesting that it's suddenly fine that we can help—when it suits *your* needs."

He glanced in the rearview mirror. "Why do you always insist on fighting in front of our mothers?"

"Don't mind us back here, go right ahead," her mom said before hiccupping.

Dani laid a hand on his arm. "Look, I understand this has all been a shock, but can't we just move on now?"

"You've lied to me for twenty years, Dani. That's not an easy thing to forgive."

"Fine." She threw her hands up in the air. "Yes, I lied to you, Michael. Don't you realize that beyond the fact that I was told not to tell anyone, I always knew—and not by using any special powers—that you would react this way? Don't you see? I didn't want to—" She cut herself off. She wasn't ready to tell him that part. It was the alcohol's fault that she'd almost let it slip.

His forehead creased. "What?"

"Nothing. Never mind. Maybe your truce idea is a good one." She crossed her arms and stared straight ahead. Things were getting serious, and as much as she hated to admit it, she *was* a drunk girl.

She needed to watch her step.

"Finish what you started, Dani."

Her mom called out from the rear, "I think what Dani—"

Grandma shushed her. "Stay out of this, honey."

Dani turned and stared at the two stooges in the back seat. Something was up, but neither was willing to let her in on it.

Suddenly Dani was tossed against her seat belt when Michael pulled off the highway.

He tilted her chin, forcing her to look him in the eye. "Focus, Dani. What were you going to say?"

"I forget."

"Tell me."

She stared into his eyes for a moment, debating. Should she tell him? It was her last defense, and she'd been saving it up. If it didn't work, she was afraid nothing would.

She cleared her throat and forced her mind to stay on track. She needed it to come out right.

"When you asked me in your office if I had any secrets, it killed me to lie to you. But I'm a coward. I was afraid if you found out, you'd leave me, and I can't imagine the rest of my life without you in it. I love you, Michael."

His shoulders slumped; then he shook his head and pulled back onto the freeway. When she attempted to say something, he lifted a hand to cut her off again. "Let's find my mother. We'll talk about the rest after. When you're sober."

Dani's eyelids, along with her heart, were too heavy. She couldn't think about things anymore, so she laid her head back, instantly falling sound asleep.

Later, the sound of Michael's voice woke her. "This is the town, but I can't remember which gas station we turn at. Let's keep going. Maybe I'll recognize it." Then he glanced at her, and a small grin tilted the corners of his sexy mouth. "Welcome back."

She had a sudden need to tell him the urgent thought floating in her mind. Threatening tears had her clearing her throat before she whispered, "In case I forgot earlier, I meant to tell you that I'm sorry I lied to you, Michael. I'll never do it again."

His jaw clenched before he turned and studied the road ahead, but he didn't respond. When they'd almost reached the end of the small town, another gas station appeared. Its logo had a cute purple dinosaur on it.

Michael murmured, "Well of course. Here's where we turn." Then he whispered, "You're damn good, Botelli."

It made her heart swell. Hope that they could get past the lies she'd told him made her smile.

Feeling a burden lift from her shoulders, like a phoenix rising from the fire, Dani turned and met her grandmother's amused gaze. "Amateur, my butt."

That drew smiles from the back seat as they made their way up a bumpy gravel lane.

Dani peered into the dense forest lit only by the moon and stars as they navigated the long winding road. Finally, they spotted the cabin, and it was just as her grandmother had described it. A few lights were on, and Maeve's car stood out front.

Michael killed the headlights and let the moon guide them near the front door. "You ladies stay here." He opened his door, then let it quietly close behind him.

Dani squinted into the darkness. What if Ron was there and had Maeve inside? What if he'd hurt her? What if Michael got hurt?

She was just about to open her door when a bank of bright lights illuminated the front porch. Maeve, smiling, waved them inside.

As they slid out of the car, Dani almost missed her mom's quiet whisper to her grandmother, "It's showtime."

After a much-needed bathroom break, they were all directed to the cozy living room and instructed to sit in front of a blazing fire. Dani drank deeply from the mug of coffee Michael's mom insisted she accept before she asked, "So how come you didn't let Michael know where you'd be, Maeve? He was worried sick. We all were."

She waved a hand impatiently. "I meant to leave a note on his door. I figured he'd see it when he got home. But in my rush to leave town before Ron got home, I forgot."

So that's why the notepad was so hot with information: she'd used that to write the note. But it still didn't make sense. Who'd leave a note in this day and age?

Then Dani recalled her mother and grandmother standing with their eyes closed in Maeve's kitchen. That had been strange, too. They usually had to hold something to read its energy.

She glanced up in time to see a smug look pass between Maeve and her mom, and it all became clear.

"Oh my God." She turned and faced Michael. "You need to know I had nothing to do with this." Then she leaned into her mom's personal space. "You guys cooked this whole thing up, didn't you? We're not sixteen, *Mother*."

Dani turned and met Michael's confused expression. "You've figured out by now that I'm not a charlatan, haven't you?"

He nodded. "Yeah, but I still don't understand. What's going on?"

"You should ask our mothers."

Michael crossed the room and stood in front of Maeve. "What is Dani so upset about?"

Maeve sighed and took Michael's hand, tugging him onto the couch beside her. "Annalisa and I thought you'd better understand the wonder of Dani's powers if you had a need for them yourself. We knew you'd be worried when I didn't call, and we planned this little escapade to show you just how pigheaded you're being about Dani."

"You knew?" His faced turned five shades of red before he launched himself off the couch. "And you didn't tell me? How long have you known?"

Maeve lifted her hands, then let them drop. "For years. Annalisa and I are good friends, and she needed someone to talk to about it, just as Dani needed Zoe. And as you can see, Dani just figured that out, which proves she can't dip into my mind. A little trust goes a long way, Michael." Maeve stood and drilled a finger into his chest. "Dani isn't a liar like Heather is. *Dani* had valid reasons for not sharing every part of her life with you." She poked him again, even harder. "I've watched you stew for days over this, and, frankly, I'm getting tired of it. You need to get over yourself and accept Dani for what she is. You love her!"

Dani was tempted to scream "Amen" after that sermon.

Michael grunted and ran his hands down his face. "I can't believe you two did this." Then he stalked out the front door, slamming it shut behind him.

Dani dropped her head into her hands and moaned. "That was about the most stupid, idiotic idea ever. I had it under control—"

Before she could finish, Michael strode back inside, heading straight for her. Dani stood and crossed her arms, prepared for the battle.

He pointed to the door. "Outside. Now!"

"If you can't speak to me in a civil—"

"Just *once* could you do as I ask?" She didn't have time for a retort before Michael picked her up and threw her over his shoulder. "What I've got to say I'm not saying in front of our mothers."

She'd never been thrown over a man's shoulder before. It was kind of exciting and . . . sexy. But for form, she pounded on his back. "Put me down, you baboon."

The world did a quick flip, and Dani found herself on the front porch, staring into the angriest set of green eyes she'd ever seen.

"I've had all I can take. Touch me or something so you can know for sure what I feel for you."

That was the last thing she wanted to do when it looked like he was going to hit something. "No, thank you." Unlike her random dreams and visions, to read people she had to touch them and then open her mind. She'd never done that before because she'd been respecting his privacy.

He leaned closer, and his tone turned the corner to dangerous. "Do it."

"Oh, for God's sake." Dani laid her hand on his arm and stared into his eyes for a moment before she blinked in confusion. The prettiest kaleidoscope of colors she'd ever seen swirled from her head and then moved straight to her heart. He still loved her.

Sensing victory, she stood on her tiptoes and whispered in his ear, "So does this mean I'm forgiven, and you're done being difficult?"

He glanced at the stars and shook his head. "Why do I *know* that's not the last time I'll hear that?"

He was bossy even when he was sort of telling her that he loved her. The funny part was she kinda liked that cranky, stick-up-the-butt side of him. So maybe she'd do him a favor and keep that fine sorry ass of his. Forever.

"You're sure you still love me? Even after all I've put you through?" She needed him to confirm it out loud.

"Yes." He cupped her face with his big hands. "God help me, I can't seem to make it go away. I do love you, Dani Botelli." Then he kissed her.

Michael's sweet, gentle touch sent a wave of warmth through her veins like a shot of old Irish whiskey. He was definitely going to be worth all the fights they'd surely have in the future.

When his lips left hers, she leaned back and asked, "When did you change your mind about us? Did the cinnamon rolls do the trick?"

"No. But I hope you'll make them for me again soon." He took her hand, leading her toward the front door. "It was right after you gave me the finger. It's when I realized I'd miss you and that attitude of yours way too much if I let you go. You're stuck with me forever, Botelli."

"Well, if flipping you off made you realize how you really feel, then that makes my sudden attraction to being thrown over your shoulder not quite so weird, I guess."

He started to open the door for her but stopped. "Instead of my shoulder, why don't we try my knee next time? You deserve a good spanking." His hand connected with her rear end, giving her a sharp pat.

"Mmmm, might be fun. But not in front of our mothers." She gave him a quick kiss.

God, she loved him.

After he kissed her back, he whispered, "So is that a yes?"

"To kinky sex? I guess I could give it a try." He'd been referring to his earlier comment about being stuck with him forever, but she couldn't resist teasing him.

He slipped his hands on either side of her face and gently lifted it up. "I'll only have kinky sex if it's with my wife. So what do you say? Will you marry me, Dani?"

She chewed her bottom lip, pretending to think about it, when inside she was finding it hard to contain the urge to jump up and down.

Her heart swelled so big with love for Michael sometimes, but the thought of always being with him made everything else inside melt, too. She'd never loved anyone like she loved him. "We'll drive each other crazy, you know. Daily."

His lips tilted into a slow, sexy smile. "Daily makeup sex sounds pretty good to me."

Yeah, because that was the thing about them. They were opposites in so many ways, and they'd surely disagree on about half of everything, but in the end, their love for each other always won. They'd both taken little detours with others that had only made them both see more clearly that there was no one else better suited to be together than they were. "Okay. I'll marry you. But don't forget. You asked for this."

He tucked a stray hair behind her ear and whispered, "How could I ever regret even a single moment with you, Dani?"

That made her knees literally grow weak.

Before her whole body threatened to turn into a big, sentimental glob of mush, he picked her up and threw her over his shoulder. "My mom can give them a ride home. Let's go back to my place. You've got a lot a making up with me to do, Dani."

"Can't wait." She smiled at the thought of the making up as she admired his fine rear end.

He flipped her back to her feet and then helped her into his car. When he slid into the seat beside her, he held out a hand. "I haven't had dinner. Hand one over please."

He must've seen the snack cakes she'd stuffed into her jacket pocket as she'd run out the door in her drunken state. "Seriously? You want this lovely, sweet, delicious, fun but extremely-bad-for-you treat?" She slowly unpeeled the wrapper, like a sexy strip tease. "Eating these on a regular basis might even take ten years off your life." She leaned over and hand-fed the decadent treat into his mouth.

He took a big bite and grinned. "I figure being married to you will probably have about the same risks, so why not?" He took her hand and whispered, "Thanks for bringing the life back to my life, Dani."

She gave his hand a squeeze. "Thanks for bringing the Michael back to mine." She kissed him softly, then whispered, "So can we forgo that spanking you talked about earlier? I have an aversion to pain."

"Me too." Michael grinned as he started the car. "But I still want to marry you anyway."

"Very funny." She swatted his arm for form but smiled as they drove home. She had her best friend back.

They'd figure out the rest.

Thanksgiving

Dani had never looked more beautiful to Michael as she slipped through the swinging kitchen door with a platter that held an enormous turkey. Even in an apron, which was oddly sexy, Dani was the most gorgeous woman he'd ever known. And she belonged to him. That still took him by surprise sometimes. He'd never been happier.

When Dani laid the platter on the dining room table, Emma gave everyone her trademark "ta-da!"

Dani had insisted on cooking the whole meal herself, and it looked incredible. She'd also insisted on inviting too many people. He'd only been in his new house two weeks, and Dani had run him ragged, getting everything ready for the holiday.

And most nights, she'd gone home to sleep in her own bed. They were trying to set a good example for his girls, but he wanted her with him full-time. So he could wake up every morning to her smile.

And it'd be easier to see she stayed out of trouble that way.

He needed to put more pressure on her to set their wedding date, Annalisa's busy schedule be damned. But first he was going to talk her into having a couple of kids. Dani would make the most incredible mother. She just didn't see it that way.

It wasn't going to be easy—she'd made her views clear on that subject every time he'd brought it up—but he had a plan. He was going to ask again while her defenses were low after spending the day with the family and friends she loved.

At the dining room table, Annalisa was convincing Julia to use her agent to represent Emma, who couldn't have cared less and was playing with the marshmallows on her candied yams, while Mario and Jerry discussed guns. Maeve and Mrs. Wilson admired the beautifully prepared food as it was passed around, and Eva rubbed her hands together with glee as she stared at her full plate.

At the spare round table in the den, he sat between his girls, Amanda and Carly, with Dani on Carly's right. Dani's sister and her friend, Rick, sat next to Dani, making cow eyes at each other, and Jake and Darlene the dispatcher rounded out the guest list. Dani had invited Zoe and her family, but they'd gone north to a hippie commune to be with Zoe's parents.

He hadn't even known communes still existed.

While Darlene buttered a roll, just as Michael was doing for his kids, she stared adoringly into Jake's eyes. When she fed him a bite of steamy buttered bread, Michael cringed. If Dani ever did that to him in public, he'd kill her.

He turned to hand Carly a roll when she suddenly hopped out of her seat. "I have to go potty."

He jumped up and reached for her hand. At three years old, Carly had a habit of waiting too long. But Carly's hand was extended toward Dani's.

Instead of taking her hand, Dani scooped Carly up and jogged away. "Come on, tiny tanks, let's go." Dani had witnessed Carly's bad habit the previous week and was a fast learner.

After he sat down, Amanda asked, "Daddy, could Dani pick us up from dance again next week?"

"We can ask if she's free. Why?"

"She's fun. The last time, the policeman made his siren go, and then we all went down to the police station. Uncle Jake bought us ice cream while Dani went away for a while. Then we got hamburgers for dinner. It was when you were gone to Texas that night, remember?"

"*Uncle* Jake?" Michael met Jake's amused gaze.

Amanda pointed across the table. "Yeah, him."

Jake winked at her. "We both like rocky road the best, don't we, sweetheart?" Then he turned to Michael. "It wasn't Dani's fault this time. An inept cop who hates me and was looking for a little retaliation pulled her over. She had some outstanding paperwork, but that's all cleared up now."

Before he could get more details, Dani and Carly returned.

He'd only been out of town for one night. How Dani got herself into these situations was beyond reason.

But she'd stepped up to help when he'd needed it, so he was grateful to her. Dani had agreed to stay with his kids, instead of sending them back to Heather, for one night in the middle of their time with him. "Amanda was just telling us all about your trip to the police station last week?"

Dani shrugged and sat down. "I told you about that." She picked up a bowl and shoved it at him. "More candied yams?"

He ignored the yams. "When did you tell me?"

She cleared her throat and leaned behind Carly's chair, whispering in his ear. "We were in the hot tub, remember?" When he didn't respond, she leaned even closer, "Right after my suit landed on the deck?"

A vague recollection of her telling him some watered-down version of the story he'd just heard niggled at his brain. Dani naked and distracting him was what he lived for. "Okay, rule number eight."

Dani rolled her eyes before he leaned close and whispered in her ear, "No more telling me important stuff when you're naked. That's cheating."

◦

As the last of the plates were loaded into the dishwasher, Dani contemplated rule number nine. Michael thought he was being so clever by never asking her to make dinner for him and the girls. He knew she'd be stubborn, just for good measure, but she was onto him.

He'd coyly start to prepare a meal, and when she couldn't stand to watch him mess it up any longer, she'd kick him out of the kitchen and finish it. The funny thing was she'd actually begun to enjoy the challenge of making food the kids would eat.

But she hated doing dishes, so rule number nine was that she'd cook, and he'd be on permanent dish duty. Especially on national holidays.

When the door swung open, she turned to tell Michael the new plan, but it was Jake who strolled in with a dirty plate she'd missed. "That was awesome, Dani. Thanks for having us."

Neither Jake nor Darlene had any family in town, so, naturally, she'd extended the invitation. Michael hadn't been happy about it, and she'd probably have to smooth it over later when everyone was gone and the kids were tucked in.

"You're welcome. I'm glad you both could come." She took the plate and filled the sink with soap to wash it by hand. "You and Darlene look good together."

"Yeah, she's great." He leaned against the counter and grinned. "She's not you, but then no one else could be."

Dani turned her attention to the dirty plate. "Yeah, but I'll bet when she calls, you don't wonder if you're going to have to bail her out of jail."

"There's that."

"And when you have plans to go out and come to her door, looking like you've been wrestling with a crack addict, I'll bet she doesn't even whine about her ruined evening. She probably hands you a cold beer, offers to make you dinner, and suggests you stay in. And while you watch a movie, she massages your tired feet."

"Hmmm." He rubbed his chin. "I'll have to suggest the foot rub next time."

Dani smacked him with a wet towel. "You have a stressful job that kicks your butt, even though you'll never admit it. And what you need at the end of the day is someone nurturing and peaceful. We both know that was never me."

"True. So, are you saying Michael likes chaos?"

"No. He likes a challenge." Dani couldn't help giving up a smile as she wiped the counters down. "He thinks it's fun to take on a seemingly insurmountable problem and solve it. Hence, me. And by the way, I'm still calling you if I need to be bailed out of jail. I have a feeling Michael would make me spend the night just to teach me a lesson."

He leaned down and laid a quick kiss on her cheek. "That's a deal. And speaking of people in jail—"

"Don't you even think about dragging me into another one of your cases." She poked him in the chest. "Believe me, I'm going to hear about the police-station thing long after everyone's gone tonight. I've used up my quota for the week."

"It's Mrs. Granger."

"Your neighbor? She must be seventy years old. What kind of trouble could she be in?"

"Attempted murder. Her husband claims she tried to kill him with a cherry pie."

"Ralph is an idiot and treats her like dirt. The cherries were probably just bad."

"All the evidence points her way, but I can't get my head around this one. I don't want to see her sit in jail for the holiday while we figure it out. Especially if she's innocent. Come on, Dani. It'll just take a few minutes. Please?"

Before she could answer, Michael strolled in.

Jake glanced Michael's way and then started for the door. "I'll be ready to go in five minutes. Thanks, babe."

After Jake was gone, Michael pulled her close. "I thought you had a talk with him about the 'babe' thing."

"I did." She circled her arms around his waist and gave him a quick kiss. "He doesn't call me that anymore unless you're around. He knows it annoys you." Dani bit her lip to contain her laughter at his obvious attempt for patience.

After he struggled for a moment, Michael's lips morphed into an overly zealous grin. Then he ran his hands through her hair and tilted her head back. "Have I told you how beautiful you are lately?"

Wary, she replied, "Yes, and thanks, but we have a house full of people. You need to behave."

His eyes lit with mischief as he backed her against the counter. Then he drove her nuts by nibbling on her neck. "I just want you to know how appreciated you are. You handled all the details and made this a great holiday. Thanks for a fantastic meal today."

"You're welcome."

He switched to the other side of her neck, and her eyes nearly rolled back into her head. "And thanks for being so good to my kids. They've already fallen for you." His lips brushed against the spot in front of her ear he knew drove her wild, making her knees buckle.

Michael was up to something, but she couldn't work up the energy to care. She tilted her head to give him greater access and played along. "It's no trouble. They're fun."

"That's what they say about you. You're going to be a great mom, Dani." He moved his attention to her earlobe and sent a sweet shiver up her spine. "And thank you for a relatively calm week."

That did it. He was definitely after something.

"It's only Thursday. Maybe you'd better wait on that one until Sunday. Especially after I tell you that I need to go out for just a bit to help a frail seventy-year-old murder suspect."

His head popped up. "Oh no, you don't. It's Thanksgiving, Dani. You are *not* running off with Jake to solve a crime, leaving me here alone with your entire family. We haven't even had dessert."

"Did I mention she's *seventy*? And I'll only be gone forty-five minutes. An hour, tops. We'll have dessert when I get back."

He stared into her eyes, and she could practically see the wheels turning in his scheming brain. "If I agree to entertain them while you're gone, then you're going to owe me. Big."

"Name your price."

His lips slowly tilted into a wide grin. "I want a baby."

Her stomach took a fast dive. "So that's what you were softening me up for?" She placed her hands on his chest and gave him a hearty shove. It was as ineffective as shoving at a solid brick wall. "That's so *not* going to happen. I'm not bringing any more freaks into this world. Name something else."

Michael pulled her more firmly against him. "Wouldn't it be fun to have a son who played football, and who could step up to the line of scrimmage and actually feel what the defense is going to do every time? He'd earn a Super Bowl ring for sure."

"No. That'd be cheating."

"Or how about a daughter who becomes a stockbroker, making a killing on Wall Street? She could retire early and live the life of luxury."

What was he saying? Michael didn't believe in cheating any more than she did. She couldn't figure out his angle but knew there had to be one. "I'll be happy to help with your girls in any way I can. They're great kids. But I don't want any of my own. I wouldn't want them to grow up like I did and have a huge secret all their lives. It'd make them unhappy, and I won't do that to anyone else on purpose."

"Okay, then. Our kids won't cheat. They'll just help others and make the world a better place. Like you do." He kissed her so gently she nearly sighed. Then he whispered, "Are you happy, Dani? With me and with the life we're going to make together?"

She had a sneaking suspicion he'd just backed her into a corner, and even though she saw it coming hard and fast like an out-of-control freight train, she couldn't stop it. "Yes, but—"

"Then there's nothing stopping any children we might have from being just as happy as we are right now. Have kids with me, Dani."

He'd done it again. The man had a way of twisting things around so fast a mere mortal couldn't keep up. The cheating angle was just a smoke screen to distract her so he could go for the kill. She was going to have to step it up if she wanted to stay in the competition.

She opened her mouth for a rebuttal but quickly snapped it shut again.

Michael's sweet, hopeful expression made her take his request seriously.

He loved kids, and his girls adored him. Could Michael make up for her ineptitude?

Spending time with Emma, and then with Michael's girls, hadn't been so bad, really. In fact, if she were honest, she'd had fun when she was with them. They made something inside her go all soft and gooey whenever they beamed those cute little trusting grins at her.

If those kids only knew what a disaster she was.

But her sister didn't have any extra abilities, and that shot a renewed spurt of optimism through her. There'd probably be a fifty-fifty chance that a child with Michael wouldn't have her affliction.

Huffing out a breath, she untied her apron and tossed it on the back of a chair.

She'd wanted a new start in life. Her plan included getting Jake to sign the papers and finding a man she was compatible with.

She could check those off the list.

Second, she wanted to keep her job and thrive at it.

Double check. After Carlos Watts had been dealt with and the news media had made such a big deal about her, she'd ended up with three pending sales and had taken four new listings in the last month.

And third, she'd vowed to stop helping Jake with his cases, therefore staying out of trouble for more than a day or two at a time.

Well . . . two out of three wasn't so bad.

"I'll be back in an hour. And I'm only committing to *one* kid! She headed for the door.

"Dani?" Michael called out.

She stopped and crossed her arms. "What?"

"Thank you." He picked up the pot of coffee and joined her. "We'll pick a wedding date when you get back—in an hour or less, or it'll be two kids you're agreeing to." He kissed her sweetly, then headed for the door.

"Hey. That's not fair."

He glanced over his shoulder with a panty-melting grin on his face. "That's what you get for dating a damn lawyer."

Yeah, she supposed it was.

But he was totally worth it.

Acknowledgments

As always, many thanks go out to my tireless critique partners, my writing friends, and my family. And mostly to the whole team at Montlake Publishing, who support me and help me live my dreams. Last, I'd like to send to my loyal fans, the ones who make writing books for them such a pleasure, a big hug of gratitude from the deepest part of my heart.

About the Author

Photo © 2012 Robyn Adams

Tamra Baumann became hooked on writing the day she picked up her first Nora Roberts novel from her favorite bookstore. Since then, she's dazzled readers with her own lighthearted love stories. She's a Golden Heart winner for Contemporary Series Romance and has also received the Golden Pen Award for Single Title Romance. Born in Monterey, California, Tamra led the nomadic life of a navy brat before finally putting down permanent roots during college. When she's not attending annual Romance Writers of America meetings, this voracious reader can be found playing tennis, traveling, or scouting reality shows for potential character material. Tamra resides with her real-life characters—her husband, two kids, and their allergy-ridden dog—in the sunny Southwest. Visit her online at www.tamrabaumann.com and on Facebook at www.facebook.com/author.tamra.baumann.